When a Princess Proposes

Also by Kerrelyn Sparks:

How to Love Your Elf

The Siren and the Deep Blue Sea

When a Princess Proposes

kerrelyn SPARKS

KENSINGTON
PUBLISHING CORP.

www.kensingtonbooks.com

KENSINGTON BOOKS are published by

Kensington Publishing Corp.
119 West 40th Street
New York, NY 10018

ISBN: 978-1-4967-3585-0 (ebook)

ISBN: 978-1-4967-3584-3

First Kensington Trade Paperback Printing: May 2022

10 9 8 7 6 5 4 3 2 1

Printed in the United States of America

*In loving memory of
our dear friend, Paul Steward.
He adored his wife, treasured his family,
and was always ready for the next grand adventure.*

Acknowledgments

I would like to thank my editor, Alicia Condon, and everyone at Kensington Publishing for graciously allowing me all the time I needed to write this book while I have been helping my husband in his struggle against stage four colon cancer. There were weeks, even months, when the battle was so intense and devastating that I could not manage a page. But my brave husband refuses to be defeated, so I have taken inspiration from him and persevered. Slowly, *When a Princess Proposes* came to life and comforted me with the knowledge that love can still conquer adversity and emerge victorious.

And so, obviously, I wish to express my love and gratitude to my husband, who has fought so hard to stay with me. I'm also grateful to all the wonderful doctors and medical staff at M.D. Anderson. Meanwhile, my best friends and critique partners, MJ and Sandy, not only vetted each chapter but kept me reasonably sane. Love you both! My love also to dear friend, Diana Steward. And as always, my agent, Michelle Grajkowski of Three Seas Literary Agency, has been a pillar of loving support. Thank you!

My final thank you goes to all the fabulous readers who have continued to support my books over the years. My first published book was released in 2002, so some of you have been with me for twenty years! I would have never lasted this long without you. And I really appreciate your patience over the last few years. Many thanks to you all! May you always feel Embraced.

Prologue

In another time, on another world called Aerthlan, there are five kingdoms. Four kingdoms extend across a vast continent, and the fifth, an island kingdom, lies in the Great Western Ocean.

Twice a year the two moons eclipse each other in what is called an Embrace. Any child born on the nights of the Spring or Autumn Embrace will be gifted with a magical power. They are known as the Embraced. Once feared by the people on the mainland, they are now widely accepted. After all, it was the Embraced kings and queens who defeated the worst danger ever to threaten Aerthlan—the Circle of Five.

After seven hundred years of war and destruction, the world is at peace. According to the new Seer, Queen Maeve, this era of peace should last another seven hundred years.

Or so she once believed. Twenty years after the demise of the Circle of Five, she is now haunted with a mysterious and unsettling dream. A dark cloud is growing, but she's been unable to see where it comes from. Or who is behind it. She only knows that the people of Aerthlan are once again in danger.

Especially the Embraced.

Chapter 1

Year 720
Ebton Palace, Eberon

The torture would be over in an hour or two, Quentin reminded himself as he watched her move gracefully through another dance. She was dressed in a brilliant green gown to match the color of her sparkling eyes, and she was so beautiful, he was tempted to shift into his eagle form and fly far, far away. But in his heart, he knew there was no escape. Running away would not erase the image of her lovely face from his mind, nor the memory of her sweet laughter. It would not keep his heart from wishing for the impossible.

So he stayed put, lurking behind a marble pillar in the Great Hall of Ebton Palace, half-hidden so he could still see *her* and the grand ball taking place. Such was his life, always present at any important event, but remaining as invisible as possible while he watched, listened, and gathered information.

As the official messenger and unofficial spy for the kings and queens of Aerthlan, he was a frequent visitor at all five royal palaces. But it was only twice a year, during the Spring and Autumn Embraces, that he found himself obliged to attend birthday parties such as this one. Tonight, at the Autumn Embrace, King Leo of Eberon was turning fifty-one.

Quentin glanced over to the dais where Leo and Luciana

were seated next to each other on their thrones. Leo glanced at his wife, and with a smile took her hand. Love everlasting, Quentin thought with a pang of envy as his gaze shifted back to the dance floor. *She* was now dancing with suitor number eleven.

Similar celebrations were happening in all the royal palaces tonight, since it was also the birthday of Queen Brigitta of Tourin, Queen Gwennore of Norveshka, King Brennan of Woodwyn, and King Brodgar of the Isles. It was a shame, Quentin thought, that he couldn't have stayed another night on the Isle of Moon. Then he wouldn't be here enduring this torture tonight. But the island queen, Maeve, had insisted he leave immediately to warn Leo and Luciana about her latest dream. A nightmare, she had called it. A dark cloud was hovering over Eberon, poised to unleash death and destruction.

As the Seer, Queen Maeve was rarely wrong, but Quentin had his doubts about this latest prediction. The country of Eberon was prosperous, full of well-fed and happy people. All the nobles here in the Great Hall were well dressed and making merry. A little too merry, he thought as he watched a tipsy baron try to impress his dance partner by leaping into the air, only to fall *splat* on his rear. The room erupted in laughter, and Quentin's gaze shifted back to catch a lovely but fleeting smile on *her* face. Damn, but this was torture.

Don't think about her. He focused his thoughts once again on the unlikelihood of Eberon being in danger. In recent years, the country had become so safe that General Nevis Harden had let most of the army return home. A few manned forts across the countryside were enough to apprehend the occasional thief.

In reward for his service, Nevis had been named Lord Protector of the Realm and given an earldom, along with Benwick Castle and the surrounding land. He and his wife, Princess Elinor, ran an academy and training camp there for royal and

Embraced children. Leo's two sons—Eric and his younger sibling, Dominic—were both studying at Benwick Academy, but they had returned home for their father's birthday.

Once again, Quentin wondered why *she* had never attended the academy. She was both royal and Embraced, so it would have made sense for her to go. Other Embraced females studied there. But whereas her older twin, Eric, had the impressive gift of being able to melt metal, Princess Eviana's magical power was a carefully guarded secret. What the hell could it be?

As someone who earned his keep gathering information, it irked him that this was one secret he'd never uncovered. He snorted. Knowing the truth would be utterly useless. To whom would he report it? Obviously, Leo and Luciana already knew their daughter's gift. The other royals probably did, too. But Quentin didn't dare reveal his curiosity by asking any of them. They might suspect his most carefully guarded secret: his unfortunate longing for the beautiful but impossible Eviana.

She'd turned twenty-three at the last Spring Embrace, and apparently her mother had decided she was in imminent danger of spinsterhood if she wasn't matched with a suitable man tonight. The ball that was meant to celebrate Leo's birthday was crowded with eligible Eberoni noblemen, all eager to pursue the royal princess and heiress to the Duchy of Vindalyn. The line to dance with Eviana was so long that she was dancing only half a tune with each man. And in that short time, each was desperately attempting to impress her.

"Go get in line. You know you want to," a female voice whispered behind Quentin, and he spun around to see who knew the secret he'd been hiding for six years.

"Oh, Lady Olana." He took a step back as he greeted her, then winced at the injured look on her face. "I'm sorry."

She shrugged. "No need to apologize. Everyone does it."

Even so, he felt guilty. It wasn't Olana's fault that she had such a terrifying power. Twenty years ago, when he and Olana had left the Isle of Secrets, they had been too young to know what their Embraced gifts would be.

He had been lucky. Damned lucky. As an eagle shifter, he'd been the logical choice to step into King Brodgar's old job as official messenger to the kings and queens of Aerthlan. And, just like Brody, he'd also learned how to gather information. By the time he was twenty-two, he'd made himself an invaluable member at all five royal courts.

Olana had also made herself invaluable to royalty, but he seriously doubted she considered her gift a blessing. At the age of fifteen, she'd taken employment as a lady-in-waiting to Queen Luciana, and that was when her Embraced gift had manifested itself. It was a downright sneaky power, and it had taken several weeks before the queen and Olana had realized what was happening.

Seven-year-old Eric had accidentally cut his finger during an archery lesson, and Olana was treating his wound when he suddenly blurted out that he was the one who had broken the vase in his mother's workroom. Two weeks later, when Olana was brushing Eviana's hair, the young princess had broken into tears, crying that she'd torn the lacy hem of her mother's shift while playing dress-up.

A week after that, a servant had accidentally touched Olana's hand while serving her tea, then had suddenly admitted to stealing five silver spoons. Curious, Luciana had taken Olana to the servants' quarters, and with a simple touch from Olana, each servant had blurted out his or her worst secret.

Now she was called the Confessor, and everyone gave her a wide berth in the hallways of Ebton Palace. Some even screeched and ran away the second she was spotted.

The kings of Aerthlan had soon realized that interrogating

prisoners was no longer necessary. They simply called in the Confessor. Over the years, Lady Olana had become so famous, all it took was the threat that she was on her way for a criminal to blurt out all his misdeeds.

But what was good for the kingdoms was not necessarily good for Olana. No one wanted to marry her or even befriend her, so now she lived alone in the east tower at Ebton Palace. About a year ago, Quentin had grabbed her when she'd tripped on the stairs, and that had caused him to blurt out his secret. Fortunately, no one else had heard, and she'd assured him she wouldn't tell anyone.

With a sigh, Quentin realized she was currently hiding in the shadows just as he was. No one was going to ask Olana to dance. She was valued and shunned at the same time.

He glanced back at the dance floor. The princess was still dancing, now with suitor number seventeen, Earl Baedan. About thirty more men were lined up, waiting their turn.

"Why don't you get in line?" Olana asked softly. "I doubt she would refuse to dance with you."

He snorted. No, she wouldn't refuse someone like him. She'd been raised to have better manners than that. But she would see it as part of her royal duty. Even now, as he studied her face, he had a distinct feeling that her smile was forced. She was not enjoying the evening, but simply going through the motions as she was expected to do.

Why would he add to her misery, forcing her to dance with him? *Not happening*, he told himself as he nabbed two goblets of wine from the tray of a passing servant. "Actually, Olana, I'm quite happy to remain here with you. What have you been up to?"

With a smile she accepted one of the goblets. "I've been working in the library. There are a huge number of books, but some of them have yet to be properly catalogued. And in the workroom, I'm weaving a tartan that I'm very pleased with. Beautiful colors."

Obviously, books and cloth were safe from her touch. "I'd like to see it when you're done."

Olana's smile widened. "That's kind of you." She took a sip of wine. "Can you believe it's been twenty years since we left the Isle of Secrets?"

Quentin nodded. It was a lonely life for Olana, so he understood why she enjoyed exchanging letters with all the other Embraced children who had grown up on the Isle of Secrets. "Have you heard from anyone lately?"

"Aye. I received a letter from Irene yesterday. She's the head gardener now at Wyndelas Palace in Woodwyn. She married a fellow named Halfric and they have two lovely children." Olana's smile slipped as a hint of regret glinted in her blue eyes.

She had probably wanted to have children of her own, Quentin thought. He refrained from telling Olana that he'd met Irene and her family the last time he'd visited Wyndelas Palace. It would only cause Olana more regret because she rarely saw any of their old friends.

She heaved a sigh. "A letter from Peter arrived two days ago. He had some terribly tragic news."

Peter was now a farmer just south of the Ron River, Quentin recalled. "What happened?"

"Do you remember Uma? She was only four when we left the Isle of Secrets."

"Barely." Uma and Victor had lived in the nursery at Aerie Castle, too young for the manual labor required of everyone who had resided in the village.

"Well, it turned out that Uma is actually the third daughter of Earl Ronford."

"That doesn't sound tragic," Quentin muttered. Much better than his own situation. Discovering he was the illegitimate and unwanted son of a stable hand and scullery maid had certainly taken a chunk out of the smart-assed attitude he'd had as a youngster.

"It *is* tragic," Olana insisted. "She passed away. And she was only twenty-four."

Quentin blinked. *Damn.* "How? How did she die?"

Olana shrugged. "I don't know. Peter just said it was a terrible accident."

Quentin narrowed his eyes. Maybe he needed to pay Peter a visit.

"What about you, Quen?" Olana gave him a curious look. "What have you been up to?"

"I arrived about an hour ago from the Isle of Moon." He adjusted his black leather belt. Since he was a frequent visitor to all the royal palaces and Benwick Academy, he kept a small trunk of clothing stashed in a tower room of each castle. For the party tonight, he was wearing his best: a dark blue velvet tunic with black breeches and boots. "I need to talk to His Majesty, but he won't be free till tomorrow morning."

Olana nodded. "It's always like this on the nights the moons embrace."

"Oh, that reminds me." Quentin tapped his goblet against hers. "Happy birthday."

"Thank you." Olana smiled as she smoothed down the skirt of her lavender silk gown. Her long blond hair had been braided with a matching silk ribbon. "The queen gave me this gown for my birthday." Her smile faded. "Though I have to admit I'm not terribly pleased about turning thirty-three."

"You don't look a day over twenty-three."

She scoffed, but her eyes twinkled with amusement. "You should practice your flattery on someone who will believe it."

He affected an injured look. "Would I lie to the Confessor?"

"Shall I touch you and find out?" She laughed when he jumped back with feigned horror. "Oh, Quen, it is good to see you again."

"Likewise." He nodded, grateful that he could ease her loneliness.

"You were born on the Spring Embrace, weren't you?"

When he nodded, she asked, "You must have turned twenty-nine?"

"Yes." Quentin glanced over at the dance floor. Eviana shared his birthday, not that she would have ever noticed.

"And you've never wanted to marry?"

He winced inwardly. Who would want to marry the unwanted bastard son of servants? He'd been damned lucky that King Silas and Queen Gwennore of Norveshka had taken him in. In gratitude, he'd worked hard, mastering all four Aerthlan languages along with all the other necessary skills that were required for the position he held today. "Whenever Gwennore asks me that, I always say I have yet to find the right woman."

Olana glanced at Eviana. "Perhaps you have found her."

He scoffed. "A princess? Leo would strike me with lightning if I even dared to approach her."

Olana nodded. "That may be true. He doesn't think any man in the entire world is good enough for his daughter."

"Apparently, Luciana thinks more than fifty men are good enough for her," Quentin muttered. "Look at her now. She's dancing with suitor number twenty-one."

"You're keeping count?"

He shrugged. "It's part of my job to know how to protect the royal families. For instance, her current dance partner is Baron Northam, who is fond of escaping to his bedchamber so he can dress up as a milkmaid."

Olana gasped. "What?"

Quentin gave her a knowing nod.

She winced. "You must be jesting."

"If you don't believe me, go touch him. He'll confess it for everyone to hear."

She heaved a sigh. "This is terrible. It makes me wonder how many of these noblemen could be totally unsuitable for the princess."

A brilliant idea popped into Quentin's mind. "We could find out."

Olana's eyes widened. "Now? In front of everyone?"

He extended a hand to her. "Lady Olana, would you give me the pleasure of this dance?"

She gave his hand a wary look. "Quen, if I touch you, you'll announce your secret."

"I'll whisper it. Besides, you already know it."

She bit her lip, considering. "It would be nice. I haven't danced in years. Everyone is too afraid—"

"I'm not. Let's do it."

"It might cause a disturbance."

"I'm counting on it."

She snorted. "You want the king and queen angry with you?"

"They might be angry at first," Quentin conceded as he set their goblets down on a nearby table. "But if we reveal which suitors are entirely unsuitable, we'll be doing them a favor, and eventually they will thank us for it." He offered his hand once more and braced himself, clenching his mouth shut. When her hand touched his, he ground out the whispered words, "My heart is forever lost to Eviana."

Olana gave him a sympathetic look. "Then let's see what we can do for her."

He led Olana to the edge of the dance floor. Luckily, the other dancers were too drunk or occupied to notice them. It also helped that there were shadowy spots not well illuminated by the candles, and that Olana was petite enough that Quentin could use his own body to block her from most people's view.

After letting Olana enjoy a few measures of a lively waltzing dance, he maneuvered her closer to Eviana. So far, so good. No one had noticed them. Suitor number twenty-two was completely focused on his attempt to impress the princess.

"Ready?" Quentin whispered and Olana nodded, an excited glint in her eyes. He swirled her around, and she quickly tapped the suitor's shoulder. Just as fast, Quentin moved her away, headed once again for the shadows.

Eviana's partner stopped dancing with a jerk, then announced in a loud voice, "Actually, I'm already married, but if I have a chance with Your Highness, I'll make sure my current wife has a fatal accident."

Eviana gasped, and all the dancers around her stopped to stare at her partner.

He slapped a hand over his mouth, his eyes wide with horror, then bolted for the front door.

Meanwhile, suitor number twenty-three saw his chance to take advantage of the last suitor's disaster, and he dashed toward Eviana, a hopeful grin on his face. Quentin steered his dance partner toward him, and Olana touched his arm.

"I still wet my bed!" he announced, then gasped. "No! No, I don't! I haven't done it in a week . . . Ack!" He also sprinted toward the front door.

The rest of the suitors stampeded toward Eviana all at once. As Quentin and Olana danced toward them, those who knew who she was screamed and ran for the door. The others, still intent on winning the princess, pushed and shoved at one another in an attempt to reach her first. As they streamed past Olana, she extended her hand, touching one after another.

"I want your money!"

"I want to marry royalty!"

"Once I'm in charge of the Duchy of Vindalyn, I'll lock you in the dungeon."

"I like to set things on fire."

"I'm afraid of my own shadow."

"I'm missing half my brain . . . I think . . ."

"I talk to chipmunks. And they talk back."

"I snore so loud, the windows shatter."

"My feet stink."

"My whole body stinks!"

"I love my mommy!"

With gargled sounds of horror, they all scrambled for the front door.

A shock reverberated around the room as everyone gasped and fled to the edges of the dance floor, far away from Olana. She and Quentin were left in the middle of the Great Hall with only Eviana close by, frozen in place with a stunned look on her face.

When Leo and Luciana jumped to their feet, the music screeched to a halt. Then the gossiping and laughter began, growing louder and louder. Eviana blinked, coming out of her state of shock to cast a wary glance at the snickering crowd.

Quentin winced at the injured look in her eyes and the deepening blush on her cheeks. Dammit. He hadn't helped her one bit. He'd embarrassed her. Hurt her.

Luciana strode across the dance floor, her expression a mixture of horror and outrage. "Lady Olana, how could you?" Without waiting for an answer, she turned to her daughter. "Are you all right, dear?"

Eviana shook her head, then gathered up her skirt and dashed for the door leading to the private rooms of the royal family. Upon reaching the portal, she glanced back at Quentin.

His heart tightened in his chest. She was seeing him, finally seeing him, but dammit, the look in her eyes was hurt and angry. He wasn't sure how he could apologize, but he had better do it quickly. Once she left, it might be months before he saw her again. He stepped toward her, but she slipped through the door and slammed it shut.

Dammit. He'd screwed up royally.

And the royal princes knew it. Both Eric and Dominic stalked toward Quentin, their eyes narrowed and their fists clenched as if they were planning to clobber him.

Quentin bowed his head. "I apologize—"

"You think that's enough?" Eric growled as he stepped closer, but his mother raised a hand, stopping him.

"Let's not make matters worse," Luciana said quietly.

Olana sank into a deep curtsy. "I am deeply sorry for the distress I have caused."

"It was my idea," Quentin insisted, not wanting Olana to take the blame. "I talked her into it, but I regret it now."

With a sigh, Luciana regarded them both sadly. "It is Eviana you should apologize to." She stepped closer, lowering her voice. "We will appreciate your efforts at a later date, but for now, I would like my husband's party to continue without any more disruptions." She glanced at her sons. "Understood?"

Dominic motioned to the front door where so many suitors had fled. "We're not inviting those scoundrels back, I hope."

"No. They will be banished from court. I'll warn the Captain of the Guard." Luciana turned toward Olana. "And I need to go to the kitchen to make sure Leo's cake is ready. Will you come with me?"

"Of course, Your Majesty," Olana replied.

"Quentin, I'll have a word with you," Leo called across the room as he strode toward his privy chamber. "*Now.*"

Quentin winced. He wasn't out of trouble yet.

Olana shot Quentin a sympathetic look, then accompanied Luciana toward the front door.

Eric waved for the musicians to resume their playing, then he and his younger brother moved toward the crowd. Young noblewomen rushed toward them, each one hoping to dance with a prince. While everyone filled the center of the room, Quentin skirted the edge of the dance floor, headed for the king's privy chamber.

Baron Northam stepped in front of him, and the would-be

milkmaid gave him an amused look. "You're in big trouble now, Messenger Boy."

"Yes, and it's given me a terrific thirst," Quentin replied with a bland expression. "Do you make milk deliveries, my lord?"

Baron Northam gasped, then glanced nervously at his dance partner. "I-I have no idea what you're talking about."

With an inward wince, Quentin kept walking. Now he'd let his frustration cause him to make a second mistake. He shouldn't have let the baron know that he was aware of the man's secret.

Even so, making new enemies was the least of Quentin's problems. Most probably, he had angered the king, but he doubted Leo would remain angry for very long. No, the worst thing to happen tonight was the look Eviana had given him.

How many times over the last six years had he hoped that she might notice him? Well, now she had.

And he had a sinking feeling that she hated him.

Chapter 2

Quentin tapped on the door to the privy chamber, then slipped inside. He expected to see Leo in his usual place, seated behind his desk, but the king was standing by a window, gazing at the stars.

"I remember the first time I met you," Leo said softly. "We had just defeated the Circle of Five on the Isle of Secrets, and Nevis was bragging about the group of children who had helped him capture the guards. He spoke very fondly of you, said you were the youngest of the group, yet you considered yourself his second-in-command."

Quentin winced, not wanting to remember how obnoxious he had been. "Nevis should have clobbered me."

Leo snorted. "You've proven yourself many times since then. We've come to depend on you."

"Thank you, Your Majesty." Even though Quentin's heart swelled at the compliments, he couldn't help but wonder when the scolding would begin.

Leo slanted him a stern look. "This is the first time you've given me cause to complain."

Now it was beginning. Quentin quickly bowed his head. "Please accept my apologies for disrupting your birthday party."

"I'm turning fifty-one. Do you think I'm eager to celebrate that?"

"You are in excellent health," Quentin murmured. "That is always a reason to celebrate."

"An answer befitting a diplomat." Leo's eyes narrowed. "You've always displayed a great deal of intelligence and caution, so I can't help but wonder what happened to you tonight. What inspired such reckless behavior?"

Quentin swallowed hard. He could hardly confess to wanting to destroy Eviana's suitors. "I am sorry . . ."

"So am I." Leo clenched his gloved hands into fists. "In fact, I'm bloody upset."

"I apologize—"

"How could this happen?" Leo stalked toward his desk and pounded a fist on the wooden surface. "How can my country have so many nobles who are anything but noble?"

Quentin blinked, surprised by the sudden turn of the conversation. "That is why you're upset?"

"Of course! How many men did Olana touch?"

Quentin thought back. "Thirteen, I believe, in all."

Leo gritted his teeth. "Thirteen."

"And then there were another dozen who ran away before Olana could touch them."

"So they're hiding something shameful, too." Leo groaned. "That's a total of twenty-five. How can there be so many worthless noblemen? What does that say for the future of this country?"

Quentin paused for a moment, not sure how to respond. As the bastard son of servants, it had always aggravated him that a nobleman was considered more worthy than he simply because of an accident of birth. "I realized long ago that life isn't fair."

Leo scoffed. "True. At my age, I should know that."

"But a good king will always strive for a more just world." Quentin stopped with a wince. Damn, he'd overstepped himself, daring to advise a king how to rule. Fortunately, Leo didn't seem to mind. He remained quiet, watching Quentin closely.

This would be a good time to change the subject. Quentin cleared his throat. "Queen Maeve sent me here with some urgent news. She has experienced a bad dream about Eberon."

Leo's eyes widened. "What did she see?"

"A dark cloud hovering over Eberon. She believes it will bring death and destruction."

Leo stiffened. "How does that make sense? We're in the midst of prosperity."

"That's what I was thinking," Quentin admitted.

"Did Maeve have any idea when we could expect this death and destruction? Could she be seeing something a hundred years from now?"

Quentin shook his head. "She didn't say, but she urged me to come here immediately—"

"So it will happen soon," Leo concluded with a frown. "Or it has already begun."

Quentin thought back over all the information he'd gathered in the last few weeks. The only odd news he'd discovered was Baron Northam's secret life as a milkmaid. The worst news was the death of Uma. "I'll leave in the morning to take a tour around Eberon. I might learn something useful."

Leo nodded. "Thank you. And I'll ask Nevis if he's heard anything. He receives reports from the different forts around the country." Still deep in thought, Leo wandered toward the door leading to the Great Hall. "For now, we will continue as normal. Watch and listen, but remain prepared."

"Aye, Your Majesty."

With a sigh, Leo rested a gloved hand on the door latch. "We should get back to the party. Luciana will be upset if I'm not there for the arrival of the cake."

"My apologies once more for disrupting your party."

Leo snorted. "I don't give a damn about the party. But I do

care that my daughter was humiliated. And embarrassed to the point that she ran away."

Quentin felt his face growing hot. "I truly regret that. The last thing I meant to do was to hurt her."

Leo tilted his head. "Then why did you do it? Were you trying to protect her?"

"I—" Quentin shifted his weight. "I would apologize to her if I could."

There was a pause as Leo studied Quentin closely. "Then do it."

Quentin blinked. "Excuse me?"

"Apologize." Leo motioned to the door behind his desk that led to the royal family apartments. "Go down the hall-way there till you reach a private garden. It's her favorite place, so I suspect she's there, along with a maid or two."

In a daze, Quentin looked at the door. He would be al-lowed to see her? Actually talk to her?

"But if you'd rather return to the party, I understand," Leo muttered. "There's food and wine—"

"No! I-I'll go see her. Right away." Quentin strode around the desk to the back door. With his hand on the latch, he glanced back to find the king still studying him.

Suddenly Leo gave him a curt nod, as if he'd reached some sort of decision, then turned to go into the Great Hall.

Relieved that the king no longer seemed angry with him, Quentin opened the door and headed into the hallway. Im-mediately his thoughts turned toward Eviana, and his heart began to race. What the hell should he say to her? How angry would she be? What would he do if he found her in the garden crying?

He glanced nervously around the hallway, noting the can-dles flickering in golden sconces and the ornately carved wooden doors. Normally, only the royal family and their per-sonal friends and servants were allowed here. He spotted a stone staircase leading up to the next floor. Was Eviana's bed-chamber there? She had grown up here in the private apartments, rarely viewed by the outside world.

The first time Quentin had seen her was twenty years ago in Aerie Castle on the Isle of Secrets. The Circle of Five had just been defeated, and Maeve had inherited some powerful magic from her deceased mother, the Sea Witch. Prior to that, King Leo had been unable to touch his own children for fear of killing them with his lightning power. But that day in the Great Hall, Maeve had used her magic to render Leo safe, and Quentin had been in the crowd of people who had witnessed him finally able to hug his three-year-old twins.

There had been laughter and tears of joy from all the kings and queens. And even though Quentin had just met Leo and Luciana and hardly knew them, he had been brought to tears by the obvious love Leo bore for his children.

That touching scene had sparked a desperate hope in nine-year-old Quentin. In the following months, while Luciana and Elinor tracked down the parents of the children from the Isle of Secrets, he had prayed that when his parents were found, he would receive the same sort of tearful and joyful embrace as the royal twins. But that had never happened. His parents had wanted no reminder of a shameful affair or the illegitimate child that had been the result, so they had refused even to meet him.

At first, he'd been devastated, but eventually, he was able to tell himself that it had all worked out for the best. King Silas and Queen Gwennore had taken him in, and all the kings and queens of Aerthlan had treated him well. He'd been determined to succeed in life, in spite of his unfortunate beginning, so he'd immersed himself in his studies and military training. The royal Eberoni twins had been mostly forgotten.

That had changed when he'd begun his job as official messenger. The day he'd turned twenty-three, he'd attended the

Spring Embrace party at Ebton Palace, where Prince Eric and Princess Eviana were celebrating their seventeenth birthday. The minute he'd laid eyes on the princess, he'd fallen hard. How could he not when she was the most beautiful and most vibrant young woman he'd ever seen? Her green eyes had sparkled, and her creamy skin had glowed with good health. Her long, shiny black hair had swayed and bounced as she'd moved through one dance after another with grace and boundless energy. Her laughter and sweet smile had pierced his heart.

For the next four years, he'd made sure he was always at Ebton Palace for the Autumn and Spring Embrace parties, so he could catch a glimpse of her. In the summer, she usually traveled with a regiment of guards to Draven Castle in Norveshka, where she would visit Gwennore for a month. The two had always been close, and of course, Gwennore made sure that her niece met all the eligible Norveshki noblemen. At the banquets, Quentin had always been seated far down the table, too far away to talk to the princess.

He'd been introduced to her a few times, but all he'd been able to do was bow and say "Your Highness" before she'd been whisked away to meet someone more important. Still, he'd enjoyed watching her from a distance.

But two years ago, he'd realized the hard truth. No matter how fondly the kings and queens might regard him, he was still basically a servant. That meant his feelings would lead nowhere and he was only torturing himself. So he'd stopped going to the parties at Ebton Palace. Out of sight, out of mind, he had hoped.

But it didn't work. Memories of her still flitted through his mind every day, and he never fell asleep at night without thinking of her.

He refused to call it love, though. How could it be love when he didn't actually know her? No, it was simply an infatuation. An unfortunate longing. Over the years, she had come to represent all the things in life that he might wish for but could never have. A real family. A future. A home and land of his own. Respect. Hope. Love.

But that was all as impossible as she was. In reality, she meant nothing more than torture to him. He knew it. He reminded himself of it every day.

And yet, he was still drawn to her.

As Eviana strode into the family's private garden, two ladies-in-waiting followed behind her at a distance, presumably to allow her some privacy, but she knew perfectly well they were lagging behind so they could gossip about the night's disastrous turn of events.

"I'm absolutely stunned," Vera whispered to the other young woman. "How could Lady Olana do something so outrageous?"

"I know," Willa agreed. "She's never caused trouble like this before."

"I wonder if the queen will punish her?"

"Oh, goodness, I hope not," Willa murmured.

Vera huffed. "Mark my words, it was that eagle shifter who goaded her into it."

"You mean Quentin?" Willa asked.

Eviana slowed her steps so she could hear better.

"Of course," Vera replied. "It's precisely the sort of ill-mannered behavior you might expect from someone as low-born as he."

"Is it true, then?" Willa asked. "He's the bastard son of a stable hand?"

With a wince, Eviana stopped in the middle of the garden path. Behind her, the ladies' footsteps crunched in the gravel as they continued to walk, completely immersed in their gossip.

"They say his mother went on to marry a sheepherder and have five children," Vera whispered. "Normal children, so she didn't want anything to do with the shifter."

Willa scoffed. "I'm not surprised. Who would want anything to do with him?"

Eviana whirled around, surprising the two women, who
skidded to a halt.

Willa gasped. "Your Highness, your face is more flushed
than ever! Are you all right?"

Vera gave the other woman an incredulous look. "Of course
she's not all right. She must be suffering something terrible
after being so horribly humiliated!"

Eviana gritted her teeth. "I am not humiliated."

"You poor thing." Willa's eyes filled with tears. "You're
putting up such a brave front."

"But we can tell how upset you are." Vera gave her a sympathetic look. "And no wonder, since you had to endure that
most wretched humiliation in front of the entire court."

Willa tsked. "Your cheeks are still pink. Shall we bring you
a cup of tea?"

Eviana took a deep breath to keep from screaming. "I wish
to be alone. Please retire for the evening."

Their eyes widened.

"How will you get ready for bed?" Willa asked.

"I can undress myself," Eviana ground out. "Please go!"

With a huff, the two women dashed toward the garden entrance.

"The poor thing must be feeling absolutely dreadful," Willa
whispered. "She's never snapped at us like that before!"

With a groan, Eviana turned to pace across the garden. Before the night was over, Willa and Vera would make sure
every servant in the castle knew all the juicy details of her
so-called wretched humiliation. And they would blame the
entire affair on Lady Olana and the eagle shifter while repeating all the bad gossip they'd ever heard about them.

Eviana had learned at a young age how much pain could
be inflicted by wagging tongues. After being kidnapped at

the age of three, she'd endured thousands of comments from courtiers and servants as they expressed their heartfelt sympathy over the horrific trauma she'd experienced. Of course, she hadn't really wanted a constant reminder of just how awful the ordeal had been, especially since it seemed to feed the nightmares she was experiencing at night. Her parents had assured her that the ordeal would soon become old news and be forgotten.

Unfortunately, it did not.

In order to impress her parents, the expressions of sympathy devolved into a contest, with each new player trying to outdo the last for the dubious honor of being the Person Most Devastated by the Princess's Trauma. Never mind that the constant wailing, chest-thumping and swooning could only add to the young princess's trauma.

To put a stop to the theatrics and protect Eviana, her parents had banned the mention of her kidnapping and kept her isolated in the private apartments of the palace. Unfortunately, that had only fed the gossip that she'd been locked in the nursery because her emotional and mental well-being were hanging by a mere thread. She'd grown up feeling as if she were constantly being watched to see when she would crack.

Thank the Light and goddesses the servants didn't know about the other traumatic event. She'd been thirteen when that fiasco had happened, but her parents had managed to keep it a secret.

It took only a dozen steps to reach the far wall of the garden where the citrus trees were located. The lemon tree was flowering once again, and she pulled down a bough to sniff the fresh scent. Then she headed down the path that circled the perimeter of the garden.

Seventy-two steps. How many times had she walked this circle? As a child, she'd always loved this peaceful and fragrant oasis, but now, it was starting to annoy her. With a snort, she realized that everything was annoying her. Her life felt as hemmed in as this garden with its four surrounding walls.

Even when she spent three months each winter in the southern duchy of Vindalyn, she felt confined. She loved visiting her grandfather, but Grandpa's health was not good these days, so they passed all of their time in his privy chamber, where he taught her how to manage the large and wealthy duchy she would inherit someday.

Please keep Grandpa healthy, she prayed to the Light and the Moon goddesses. Not only would she sorely miss him, but she was in no hurry to spend the rest of her life trapped behind his desk.

Her eyes had been opened five years ago, when she'd made her first official visit to Norveshka to see Aunt Gwen. The vastness of the Norveshki mountains had pulled at Eviana's heart, amazing her but also making her realize just how tiny this garden was. Or how small Grandpa's privy chamber felt.

In the mountains, if she felt frustrated, she could simply let out a scream. But if she screamed here, a dozen guards would appear. Then they would report it to her parents. And then her mother and father would wonder why she wasn't happy. Or grateful for all she had.

In truth, she *was* grateful. She adored her family. She was truly blessed, so she knew she should be happy. She told herself that every day, yet she still felt . . . annoyed. Confined. Overly crowded and perpetually on display.

The highlight of the year was the month she was allowed to spend in Norveshka every summer. She loved wandering into the forest and hiking along the mountain streams. Aunt Gwen could communicate with the redwood trees and the dragons there, and her daughter, Lenushka—or Lennie, as Eviana called her—was not only a trained soldier but the first female dragon shifter in the world. When the three of them ventured off by themselves, they had such glorious adventures!

Six weeks ago, Eviana had returned home, and already she felt trapped. She tilted her head back to gaze at the night sky. The Embraced moons shone down with an extra brilliance, tinting the gray stone walls and green plants with a glint of silver. Stars twinkled at her, beckoning her to break free. If only she could fly away like her dragon uncle, Silas. Or like her best friend, Lennie. Or maybe . . . like an eagle.

An eagle with golden eyes who always watched her.

She'd been aware of him for several years now. How many times had she caught him looking at her? Curious, she'd started glancing his way every now and then. But then she'd realized, with some dismay, that he was watching everyone with those startling golden eyes. It was simply his job. Messenger and spy. He traveled all around the world, gathering information. That much freedom had to be amazing. And intriguing.

Usually, he remained in the background, as if he were trying to disappear into the shadows. No doubt, he considered inconspicuousness to be the best strategy for a spy, but Eviana had always felt it lent him an aura of mystery. As much as she hated gossip, she still found herself listening to any she heard about him. Rumor had it that his eyes were genuinely the eyes of an eagle, and he saw much more keenly than the normal human being.

There were a few times in Norveshka when she'd spotted him flying overhead. As an eagle, he was golden in color, but in human form, with his long wavy hair of burnished gold and tanned skin, she'd always thought of him as bronze. How had the silly man ever thought he could disappear into the shadows? She'd always been able to see him.

Knowing that he'd grown up with Lady Olana on the Isle

of Secrets, she'd encouraged Olana to talk about their childhood. Eviana found the story fascinating. Embraced babies had been taken from their families and shipped off to an unknown island in the Great Western Ocean, and there, they had been trained as an army to help the evil Circle of Five take over the world.

But according to Olana, their lives had been anything but exciting. She and the other children had lived in a village, forced to do labor while receiving no education and very little in the way of food or clothing. How alone and trapped they must have felt!

They were no longer trapped, but Eviana suspected they still felt alone. Did Quentin feel unwanted and rejected by society because of his birth? He had been lucky that Silas and Gwennore had taken him in. But that was hardly surprising, since Eviana thought her favorite aunt and uncle had the biggest, most generous hearts in the world.

She settled onto a stone bench, and, closing her eyes, breathed in the scent of the flowers around her. Roses and chrysanthemums. The night air was chilly, but she enjoyed the coolness against her cheeks. Soon, winter would come and the gardeners would extend a glass roof over the top of the garden to keep snow from falling inside and the frosty air from killing some of the garden's more tropical plants.

And once winter had arrived and the snow was deep on the ground, she would make her annual trip south to Vindalyn to see her grandfather. This year, her mother was planning to come with her so she could host a few balls at Vindemar Castle and invite all the nearby noblemen to try their hand at winning a princess.

With a groan, Eviana lowered her head into her hands. So she would spend her days trapped in the privy chamber and her evenings hounded by men who saw only her title and wealth.

But maybe it wouldn't be so bad! All those men who had embarrassed themselves tonight would never try to court her now. She smiled. Tonight's disaster was actually a blessing.

And how strange those men were! *I still wet my bed. I'm afraid of my own shadow. I'm missing half my brain . . . I think . . .*

A chuckle escaped. She pressed a hand against her mouth as her shoulders shook. *I talk to chipmunks. And they talk back. I snore so loud, the windows shatter. I love my mommy!*

"You're crying," a male voice said behind her, and she froze.

Who was that? He didn't sound like one of her personal guards. They were trained never to start a conversation with a member of the royal family. She heard the crunch of gravel as he entered the garden.

"I never meant to hurt you. I was trying to . . . well, there's no excuse for what I did. I am truly sorry."

He had a lovely, deep voice, but not one that she recognized. He wasn't one of the nobles she was acquainted with, so who . . . ? Quentin? Surely not. She glanced over her shoulder.

Holy goddesses! She jumped to her feet. The eagle shifter stood right behind her.

"I didn't mean to alarm you. I . . . I came to apologize."

She took a deep breath and turned toward him slowly. "How did you know to come here?"

His eyes widened as they stood face-to-face; then he quickly bowed his head and lowered his gaze. "Your father told me to come. He also believed that I owed Your Highness a—"

"My father sent you here?"

"Yes. He said you would be here with a few . . ." His gaze searched the garden. "Servants."

"I sent them away." Eviana's breath caught when he suddenly focused those startling golden eyes on her. Could he actually see better than everyone else? He seemed to be looking straight through her. Or deep into her heart.

He took a step back. "We shouldn't be alone."

Was he going to leave? "Papa sent you here, so it's all right for you to . . . stay." Good goddesses, did that sound desperate? She felt her cheeks growing warm.

"You're still embarrassed." He looked away, wincing. "I didn't mean to cause you pain. I am truly sorry—"

"Please stop apologizing."

He glanced back at her with a surprised expression.

She waved a dismissive hand. "You have nothing to be sorry for. As far as I'm concerned, you did me a great favor."

"But I thought you were embarrassed. Humiliated."

"I am not humiliated!"

His eyes glinted as he watched her closely. "I saw the look you gave me. You seemed hurt and angry."

With a huff, she planted her hands on her hips. "Yes, I admit I was embarrassed at first. Everyone was laughing. But now I realize there's no reason for me to be embarrassed. I don't converse with chipmunks or set things on fire. And as far as I know, I don't snore. Nor have I ever wet my bed!"

A corner of his mouth curled up. "That is quite a lot to be proud of."

"Yes." Her mouth twitched. "I consider it an amazing accomplishment."

His smile widened. "Worthy of a knighthood, at least."

"Exactly." She grinned, then realized they were standing there smiling at each other. And good goddesses, the man had dimples.

She schooled her features and turned away. "So . . . as I was saying, you did me a great favor. Those men won't be back, so that's twenty fewer suitors I have to contend with in the future."

"Twenty-five, to be exact."

"Oh." She wandered down the center garden path. "Well,

that is a great relief. I've grown rather tired of my mother's matchmaking efforts."

He followed her slowly. "I suspected you weren't enjoying the ball."

He knew that because he always watched her. Eviana stopped by a rose bush and stroked the velvet petals of a yellow rose. "Is—is it true, what they say about you?" She glanced at him and saw his jaw clench. Oh, no! He must think she was referring to his low birth.

But obviously, he'd done well for himself. His clothes looked rather expensive. Not as flamboyant as those worn by a nobleman, but they had a simple elegance that she found appealing. Most probably, he was wearing those dark colors so he could blend into the shadows and watch everyone with those amazing golden eyes.

"What I meant was . . ." She motioned toward his face. "I was wondering if your eyesight is truly superior."

"Oh." He seemed to relax a little bit. "I cannot say."

"It's a secret?"

"No." He smiled. "I can't compare my eyesight to someone else's when I don't know how well another person can see."

"Ah." She tilted her head, considering that. "I know! We'll test your eyesight against mine."

"We will?"

"Yes! I've been told my vision is excellent." She glanced around the garden. "There!" She pointed at the citrus trees planted along the left half of the far wall. "There are plaques on the wall behind those trees. From here, I can't make out the words. Can you?"

With his eyes narrowing, he took a step toward the trees.

"No fair getting any closer." She stopped him by placing a hand on his chest.

He stiffened, and suddenly, she was aware of how broad his chest was. And firm. Beneath the dark blue velvet, he was hard with muscle.

She removed her hand and turned away as heat rushed to her cheeks.

"The plaques are in shadow," he murmured.

"Yes." She waved a hand nervously at the opening above them. "But the Embraced moons are very bright. So . . . what can you see?"

He focused a moment. "The lemon tree on the left is dedicated to your brother, Prince Eric."

"You're right!" She smiled at him. "You can read the words?"

"The plaque behind the middle tree says 'I, King Leofric of Eberon, plant this orange tree in the year 697 to commemorate the birth of my daughter, Eviana.' "

"You *can* read it!"

He nodded. "And the lime tree is dedicated to Prince Dominic. Apparently, His Majesty expected his children to have sour dispositions."

She laughed. "Don't tell my father that. But this is truly amazing! You really do have the eyes of an eagle."

He shrugged, his bronze cheeks turning slightly pink. "I've never seen citrus trees this far north. Do they actually bear fruit?"

"Yes." She motioned toward the right side of the wall, which was empty. "My mother keeps hinting that she needs grandchildren so they can plant more trees."

"Then your brothers should hurry up and get married."

"Yes!" With a grin, she turned toward Quentin. "That's what I always say. But my parents think I should get married first because I'm female." She shuddered. "It's so annoying."

"You—you've never met anyone you would consider?"

"No." She leaned over to sniff at a red rose. "How could I consider any of those suitors? They're more interested in my inheritance than in me."

"Then they are fools."

She gave Quentin a curious look. "Why is that? Any man with intelligence would want the Duchy of Vindalyn."

"Then I suppose you'll have to marry the man who's missing half his brain."

"Ha!" When she gave his shoulder a light swat, he smiled. Good goddesses, there were his dimples again! He was more handsome than she had realized. And he was so easy to talk to.

She wandered down the path. Why was she enjoying herself so much with this man? He was nothing like the suitors her mother was always pushing on her.

That was it! He wasn't a suitor. Quentin was so completely unsuitable for her, she didn't feel pressured in any way. She didn't have to play the role of a princess, but instead, was free to say whatever she wanted.

She spun around to face him. "Quentin."

He blinked. "You know my name?"

"Of course. We've been introduced a few times, have we not?"

"Yes, Your Highness." He bowed his head.

"Very well, then." She took a deep breath. "I have a proposition for you."

He glanced up quickly. "Excuse me?"

"We should be friends."

He blinked once. Twice. "Friends?"

"Yes." She shrugged. "Not that we'll see each other very often, but from time to time, I think it would be rather pleasant for us to have a talk."

He grew still, his golden eyes watching her closely. "You want to talk?"

"Yes. I found our conversation amusing. Didn't you?"

His eyes narrowed.

Her heart raced. She'd never been this forward with a man before. "So shall we be friends?"

"I am deeply honored, Your Highness." He bowed his head once again. "But no thank you." He turned on his heel and strode toward the entrance.

What? Eviana's mouth dropped open. He . . . he had turned her down? Who in their right mind refused a request from royalty?

She stepped forward, lifting a hand to stop him. But what could she say? *I'm a princess so you have to do as I say?* How awful was that? Especially when the main reason she had enjoyed his company was because she had felt free from her usual role.

Her hand dropped to her side as he disappeared into the hallway. Perhaps he hadn't enjoyed talking to her. Perhaps he had forced his smile just as she did when confronted by an unwanted suitor. Perhaps he didn't even like her.

But then why did he watch her so much?

Tilting her head back, she gazed up at the moons. This was so confusing. But one thing was definitely clear.

Even a princess couldn't get everything she wanted.

Chapter 3

By the time the sun breached the horizon the next morning, Quentin was already flying to Peter's farm just south of the Ron River. After tossing and turning most of the night, he'd finally given up on sleep.

Friends? How could she suggest such a thing? It was wrong on so many levels. First, there was the most obvious problem. She was a princess and he was a servant.

Then, there was the second problem: propriety. Single young women didn't have male friends. Was he so unsuitable she didn't even see him as a man? *Dammit to hell.*

And the last-but-not-least problem: the undeniable fact that spending time with her would be torture for him. She'd found their conversation *amusing. Bah!* How many years had he waited for a chance to talk to her? Finally he had, and dammit, he had really enjoyed it. She'd smiled at him. She'd laughed. She'd even touched him.

It was a potential disaster. Admiring her from afar was bad enough, but if he became better acquainted with her, he ran the serious risk of falling for her even more. How could he let his infatuation turn into love when he knew it was impossible?

He'd done the only thing he could. Walked away. But then he'd stayed up most of the night, questioning his actions. *Fool,* he reprimanded himself for the fiftieth time.

It had always been this way with him, even as a child.

He'd always wanted more than his circumstances justified. Nevis had been right about him. As a nine-year-old, Quentin had wanted to be Nevis's second-in-command, even though he'd known eighteen-year-old Elam was much better suited. He'd also wanted to be a dragon, even though Silas had gently explained that only a Norveshki who was born from one of the Three Cursed Clans could ever be a dragon shifter.

Even so, Quentin had learned over the years that with hard work and perseverance, he could still succeed in spite of any limitations or disappointments that life threw his way. Sometimes he had to readjust his goals. Sometimes he had to be flexible. But never did he have to give up.

Unfortunately, that strategy did not apply to Eviana. He knew it, but he still longed for her. *Fool.*

A long ribbon of water came into view, and Quentin recognized it as the Ron River, which cut across the middle of Eberon. To the west, Ronford Castle was perched on a hill overlooking the river. Even farther to the west was the main road to Vindalyn and the ferry that crossed the Ron River.

Quentin veered right, flying toward the castle where Earl Ronford lived. Black flags whipped in the breeze from the tops of the castle's six towers. He circled the old stone fortress, peering down into the inner bailey. A few servants moved about, their demeanor quiet and subdued. The whole castle appeared to be in mourning for Uma.

Once again, he wondered how she had died. He had no clothes stashed in this castle, so he didn't plan on stopping. In his experience, people didn't want to talk to a naked person who had been a bird just moments before. They were much more likely to screech and run for the hills.

Peter's farm was not far away, situated east and south of Earl Ronford's land. Quentin swooped around, headed east. Peter had been one of the lucky ones from the Isle of Secrets. His parents weren't nobility, but they owned a nice tract of land that included a cornfield, a large vegetable garden, a few animals, and an apple orchard. They had been eager to have their only son back to help them on the farm. Peter had married ten years ago, and even though he was only a year and a half older than Quentin, he already had five children.

As Quentin flew over the cornfield, he noticed the corn had already been picked. He descended gradually until he was skimming over the apple orchard. There, he spotted Peter with seven boys. Four of them looked about sixteen, too old to be his sons. The youngest three, ranging in ages from three to nine, all had Peter's brown eyes.

The four older boys were holding a blanket under an apple tree, while Peter, on a ladder, was shaking the boughs to cause ripe apples to fall. His three sons were picking apples off the ground and depositing them into baskets. The youngest looked up as Quentin flew by.

"Daddy, a big bird!"

Peter spotted Quentin as he settled on a high branch of a neighboring tree. "Quen, is that you?"

Quentin nodded his head and let out a squawk.

"You know that bird?" one of the older boys asked.

"Yes." Peter descended the ladder. "Set the blanket down."

When the boys did, he grabbed an edge and pulled it out from under the pile of apples. "Here, Quen. You can use this."

"Why does the bird need a blanket?" another boy asked.

"He's a shifter," Peter explained, then motioned to the apples rolling about on the ground. "Get them into baskets. Then you can take a break for a little while."

"Yes, sir!" The boys scurried about, grabbing all the apples.

Quentin flew down to land next to the blanket and shifted. While the boys gasped, he pulled the woolen material around his waist and tied it. "Good morning, everyone."

"I remember him!" Peter's oldest boy exclaimed.

"Me, too." The middle son grinned. "He's the Bird Man."

"And he's naked!" The youngest pointed at him.

"Liam." Peter turned to his oldest son. "Take your brothers to the house and tell your mother to put on the kettle. We have a guest."

Liam and his brothers scurried off.

With a smile, Quentin shook Peter's hand. "How have you been?"

"I'm fine." Peter gave him a wry look. "But it's been too long since you came to see us. My youngest boy didn't know about you."

"I've been busy." Quentin adjusted the blanket around his waist as he walked beside Peter, headed toward the house. "You've hired some workers for your farm?"

"Oh, the boys?" Peter glanced back to check on their progress. "There's too much for me to harvest by myself in the fall, and my boys aren't quite old enough to be of much help. So I told the village boys if they helped me, they could each take a bushel of apples home to their families."

"Sounds like a good plan."

Peter slanted him a curious look. "You didn't come here to talk about my farm. What's going on?"

Quentin shrugged. "Just the usual information gathering."

Peter snorted. "I can't imagine that I know anything important."

Ahead of them, Peter's three sons approached the back door of his house.

"Mama!" the youngest one yelled. "Daddy's in the orchard with a naked man!"

"*What?*" a female voice answered; then Peter's wife peered through the open doorway. "Oh, Quentin!" Suzy smiled and waved at him. "Make yourself at home."

Quentin waved back at her. "Thank you."

Peter motioned to an outdoor table and chairs beneath an arbor covered with grapevines. "We can sit here."

Quentin plucked a grape off and popped it into his mouth. "You have a wonderful home and family."

With a smile, Peter sat at the table. "Yes, I've been blessed."

Quentin sat across from him. "Last night at Ebton Palace, I was talking to Olana at the Autumn Embrace party. Oh, happy birthday, by the way."

"Thank you. How is Olana doing?"

Quentin shrugged. "As well as she can. Thank you for writing to her. She really enjoys the letters she receives."

Peter's smile faded. "It's the least I can do. She writes often, and I can tell that she's lonely."

"She mentioned something from your last letter. Uma passed away?"

Peter winced. "Yes. Just over a week ago. The Earl of Ronford and his wife are devastated."

"Do you know what happened?"

Peter frowned. "I've heard some odd rumors, so I'm not sure how true this is, but apparently she tried to jump all the way up to one of the castle towers."

"What?"

"That was her Embraced gift. She could jump extremely high." Peter shrugged. "So many Embraced gifts are completely useless. Look at mine. I'm a farmer who can make it hail. How ridiculous is that?" He shook his head. "She should have just ignored her gift and lived a normal life the way I do."

"Why would she try to jump up to a tower?"

Peter set his elbows on the table and leaned forward. "Rumor has it that she was trying to impress a young guard. He was on duty at the top of the tower, and he teased her that she couldn't reach him. So she tried it, and she did make it, from what I heard. Her feet were on the battlements, but then she lost her balance and fell."

Quentin narrowed his eyes. "She fell even though the guard was there?"

"Aye. It was a shame he wasn't able to pull her to safety."

Or he had wanted her to fall, Quentin thought. "I need to talk to this guard."

"You're not alone," Peter muttered. "The earl wanted to question him, too, but he disappeared right after the accident. He was found three days ago in the village of Arondale with his throat slit."

Quentin sat back. So the guard had been murdered to keep his mouth shut. "He either let Uma fall, or he pushed her."

"You think she was murdered? But why—" Peter hushed when his oldest son rushed toward them, holding a pair of breeches.

"Mama told me to give these to you," Liam said.

"Thank you." Quentin slid his feet into the trouser legs.

"Do you like being an eagle?" Liam asked. "Is it fun to fly through the air? Do you ever fall down?"

"Liam," Peter said. "Can you go see if the tea is ready?"

"All right." Liam trudged back to the house.

"Uma was only twenty-four," Peter muttered as Quentin stood and turned around to pull the breeches up to his waist. "Why would anyone want to kill her?"

"I don't know." Quentin buttoned the waistband, then sat back down with the blanket around his shoulders.

Peter shook his head. "It doesn't make sense. If someone wanted to murder her, he could just stab her or choke her to death. Why wait until she was making a jump?"

Quentin tilted his head back to gaze at the grapevines overhead. If the guard had teased her, then he'd been trying to make her jump. "She was killed while using her gift."

"A strange coincidence," Peter muttered.

"Or payback for being Embraced."

Peter scoffed. "How can that be? The Embraced have been accepted for over twenty years now. And why would anyone target Uma? She jumped into trees to rescue kittens and lost kites. There was nothing dangerous about her gift."

They grew quiet as Suzy emerged from the back door, carrying a tray.

Quentin drank tea and ate biscuits, making small talk with Peter and his wife, while his mind swirled around the possibility that Uma could have been murdered because she was Embraced, executed on purpose by using her own gift. And then the guard had also been murdered so he couldn't talk . . . about what? Who was behind this? Did it have something to do with the dark cloud Maeve saw hovering over Eberon?

Before noon, Quentin was flying once again, this time headed upstream to the small village of Arondale. He'd never been there before, but Peter had told him it was located in a hilly area where a series of hot springs fed into the Ron River. Centuries ago, the local chapel of Enlightenment had claimed the springs were medicinal, so sickly people from all over Eberon flocked there to bathe in the healing waters.

According to Peter, one of the Embraced children from the Isle of Secrets was living there: Victor, the young boy who had been in the nursery with Uma. After investigating the death of the guard, Quentin planned to locate Victor to tell him the sad news.

The hot springs came into view: five pools on a hillside connected by small waterfalls. Steam hovered on the surface of each pool, but he could still see people relaxing in the hot water. At the base of the hill, the spring water emptied into the Ron River, turning it from a small creek into a small river. A quaint village hugged the banks of the river with stone bridges arching over the rushing water. Close to the springs, a Chapel of Enlightenment stood, its spire reaching toward the heavens and the sun god that was worshipped inside the stone walls.

A crowd of people was gathered around one of the bridges, and as Quentin drew nearer, he could hear the shouting of agitated voices, pierced by a female's mournful cry.

"Save him!" she screamed. "Please save him!"

Quentin zoomed down for a closer view. Several village men were dragging a young man from the rushing stream onto the grassy bank. One of the men kneeled down and began to press against the young man's chest.

"No!" the woman wailed as she fell to her knees beside them. "Victor, don't leave me."

Victor? Quentin landed on the branch of a nearby tree.

The man who was doing chest compressions stopped, tears running down his face. "I'm trying to push the water out of him, but it's not working."

"No!" the woman cried, then turned to the nearby priest. "Father, can you save our son?"

"I'm not sure." The priest kneeled beside Victor to examine him. "He's not breathing."

The woman burst into tears. She must be Victor's mother, Quentin thought, while the crying man was no doubt his father.

"How could this happen?" a villager asked.

"I thought Victor could hold his breath for over an hour," another said.

"Aye," another villager agreed. "That was his gift."

Victor's father frantically started pressing on his son's chest again. "You can't drown, Victor! How could you drown?" He rolled his son over to pound on his back.

Everyone gasped, and Victor's father fell back onto his rear in shock.

The back of Victor's head was smashed in.

Murder. Quentin's thoughts raced. If Victor's Embraced gift was the ability to hold his breath for over an hour, he should never have drowned. But someone had made sure he would, after bashing him in the head to render him unconscious.

A death caused by the failure of his own gift. Much like what had happened to Uma. What were the chances of two

Embraced people being murdered in such a way within a fortnight?

After a moment of hesitation, Quentin took off, flying north. He was tempted to remain in Arondale to gather more information, but at the same time, he felt that Leo needed to be warned at once. The Embraced were being targeted for death.

Nevis. That was where he needed to go first. Nevis could send some soldiers to Arondale to investigate Victor's death and the death of the guard. And Nevis needed to be warned first because the greatest number of Embraced were gathered at his academy. After reporting to Nevis, Quentin would head on to Ebton Palace to tell Leo that the Embraced were all in danger.

Damn. Eviana was Embraced.

Don't panic, he thought as he ramped up his speed. Whoever was behind this would have a hard time using her gift against her. For, as far as he knew, only her family knew what her gift was.

There was a bounce in Eviana's step as she sauntered along the deck of the royal barge. What a glorious turn of events! Who would have believed that today she would be sailing up the Ebe River on her way to Norveshka? A regiment of soldiers and sailors were accompanying her: the soldiers to keep her safe and the sailors working hard on the poles and oars to move the barge upstream.

It had all started that morning at breakfast, which had been a rather strange affair. Between bites of food, her father had kept muttering that the country was overrun with worthless noblemen. Her brothers, always competitive, had tried to outdo each other with their plans to thrash the worthless noblemen who had run away the night before. And her mother had sighed and looked forlorn as she pushed her food around her plate.

Eviana hadn't felt well, either, since she'd tossed and turned all night, unable to sleep. She'd slumped in her chair, her bloodshot eyes burning as she gazed at her food with no appetite.

Her mother had taken one look at her and gasped. "Oh dear, I'm afraid this disaster has taken a terrible toll on you. What can we do to help?"

The only disaster that had popped into Eviana's mind was Quentin's refusal to be her friend. After all, it was his rude rejection that had kept her up all night. Of course her parents had assumed her haggard appearance was due to her so-called wretched humiliation. They didn't realize she was grateful to have twenty-five fewer suitors.

But there would be more. Once she and her mother arrived at Vindemar Castle, her mother would start planning more balls and finding new men who wanted a share of her inheritance. If Eviana didn't want to feel trapped, she had to escape.

So she had heaved a pitiful sigh and mentioned how much happier she might be in Norveshka. To her amazement, her parents had immediately agreed and ordered the royal barge to be made ready for departure. Eviana had been so surprised, she'd nearly fallen out of her chair. She was actually going to Norveshka!

Her father had warned her to stay no longer than two months, since it was still her duty to spend time with her grandfather in Vindalyn. But two months of freedom! Eviana grinned as she sauntered along the deck of the barge. She'd heard Aunt Gwen complain in the past that the Norveshki winters were bitterly cold, but Eviana was too excited to let that bother her. She'd had all her warmest clothes packed into two trunks, and within an hour, she was ready for this glorious new adventure. How would the mountains and forest look when covered with snow?

Norveshka, land of dragons. She stopped by the barge's

railing and took a deep breath of the crisp autumn air. Would her best friend, Lennie, be there? Or was she back at Benwick Academy? Either way, Aunt Gwen would make sure Eviana met some young and handsome dragon shifters. She might even make some new friends.

Quentin. He lived at Draven Castle when he wasn't busy roaming about.

Her smile faded. Would he still refuse to be her friend? Why had he refused? She'd wondered about it all night, but she'd never been able to figure out a reason other than the most obvious one. He simply didn't like her.

Blast him. She turned to walk along the deck. *Don't even think about him.* Her life was taking an exciting turn, and she would not let that scoundrel cast any darkness on her bright and sunny day.

She entered the large cabin, decorated with the official colors of Eberon—red and black. Comfy chairs and footstools, upholstered in red velvet, sat atop a thick red carpet. A carved black table was covered with a small buffet to provide sustenance during the journey, which would take most of the day. By this evening, she would arrive in the town of Vorushka on the border of Eberon and Norveshka.

Her appetite had returned so she helped herself to a plate of cold meat, cheese, and fruit. Then she settled on a comfy lounge chair. Soon, the gentle sway of the barge lulled her into a light sleep.

She woke when the barge suddenly rocked hard and the soldiers shouted in alarm. What on Aerthlan . . . ? She rose to her feet, but the barge lurched once again, nearly causing her to fall over.

A man screamed in pain.

Good goddesses, were they under attack? She ran to the door and cracked it open. The servants were no longer poling the barge up the river, but were huddled on the deck floor.

The soldiers were shooting arrows toward the southern bank.

Who in Eberon would dare attack the royal barge? Eviana opened the door wider and spotted a group of men and horses on the southern shoreline. Three of them shot arrows with tethering ropes attached, and the barge shuddered when the arrows hit the side. They meant to drag the barge ashore?

Meanwhile her soldiers were busily shooting arrows, and the group onshore was taking casualties. She gasped when she spotted one of her own men sprawled on the deck, an arrow in his chest.

"Your Highness, go back inside!" the captain shouted. An arrow hit his shoulder, knocking him back against the cabin.

Panic ripped through Eviana as she slammed the door shut. Holy Light and goddesses, she couldn't allow her men to be injured or killed. What did the attackers want?

Her? She gulped.

The barge groaned as it was dragged toward the shore. Did they mean to kidnap her? Kill her?

She jumped when a nearby window shattered. The arrow that had burst through struck hard into the lounge chair where she had been asleep just a few minutes before. She had to put a stop to this.

There was a way. Her Embraced gift.

She had to use it now.

Chapter 4

When the Ebe River came into view, Quentin turned left to follow it downstream to Benwick Castle, located where the South Fork emptied into the Ebe. After a short while, he noticed a small herd of horses ambling upstream. Each one was saddled but had no rider. *Strange.*

After a few minutes he spotted about two dozen men he supposed were the owners of the escaped horses. They were resting on the grassy southern bank of the Ebe. Asleep? Two of their horses had remained close by, and they lazily munched on grass while the men remained motionless.

He dipped lower for a closer view. Arrows! Seven of the men had arrows embedded in their chests and appeared to be dead. The others were not wounded, as far as Quentin could tell, but they were not moving. This was definitely strange.

Whoever had attacked these men had moved on, so he circled upward for a more panoramic view. To the west, he spotted a barge drifting slowly downstream. Its flag, hanging limply along the pole, was red and black, identifying this as an Eberoni vessel. It had rotated sideways as if no one was piloting it.

His vision zeroed in on the arrows shot into the side with tethering ropes attached. *A-ha.* The group of men lying on the southern bank must have attacked this barge with the intent to drag it ashore. Why? To rob the passengers onboard?

A breeze caught the vessel's flag, unfurling it, and his breath caught. *The royal barge!*

His heart pounded as he picked up speed, headed to the vessel as quickly as possible. Who in their right mind would attack the royal barge? They had to know that attacking a member of the royal family meant a death sentence if they were caught. And which member of the royal family was onboard?

As he swooped down, he spotted guards in the official Eberoni uniform sprawled about on deck. In fact, all the soldiers, servants, and sailors were just lying there. Some appeared wounded, some not, but none were moving. Were they all dead?

He landed, quickly shifted, then checked the nearest guard. The man was breathing and had no visible wounds, but no matter how much Quentin shook him and yelled at him, he seemed incapable of waking up. What on Aerthlan had caused all these people to lose consciousness?

Quentin threw open the door to the cabin. Empty inside. *Dammit to hell.* Who was onboard? As far as he knew, Eric and Dominic were supposed to return to Benwick Academy today, but they usually traveled by horse. Besides, the barge had already gone past Benwick Castle. Who could . . . ?

Eviana?

His heart tightened in his chest. *Oh hell, no.* He dashed around the deck, searching for her.

A raven landed on one of the unconscious guards and, with its beak, poked at the man's chest.

"Shoo!" Quentin yelled. "He's not dead!"

The bird tilted its head to look at Quentin with its black eyes. Then, with a gargled caw, it flapped its large black wings and flew away.

"Damned bird," Quentin muttered as a pile of white clothing drew his attention. He ran over to inspect it. Wool and lace . . . petticoats? If Eviana had taken these off, then she must have . . .

The river! He leaped into the air, instantly shifting and gaining altitude so he could scan the river.

There! He spotted a head of black hair and zoomed toward it. Eviana was desperately trying to reach the southern bank, but the strong current was carrying her downstream. His heart clenched when he saw her fighting to keep her head above water.

He dove into the water, shifting into human form at the last second. When he grabbed her from behind, she let out a cry and kicked at him. Damn, she must think he was one of the enemies who wanted to kidnap her.

"Eviana, it's me!"

With a gasp, she stopped wriggling. "Quen—" She went under, and he pulled her back up.

Shit. Her woolen gown had soaked up a ton of water. No wonder she was struggling to swim. At least she'd had the foresight to remove those petticoats.

Coughing, she grabbed onto his shoulders.

Luckily all the years of flying had given him extremely strong arms and shoulders, and he managed to maneuver them toward the southern bank. When he was able to stand, the water reached to his chest and he suddenly remembered he was naked. Damn, this was going to be awkward. He swept her up into his arms so the fall of her skirt would cover his private parts.

"You don't need to carry me. I can walk."

He scanned his surroundings for an excuse to keep holding her and spotted a patch of reeds along the shore. "Your shoes have fallen off. There could be broken reeds in the riverbed that would stab your feet."

"But—" She shoved a tendril of wet hair away from her mouth. When she returned her hand to his shoulder, she hesitated, her palm a few inches from his skin. "You don't have shoes, either."

Had she realized he was naked? He glanced at her and saw her gaze sweep over his bare chest before she settled her hand back on his shoulder. Her fingers were icy cold, and the light shudder that skittered through her body made him wince. How could he protect her from catching a cold? "I'm afraid I don't have any dry clothes to offer you."

"I'll be all right. My gown will dry . . . eventually."

Unfortunately, a jumble of wayward thoughts crowded his mind. Why not offer to warm her up? No, heat her up. Set her on fire. *Stop it. You're an eagle, not a pig.* As he moved forward, the water level dropped to his thighs, and her sodden gown molded itself against his groin. Damn, that was cold. "Once we reach the shore, you can rest while I fly upstream to grab some horses. I'll try to find you a blanket." *And some clothes for myself.*

Her hand on his shoulder flinched slightly. "You're going to the men who attacked the barge?"

"Yes. I don't know why, but they're not moving."

"They're in a deep sleep."

He halted. "Do you know how that happened? And why you weren't affected?"

She winced. "I did it to them. They'll be unconscious for several hours."

Holy goddesses. "That is your Embraced gift?"

She nodded, glancing away with an embarrassed look. "I know it's not a good one."

"Are you serious? You saved yourself from being kidnapped." Or worse, though he didn't want to mention that. "Thank the goddesses you have such a powerful gift."

She frowned. "I'm afraid it creates as many problems as it solves. Everyone fell asleep, including the sailors, so there was no way to control the barge. I didn't know what to do. It could take hours for the barge to float back to Ebton Palace, and meanwhile, there are injured men onboard who need help. The only recourse I could think of was to swim ashore, steal a horse from the attackers, and ride straight to Ebton."

With a nod, he started walking again. "That was a good plan."

"Thank you." She slanted an apologetic look at him. "I'm sorry I kicked you. I-I guess I panicked."

"You were under attack. No need to apologize."

She sighed. "I wish I had a better gift. If I could fly like you, I could have escaped much more easily."

"No. If you had taken to the air, they would have shot you down with arrows. I've been shot at before, and it's not fun."

"Someone tried to shoot you?"

He shrugged as he reached the shore. "Believe me, your gift is much safer."

A pained look glinted in her eyes. "It's far from safe. I've been told many times that it's dangerous. And cowardly."

Who the hell would tell her that? He tamped down a burst of aggravation as he stopped and gave her a stern look. "Would you have preferred a prolonged battle where more of your men were injured or killed? You were outnumbered and completely vulnerable in the river, like a sitting duck. There's a difference between being cowardly and foolhardy."

"I know that, but I hate the fact that all my gift allows me to do is to stop something from happening and then run away."

"You're not running away. You avoided capture and made a plan to save your people. I think your gift is amazing. You can escape any bad situation. No one will ever be able to hurt you."

Her eyes glimmered with tears, and she blinked them away. "You make my gift sound like it *is* amazing."

"It is."

"If I use it, I end up all alone."

"You're not alone now." *Damn.* He shouldn't have let that slip out. When he cast a wary glance at her, he found her staring at him, her gaze searching his.

"You rescued me last night and now, you've done it again."

"I—" He lowered his gaze but caught a glimpse of her sodden gown molded to her breasts. The cool air had caused her nipples to pucker. *Damn.* He shifted his focus to a row of poplar trees growing on the ridge above the southern bank. "I was just lucky that I happened to come along when I did."

"Quentin," she said softly, and he glanced back at the lovely green eyes that were still studying him. "Thank you."

A frisson of desire shuddered through him, and his grip on her automatically tightened. A surge of heat shot to his groin, and he winced. At this rate, there would be steam coming off her wet skirt.

"I must be too heavy for you."

"No, not at all." He focused once again on the trees.

"But you're frowning. I know my gown weighs quite a bit."

"I'm perfectly fine." He glanced at her and his heart swelled once again with desire. "I'm going to lay you down." *Damn, that sounded forward.* "I mean, I'll set you down." He fell to his knees, leaning over to place her gently on the grass, carefully turning her on her side so she would face away from him. "I'll be right back. Rest here."

"Quen—" She glanced back at him, but he'd already shifted.

He hopped back to give his wings room to extend, then took off, headed upstream to the group of ruffians.

Rest? How could she rest at a moment like this? She sat up to watch Quentin fly away. She'd never seen him in eagle form so close before. Why, his wingspan had to be at least eight feet! And she'd never noticed before that his head was white while the rest of his body was gold. He was truly a magnificent creature. Were his feathers as soft as they looked?

Stop thinking about him! Why would she waste any time over a man who had rejected her? Unfortunately, the only way she could lessen the sting was to remind herself how completely unsuitable he was, and that just made her feel snobbish. Rejected and snobbish.

And cold. She crossed her arms, hugging herself as a chilly breeze made her shiver. Rejected, snobbish, and cold.

And wet. Rejected, snobbish, cold, and wet.

Get a grip, Evie! It was better than being dead. If Quentin hadn't come along when he did, she might never have made it ashore. She shuddered, not even wanting to think how close she had come to drowning.

Thank you, Light and goddesses, for sending Quentin. It was embarrassing that she'd flailed and kicked at the poor man when he was only trying to save her. But ever since her childhood kidnapping trauma, she tended to react poorly if she was grabbed from behind without warning. Fortunately, Quentin had still managed to hold her up and swim ashore. Not surprising, though, when she could see *and feel* the strength in his arms and shoulders.

She'd let him think her cold, sodden gown was to blame for the first shiver that had coursed through her body, but the cause had been something else entirely. In one fell swoop, she'd realized two shocking things: one, he was naked, and two, he possessed an astonishing amount of strength.

After talking to him, she'd learned even more about him. He was thoughtful and kind. Her brothers had always teased her, claiming her gift was only good for taking the easy way out of any situation. She knew deep down why they made light of her gift. Their father had reacted so strongly that it was their way of trying to soften the impact. But when

Quentin had made her gift sound wonderful, her heart had been touched. And the way he had carried her ashore had seemed so . . . caring.

Was she wrong to assume he didn't like her? But what other reason could there be for refusing her friendship?

Ugh, she was still thinking about him! Why should she care how he felt about her? Obviously, he had saved her because it was the right thing to do. He was simply doing his duty. After all, he was paid to serve the royal families.

Meanwhile, the barge had drifted into view, and she chastised herself for sitting onshore doing nothing while her wounded men needed help. As she scrambled to her feet, her wet skirt tangled with her legs.

"I'm going to do like Lennie and start wear breeches," she muttered as she wrung excess water from her gown.

Before abandoning ship, she'd twisted the skirt up and tied it around her hips so she'd be able to swim. But once she'd jumped overboard, the skirt had soaked up so much water that it had unfurled itself and nearly caused her to drown.

Shaking the skirt out as she walked, she headed upstream. Since her feet were bare, she picked her path as quickly and carefully as she could, avoiding rocks and gnarled tree roots.

She reached a large willow tree growing along the shore and ducked underneath its canopy of dangling leaves, painted yellow and gold for autumn. How lovely. And peaceful. A light breeze fluttered the leaves, making them shimmer in the sunlight. It was such a sheltered place she could almost forget the terror she'd just endured.

But how could she forget her wounded guards? She snapped off some pieces of a dead branch. Aunt Gwen had taught her how to make a concoction with willow bark that could relieve pain and lessen a fever.

She lifted her damp skirt to make a small pouch for the bark pieces. Hopefully she'd be able to find some sort of canvas bag once she reached the group of ruffians. Holding the pouch closed with one hand, she reached with the other to sweep aside a few dangling branches.

Holy Light and goddesses, she was closer to the ruffians than she'd realized. Only twenty feet away from her, a man was sprawled on the ground with an arrow in his chest. His head was turned in her direction, his glassy, unseeing eyes staring right at her. She jerked back, letting the leaves fall back into place. The golden canopy surrounded her once again, but the peaceful feeling had completely fled.

She clutched her skirt tightly as her heart began to pound. Up until this moment, she'd been so occupied with her struggle for survival and Quentin's dashing rescue that she'd managed to avoid dealing with the harsh truth. But she could no longer escape it. It slammed into her, making her head reel.

These men had planned to capture her. Had they intended to hold her for ransom? Or use her to force her father to do their bidding? Had they planned to abuse her? Kill her?

Light, help me. The thundering of her heart became so loud, it echoed in her ears. The horrid memory of that first kidnapping flooded her mind, taking her back to her third birthday when a Norveshki dragon had swooped down and captured her.

She squeezed her eyes shut, trying to block the memories, but still she felt the dragon's arms locking her in a tight vise, squeezing the breath out of her as its talons dug into her tender skin. She'd been so afraid. Afraid she would die. Afraid that Aunt Gwen would die, trying to save her. The terror had been so overwhelming, she'd lost consciousness.

That is all in the past, she reminded herself. *All in the past.* She inhaled deeply to calm her nerves. The nightmares had stopped years ago. She was over the kidnapping now. And besides, it had all worked out. Aunt Gwen and Uncle Silas had fallen in love and were happily married with two children. And now, Norveshka was Eviana's favorite place to visit.

But as soon as she managed to squelch the memory of her first traumatic event, the second one crept into her thoughts. She'd been thirteen when that one had happened. And she'd been left all alone to deal with it.

She shook her head. She wasn't alone now. Quentin was with her.

Three. Thirteen. And now she was twenty-three. Was she doomed to have some sort of horrific experience every ten years?

Fear seeped, icy cold, into her bones, and she struggled against the panic, concentrating on slow, long breaths. She'd overcome adversity as a child and a youth. She could certainly do it again as an adult. *You're the daughter of King Leo and Queen Luciana. You have the blood of heroes in your veins.*

With her nerves steeled, she swept the curtain of leaves aside and lifted her gaze past the dead man with the glassy eyes. *I can face any danger. I have nerves of . . . Crap!*

Quentin was in human form, pulling on a pair of borrowed breeches, the worn leather gliding over his bare buttocks. With a choked yelp, she jumped back and slapped a hand over her mouth. Oh, dear goddesses, she hoped he hadn't heard that!

Thankfully, the curtain of leaves had fallen back into place. She groaned inwardly. Maybe she was a coward after all. One look at a man's bare buttocks and she'd gone into hiding? But how could a man be so beautiful?

An image popped into her mind of a bronze statue of the sun god she'd seen a few years ago. At the time, she'd thought the artist had done an excellent job of representing a god, for no mortal man could actually look that perfect.

But Quentin did. He was bronze all over. Muscular all

over. When he'd straightened, the muscles in his rump had flexed and tightened. *Good goddesses.* She pressed her other hand against her pounding heart.

Wait a minute. *Blast it.* She'd dropped all the bark she'd collected. Because of a man's arse?

How embarrassing. She knelt on the ground to gather the pieces. But as she glanced down, she realized her wet gown was glued to her breasts, leaving nothing to the imagination. Holy Light, this was mortifying! Had Quentin noticed? She plucked at the fabric, trying to pull it away from her skin.

The leaves suddenly parted, and a long, vicious-looking blade whipped through them to point at her face.

"Oh!" She fell back on her rear. Quentin was there, his breeches half-buttoned, his chest bare.

"Evi—Your Highness." He tossed the dagger onto the ground behind him. "I heard a noise and thought someone was planning to steal the horses before we could."

"I—" She scrambled to her knees, hunching over so he couldn't see her wet bodice as she quickly picked up the fallen pieces. "I must have gasped when I accidentally dropped all this willow bark. It can be used to treat any pain my guards might be feeling once they wake."

"Oh, that's clever of you."

She fumbled with her skirt to make a pouch for the bark. Why did the man compliment her if he didn't like her? She glanced up and realized his breeches were right at eye level. Three buttons done. The top two still open.

"And it's very thoughtful of you to be concerned about your guards."

She blinked. Guards? What guards? "Oh." Instead of thinking of her guards, she'd been ogling this man. How embarrassing!

"Are you all right? You look a bit feverish."

"I'm fine. But I could use a bag for this—"

"I'll find one." As he turned away, the leaves fell back into place, and she was alone once again.

With a groan, she rose to her feet. Hopefully, he hadn't noticed how clearly her breasts were on display. But she'd certainly noticed him—the dips and swells of his muscular abdomen, the wide expanse of his chest, his toned arms.

She shook her head. Why was she becoming so obsessed with the man's body? Nearly drowning must have addled her brain.

"I found a bag," he announced.

She gave her bodice one last tug. *Just act regal and he won't notice.* She swept aside the leaves and stepped out.

Quentin was waiting for her, a canvas bag in his hands and a blanket tossed over a shoulder. "The bag has a few apples inside, but it should work."

"Yes, thank you." She emptied the bark into the bag as he held it open. A quick glance confirmed that he had also finished buttoning his breeches.

"Here." He handed her the blanket, then strode toward the horses that were tethered to a nearby tree.

With a silent groan she wrapped the blanket around her shoulders. Of course he'd noticed her breasts. Since when did the man miss anything with his superior golden eyes?

He hooked the bag onto the back of the saddle, then grabbed the coil of rope next to it. "Before we leave, I'm going to tie up the ruffians who are still alive."

She glanced at the men and suppressed a shudder when she realized there were at least seven dead bodies close by. "You needn't worry about the survivors. They'll be asleep for hours."

"Yes, but it may be several hours before any soldiers can collect them." He retrieved the dagger he'd dropped on the ground. "We can't let them escape. They attacked the royal barge to do you harm. They must pay for their crime."

"Aye." She watched as he sliced off a section of rope and tied a man's hands behind his back. "How can I help? Should I collect all their weapons?"

He nodded as he tied the man's ankles together. "Good plan. We can't leave them with the means to cut themselves free."

She scurried about, focusing on the weapons instead of the dead bodies. It was so much easier to keep any anxiety at bay as long as she stayed busy. Soon, she had every quiver, bow, and sword stacked into a small pile. When she discovered a dry handkerchief next to one of the men, she tied the red cloth around her head to keep her wet hair from dangling in her face.

Meanwhile, Quentin had tied up the survivors and dragged them far away from each other. Any knives he found concealed on their bodies, he added to her pile.

"You should keep this for yourself." He offered her the dagger he'd been using.

"But don't you need it? I can protect myself by clapping my hands."

"Is that how your gift works? You clap your hands?"

She nodded. "Three times in a row. So I can't do it holding a knife."

"You should still have one, just in case. Let me find you a belt." He strode toward a ruffian who had a belt with a sheath. After pulling off the man's belt, he handed it to her.

She looped it around her waist, but it was too big.

"I could cut it shorter," he suggested.

"No, I'll make it work." She crossed the ends of the blanket and stuffed them under the belt, then slid the dagger into the sheath.

His mouth curled up. "You look like a pirate."

"A lady pirate?"

He feigned a shudder of horror. "That's the worst kind."

She snorted. "How would you know? Have you ever met one?"

"Aye." His golden eyes twinkled. "Just now."

Her mouth twitched as she rested a hand on the knobbed handle of her dagger. "Then I'll make you my first mate."

Something intense flared in his eyes. It only lasted for a second, but it was long enough to make her heart flutter. *Good goddesses, what was—*

"We've wasted enough time here." He looked away, scowling.

She blinked. Why did he seem angry all of a sudden?

"That damned bird," he whispered, his eyes narrowing on the row of poplar trees growing along the nearby ridge.

"Excuse me?"

"The raven." He pointed at one of the trees, and with a gargled caw, a large black bird took to the sky and flew away.

She shuddered. "It was probably attracted to the dead bodies here." He continued to stare at what looked like empty blue sky to her. "Can you still see it?"

He nodded, then motioned to the pile of weapons. "We should hide these before we go. Otherwise, the ruffians might manage to scoot over here and free themselves."

"You're right." She looked around. "I know!" She grabbed several swords and hurried back to the willow tree. From past floods, the river had eroded the soil around an exposed root, leaving a hole underneath. She slid the swords into the hole.

"Good plan." Quentin tossed in an armful of quivers. Soon they had transferred all the weapons to the hiding place.

"All done," she announced as she tossed several dead, leafy branches on top. "Every lady pirate should have a hidden treasure, don't you think?"

He smiled at her. "Definitely."

She smiled back, relieved to see him being friendly again. And showing his dimples. "So, are we ready to go?"

"Almost. I discovered a bag of gold on one of the ruffians. I'm guessing he's the ringleader. I want to take him with us, so he can be questioned first."

A bag of gold? "Then you believe he was paid to kidnap me? Who would do that?"

"I don't know, but we'll hear the truth once Lady Olana touches him. After you." Quentin swept aside some willow branches and motioned for her to pass through.

She strode toward the horses. "I assume we're riding straight to Ebton Palace?"

"No. Benwick Castle."

She halted with a jerk.

"Is something wrong?" He stopped beside her, giving her a curious look.

"I-I think we should go to Ebton. Lady Olana is there."

"Benwick is much closer. And General Nevis is there with the army. We need him to—"

"I can't go there."

"Of course you can. It's downstream a short—"

"You don't understand." Oh, dear goddesses, she hated having to admit this. "I can't go to Benwick. I was . . . banned."

"What?"

"Banned." She gritted her teeth. "As in not allowed to set foot there. My gift is considered too dangerous."

He gave her an incredulous look. "That's bullshit."

She scoffed. "Is it? How could I go to the academy with the other Embraced? When it came time for everyone to practice their gift, I would have knocked them all out. Along with the general and the entire army. I would have caused the country to be completely vulnerable"—she motioned to the ruffians—"to people like this."

"So that's why you never went to school there?"

"Yes." With a sigh, she hugged the blanket tighter around her shoulders. "Not only could the country be in danger, but I could be, too. If the nature of my gift became known, I could be kidnapped and used as a weapon. So I was confined to the private apartments—"

"That's bullshit."

"Why do you keep saying that?"

"Do you have no control over your hands? Do you clap them accidentally in your sleep? Or when you sneeze or hiccough?"

"Of course not."

"Then it's bullshit." With a frustrated look, he dragged a hand through his long blond hair. "I can't believe General Nevis made such a ridiculous decision."

"My father made it."

Quentin blinked. "King Leo?"

She nodded. "Just to be safe." Her father's decision had kept her and the country safe, but it certainly hadn't safeguarded her feelings. Her parents had always been apologetic and hired the best tutors they could find, but she'd always felt dejected whenever she'd heard stories about all the other Embraced and royal children spending time together at the academy. "It was one of the lessons I learned at a young age: to put the well-being of the country and its people before myself."

Quentin stared at her, then said softly, "I'm sorry."

His unexpected sympathy brought tears to her eyes, but she blinked them away and forced a smile. "It's part of the price of being a princess."

He nodded slowly. "I never realized that before."

Was he going to keep staring at her? "Then we're going to Ebton?"

"No. We're going to Benwick, and if they don't like it, they can go to hell." As he stalked away, her heart tightened in her chest.

He was on her side. Even if he didn't want to be her friend, he was still on her side. Even though he was unsuitable, he was, thankfully, still on her side.

So they would go to Benwick Castle. The eagle and the outcast. She smiled to herself, imagining how her brothers would react. "Then let's go."

Quentin hefted the ringleader over his shoulder, then carried him to the larger of the two horses.

Once again she was impressed by Quentin's strength as he easily handled the dead weight of the large unconscious man. And once again, she wondered who would have paid this man and his gang to kidnap her.

After tossing the ringleader across the saddle, Quentin quickly tied him in place. "Once we arrive at Benwick, we'll send someone to Ebton to let your parents know what happened. And we'll request Lady Olana's assistance."

Eviana nodded. "I'm still wondering why someone would want to kidnap me. No one knows about my gift, so that couldn't be the reason. Are they seeking revenge against my father, or trying to use me in order to control him? Or could it be an act of revenge by one of the suitors who was humiliated last night? Or perhaps a nobleman who believes he could take me away and force me into marriage?"

Quentin's eyes widened. "I hadn't thought of that. I . . ." He looked away, frowning.

She stepped closer. "What do you think?"

He slanted a worried look at her. "While it is possible you may have been targeted because you're an heiress, it could also be because you're Embraced."

She blinked. "But there must be dozens of Embraced people in the country."

"Yes. And two of them have been murdered in the last fortnight."

She gasped. *Murdered?*

Quentin touched her arm. "It's all right. No one can hurt you, remember? You have your gift to protect you."

She nodded, her heart pounding. Yes, she had her gift. And she had Quentin, thank the Light and goddesses. She hurried over to the tree to untether the horses. "Do you want to ride with me?"

"Actually, I plan on flying. That way, I can spot an ambush from far—"

"*Ambush?*" Her hands fumbled as she untied the reins.

"Whoever paid for your capture might have an alternative plan. So we need to have a plan, too."

She swallowed hard. "All right."

"I'll keep a lookout from above, while you ride as quickly as you can, towing our prisoner here." He tied the reins of the larger horse to the saddle of the smaller one. "If I spot any danger, I'll land on the back of our prisoner, and that will be your cue to use your power."

"What if it puts you asleep?"

"If it does, I'll take a nap along with everyone else, while you keep moving. But I don't think I'll be affected while I'm an eagle. The horses didn't fall asleep."

"That's true. My gift has never worked on animals." She gave him a hopeful look. "So you should be immune."

"Then let's get going. Mount up." He held her horse steady as she swung into the saddle.

She took a deep breath to steady her nerves. What a sight she must be with her wet gown and bare legs showing from the knees down. This would be considered quite scandalous at Ebton Palace, but now, with dead bodies nearby and a possible ambush ahead, it hardly seemed to matter.

How quickly her life had changed. Danger had hooked its claws into her, leaving her with one goal: survival. But at least she wasn't alone.

Quentin led her horse up the ridge to the nearby road, then handed her the reins. "Go ahead. You'll see me soon."

"Aye." She urged her horse into a slow trot. *I'm not alone,* she thought as she glanced back to make sure the second horse was following along with their prisoner.

The shadow of a large bird moved along the dirt road, and she glanced up to see Quentin soar past her. What a relief it was, knowing that if she had to use her gift, it would probably not affect him. He would still be by her side. In all of Aerthlan, there could be only a few men with that ability.

With a small gasp, she realized something new and astonishing.

Quentin was not so unsuitable after all.

Chapter 5

Thankfully, the journey to Benwick Castle passed without incident. For the length of the one-hour trip, Quentin flew in a zigzag pattern, carefully scanning the woods that lined the road while he kept an eye on Eviana's progress. He also searched the sky periodically for any sign of the raven he'd seen earlier. Something about that bird was bothering him.

Since Quentin was a bird shifter and a spy, he had to acknowledge the possibility that another Embraced person could possess similar gifts. But as far as he knew, all the Embraced children who had exceptional gifts were either currently students at Benwick Academy, or had studied there in the past. He had never heard of the existence of another bird shifter.

Stop worrying over nothing. It's just a bird, he told himself for the fiftieth time. Ravens were known to eat carrion, so it made sense for the bird to have been there. But ravens were also curious and intelligent. Some were even able to speak a few words and mimic other animals. Was one capable of being a spy? Had this raven purposely eavesdropped on them?

If that was true, was the raven flying back to whoever had paid the men to attack the royal barge? Who exactly was behind the attack? Had they known Eviana was onboard? Her trip had not been planned in advance, so if she was actually the target, then the news of her voyage had leaked from Ebton Palace. Was there a spy at Ebton? And what was the purpose of the attack? Could it be as Eviana had feared, and some bastard was trying to force her into marriage? Or was it as Quentin suspected, and she'd been targeted by the same person who had murdered Uma and Victor?

Down below, Eviana sneezed, and Quentin glanced back at her, worried once again that she would catch a cold. Her hair and gown were probably still wet, and her lovely, long legs were exposed from the knee down to the chilly autumn air. Dammit, he should have stolen a pair of boots for her, even though they would have been far too large.

A crosswind caught him, nearly flipping him over, and he dipped down to right himself. *Dammit, pay more attention to what you're doing.*

He gained altitude and spotted the towers of Benwick Castle three miles away. Surrounding the castle was an army encampment of over fifty tents and a dozen practice fields. Numerous soldiers were out, working on their fencing, archery, and wrestling skills.

From the castle's highest tower, the Eberoni flag flapped in the breeze. Down in the army encampment, he spotted the flags of Woodwyn, Norveshka, Tourin, and the Isles. Each kingdom had been invited to post some soldiers here, a move that had encouraged camaraderie amongst the armies from the five different kingdoms.

When Nevis and his wife, Princess Elinor, had decided to open this academy, they had wanted to welcome the young Embraced from the entire world of Aerthlan. The five kings and queens had readily agreed, and had decided to send their children there, too, whether they were Embraced or not.

For the last twenty years, Aerthlan had enjoyed peace, primarily because the five queens had grown up as sisters and their husbands had followed suit, declaring themselves brothers. They had soon realized, though, in order to keep this peace continuing into the future, they needed their children to grow up with the same feeling of family. So, at the age of fourteen, all the royal children were sent to Benwick.

All except Eviana.

Quentin made a hissing sound through his beak, and his talons curled tight. *Too dangerous, his feathered ass.* How could her own father have made such a decision?

Well, who else would? A king would always have the last word when it came to his country's security. *But damn!* Did her family have any idea how much they had hurt her? Quentin's heart had clenched when he saw the pain in her eyes. Couldn't her family see what they'd done?

He'd always thought she'd lived a carefree life, her every whim quickly fulfilled by servants. No doubt, she had been pampered to some degree, but she'd also been judged unfairly and isolated from her peers. She had an amazing gift, but she'd been made to feel ashamed of it. She must have felt lonely.

Dammit to hell! Quentin huffed another angry breath. They'd made her feel like an outcast. Who would have believed that he would have something in common with a princess? Over the last twenty years, he'd heard his share of whispered gossip and to-his-face insults regarding his heritage. He'd learned to grit his teeth and ignore them. But how could he ignore Eviana's pain? It made him want to pummel something.

Even so, she'd endured the situation without letting it tarnish her positive and cheerful spirit. Indeed, it was that joyful vibrance that had first drawn him to her. But now he realized the true depth of her courage and strength. There was so much more to her than he'd ever imagined. She might not know it, but she could take on the world.

You fool, you're falling for her even more. Once she was

safely inside Benwick, he needed to step back. Even so, if any-one at the castle tried to ban her entry, Quentin was tempted to punch the bastard. Even if he happened to be royal.

After one last check of the forest, he put on a burst of speed and zoomed toward the highest tower of Benwick Cas-tle. He had a trunk of clothes stashed inside, and the minute the guards on the battlements saw him landing, they would alert General Nevis of his arrival.

Elam actually spotted him before he landed, so by the time Quentin had shifted, his friend was waiting for him by the tower entrance.

"Send for Nevis right away," Quentin said as he dashed into the tower.

"I already have."

"Good." Quentin's trunk of clothes was sitting next to the two that belonged to the prince and princess of Norveshka. They normally flew here as dragons and needed clothing once they arrived. He retrieved a pair of brown leather breeches from his trunk and pulled them on. "Princess Eviana is about two and a half miles away with a prisoner. Can you have a troop escort her in?"

"Princess Ev—a *prisoner*? What the hell is going on?"

Quentin glanced over his shoulder as he buttoned up his breeches. He'd known Elam all his life. They'd grown up to-gether on the Isle of Secrets, and since Elam's gift had been considered too inferior for the Embraced army, he'd been rel-egated to a life of hard labor in the village blacksmith shop. When Nevis and Princess Elinor had arrived on the island to defeat the Circle of Five and their Embraced army, Nevis had made eighteen-year-old Elam his second-in-command.

Now, twenty years later, Elam was a tall, muscular colonel in the Eberoni army, still devoted to the general who had rec-ognized his potential when no one else did.

"The royal barge was attacked." Quentin retrieved a cream-colored linen shirt from the trunk while Elam's eyes widened with a stunned look. "Her Highness is all right, but I would appreciate an escort—"

"Of course." Elam snapped out of his shock, then darted back onto the battlements to deliver his orders.

By the time Quentin had pulled on a pair of leather boots and joined Elam on the battlements, a troop of soldiers was charging through the castle gate, drawing the attention of all the soldiers outside the walls. They immediately grabbed their weapons in case they were needed.

As Quentin tucked in his half-buttoned shirt, he spotted Eviana in the distance. The soldiers would soon catch up with her. She was safe.

With a sigh of relief, he turned to peer down into the inner bailey of the castle. Normally, there would be students milling about the courtyard between classes and enjoying a few snacks from the nearby kitchen. But today, only a few guards were stationed by the gate and along the ramparts. The tables by the kitchen were empty.

Every year, the academy closed for two weeks around the time of the Spring Embrace and for another two weeks at the Autumn Embrace. That way, the students could go home to celebrate Embraced birthdays with their families. Since Ebton Palace was less than two hours away, the Eberoni princes were usually the last to leave and the first to come back.

"I assume Eric and Dominic have already returned?" When Elam nodded, Quentin continued. "Did they mention anything about the party at Ebton Palace last night?"

"No. Why? Did something happen?"

"No." Quentin shook his head. "Nothing important." So the brothers were staying quiet about the scandal in order to protect their sister. Even so, the news would eventually make its way here.

He spotted the two princes exiting the large kitchen, carrying a pitcher of cider and a stack of wooden plates and cups. They were followed by Nevis's seventeen-year-old daughter,

Faith, who held a bowl of fruit, and the Norveshki prince and princess, who were toting platters of bread and cheese.

"When did Pendras and Lenushka arrive?" Quentin asked as the group of five plunked their food on a table and passed out the wooden plates and cups.

Their actions reminded him of one of the rules Nevis had always insisted on at the academy. The royal children were expected to fetch their own food, wash their own clothes, and make their own beds, just like the other Embraced students. There were servants, of course, in order to keep the castle functioning and to assist Nevis and his wife, Elinor, but they were not at the beck and call of the royal children. All students were treated equally here, but when it came to socializing, Quentin had noticed that the royals tended to spend their free time with one another. After all, the other Embraced could end up serving them at some point, much as Quentin did.

"They flew in a few hours ago," Elam replied as the group sat down to begin eating.

So the two from Norveshka had traveled early enough to have missed seeing the attack on the barge, Quentin thought as he followed Elam down the stairs. He knew from experience that the flight from Draven Castle took several hours. As dragon shifters, Pendras and Lenushka could manage the trip a bit faster than he could. "They must have left home at dawn."

"Aye," Elam agreed. "They said it was already snowing there, so they were happy to come south."

No doubt, the next to arrive would be Prince Reynfrid from Tourin. His younger sister, Roslyn, would not be returning to Benwick. The twenty-year-old Tourinian princess was remaining in Lourdon to prepare for her spring wedding to a wealthy nobleman.

It was the next big event at which all the royal families and nobles would gather to celebrate. Quentin knew all about it since he had been the one to spread the news and extend the invitations. He'd even been invited himself, no doubt so he could spy on any attendees whose loyalty was in question.

The last royal children to return to Benwick would be the ones from Woodwyn and the Isles. Prince Brendelf and his younger sisters Kendall and Glenda would make the long journey from Woodwyn on horseback, while Princess Julia and her younger brother, Rudgar, would travel by ship from the Isle of Moon to Ebton Palace before continuing the rest of the way on horseback.

As Quentin reached the base of the stairs, Pendras and Lenushka spotted him and waved. Of all the royal children, they were the ones he knew best, since he'd lived at Draven Castle the last twenty years. Pendras had inherited his black hair from his father and his lavender eyes from his mother, while Lenushka had her father's green eyes and her mother's white-blond hair.

Eric turned his head to see whom they were waving at, and he immediately stood, pushing his chair back to aim a steely-eyed glare at Quentin. Dominic quickly followed suit.

So they were still angry about last night.

"Quentin!" Nevis called as he exited the Great Hall with Elinor. With a big smile, he hurried down the stone steps to the courtyard. "How are you, my boy?"

Quentin smiled back. "Very well, my lord."

Nevis clapped him on the back. "Always a pleasure to see you. You bring back good memories. Right, Elinor?" He turned to his wife.

She gave him a dubious look. "You mean the time when our lives were in imminent danger and the world nearly succumbed to the forces of evil?"

Nevis shrugged. "Aye, but it wasn't all bad. That's when I met you."

"True." With a grin, she gave Quentin a hug. "It's good to see you again."

"Why are you here?" Eric demanded as he and his younger brother stalked toward them.

Nevis gave the prince a disapproving look. "Quentin is a good friend. He doesn't need a reason to visit." He turned to Quentin. "Although I would wager that he has a good one."

"He does," Elam agreed, but before Quentin could explain, Dominic interrupted him.

"We've already warned the general about Aunt Maeve's prediction." The twenty-year-old prince glowered at Quentin.

"What prediction?" Pendras asked as he approached with his sister and Faith.

Lenushka's eyes narrowed. "Is it bad?"

"It is," Quentin agreed, "but we have a more urgent matter at hand. Princess Eviana is on her way here, about a mile aw—"

"Evie?" Eric snorted. "You're mistaken. She's on her way to Norveshka."

Lenushka nodded. "I've already sent a mental message to my parents to expect her."

"Besides, she can't come here," Dominic added. "She's not allowed—"

"Don't even say it," Quentin growled at the young prince, who stiffened with a stunned look.

Eric scoffed. "You dare talk to royalty like that?"

"I speak as I see fit," Quentin replied, and Eric drew in a hissing breath.

"Get over it," Nevis ordered, and Eric turned away with a muttered curse. "Are you sure, Quentin, that she's coming here?"

"Aye." Quentin nodded. "The royal barge was attacked."

A series of gasps sounded around him.

"*What?*" Eric spun back toward him, his eyes widening with horror. "Attacked? With my sister onboard?"

"Is she all right?" Dominic demanded, his voice strained.

"Yes." Quentin felt a small measure of gratification when

he saw how upset Eviana's brothers were. "Elam has already sent a troop to escort her in. She's unharmed, but after the barge was attacked, she had to swim ashore. Her gown is soaked through, so she's most likely chilled to the bone."

"Oh dear," Elinor murmured, then turned to her daughter. "Faith, we need lots of hot water."

As Faith ran to the kitchen, Eric snapped out of his state of shock and sprinted toward the open gate.

"Where is she?" he yelled as he peered through the gate. "I don't see her!"

"She should be less than a mile away," Quentin called back, surprised by how agitated the prince was. Eric had been well trained as a soldier, and with his Embraced gift of being able to melt metal, he was practically invincible on the battlefield. He'd also been raised with the knowledge that he would inherit the throne, so his usual demeanor was one of strength and confidence. But now, as he paced back and forth at the gate, he looked downright frantic.

"Who would be crazy enough to attack the royal barge?" Frowning, Nevis crossed his arms over his broad chest. "Do you think they knew Eviana was onboard?"

"If they did, then someone at Ebton told them," Quentin replied.

Everyone winced at the thought of a spy in the royal palace.

"So they were trying to kidnap Eviana?" Dominic asked, his face pale. "She was kidnapped once before . . ."

"My mother told us about that," Lenushka said quietly. "Evie doesn't like to talk about it."

"Nay, she had nightmares for years." Dominic glanced at his brother with a worried look. "She wasn't the only one."

So Eric had been traumatized, too, Quentin realized. Gwennore had told him the story years ago, and it had upset him to imagine a young Eviana so terrified that she'd lost consciousness. But he'd never considered how horrifying it must have been for a three-year-old boy to witness a dragon carrying off his twin sister. And then he would have watched his parents fall apart.

And now it made perfect sense that the attackers had gone after Eviana. For when it came to King Leo and his two sons, they all clearly shared a major weakness: the princess.

"I see her!" Eric waved at his sister. "She's fine! She's waving back!" He stalked back toward the group with a determined stride. "Tell us everything you know, Quentin. Who attacked the barge? Did the bastards get away?"

"No, they're still there, unconscious and tied up." Quentin turned to Nevis. "We'll need to send someone to collect them."

"I'll go," Elam volunteered. He motioned to a soldier and gave orders for a troop to saddle up and ready extra horses.

"Poor Eviana. What a terrifying experience for her." Elinor patted Quentin on the shoulder. "I'm glad you were there to help."

"Aye," Nevis agreed. "Very fortunate that you were there."

Dominic extended a hand toward Quentin. "Thank you for coming to her aid."

"Aye, thank you." Eric shook his hand next.

Damn. Quentin gritted his teeth. Did everyone assume Eviana was helpless? Did they not realize how brave and strong she was? "I'm afraid you're all mistaken. I was on my way here, flying along the Ebe River, when I came across the battle scene. By the time I arrived, it was all over. Eviana had handled the entire situation herself."

Eric blinked. "What?"

Lenushka's eyes lit up. "Did she really?"

Quentin nodded. "Aye. She used her gift to stop the attack. Not only did she protect herself, but most likely, she saved the lives of her guards and crewmen."

The men in the group appeared stunned, but Elinor and Lenushka exchanged excited looks.

Eric frowned. "So you know what her gift is?"

"I do now," Quentin replied. "Since no one was awake to pilot the barge, she decided to abandon ship. Her plan was to swim ashore, steal a horse from the attackers, and ride straight to Ebton Palace."

"Yes!" Lenushka clapped her hands.

"Good for her." Elinor grinned.

"That's when I arrived," Quentin continued. "I helped the princess tie up the attackers so they couldn't escape. It was her idea to confiscate all their weapons and hide them under a willow tree by the riverbank. Elam, when you collect the attackers, you should bring back their weapons."

"Will do." Elam dashed off to join the troop that was preparing to leave.

"I'll go, too," Pendras offered. "I can fly upstream and spot them." He darted up the stairs so he could shift on the battlements.

"Eviana is bringing a prisoner with her," Quentin told those who remained. "We believe he could be the ringleader, but we won't know for sure until he's awake and can be questioned. I suggest we send for Lady Olana."

Nevis nodded. "Good idea. We also need to tell Leo and Luciana what happened."

"I'll do it." As Dominic dashed off to the stables to ready his horse, he called for some soldiers to join him. Since the younger prince was in training to become the next Lord Protector of the Realm, his orders were quickly followed.

A shadow raced across the courtyard as Pendras shot across the sky in dragon form, headed up the Ebe River. While the two groups of soldiers gathered by the gate, preparing to leave, Quentin told Nevis and the rest of the group about the deaths of Uma and Victor and how he suspected they had been targeted because they were Embraced.

"Then the attackers may have fired upon the royal barge because Eviana is Embraced?" Elinor asked.

Eric hissed in a breath. "They may have intended to kill her."

Lenushka winced. "Thank the Light she was able to use her gift."

The group went silent, and Quentin assumed they were all realizing the depth of this new threat. None of them knew who this new villain was or why he or she was targeting the Embraced. But they knew that nearly every student at Benwick was Embraced, and many were on the road right now, traveling back to the academy.

They could all be in danger.

Chapter 6

During the trip, Eviana had pulled her blanket up to cover her head, but her bare feet remained so cold, they had started to throb. The pain didn't seem the worst of her problems, however, not when she considered the possibility that some mysterious person or group of people wanted her dead.

A shudder racked her body when she could no longer see Quentin overhead. Where was he? She couldn't imagine that he would abandon her. He was a man of honor; she was sure of it. There had to be a reason why he'd flown ahead of her.

As she came around a wooded bend in the road, she spotted the towers of Benwick Castle in the distance. Of course! Quentin was there, warning everyone of her imminent arrival. Would she be stopped outside the gate, barred from entry? That would be humiliating.

But at least she should be safe from attack now. She let out a shivery breath of relief when she spotted the armed encampments of the five different kingdoms. Surely she was safe.

Her heart lurched when a troop of soldiers charged through the gate. Were they coming to stop her? As the troop advanced toward her, time seemed to crawl more and more slowly. What if they meant to turn her away? *You're a princess. You can demand entry.* She had to, or her feet would surely be nothing but frozen chunks of ice.

Finally, after what seemed an eternity, the troop halted a few yards in front of her.

"Welcome to Benwick, Your Highness," the leader announced. "Please allow us to escort you inside."

After an hour of fear and cold, she nearly wept. "Thank you." She moved her horse into their group, along with the horse she was leading. "Could you see to the prisoner?"

"Aye, Your Highness." The leader whipped out a knife, cut the tethering line, and passed it to another soldier.

She glanced toward the open gate and spotted her brother, Eric, waving madly at her, and she waved back. A sudden, glorious feeling of elation swept through her, and she urged her horse into a gallop. She was safe. She was welcome. Quentin must have explained what had happened.

The troop's leader raced alongside her as they sped past the army encampments. Soldiers waved at her as she passed by.

After a few minutes, she surged through the gate and quickly reined in her horse since the courtyard was full of soldiers, readying their horses for departure. She glanced around, searching for anyone she knew.

"Evie!" Dominic tossed his reins to another soldier and dashed toward her. As she started to dismount, her cold limbs refused to cooperate as if they'd been frozen in place.

"Evie." Dominic pulled her off the horse. "By the Light, you're practically blue."

Twin bursts of pain skittered up her legs as her frozen feet hit the hard flagstone surface of the courtyard, and she hissed in a breath. "I—I'm fine."

"No, you're not," Dominic growled as he gripped her by the shoulders to look her over. "When I think about those bastards attacking—"

"Evie!" Eric yanked her into his arms. "Thank the Light you're all right. I won't let anyone hurt you again. Never!"

Tears stung her eyes as she recalled how her twin brother

had latched onto her after Uncle Silas had taken her back to her family after the kidnapping. For months afterward, he'd crawled into her bed at night to hold her hand. And when she'd suffered from nightmares, he had, too.

"Evie!" Lenushka pushed Eric aside and hugged her. "By the Light, you're frozen!"

Eviana blinked back tears as she returned Lennie's hug.

Elinor grabbed her hands and rubbed them with her own. "My poor dear, we'll have you in a hot bath soon."

Nevis gave her a pat on the back. "It must have been quite a frightening ordeal for you."

"I'm fine, really." Eviana searched the small group surrounding her. What had happened to Quentin? Was he all right? The clatter of horse hooves behind her drew her attention, and she turned to see the rest of her escort coming through the gate, towing the prisoner.

When Quentin appeared and strode over to the prisoner to check on him, she noted he looked well. More than well. His cream-colored shirt, although tucked in, was mostly unbuttoned, giving her an excellent view of his muscular torso. And those tight leather breeches—her mind flashed back to how she'd caught him pulling on the last pair of breeches on the riverbank.

He must have felt her gaze upon him, for he suddenly looked straight at her with those mesmerizing golden eyes. She felt frozen in place, unable to look away as a peculiar sensation fluttered in her chest. *Good goddesses.* What was coming over her? Was she actually attracted to this man? Why? Because she'd seen him naked and he was beautiful? That seemed terribly shallow of her. But he'd also come to her rescue. He'd defended her. Protected her.

Because it is his duty, she reminded herself. As if to emphasize that point, he turned away from her and began untying the knots that held the prisoner secure to the saddle. He was obviously more interested in the prisoner than in her.

"Evie," Dominic said, drawing her attention. "I'm leaving now for Ebton."

"Oh." She noted the small group of soldiers ready to accompany her brother. "Tell our parents that I'm all right and perfectly safe."

"They're still going to be upset," Dominic grumbled.

"I don't want them to worry about me," she insisted. "The main problem now is the barge. They need to bring it into port so they can tend to the wounded soldiers." She unhooked the bag from the saddle of her horse and handed it to her brother. "The willow bark in here can be used to ease the pain of the wounded."

"All right." Dominic looped the drawstrings over his saddle horn, then mounted his horse. He and his troop charged through the gate.

As a second group saddled up, Nevis explained, "Elam is going upriver to collect the rest of the criminals."

Eviana spotted the leader, who was wearing the uniform of a colonel. "Don't forget their weapons. We hid them under the willow tree."

"Aye, Your Highness." Elam nodded, then rode through the gate with his troop.

"We heard about the weapons you confiscated," Lennie said, looping an arm around Eviana's shoulders. "And how you tied up the attackers so they couldn't escape."

Eviana blinked. "Excuse me?"

"Quentin told us all about it," Elinor said with a grin. "How you halted the attack and swam ashore to steal a horse."

"We're all so very proud of you!" Lennie added.

Quentin had made it sound as if she'd done everything on her own. Why? She glanced back at him and caught him watching her. Quickly, he turned his attention back to untying the prisoner.

Eric grinned at her. "It's good to see that you can still be tough."

"Of course she can," Lennie insisted.

"She's going to be frozen solid if we don't get her inside." Elinor took Eviana's arm to escort her toward the Great Hall. "Lenushka, could you check on the hot water? And have it brought to my bedchamber."

"Yes, my lady." Lennie dashed off to the kitchen.

"We'll put you in my bedchamber," Elinor said with a smile. "My husband won't mind at all if I share his room for a few days."

"Thank you." At the foot of the steps leading up to the Great Hall, Eviana glanced back.

Eric, Nevis, and Quentin had laid the still-unconscious prisoner out on the flagstones and were searching through his pockets. Nevis removed a bag of gold from an inside pocket of the man's jacket and upended it into his hand.

A dozen gold coins rained down, some landing in the general's hand, others falling onto the ground.

"Dammit to hell," Eric growled. "Someone paid a high price for my sister's capture."

"Aye." Nevis tossed the leather pouch down with disgust.

Quentin's eyes narrowed on the pouch, then he suddenly grabbed it and reached inside to pull out a small, crumpled piece of paper.

"What is that?" Eric peered over Quentin's shoulder. "*Father Saul, Bramblewood.* That's all it says."

A priest? Eviana's mind raced. Had a priest paid for her kidnapping?

Nevis took the piece of paper and examined it. "Bramblewood is a small village about fifteen miles east of here."

"I'm going." Quentin dashed up the stairs to the battlements.

"I'm right behind you!" Eric shouted as he sprinted to the stables.

"Come, dear." Elinor led Eviana up the stone steps to the wide double doors of the Great Hall.

At the top of the stairs, Eviana glanced back once again. On the battlements, Quentin had removed his clothes, although with the stone parapet blocking her view she could only see his chest. His body wavered for only a second, then he was gone, and a magnificent eagle soared into the air. Meanwhile, Eric and three soldiers led their saddled horses from the stables. "I should be going with them."

With a scoff, Elinor opened the doors. "You've done quite enough today already. You need to rest. And we need to warm you up before you catch your death of cold."

A hot bath did sound wonderful. And warm clothes and a warm bed. But Eviana seriously doubted she would be able to rest. Quentin and Eric could be in danger as they hunted down whoever had ordered her kidnapping. Or murder. And if this unknown villain was intent on killing the Embraced, he now had two more Embraced targets headed his way: her brother and Quentin. This ordeal was not over.

It was, in fact, just beginning.

Quentin flew east over patches of forest and quilt-like blocks of fields that were being harvested until he spotted a small village situated on top of a flat-topped hill. As he swooped down for a closer look, he noted the square-shaped village green. In the southwest corner, a small group of women had gathered around the stone well to gossip. He dropped onto a nearby rooftop to listen while he scanned the surroundings. The discussion had to do with a young farmer's unfortunate attraction to one of the women's daughters. Two of the women thought Bert was a good catch, but the other three disagreed. And most important, Bessie's mother insisted, was the fact that Bessie wanted nothing to do with the young man.

At least the poor sap hasn't fallen for a princess, Quentin thought as he turned his attention to the east side of the green. A wooden church of Enlightenment sat there, its steeple reaching for the heavens.

He soared into the air, then circled the church to peer through the windows. The largest windows faced east, so worshippers inside could watch the rise of the sun god, Light, at dawn. The building appeared empty, and there were no living quarters attached to it. Did Father Saul live elsewhere?

There were several dozen houses built along the southern and western edges of the village green. To the north, sprawled a wattle-and-daub two-story building. He narrowed his eyes at the letters above the wooden door. The Bee and the Bramble. The village pub and inn. It would be the best place to gather information.

After landing on a wide windowsill, he peered through the partially open window. No priest in sight. An older man sat alone in front of the fireplace, nursing a tankard of beer and mumbling to himself. At a nearby table, four young men were sharing a pitcher of beer. From their ruddy faces and slurred speech, Quentin figured the foursome had been imbibing for several hours.

"I sold a whole cartload of radishes and cabbages in Mount Baedan," one of the men boasted.

"Then you can buy us the next round," a second one declared, and they all laughed.

"I bought the last two," the first one protested.

"And we're barely getting started," a third one chimed in.

"Can't do it," the first man replied. "I've already spent most of my earnings. Bought some of the finest clothes you've ever seen. Bessie will be so impressed at church on Sunday."

"Then you're a fool, Bert," the fourth man grumbled. "If you truly wanted to impress her, then you would buy *her* some fine clothes."

So this was the infamous farmer Bert who was smitten

with Bessie, Quentin realized. Sometimes he could learn important information by simply listening in, but today, he was getting an earful of useless gossip. He needed to ask questions, and that meant he needed some clothes. With a flap of his wings, he took off toward the village houses.

Clotheslines crisscrossed all of the backyards, but only a few had clothes attached. A woman's shift and gown. Not happening. A child's shirt and breeches. Too small.

Good goddesses. He cringed when he spotted the only clothesline that held men's clothing. Red-and-yellow-striped breeches and a green linen shirt, the color reminiscent of a smashed insect. Ugh.

Beggars can't be choosers, he reminded himself as he landed in the backyard next to an empty cart. He quickly dressed, but with no shoes available, he had to walk barefoot across the village green to the pub. In the distance, the women at the well snickered. *Dammit.*

He opened the pub's heavy wooden door and stepped inside, his eyes quickly adjusting to the low light. The old man by the fire had fallen asleep, and the four young men were still arguing over who would buy the next round.

A young waitress with curly brown hair and pink cheeks approached him, her gaze traveling over his strange appearance. She stopped a good twelve feet away, as if afraid he might be diseased or insane. "I've never seen you here before."

He gave her what he hoped was a charming smile. "I'm just passing through."

She glanced at his bare feet. "Without shoes?"

He motioned toward the door. "I left them outside. I had an accident earlier with a cow patty and didn't want to bring the foul smell inside your fine establishment."

"Oh." She nodded with a relieved smile. "I suspect you must be hungry and thirsty. What can I get for you?"

"Actually, I—" Quentin began, but stopped at the clatter of a chair being knocked over.

"What the hell?" Bert lurched toward him. "What are you doing, wearing my new clothes?"

Oh, shit. These *were the fine new clothes he'd been boasting about?* In all his years of borrowing clothes, Quentin had never encountered this problem before. But then, he normally managed to dress inconspicuously. He gave the drunkard a dumbfounded look. "You mean you own a shirt like this, too?"

"That *is* my damned shirt! And those breeches are mine, too!"

"What the hell?" The second drunkard stumbled to his feet, pointing at Quentin. "That man's a thief!"

The third man joined in. "We should lynch the bastard!"

The fourth one snickered. "Those are the most hideous clothes I've ever seen."

"What?" Bert whirled toward his friend and nearly fell over.

The fourth man shrugged. "The way I see it, you're damned lucky the thief relieved you of those clothes before you embarrassed yourself."

"I am not a thief!" Quentin pretended to look affronted. "I just came from Mount Baedan, where I purchased these fine clothes this morning, and the lady there assured me they were one of a kind."

"*What?*" Bert bellowed. "That's what she told me!"

Quentin huffed. "Well, she must have lied to us. I have a mind to return these."

"You should," the fourth man grumbled. "They look like they belong in a traveling circus."

Quentin glared at him. "It's obvious that you don't recognize fine fashion when you see it."

"Exactly!" Bert agreed, giving Quentin a grin.

The fourth man shook his head. "I can't believe there are two people in this world with the same horrid taste."

"He must be related to me!" Bert announced. He pounded on their table. "Come, cousin, join us for a drink!"

"Yeah," the second one agreed, then hiccoughed. "Can you pay?"

Quentin exhaled with relief. He'd escaped a lynching for now. It was a shame, but far too often his job required him to lie his ass off, and over the years he'd learn to do it well. "I would love to, but first I have some business I must attend to." He turned back to the waitress. "I have an urgent message for Father Saul. Do you know where I might find him?"

"Aye, I do." She nodded, then motioned toward a hallway. "He's in the back room with two other priests." She lowered her voice to a conspiratorial whisper. "A very important meeting, Father Saul said. He asked that they not be disturbed."

"I believe he will want this message," Quentin insisted.

"All right, then." The waitress waved for him to follow.

"Come back when you're done, cousin!" Bert yelled as Quentin headed down the dimly lit hallway.

"Do you happen to know the two priests who are meeting Father Saul?" Quentin asked.

The waitress shook her head. "Nay, I've never seen them before. They were both rather young, midtwenties, I would say, but the taller one . . ." Her steps slowed to a stop as she let out a dreamy sigh. She lowered her voice to a whisper. "'Tis a pity when a man that handsome becomes a priest."

"Perhaps you haven't heard, but priests are allowed to marry now," Quentin whispered back. As the head of the Church of Enlightenment, Leo had made the new ruling after receiving multiple complaints about priests living with mistresses. Leo had hoped the new law would lend some protection to the women and their children, who had been viewed before as unlawful and illegitimate.

"Really?" The waitress's eyes lit up. "Then I should bring him an extra slice of pie. I made it myself."

"Great idea." Quentin approached a nearby door. "Is this the room?" When the waitress nodded, he paused, wondering what kind of approach he should take with the three priests. Luckily, Eric and his soldiers would be here soon.

He rapped on the door, then cracked it open. At first glance, the room appeared empty. "What . . . ?" He swung the door open wide and froze.

"Is something wrong?" The waitress peered around him. "Oh, where did they go? I never saw them leave."

"One is still here." Quentin pointed at the body on the floor, partially hidden behind the table.

The waitress stiffened with a gasp.

As Quentin strode inside, he quickly noted the half-eaten meal on the table and the open window with lace curtains fluttering in the breeze. Had the remaining two escaped after murdering their fellow priest? "Is this Father Saul?"

"Aye." The waitress nodded, her eyes growing wide with horror. "Is he . . . is he . . . ?"

Quentin stooped over the body, noting the glassy, unfocused eyes. A quick check verified there was no pulse at his wrist, nor any breath coming from his nostrils. His face was red and contorted with foam-like dribbles around his mouth. "He's dead."

With a strangled cry, the waitress stumbled back. "How . . . why?"

"Miss."

"This is terrible!" Her hand fluttered over her chest as she breathed too rapidly.

He stepped toward her. "Miss, do you have a name?"

She blinked at him, her face turning pale as she struggled to breathe.

"Take slow, deep breaths. In. And out. Do you have a name?"

She drew in another long breath. "P-Polly."

"That's good, Polly. Do you have a local constable?"

"Ah, yes." Color crept back into her cheeks. "He's asleep by the fireplace. Should I fetch him?"

The old drunk was the constable? Quentin sighed. Luckily Eric was on his way. He could take charge of the investigation. "If you can manage to wake the constable, that would be good. Thank you, Polly."

She darted off.

Quentin returned to the dead priest and hunkered down for a closer inspection. The man appeared to be about thirty years old and in fit condition. There were no wounds or sign of an attack. Given the foam around his mouth, he'd most likely been poisoned. A quick look at the table confirmed that all three men had partaken of the same meal with a few bites left on each plate. All three had drunk from the same bottle of wine. So the poison had come from somewhere else.

A ring on the priest's left hand drew his attention. The top part was flipped open, revealing a hidden compartment. Thanks to his superior eyesight, he could discern a few tiny grains of white powder caught in the latch.

So Father Saul had carried a supply of poison on his person? Why would anyone do that? Only for some nefarious purpose, Quentin concluded. And indeed, if the priest had paid for Eviana's kidnapping, then he was guilty of criminal activity. In fact, all three of these priests were most likely involved.

Had Father Saul been prepared to poison himself if he was captured? What sort of secret was worth dying for? Or was this death a punishment for failing to kidnap the princess? Had the priest willingly poisoned himself or had the other two priests forced him to do it?

Quentin lifted the man's hand to see if there were any bruises around the wrist to indicate he'd been coerced. None.

As the robe's loose sleeve fell back, the priest's forearm was exposed, and on the underside of his arm, a tattoo was visible. A circle with rays emanating from it like those of a sun.

Was this a portrayal of the sun god, or did it have deeper meaning? Quentin had heard that the Circle of Five had used a similar pictograph, a sun with five rays, to symbolize their movement. He counted the number of rays on this one. Eight.

"Hey, cousin!" Bert's voice sounded in the hallway. "Why is Polly shaking the constable and saying someone is dead?"

Quentin straightened just as the drunk foursome crowded around the open door.

"Holy Light!" Bert jumped back, causing the other three to stumble about and bounce off the walls.

The second drunkard pointed a trembling finger at the body. "Is . . . is that Father Saul? He looks dead!"

"What?" The third one peered through the doorway, then choked as if he was about to throw up.

Quentin nodded. "I believe he was poisoned."

"By the food?" Bert asked. "Oh, shit! We ate here today, too!"

The third one moaned, slapping a hand over his mouth.

"What is all the ruckus here?" queried a new male voice in the hallway. "Move aside."

"Father Saul is dead!" the second drunkard announced.

"What?" The newcomer shoved his way into the room, took a quick look at the priest, then glowered at Quentin. "How dare you murder our priest!"

Quentin stiffened with surprise. "I didn't do it. I just got here."

"That's true," the fourth drunkard insisted. "He's not a murderer. He's a thief."

"He's not a thief!" Bert hiccoughed. "He's my cousin."

The newcomer glared at the four men. "Then which one of you murdered the priest?"

"We didn't do it!" the second drunkard claimed, and the third drunkard choked once again.

"Dammit," the newcomer growled. "If you're going to vomit, do it outside!"

"Who are you?" Quentin asked.

"I'm the owner of this fine establishment. I was down the hall in my office when I heard all the noise." The newcomer strode over to the table. "Ah, thank the Light they still paid their bill!" He grabbed the small stack of coins off the table.

"Is there a back door where the other priests could have made a quick exit?" Quentin asked.

"There is," the owner replied as he pocketed the coins. "But it's right next to my office and I didn't see anyone leave."

So they must have escaped through the open window, Quentin thought, as he glanced that way.

"Who are you?" the owner demanded.

"An official courier for the king," Quentin replied.

The owner scoffed. "I doubt that. You're dressed more like a clown."

"Hey!" Bert protested. "Those are fine clothes."

"Move aside!" a voice barked at the crowd around the door.

"Constable," the fourth drunkard greeted him. "Someone has murdered Father Saul!"

The third drunkard groaned, rubbing his belly.

The old constable lurched into the room, took one look at the dead priest and belched. He glared at Quentin. "You bastard, why did you kill him?"

Before Quentin could reply, Bert and his companions yelled, "He didn't do it!"

The pub owner waved at Quentin. "He's not a murderer. He's an official clown for the king."

"I'm not—" Quentin started.

"He looks like a jester," the constable mumbled.

Quentin gritted his teeth. "I'm the official courier. I deliver messages and collect information—"

"Like a spy?" the fourth drunkard interrupted.

"Did you know our priest was going to be murdered?" Bert asked.

"No," Quentin replied. "But I know that you're smitten with Bessie, and she wants nothing to do with you."

Bert hissed in a breath. "How do you know that?"

"In fact," Quentin continued, "three out of five village women disapprove of you. I suggest you and your companions stop getting inebriated during the day."

"Whoa," the second drunkard whispered. "How does he know so much?"

"I also know some soldiers from Benwick Castle should be arriving any second now," Quentin continued. The sound of boots came from the hallway. "Ah, they're here."

"Damn," the fourth drunkard muttered. "He knows everything."

"Let me through," Prince Eric said as he eased his way through the crowd. He spotted Quentin and lifted a hand in greeting. "The waitress told me Father Saul was murdered." He turned to address the crowd. "I'll be in charge here, so if you would all move—"

"No, you're not," the old man interrupted. "I'm in charge. I'm the constable!"

"I appreciate that," Eric replied, "but your assistance will not be needed."

Bert scoffed. "Who is this uppity fellow?"

The fourth drunkard narrowed his eyes as he studied the prince. "He looks somewhat familiar."

"I should," Eric replied. "I pass through this village regularly."

"I know!" the second drunkard exclaimed. "You're the traveling tinker. Thank the Light you're here. My chamber pot has a hole in it."

"He's not a tinker, you fool," the owner snarled. "He's traveling with soldiers."

"Well, he's not in uniform," the second drunk defended himself. "If he was somebody important, he'd be wearing a uniform."

"Yeah," Bert joined in. "Who does he think he is, waltzing in here and ordering everybody around? My cousin should be in charge—"

"Enough," Quentin interrupted. "This is His Highness, Prince Eric."

Everyone gasped.

"*He's the crown prince?*" the second one shrieked.

"Your Highness!" They all quickly bowed. Unfortunately, when the third drunkard leaned over, he threw up on the floor.

Eric jumped back to keep his boots from getting splattered, while the owner muttered a curse.

The fourth drunkard winced. "I thought you looked familiar. Our apologies, Your Highness."

Eric gritted his teeth. "I would ask you all to wait in the front room. Please remain there in case we need to question you."

The group of men mumbled as they trudged down the hallway.

"Shouldn't he wear a sign to warn people he's a prince?"

"I didn't vote for him."

"We don't vote for kings and princes."

"Why not? We voted for the mayor and the constable."

With a groan, Eric shut the door, leaving the three soldiers outside to stand guard. He strode over to the dead priest. "So this is Father Saul?"

"Yes," Quentin replied as he approached the window. "He was having a meeting with two other priests, but they have already fled the scene."

"Then a group of priests were behind the attack on the barge? I thought they were supposed to be champions of peace, not kidnappers and murderers." Eric leaned over the dead body. "Dammit. We needed some answers from this man."

"Which could be the reason he took the poison."

"You think it was suicide?" Eric gave Quentin a questioning look, then blinked. "What the hell are you wearing?"

"It's a long story." Quentin moved aside a lace curtain so he could peer through the open window. The plants next to the building appeared trampled. The inn's stables were about twenty yards away. "I believe the priests escaped this way. They most probably had horses in the stable."

"If they escaped, why didn't they take this priest with them? Why would he kill himself?"

Quentin shrugged. "Maybe it was punishment for failing in his mission."

Eric winced. "That seems rather extreme. Who are these bastards?"

"Whoever they are, they believe in their cause enough to die for it."

Eric grew pale. "This sounds too much like the Circle of Five."

Quentin nodded. "It could be the dark cloud that Queen Maeve warned us about." He turned back to the window. "If the priests are on horseback, they could be miles away by now. But I might be able to spot them from the air."

"There are four roads in and out of this village," Eric explained as he joined Quentin at the window. "We rode in on the road to the west, so they didn't go that way or we would have seen them. The road to the north is short and dead ends at the Ebe River. Most likely, the priests escaped to the east or south. I'll have my soldiers search for them."

"Good plan." As Quentin turned toward the prince, something snagged his attention. A wad of black material had been stuffed behind a nearby chest of drawers, barely noticeable in the shadow. He pulled it out. The black robes of a priest.

"So one of the priests ditched his robe before escaping," Eric concluded. "They probably guessed we would be searching for two priests traveling together."

Quentin's breath caught as another possibility struck him. Could one of the priests be a shifter? Then he would have discarded the robe before shifting.

Quentin stepped back to more carefully scan the window and curtains. There. Something dark stuck in the white lace.

He plucked it out. A small black feather.

The Raven.

Chapter 7

Eviana woke with a jerk. The room was dark, but after a few tense seconds, she remembered where she was. Safe in Princess Elinor's bedchamber at Benwick Castle. But how could she have slept while Quentin and Eric were searching for a villain?

She sat up and noted the darkening sky outside the window. Goodness, she must have slept several hours. A candle flickered on the bedside table, and across the room, a small fire burned in the hearth.

"Evie, are you awake?" a voice whispered from a chair by the fireplace, and Eviana gasped with recognition.

"Mama?"

Luciana rushed toward her. "My dear child, how are you?"

"I'm fine." She winced. "You didn't need to come."

"Of course I had to." Luciana hugged her, then perched on the edge of the bed. "I had to see for myself that you're all right." She took Eviana's hands in her own. "You weren't injured in any way?"

"No, I'm perfectly fine. Just embarrassed that I fell asleep while Quentin and Eric are in danger."

"After what you went through, you deserved a good rest." Luciana squeezed her hands. "Besides, there's nothing to worry about. Eric is already back, safe and sound."

But what about Quentin? Eviana opened her mouth to ask, then reconsidered. Why was the man monopolizing her thoughts? Was she simply grateful that he'd rescued her, or was she actually attracted to him? Perhaps both, or it could be that his valiant rescue had inspired her attraction. If that was the case, it might be a temporary phenomenon. That would probably be for the best, as she could be fairly certain that her parents would never consider him a suitable match. Neither would Quentin, for that matter, since he didn't even like her.

All things considered, it seemed that the best course of action was to keep this unfortunate attraction to herself. After all, if it was simply a fleeting emotional response to the day's traumatic events, she would recover from it soon. Or would she? How could she forget how he'd carried her ashore, holding her in his powerful arms? Would she ever forget the way he looked at her with those beautiful golden eyes?

"Evie?" Her mother tilted her head, studying her daughter. "Is something troubling you? If you're worried about your safety, you needn't be. With the army stationed here, Benwick is the safest place in the entire country."

"Yes, I know." It wasn't *her* safety she was concerned about. Quentin was the one in danger. "Do you know if Eric and Quentin found the priest?"

"They did." Luciana winced. "He was dead when they arrived."

"What? How did that happen?"

Luciana shrugged. "Nobody knows much right now. But I can tell you what everyone was doing while you were asleep."

"Yes, please." Surely her mother would say something about Quentin, and that would save her from having to ask.

"Very well. Your brother Dominic stayed at Ebton to help Leo bring the barge into port." Luciana wandered over to a nearby table to fill a glass with water. "Lady Olana and I came here right away, along with a troop of soldiers. Of course, we're hoping she'll learn who is behind the attack. And also, if we have a spy at Ebton Palace."

Spy? Eviana inhaled sharply. She should have realized this earlier. Once the decision had been made that morning that she would travel by barge to Norveshka, everyone at Ebton Palace had known about it. The news could have leaked naturally, given the fact that servants and courtiers were prone to gossip. But the villain had known early enough that he'd been able to plan the attack, and that made the existence of a spy highly probable.

"Elam and his men brought back the criminals who tried to kidnap you," Luciana continued. "They're locked up in the dungeon, and Olana is there now, questioning them. That's everything, I suppose." She handed the glass to Eviana.

"It is?" Eviana took a sip of water. It looked as if she would have to ask about Quentin.

"Oh, I forgot," Luciana began, and Eviana perked up. "I brought you some clothes to wear."

"Oh." Eviana's shoulders slumped.

"Is something wrong?"

Eviana sighed. There was no help for it. She would have to ask. "Do you know if Quentin has returned?"

"I don't believe he has." Luciana shrugged. "The last I heard he was flying around, searching for some missing priests. It's a shame he and Eric didn't learn much, but Olana should have better luck."

"I see." Eviana took another sip of water. Missing priests? So there was more than one priest who had wanted to capture her?

With a smile, Luciana sat back down on the bed. "I heard you tied up the prisoners and hid their weapons. That was very brave and clever of you."

Eviana winced. "I didn't actually tie anyone up. Quentin did that."

"Oh?" Luciana shrugged. "Well, he couldn't have done it without you. It was your gift that knocked them all out."

"Papa always said the gift was too dangerous to use—"

"Unless you found yourself in a dire emergency, which you did. Your father and I were horrified, of course, to hear what had happened, but we thought you handled the situation brilliantly."

"I'm not so sure about that." Eviana's hand trembled as she set the glass on the bedside table. "I tried to swim ashore, but I might not have made it if Quentin hadn't come along when he did."

Luciana's face grew pale. "You . . . ?"

"I was struggling." Tears crowded Eviana's eyes, and she blinked them away. "He saved me."

"Oh, my poor dear." Luciana pulled Eviana into her arms. "It must have been terrifying."

Eviana rested her cheek against her mother's shoulder. What seemed the most terrifying now was the realization of how unprepared she was for surviving a future filled with danger. Ever since her kidnapping at the age of three and the horrible incident at age thirteen, her parents had made sure she was always safe and protected. Too protected. That had to change.

She sat back. "I need to learn how to defend myself."

"All you have to do is clap your hands."

"But what if I'm attacked while asleep or caught by surprise? You know Papa has always been worried that I could be kidnapped and somehow used as a weapon."

Luciana winced. "Don't even say something so frightening. From now on, your father and I will be even more vigilant with your safety."

A chill crept over Eviana's skin. "You mean you'll lock me up."

Luciana's eyes widened.

"Will you throw away the key so no one can get in? Will

you shutter the windows so no arrow can come through? Pad the stairs in case I fall? Mash my food into gruel so I cannot choke?"

A look of horror came over Luciana's face. "Is that . . . is that how it seems to you?"

Eviana nodded. "Aye, it does." Her eyes burned with tears. "The only time I don't feel trapped is the month I spend in Norveshka every summer."

"Oh, my poor child." Luciana's eyes glistened with tears.

"I know you tried to make my life as painless as possible. I had excellent tutors and all the books I ever wanted. It wasn't until I tasted freedom in Norveshka that I even realized I had grown up in a lovely prison. But I cannot hide from life anymore. And I don't want anyone to fear me because of my gift." Quentin's angry words echoed in Eviana's head, and she found herself repeating them. "I'm not going to clap my hands in my sleep or when I sneeze. I can control myself. You have to trust me. And give me the freedom to live."

A tear rolled down Luciana's cheek. "You're right. I'm so sorry that we . . . I'm afraid we've overreacted. We cannot bear the thought of losing a child."

"Then you need your children to be strong." Eviana recalled another statement Quentin had made that afternoon. As long as she could use her gift, no one could ever hurt her.

But that protection was not absolute. It didn't work on animals. Or shifters while in animal form. Or dragons. "My gift is limited, so I need to be able to defend myself. I was very lucky today when Quentin showed up, but I can't be sure that he'll always appear when I need him."

"Your gift didn't put him to sleep?"

"No, he was in eagle form when I clapped my hands. Thank the goddesses it has no effect on him, or he could fall from the sky." Eviana shuddered to think how such a fall could injure or even kill him.

"So he must have shifted to help you swim ashore?"

He'd swooped her up in his powerful arms and carried her, but Eviana didn't want to tell her mother that. Or the fact that he'd been naked. Just remembering it made her cheeks feel warm. "He rescued me and made sure I arrived here safely. I don't know why, but he told everyone that I did much more than I actually did. He made me sound like the hero instead of himself."

Luciana's eyes narrowed. "He did?"

"Aye. It seems very strange to me, particularly since . . ." Eviana bit her lip.

"Since what?"

"I . . . I don't think he likes me."

Luciana snorted. "Why do you think that?"

Eviana plucked at the blanket, not wanting to admit that she'd been rejected.

"Last night he rescued you from some dreadful suitors, and today, he saved you from drowning."

Eviana shrugged. "He works for the royal houses. He was merely doing his duty."

Luciana heaved a sigh, then muttered, "We have locked you up too much."

A knock sounded on the door, then it was cracked open, and Lennie peered inside.

"Oh, good! You're awake." Lennie stepped into the room, closing the door behind her. "I thought you should know that Princess Elinor is hosting a dinner for everyone, and Nevis wants to use the occasion to discuss the investigation and make future plans."

Eviana scrambled out of bed. "I need to be there."

Lennie smiled. "I was hoping you'd say that."

"We'll help you get dressed." Luciana fetched the bundle of clothes she'd left on top of a trunk.

While Eviana changed into a gown of dark green wool, she decided that she would take an active role in the discussion. After all, she had been the target of the kidnapping, so she had a bigger stake than anyone in the investigation.

She'd faced danger that afternoon and survived. There was no reason why she couldn't do it in the future. Her days of feeling trapped and stifled were over.

The sun had set and the night sky was overcast with clouds, but thanks to numerous campfires and torches along the battlements, Quentin was able to easily spot Benwick Castle. He landed on the wall walk, where he had disrobed earlier. A guard had tossed his clothes and boots back into the tower, so he slipped inside to get dressed.

"Quen?" Elam called to him from the wall walk. "I heard you were back."

"Aye." He finished buttoning his breeches.

"How can you tell what you're doing?" Elam peered into the dark tower. "I can't even see you. Do you need a torch?"

"Nay, I'm fine." *My eyes must really be different,* Quentin thought as he sat on a bench to pull on his boots. It seemed strange that it was only last night that Eviana had wanted to test his sight. So much had happened since then. Should he ask how she was faring, or would that make his attraction too obvious? He cleared his throat. "Any news?"

Elam snorted. "I was going to ask you that."

"Not much to report." Quentin buttoned his shirt as he joined Elam on the wall walk. "Did Eric make it back? And Dominic? How is Eviana doing?" He nonchalantly slipped the last question in.

"She's fine. Her mother is with her now. Dominic stayed at Ebton. And Eric brought the priest's body with him so Nevis could see the sun tattoo on his arm. His men weren't able to find the other priests."

"I couldn't spot them, either." Or the raven. But then the abundance of trees along the roads made it very easy for a bird to hide. Quentin had told Eric his theory about a raven shifter, but the prince had been reluctant to believe it. "Did you bring the criminals back?"

"Aye." Elam nodded. "They're in the dungeon. Lady Olana is questioning them now."

"Excellent." Quentin hurried down the stairs. "Let's go see how she's doing." Perhaps one of the criminals would be able to confirm that the raven was, indeed, a shifter.

"Ah, actually . . ." Elam followed him down the stairs. "Nevis is holding a strategy meeting over dinner. They've already started. He asked me to bring you right away."

"All right." Would Eviana be there? Quentin tucked in his shirt to look more presentable. As he strode across the courtyard, he realized how hungry he was. It had been hours since that small meal at Peter's house. "By the way, I saw Peter this morning. He and his family are doing well."

"That's good." Elam frowned. "But I was sad to hear about Uma and Victor."

"Aye." Quentin nodded. "Olana heard the news from Peter. She corresponds with him and some of the others from the Isle of Secrets." He glanced at Elam. "You should write to her, too."

Elam tripped slightly, but quickly righted himself, making Quentin grin.

"I thought your gift was tripping other people, not yourself."

Elam winced. "There's a loose stone in the pavement."

Quentin hadn't noticed one. "Olana must have been happy to see you again."

"I—I didn't see her." Elam's face reddened. "I was in a meeting with Nevis when she arrived. Captain Westmore took her to the dungeon."

As Quentin climbed the steps to the Great Hall, he slanted a curious glance at Elam. Why hadn't the colonel joined Olana in the dungeon as soon as possible? If Quentin had been here, he would have done so. But then, most people went out of their way to avoid the Confessor. It would be a shame if Elam did that, though, since it would hurt Olana's feelings. "You didn't want to know if she's learned anything important?"

Elam rushed up the stairs to the double wooden doors. "I'm sure we'll hear from her soon."

He's hiding something. Quentin wondered what it could be as the colonel pushed the doors open and stepped inside.

A loud banging noise drew his attention to the side of the castle. Lady Olana and Captain Westmore had exited the dungeon and the heavy iron door had swung shut with a crash. Apparently, the captain had decided to distance himself from Olana rather than remain close by to shut the door properly. Even now, he was inching farther away from her while she attempted to have a friendly conversation.

"Olana!" Quentin waved at her.

She spotted him and grinned. "Quen!"

Captain Westmore quickly bowed, then sprinted for the stables. Olana gave him a wry look as he disappeared inside.

Quentin didn't know which was worse: that people ran away from Olana, or that the poor woman was accustomed to it. It made him even more determined to remain one of her few friends. "Come join us. Elam and I are headed to the dining room."

"Elam is with you?" Her smile returned as she strode toward the steps. "How wonderful. I haven't seen him in ages."

Quentin glanced inside the Great Hall. Elam was backing up with a frantic look on his face. With an inward groan, Quen turned back to Olana. "Nevis is planning strategy over dinner, so he'll want you there."

She nodded, her blue eyes sparkling. "I must say, this has all been very exciting."

"Aye." Quentin smiled. "It's been a while since your gift was needed."

"Yes." She ascended the stone steps. "It's been over a year since I left Ebton Palace." Her smile faded. "Of course, I was horrified to hear about the attack on the barge."

Quentin nodded. "Of course."

"But I am grateful that my gift can be useful." She paused when Quentin offered his elbow to escort her inside. "Are you sure?"

"Yes." He stepped into the Great Hall, clenching his teeth as she curled her hand around his arm. "My heart is forever lost to—"

"Elam!" Olana raised her voice loud enough to drown out his mumbled confession. "How lovely to see you."

The colonel froze in the middle of the hall, his eyes growing wide at the sight of Olana. He blinked, apparently coming to his senses, then executed a quick bow. "My lady."

"Please." She grinned as she strolled alongside Quentin. "We're old friends. You must call me Olana."

Elam nodded, his cheeks growing pink.

"How long has it been since we last saw each other?" she asked. "Over a year?"

"Twenty-one and a half months," Elam mumbled.

He knew the exact length of time? Quentin thought that seemed a bit odd.

"That long?" Olana looked shocked. "My goodness, but time flies by so quickly." Her smile faded as Elam backed away.

Dammit. "Are you opening the door for us?" Quentin asked, trying to save Olana's feelings.

"Ah, yes. That's where I'm going." Elam dashed to the dining room and pulled open the door, standing halfway behind it to use it as a shield as she passed by.

He must be hiding something really embarrassing, Quentin thought, although he had no idea what it might be. He'd known Elam most of his life, and the man was as honorable as could be.

"Thank you," Olana murmured with a strained smile.

She's trying not to show her hurt feelings, Quentin thought as he led her into the dining room. Quickly, he scanned the room to see where Eviana was. Three servants blocked his view as they leaned around the diners to remove dishes and load them onto trays. Apparently, the first course was over.

As the maids retreated, he was able to see everyone. Nevis sat at the head of the table with his wife, Elinor, to his left and Luciana to his right. Next to Elinor sat Pendras, Eric, and Faith. Next to Luciana sat her daughter and Lenushka.

Eviana looked well rested and as beautiful as ever, her eyes appearing a brilliant green since she was wearing a dark green gown. *Damn.* With a gulp, he realized he was noticing her eye color because she was looking straight at him. Normally he would immediately avert his eyes to keep from being caught staring at her, but this time . . . this time, he couldn't look away. Her gaze searched his, and his pulse quickened as he held onto it. The connection lasted only a few seconds, but in his heart, it seemed to stretch into an eternity.

"Quen! Lady Olana!" Nevis smiled and motioned to the empty chairs down the table. "Please have—"

A loud clatter interrupted Nevis as one of the maids squealed and dropped her tray on the floor.

"The Confessor," another maid whispered as she backed away. She set her tray on the sideboard and ran to hide behind the curtains.

With a wince, Quentin led the blushing Olana to the foot of the table.

Seeing her chance to escape, the third maid dashed toward the door, keeping an eye on Olana. She crashed into Elam as he entered, and her tray was upended against his torso.

He stiffened in shock, but with excellent reflexes he caught the tray before it could plummet to the floor. Unfortunately, some of the dishes slid down his uniform, leaving oily strands of lettuce behind.

"Oh, Colonel!" The maid jumped back, horrified. "I'm so sorry!" She swatted at the lettuce, but the pieces simply slid down Elam's jacket to his breeches.

"It's all right," he muttered, handing the tray back to the servant.

"Oh, Elam, I do apologize." Olana grabbed a napkin off the table and offered it to him. "It is my presence that caused this mess."

The maid backed away, holding the tray up as a shield.

Elam glanced at the maid, then at Olana, and his eyes filled with regret. "It was not your fault, Olana. You should never have to apologize for being who you are." He reached up to accept the napkin. "Thank you."

"You're welcome." Tears glistened in Olana's eyes as she returned to her seat at the foot of the table.

While Elam wiped the lettuce off his breeches, the maids knelt to gather the broken dishes back onto the trays. Soon they were scurrying out the door.

Elinor sighed. "It makes you wonder what they're hiding."

"I doubt it's anything serious," Olana said from the foot of the table. "In my experience, people are often hiding things that are only embarrassing to them. For instance, one time a person was mortified to admit having a wart on her big toe."

Everyone smiled, and several new maids entered, carrying trays loaded with platters of roasted beef and vegetables. They set the platters on the table, along with a few pitchers of wine, carefully keeping a distance from Olana.

Elam had taken the seat next to Lenushka, which left an empty chair between him and Olana. Quentin sat to Olana's right, so she wouldn't feel lonesome and he would have a good view of Eviana. He filled Olana's glass with wine and then his own. Everyone enjoyed their wine while taking turns using the large serving forks to fill their plates from the platters of food.

"I can't help but be curious." Faith turned to Olana. "What do people confess the most often when you touch them?"

With a smile, Olana lifted her wineglass. "Love."

Elam dropped a piece of beef onto the tablecloth, then quickly speared it with the fork and moved it to his plate.

"They're hiding their love for someone?" Eviana asked Olana, and Quentin glanced her way. "Why would they do that?" Her gaze shifted to him, and he quickly concentrated on cutting his slice of beef into tiny pieces.

Good goddesses, does she suspect I have feelings for her?

"There could be many reasons, I suppose." Olana took a sip of wine.

"It seems cowardly to me," Faith muttered.

Damn. Quentin stuffed a morsel of beef into his mouth.

"You would know," Eric mumbled.

"I'm not a coward." Faith glowered at the crown prince, then threw a dinner roll at his chest.

He caught the roll and took a bite out of it. "Mmm. Next time, butter it for me, would you?"

She huffed. "Next time, I'll aim for your head."

"Faith." Elinor frowned at her seventeen-year-old daughter.

"Enough," Nevis grumbled. "We need to figure out who was behind the attack on the barge. Did you learn anything, Lady Olana?"

She swallowed her food, then dabbed at her mouth with her napkin. "The ruffians know only what their leader, Duncan, told them. And all Duncan knows is a fabricated story. He did verify that Father Saul paid him twelve gold pieces to kidnap a woman, but he had no idea that his target was Princess Eviana or that they were attacking the royal barge."

Eric snorted. "He's just saying that to avoid being executed."

Luciana shook her head. "When Olana touches someone, they have no choice but to tell the truth."

"So who did this Duncan think he was kidnapping?" Nevis stabbed a chunk of roasted potato and popped it into his mouth.

Olana smiled. "Shall I tell you the story Father Saul told Duncan? It's quite interesting."

Eviana's eyes widened. "Yes, please."

"Very well." With sparkling eyes, Olana set down her knife and fork.

Quentin smiled to himself. After years of loneliness and boredom, Olana was definitely enjoying the moment.

"It's the story of a wealthy old merchant and his beautiful young wife," Olana began. "The old merchant was cruel and abused his wife, so in distress, the woman fled to Father Saul and begged for his help. He did his best to protect her, and over time, he and the woman fell in love and began a passionate affair."

Nevis snorted, then ate a bite of beef. "As if an affair was going to help her."

"Shh." Elinor hushed her husband, then turned to Olana. "What happened next?"

Olana heaved a dramatic sigh. "I'm afraid the husband found out."

"Of course," Nevis muttered, but all the women at the table shushed him.

"The poor woman feared that her husband was planning to kill her," Olana continued, "so she fled by barge to Norveshka. And that was when Father Saul asked Duncan and his men to stop her and take her to a hidden farmhouse located between the Ebe River and the village of Bramblewood. And there, the priest and his lover would live happily ever after."

As the women at the table let out a communal sigh, the men shook their heads.

Pendras snorted. "And Duncan believed that stupid story?" Nevis gave him a wry look. "For twelve pieces of gold, I'm sure he'd believe anything."

Faith frowned at her father. "I think the priest had a romantic heart."

"He has a dead heart," Eric muttered, earning another glare from Faith. "I brought his body back here so we could examine it more closely. He had scars across his back as if he'd been flogged numerous times in the past."

"Oh." Faith pressed a hand to her chest. "The poor man was also tortured."

Eric gave her an incredulous look. "That 'poor man' tried to kidnap my sister! Who knows what horrific things he planned to do to her once he had her trapped in that farmhouse?"

Eviana sat back, inhaling sharply.

"Eric," Luciana muttered.

"Sorry," Eric mumbled.

Quentin noted Eviana's hand trembling a bit as she sipped some wine. He needed to change the subject. "The priest also had a tattoo on his forearm. But I'm not sure if it is the symbol of some secret organization or simply the sun god."

Luciana gave him a worried look. "Was it a circle with five rays?"

"Nay." Quentin shook his head. "I counted them to make sure it wasn't a symbol for the Circle of Five. There were eight rays."

Luciana looked a bit relieved. "That's good, but it still concerns me that this priest was so quick to poison himself."

Lenushka nodded. "It does seem terribly extreme."

"Especially when he could have fled with the other two priests," Eric added.

Quentin glanced again at Eviana as he ate some roasted vegetables. She'd stopped eating and seemed deep in thought. "I suspect the priest killed himself because he failed to kidnap Her Highness. It may be the way this organization works. And if the cost of failure is death, then each member will do anything in order to succeed. That makes them extremely dangerous."

Eviana glanced at him, then looked away, biting her lip. Once again, he wondered what she was thinking.

Nevis cleared his throat. "So we have an organization of priests who are intent on killing the Embraced."

"But we have no idea how many priests are involved," Elinor added.

Elam raised a hand. "I sent out several troops to cover all the routes leading to Benwick. Hopefully, that will give some protection to the Embraced students who are on their way back to school."

Nevis nodded. "Excellent."

Luciana took a sip of wine. "I have to say, when I heard about Father Saul killing himself, I was reminded of Lord Morris twenty years ago. When he was captured in Woodwyn, he took poison to avoid interrogation."

"Who was Lord Morris?" Faith asked.

Eric snorted. "You must have fallen asleep in history class."

"I couldn't." Faith gave him a dry look. "You were snoring too loud."

Nevis gave his daughter a warning look, then explained, "Lord Morris was one of the Circle of Five. He was King Frederic's chief counsel, and since Frederic feared that an Embraced child might grow up with enough power to oust him from the throne, he ordered Lord Morris to get rid of all Embraced children as soon as they were born."

"So terrible," Elinor murmured.

"And that's why my mother was sent to the Isle of Moon, along with her adopted sisters," Eric added. "It was the only way to keep them safe."

Luciana nodded. "But when Lord Morris joined the Circle of Five, he decided it was a better idea to keep the Embraced babies rather than kill them. That way the Circle could have an Embraced army at their disposal."

"And that's how Olana, Quentin, and I ended up on the Isle of Secrets," Elam said. "Along with the other Embraced children."

"Lord Morris didn't have any sort of magical gift himself, did he?" Faith asked.

"No," Nevis replied. "He had the power of his political position and a huge network of spies spread across the mainland."

"He probably killed himself to keep from revealing their names," Eric added.

"Wait a minute." Eviana came out of her deep thought and held up a hand. "What happened to his network of spies?"

"An excellent question." Nevis pointed at her with his fork. "Only a few were found. We believe most of them went into hiding. In twenty years, some will have died."

"But if the organization still exists, then more could have been recruited," Eviana insisted. "Like Father Saul and the other two priests."

Luciana winced. "You think Lord Morris's network has continued in secret?"

"It's possible," Eviana replied, then shrugged. "But we have no way of knowing until we investigate."

"Exactly," Eric agreed with her. "So the obvious course of action is for Dominic and myself to start investigating as soon as possible. All we have to do is check all the priests to see if they have a tattoo or one of these." He reached into a pocket and set Father Saul's suicide ring on the table.

"If it's a secret organization, they will simply go into hiding," Quentin said. "Or hide their rings."

"True," Nevis grumbled. "Any villain who sees you and Dominic arriving with a troop of soldiers will immediately hide. Even without the soldiers, they'll hide. You and your brother have toured the country so many times, almost everyone will recognize you."

Eric frowned. "Then what do you suggest?"

"I have a proposition," Eviana announced.

Quentin tensed. What was she going to propose now?

Eviana took a deep breath. "To uncover a secret organization, we need a secret investigation. Done by someone who will not be recognized, someone who has spent most of her life isolated from the public."

Quentin stiffened. *Good goddesses, no.* Now he knew what she'd been thinking, and it couldn't be more dangerous.

Eric flinched. "No. Absolutely not. You will not lead the investigation."

Eviana lifted her chin. "I absolutely will. And you can't stop me."

Chapter 8

Eviana glanced around the table to gauge everyone's reaction. Mama looked pale and worried. Lennie and Faith were clearly excited. Elinor and Lady Olana intrigued. Nevis, Pendras, and Elam stunned. Eric horrified. And Quentin was staring at her with an intense look that she wasn't sure how to interpret. Alarmed? Angry? If so, she felt a prick of disappointment. Wasn't he the one who had reassured her that no one could ever harm her? He should be supportive, like Lennie.

Eric slammed a fist on the table. "I will not have this."

Eviana gave him a pointed look. "I was the target of the kidnapping, so I have every right to be involved."

"You *are* the target," Eric growled. "That's precisely why it's not safe for you!"

"I could go with her," Lennie suggested, leaning close to squeeze Eviana's hand. "I can fly overhead to provide protection."

Pendras snorted. "A secret investigation with a dragon overhead? That would be a bit noticeable, don't you think?"

Eviana smiled at her best friend. "I appreciate your offer, but I'm afraid, even in human form, you're very noticeable."

Lennie tucked her white-blond elfin hair behind a slightly pointed ear. "I could wear a disguise."

A disguise! That would be perfect, Eviana thought, recalling Father Saul's story. "I'll disguise myself as a merchant. No one will ever know it's me, so that alone will afford me a layer of protection."

Eric scoffed. "You know nothing about business."

"I know a great deal about the wines of Vindalyn." She lifted her wineglass and swirled the wine around. "Grandfather has been teaching me for years. I'm sure I could pass as a wine merchant."

"And how would you make a priest confess to being a member of a secret organization?" Eric asked. "Would you get him drunk?"

Eviana took a sip as she pondered that question, then set her glass down. "I could bring Lady Olana with me."

Olana gasped. "Me?"

"Yes." Eviana smiled at her. "It would be quite an adventure, don't you think?"

"A dangerous adventure," Elam ground out. He gave Olana a worried look. "Two women traveling alone? Surely you're not considering it?"

Olana tilted her head, thinking. "If my gift can be used to fight evil, then I have a moral obligation—"

"You are not obliged to do anything dangerous." Elam grabbed his wineglass and gulped down some wine.

"Then you could go with them," Nevis declared, and Elam choked.

He wiped his mouth. "Go . . . with them?"

Nevis nodded. "To provide protection. You could be disguised as a servant."

"Wait a minute!" Eric lifted both hands in the air. "General, you can't possibly approve of this. It would be like sending a lamb to the wolves!"

"I am not a lamb," Eviana protested. "I protected myself today, and I can do it again. As long as I can clap my hands, no one can hurt me." She turned to Quentin. "Didn't you tell me that? You believe I can do it, don't you?"

Quentin stiffened, looking a bit stunned. He glanced at Eric, who was glaring at him, sending a message with his eyes that Quentin had better disagree with her. He cleared his throat. "I believe it could be dangerous."

"There!" Eric shot her a triumphant look. "The master spy has spoken."

A pang reverberated through Eviana. Why did it feel as if she'd been betrayed by a dear friend? Even though Quentin had rejected her friendship, she had still believed that he was on her side. She had wanted to believe that with all her heart.

A pained look crossed his face. "But I also believe that if the mission is kept secret, then Her Highness would be safe."

Yes! He did believe in her. Eviana smiled at him.

He winced. "Unfortunately, I'm not sure it can be kept secret."

Her smile faded.

"Do you suspect we have a spy at Benwick?" Nevis asked.

"That is possible," Quentin replied. "But my main concern is that Her Highness may have been seen today by one of the villains. There was a raven at—"

"It's nonsense," Eric interrupted.

"But I did see a raven by the river." Eviana gave Quentin a confused look. "Do you think he was spying on us?"

Quentin nodded. "I believe he's a shifter." As a series of gasps sounded around the table, he continued. "He may have been one of the priests in Bramblewood. There was a discarded robe—"

"It's hogwash!" Eric waved a dismissive hand. "If this organization wants to kill the Embraced, how could one of them *be* Embraced? It makes no sense."

"I realize it sounds odd," Quentin admitted, "but I'm still convinced there is more to this raven than we can see."

Elinor touched Nevis's arm. "Brody can always sense the presence of another shifter, so it could be the same way with Quentin."

"I agree." Nevis frowned. "So we had better proceed with the assumption that this raven could be a shifter in league with the villains."

Eric huffed. "If you insist. But that possibility only makes my case stronger. If the villain knows what Evie looks like, then it is definitely too dangerous for her to undertake this mission."

Eviana clenched her fists. "I can still do it. They'll expect me to look like a princess, not a wine merchant."

Quentin gave her a regretful look. "The raven saw more than your face. He witnessed your gift."

"Shit," Eric muttered.

Eviana swallowed hard. Her father had always feared that her gift could be used as a weapon. That had been the main reason for keeping it a secret. But if the villains knew . . .

"We'll have to keep Evie guarded night and day," Eric announced.

They wanted to lock her up. A chill ran down her spine as her worst fear clawed once again to the surface. Trapped. How could she live like this? This wasn't even living.

Luciana squeezed her daughter's hand. "If the villains become even more determined to capture Evie, it could be a good idea to let her take on a disguise."

Eric scoffed. "How can you suggest something that risky? Not only to Evie, but to the whole country!"

"Then you want to lock me up forever?" Eviana blinked away tears as she held tight to her mother's hand. "If I present that much of a risk, why don't you just kill me now?"

"Evie!" Eric's eyes flashed with anger. "We're trying to protect you. Don't you know how terrified I am that something bad could—"

"Then you're willing to imprison me just so you can *feel* better?" Eviana yelled, and a tear escaped, rolling down her cheek.

Eric sat back with a stunned look. "That . . . that's not what I'm doing . . ."

"It is." Eviana wiped her cheek. "I have a right to live my life, no matter how dangerous it might be. And you don't have the right to deny me the chance to do something meaningful with my life."

Her brother winced. "I don't mean to be selfish, Evie. I can handle being in danger, myself, but somehow, the thought of you being in danger nearly kills me."

"I know." Eviana gave him a sad look. Just like her, he still suffered from her childhood kidnapping.

Nevis sighed. "I realize how much you want to take on this mission, Eviana. And I appreciate your courage, but . . . for the sake of the country . . ."

They still wanted to lock her up. Another tear rolled down Eviana's cheek, and she hastily wiped it away. "I believe it will work if I'm in disguise. Elam will be with me for protection. And if my gift is no longer a secret, then there's no reason for me not to use it whenever I need to."

Eric shook his head. "I can never support this. Father won't, either."

"He will if I recommend it." Luciana squeezed her daughter's hand. "I was younger than Evie when I took on a dangerous mission. I'm sure she'll fare even better than I did."

Eviana gave her mother a grateful look.

Nevis refilled his glass with wine. "You haven't convinced me yet."

Eviana thought quickly. "The villains would never expect it."

"An excellent point," Quentin said, and she glanced at him. Was he coming to the rescue? Again? Her pulse sped up.

He pushed his plate back and leaned forward, his elbows on the table. "We should look at this from the perspective of the villains, whoever they may be. They know today's kidnapping failed, and they must know that King Leo will be outraged that someone tried to harm his daughter. So they will be expecting a quick and terrible reaction."

Nevis nodded. "Agreed."

"I suggest Eric and Dominic take a troop of soldiers and begin an official investigation," Quentin continued.

Eric pounded a fist on the table. "Exactly."

"But—" Quentin raised a hand. "They will serve as a distraction. While the royal princes put on a big show, the villains will be watching them."

"And a disguised Eviana will go unnoticed," Nevis concluded with a smile. "That could work."

"Since she was their target," Quentin continued, "and they may be eager to use her gift, they will want to know her exact location. We can't say she's safely ensconced at Ebton Palace, because their spy would report that she isn't there. We also can't say that she took the royal barge to Norveshka, because the spy would know that the barge is still at Ebton."

"We could say she is staying here at Benwick," Elinor suggested.

"We can't be sure they don't have a spy here," Nevis muttered.

"I have a suggestion," Luciana announced. "Normally, Eviana spends the winter months in Vindalyn, and everyone knows that I'm taking the trip with her this year. I could proceed with the journey and pretend she is with me. Or perhaps, someone could pretend to be Evie. Someone about the same height with long black hair." Her gaze wandered to Faith.

"What?" Eric scoffed. "Now you want to put Faith in danger, too?"

"I told you I'm not a coward," Faith grumbled to Eric, then turned to Luciana. "I'd love to do it."

Nevis and his wife exchanged a worried look.

Luciana touched Nevis's arm. "I'm sure she'll be safe. After the attempted kidnapping today, Leo will insist on our traveling with a small army. It would only take a few days to reach the Vindalyn border, and my father will have even more soldiers waiting for us. It would serve as a second distraction. If the villains believe Eviana is with me, they will not look for her elsewhere."

"You make a good point," Nevis admitted.

"Pendras and I can go with you, too," Lennie offered. "No one would dare attack you with two dragons overhead."

Luciana smiled. "That's wonderful. Thank you."

Nevis nodded. "With two dragons and a small army to protect you, the villains will certainly believe Eviana is with you." He glanced at his wife. "It will be safe for Faith."

"Then I'm going!" Faith grinned.

"And I'm going, too," Eviana said, her heart pounding. She glanced at Lady Olana. "Will you come with me?"

Olana nodded, her eyes dancing with excitement.

"Then I will be a wine merchant, traveling with my female companion and our servant." Eviana glanced at Elam, who was casting Olana a wary look.

"We'll need to find you some appropriate clothing and a horse and cart," Elinor concluded. "We have some crates of Vindalyn wine here that you can take."

"I know where I can get a workhorse and cart," Quentin offered.

"Excellent." Nevis stuffed a piece of beef into his mouth. "Let's finish eating while we iron out the details."

Eric sighed in defeat and drank some wine.

Eviana smiled as she dug into her food. Instead of being locked up in a tower, she would be undertaking a secret mission with Olana and Elam. *But what about Quentin?* He'd helped convince Nevis to let her go. Didn't he want to accompany her? She glanced at him and discovered him frowning at his plate of food. What was wrong now?

"There's another problem." He looked at her, and her heart grew still. "If the raven manages to locate you, your gift won't work on him."

Eric hissed in a breath. "I'm telling you, Evie, you can't do this."

"I can." Eviana kept her gaze on Quentin, praying that he would stand by her. "I can do it if you come with me. My gift won't affect you, either. I need you."

His eyes glinted with an intense look, but he remained silent.

Luciana gave him a questioning look. "What do you say, Quentin? Are you willing to protect my daughter?"

He bowed his head. "I will protect her with my life, Your Majesty."

He was going with her! Eviana's heart swelled, but at the same time she was sorely tempted to ask *why*. Had he agreed out of a sense of duty or did he actually care about her?

"Good." Nevis popped a roasted carrot into his mouth. "Then it's all settled. Tomorrow, Eric and Dominic will take two troops of men to begin the official bogus investigation."

Eric huffed. "We might actually discover the real villains, you know."

"That would be good." Nevis smiled as he heaped more food onto his plate. "And two days from now, Luciana and Faith will begin their trip to Vindalyn with four troops and two dragons."

"And my small group will set out in disguise," Eviana finished with a smile aimed at her cohorts. Olana smiled back, but for some reason, neither Quentin nor Elam looked excited. "We will succeed—I'm sure of it."

Quentin shot her a fierce look. "I will insist on one condition."

Her breath caught. "What is it?"

"For your protection, you must follow any directions from myself or Elam. And if we discover that the villains are on to us, we will proceed immediately to the nearest place of safety."

"A good idea," Nevis added, and Eric nodded his approval.

Eviana frowned. That was two conditions. And she had a sneaking suspicion that Quentin was trying to take control of the mission. He did have years of experience when it came to gathering information, but still, the mission had been her idea, and she didn't relish the thought of being bossed around.

"Do you agree?" Quentin asked.

She narrowed her eyes. "As long as your requests are reasonable."

He arched a brow. "I am always reasonable."

Refusing her friendship had not been reasonable. She lifted her chin. "I also have a condition."

His eyes widened.

How could a man's eyes be so beautiful? She couldn't recall ever experiencing a man's gaze that made her heart pound like this. It felt as though he was trying to look into her soul.

"What is it, Your Highness?" he asked softly.

She blinked. Goodness but her mind had gone blank for a second. "I-I'll be in disguise, so you mustn't use my title. Or my real name. I'll simply be Mistress Evie, the wine merchant."

122   *Kerrelyn Sparks*

"All right." He held her gaze. "Evie."

Her heart fluttered at the sound of his deep voice and heat rushed to her face. Oh, dear goddesses, what had she gotten herself into? How could she travel with this man?

What the hell was he doing? How could he travel with the princess? Quentin paced along the torchlit battlements of Benwick Castle. An hour had passed since the dinner where he'd foolishly allowed himself to become ensnared in Her Highness's mission.

Who are you kidding? You wanted to go with her. He'd felt an overwhelming need to protect her. But more than that, his heart had yearned to remain close to her. And so, he had to admit it, he'd been thrilled when she'd begged him to go with her.

I need you. Her words had filled him with joy. And longing.

And dread. For there was no doubt in his mind that the more time he spent with Eviana, the more his heart would be hopelessly hers. *You fool, what have you done?*

If this weren't bad enough, they would be traveling with Olana. One touch from her, and he would be confessing his unfortunate attraction for all to hear.

And then there was the danger of the mission. If the Raven reported Eviana's power to his cohorts, as Quentin suspected he would, then the villains would start a desperate hunt for her.

He had to travel with her. Regardless of his feelings, he was the best choice. Her gift wouldn't affect him, so no one could protect her better than he.

But he would have to keep a distance. The obvious solution was for him to stay in eagle form as much as possible, watching over her from above.

Noise in the courtyard drew his attention, and he saw Nevis and a small group of soldiers mounting up. Each of the four accompanying soldiers carried a torch for traveling in the dark. The gate was opened and they rode through it, taking the road headed west.

Nevis was probably going to Ebton Palace to tell Leo about their plans. By the end of dinner, they had figured out all the details. Eric would leave at dawn, taking his troops to Ebton. There, Dominic would join them, and they would travel west toward the coast. Quentin had decided that Eviana's group should travel southeast toward Arondale, the village where Victor had been murdered. So everyone had agreed that Eric and Dominic should draw the villains' attention in the opposite direction.

Meanwhile, Leo would make arrangements for a covered wagon, clothing, and supplies to be delivered to Benwick Castle. Luciana and Faith would use the wagon for their journey south to Vindalyn.

Quentin had his own plans to accomplish before the mission began. Tomorrow, he would go back to Bramblewood to strike a deal: his best clothes and a fine horse in exchange for Bert's cart and workhorse. Nevis had given him a small pouch of gold coins in case he needed to sweeten the deal.

"Quentin!"

He turned to find Eric racing up the stairs to the battlements.

"Your Highness." Quentin bowed his head.

The prince reached the wall walk and took a deep breath. "Elam told me you were probably here."

Spending time on the battlements was a habit imbedded in Quentin. As long as he was outdoors, he could shift and fly away if he needed to. "Are the preparations going well?"

"Aye. We leave at dawn." Eric motioned to the camps below. "I'm taking soldiers from every kingdom. If our enemies are related to Lord Morris and his spy network, then their scheme could affect the entire world."

Quentin nodded. "True."

With a sigh, Eric leaned against the stone wall. "I wanted to have a word with you before I leave."

No doubt he was still concerned about his sister. "I assure you I will protect Her Highness with my life."

Eric gave him a wry look. "Don't be so quick to give up your life. You're the only one who can protect her if she has to use her gift." He gazed into the distance with a faraway look. "We were thirteen years old when her gift first manifested itself. It was a terrifying experience for her. Well, for all of us." He glanced at Quentin. "She probably wouldn't like me talking about it, so I won't say more than this. It is a great relief to me, knowing that she won't be alone."

Quentin bowed his head. "I am honored to be of service." And now, his curiosity had been piqued. What had happened when Eviana was thirteen?

"I know you will protect her . . ." Eric frowned as he hesitated. "I'm not sure how to say this."

"Feel free to speak your mind."

Eric gave him a pointed look. "You'll be traveling with her. Protecting her. Night and day."

Quentin could see where this was going. "You have my word that no harm will come to her."

"Even from you," Eric added quietly.

Quentin groaned inwardly at the reminder that he was not worthy of her. "I will behave honorably."

"I'm sure you will." Eric nodded, frowning. "But you saved her life earlier today. Rescued her from a few scoundrels last night. She might mistake her gratitude for something more. In that case . . ."

Quentin swallowed hard. "You needn't worry, Your Highness. I know my place."

Eric winced. "We do value you, Quen."

"I understand." But he was still a servant. And an illegitimate son of servants. Never under the two moons would he be considered worthy of a princess.

"Very well, then." Eric laid a hand on Quentin's shoulder. "May the Light be with you."

"And you, too." Quentin turned away as the prince hurried down the stairs. *Dammit.* He would definitely have to keep his distance from the princess.

But what if Eric was right, and Eviana mistook her gratitude for affection? Or love? *Shit.* What if she purposely tried to spend more time with him? What if she actually fell for him?

How could he resist her then?

Chapter 9

It was shortly before dawn when the Raven landed on the stone ledge of a narrow window at the top of the castle tower. A lone candle barely illuminated the small circular room he shared with his two brothers. Across the room, on the third cot, his youngest brother, Zane, was lying on his stomach, wincing in pain while Arlo applied salve to his wounds.

A swell of anger made the Raven's talons scrape against the stone. While he'd been busy spying, another Loyalty Ceremony had occurred at the monastery, along with its ritual flogging. His excellent night vision allowed him to see each stripe of raw, mangled flesh crisscrossing the seventeen-year-old's back. *Dammit to hell.*

The Raven knew too well how much his brother was suffering. He'd survived the whip for ten years, himself, and the unwanted memory slithered into his mind, causing the feathers on his back to ruffle. In human form, he still had the scars. Arlo had them, and Zane would, too.

All the members of the Brotherhood of the Sun endured the flogging during their childhood years. The Loyalty Ceremony happened twice a year when the moons embraced, for those two nights marked the zenith of the moon goddesses' power, and that was when their evil influence had to be purged. Those who were Embraced, like the Raven and his brothers, received twice the number of blows: thirty, while the humans endured fifteen.

According to Master Lorne, it was the will of the Light, the sun god they all worshiped. Being Embraced meant the three brothers had been born completely permeated by the moon goddesses' evil power. They'd been born evil, and they were doomed to die evil.

The Raven had heard it for all his twenty-four years. The monks who had raised him had reminded him daily that he was not normal, but a perverse mutation that mocked the purity of those born perfectly human. He hadn't questioned the doctrine as a child, for why would a group of kindly priests who took in orphans lie to him and tell him he was evil if he wasn't?

But slowly, over the last few years, a seed of doubt had taken root inside him. It was partially due to his job as a spy, which forced him to observe the outside world. But it was also caused by his own brothers. They were Embraced as he was, but he'd watched them grow up with such compassionate and gentle souls that he could not bring himself to believe they were evil.

As for himself, he probably was evil. He had to be, didn't he, if he did nothing while his innocent brothers were whipped? But he wasn't sure how he could rescue them. They had nowhere else to go. He wasn't sure they even wanted to be rescued. They had been trained so well to be obedient. The Raven, too. For even with a kernel of doubt, he continued to do as he was told.

And he hated himself for that.

Why? he asked himself for the hundredth time. He'd been taught all his life that loyalty and obedience were the most desired virtues he could strive for, so why did living by those principles make him feel so wretched? A few months earlier, overcome with despair, he'd mentioned his pain in confession, and the monk had told him it was caused by his own evil nature. The only way he could be redeemed was by suffering for the Light and allowing his Embraced powers to be used to fulfill the holy quest bequeathed to the Brotherhood.

What exactly that quest would require him to do in the future, the Raven didn't really know, but he'd been taught all his life who the enemy was: the Embraced who lived in the outside world, and especially the Embraced of the royal families. Because of their magical gifts, given to them by the evil moon goddesses, they thought they were superior and used their powers to lord it over innocent humans.

As true followers of the sun god, the Brotherhood was naturally opposed to those who had been embraced by the moons. But Master Lorne had kept the Brotherhood hidden and quiet all through the Raven's childhood. Enclosed in his library, the master had devised his secret plans while receiving his daily reports from spies spread across the four mainland kingdoms.

Life had been dull and routine all those years, the only moments of excitement occurring during the Loyalty Ceremony when each monk could have a turn at plying the whip. But now, as the Raven, his brothers, and the other orphans reached adulthood, Master Lorne had started assigning actual missions.

Excitement was running high at the monastery now, with each priest praying that he would be selected for a mission, even though failure would mean death. Over the last few months, most of the monks had focused on the writing and distribution of hundreds of handbills, designed to turn the populace against the Embraced royal family. In the last few weeks, several monks had been tasked with more important missions: the extermination of certain Embraced young people.

But the Raven had not known that today's mission would

target the royal princess. Father Saul hadn't known, either. Master Lorne tended to be secretive, insisting the Brothers follow his orders out of strict loyalty and obedience, rather than understanding. Father Saul had successfully displayed those virtues by accepting the price for his failure and ingesting the poison, but Master Lorne had been prepared in case the priest's resolve faltered. He'd sent his favorite assassin, Father Greer, to make sure Saul was obedient to the end.

Dammit to hell. The Raven's talons curled, scratching painfully against the stone windowsill. Watching his older friend commit suicide had left him ready to explode. Saul had been only thirty-two years old, and he'd had a kind soul. He'd enjoyed being a priest and looking after his flock. He'd been the one who had smoothed salve on the Raven's back when his skin had been ripped to shreds.

With a disgusted huff, he jumped off the windowsill and landed on the cold stone floor.

Arlo spotted him and grinned. "Bran, you're back!"

He shifted into human form by the trunk at the foot of his bed. "What happened while I was gone?" He pulled out a black robe and slipped it on.

"Not much." Arlo sat on the end of Zane's cot as the youngest brother attempted to sit up. "Just the usual Loyalty Ceremony."

"Don't be so modest," Zane contradicted, then gave Bran a pained smile. "During the ceremony, Master Lorne gave Arlo a promotion! He didn't have to be whipped. He's a priest now. And one of the Brothers!"

Arlo's fair face turned pink as he shyly smiled. "I wasn't expecting it to happen until the next Spring Embrace."

"That's wonderful," Bran said quickly, then spun around so his younger brothers couldn't see his anger surging to the surface. *Dammit.* Father Greer must have raced here right away to confirm Father Saul's death. If so, then Master Lorne might have decided a replacement was needed.

"Maybe you'll be given a parish," Zane added, his voice vibrant with excitement.

This was so wrong, Bran thought as he buttoned his robe. Arlo had just turned twenty on the Autumn Embrace. He was too young for this. Being a priest of the Brotherhood meant he could be . . .

With a jerk, Bran slammed the trunk lid shut. His brother could be given a mission. *Holy Light, no.* He turned slowly to look at the small table next to Arlo's cot.

A shiny new silver ring sat there.

Dammit to hell. He dashed over to the ring and opened it up to find the white poison inside.

"Bran." Arlo strode toward him.

But Bran was too fast. In just a few seconds, he emptied the ring out the window.

Arlo sighed. "That was pointless. If I'm given a mission, the ring will be refilled."

"And I will dump it."

Arlo gave him an annoyed look. "You do missions all the time. Why shouldn't I?"

Zane nodded. "We want to be brave and virtuous like you."

With a snort, Bran slammed the empty ring onto Arlo's table. "What bravery? I take no risk when everyone thinks I'm a bloody bird. And what virtue is there in spying on people?"

"You're bringing back valuable information," Zane insisted.

"For what purpose?" Bran growled. "So more Embraced can be killed?"

Arlo winced. "How can you object? They're the enemy." He rested a hand on Bran's shoulder and gave him a pointed look. "I fear you are spending too much time with them. You must not allow yourself to be swayed."

Would his own brothers report him for disobedience? Bran's heart grew heavy, knowing that the answer would eventually be yes. And perhaps they were right. His job as a spy left him too exposed to the outside world. The lives of the people he spied upon were so different, he'd found himself intrigued. And after discovering the eagle, he'd felt . . . conflicted.

He wasn't alone. There was another bird shifter. An instant, glorious sense of kinship had filled his heart, quickly followed by a desperate need to reject it. For sadly, the eagle was one of the enemy.

With a sigh, Bran sat on his cot, ignoring the tight pull of the scarred skin on his back. "You are right, Arlo." He slipped his feet into his leather sandals. No doubt he was letting his grief over Father Saul's death cause him to think and act foolishly.

"I'll go see the master now and make my report." He strode to the door and glanced back at his brother. "Congratulations on becoming a priest, Father Arlo. I am proud of you."

Arlo nodded, his eyes brimming with tears. "Thank you, Father Bran."

The reminder that he, too, was a priest made Bran wince as he closed the door behind him. He would never be a gentle priest who gave wise counsel to his flock as his kind-hearted brothers would someday. Blinking back tears, Bran sent up a quick prayer to the Light to keep his younger brothers safe.

A torch at the base of the spiral staircase was the only light, but with his excellent night vision, he had no trouble descending the stone steps. As a bird shifter, he liked being at the top of the tower, where it was easier to come and go. The location couldn't be easy for his brothers, but even so, they had insisted on sharing the room with him.

He and his brothers had always stuck together. The rest of the acolytes at the monastery were orphans, and some of them had resented the fact that the three brothers had each other and special Embraced powers. Only two of the other orphans were Embraced: Father Horace, also called Father Hound Dog because of his gift of tracking people, and Father Greer, who treated Horace as if he were his pet. Bran had never understood why Horace went along with it, but the tracker was fiercely loyal to Greer.

Bran was the same age as Greer, and he had never liked the coldhearted bastard. Greer's gift was an ability to freeze something to death, and as a youth, he'd taken delight in practicing his gift on any small animal he could find. Bran and his brothers had stopped him whenever they could, and Greer had hated them for it.

Greer also hated them because they were actually related to the two brothers who had founded the Brotherhood and built the monastery. Bran's father, the eldest of those two brothers, had passed away, but the younger one, Master Lorne, was now in charge. That meant Bran and his brothers were next in line to continue the family legacy. One day, Bran would be the master, a position he'd never wanted, but the fact that Greer would be his subject someday filled the bastard with rage.

Bran reached the ground floor and moved through the dark hallways until he arrived at the Great Hall. It was empty at this time of night, because the monks tended to retire early so they could attend mass at sunrise. There was no furniture in the Great Hall; the priests were disdainful of comfort. The only item in the space was a huge golden gong that symbolized the sun and could be struck in case of an emergency.

His sandals clopped on the flagstones, causing an echo across the Great Hall as he strode to the master's library. He assumed Master Lorne would still be awake, for as far as he knew, the man rarely slept. Of course the main reason the master was overworked was his refusal to allow anyone else to read the multitude of reports he received. No one else even knew how many spies there were in his massive network. The master was naturally secretive, the other monks claimed, but Bran figured he was simply afraid of losing his power. He was definitely wary of Bran, his heir, so he purposely kept Bran in the dark as much as he could.

Bran knocked on the door, then cracked it open to peer inside. A fire in the hearth had dwindled down to glowing embers, casting a golden hue over the wood-paneled walls and bookcases. Far across the room, two lit candlesticks sat on an enormous desk of dark wood. Behind the desk, black curtains had been drawn across the windows. And seated at the desk, Master Lorne wore the plain black robes of a monk. Either the candlelight was tinting the color of his face, or the man was ill, because his skin had a sickly, yellowish pallor, reminiscent of the dried and fragile pages of an ancient book.

He looked up, his dark eyes narrowing on Bran.

The man was his uncle, but there would be no warm welcome here. The master reminded him of a black spider, hovering in the middle of his web, ready to strike at any moment.

Without a word, the master waved a bony hand, motioning for him to enter, and the candlelight flickered off his ring of poison. Unlike the silver ones that the rest of the Brotherhood wore, Master Lorne's ring was made of pure gold.

Bran closed the door behind him, then bowed his head to repeat the words he'd been taught to say as a toddler. "Greetings, Lord Master. May the Light be with you."

"You're late coming back," Master Lorne grumbled. "Father Greer told me an hour ago that the mission failed. If you have nothing to add, you may leave."

Bran tamped down another surge of anger. He strongly suspected that the bastard Greer had foisted the sudden mission on Father Saul, so if it failed, Saul would be the one stuck paying the price for it.

"I do have something to add." Bran approached the desk. "Father Saul shouldn't have been blamed for the failure of this mission when he was given only a few hours to prepare for it. And he was not told that the target was the princess. Neither was I. Doesn't this attack put the Brotherhood in danger? The king could find out about us."

Master Lorne shrugged. "The kings and queens are the worst of our enemies. We can hardly be at war with them while keeping that war a secret."

Then the master intended to go to battle against all the royal houses? If the kings and queens were defeated, who would take control of the world? The master, of course.

Bran's initial shock quickly faded, and he let out a sigh. He shouldn't have been surprised. After all, it was the same quest that the Circle of Five had attempted. Some things never changed. "Saul would have taken extra precautions if he had known the target was a heavily guarded princess."

The master waved a dismissive hand. "He still failed."

"It was not a failure! I watched the mission and learned something extremely valuable. But I never would have discovered it had the mission transpired in a different manner. Father Saul should have been commended, not commanded to die!"

Master Lorne's mouth thinned. "Anything else?"

"He was only thirty-two years old. He could have served you for many more years. It is wrong to expect people to kill themselves—"

"*Wrong?*" The master stood abruptly, then stalked toward

Bran. "You fool, what has happened to your concept of right and wrong? Saul's death was right because he was *obedient*. And what is *wrong*, Bran? Tell me!"

The skin on Bran's scarred back itched. "Disobedience."

"Correct." The master slapped him hard across the face. "Don't ever question me again."

Bran stood still, his head turned. His fists slowly clenched as his face burned. A spot on his cheekbone stung, and he felt the trickle of blood on his cheek. The master's ring must have torn his skin.

"Anything to say now?" Master Lorne hissed.

Bran forced his hands to relax. "I would ask—no, beg that you not give my brother any missions. He has just barely turned twenty."

The master scoffed. "So you're assuming Arlo would fail?"

No, Bran would do everything in his power to make sure Arlo did not fail.

Master Lorne shrugged one bony shoulder. "My brother was willing to take his life. Why should his sons do less?" He motioned to Bran's right hand. "Why aren't you wearing your ring? Every member of the Brotherhood wears his ring to show his willingness to give his life for the cause. Some of the monks have been complaining that you don't wear yours."

"I'm a raven most of the time. It's not possible—"

"And I've told you before, whenever you pretend to be human, you need to wear it. We can't have any of the priests thinking you're getting preferential treatment just because your father was Lord Morris."

Bran gritted his teeth. "Preferential treatment? As in receiving twice the number of blows from the whip?"

Master Lorne scoffed. "That has nothing to do with your parentage. You were whipped because you're Embraced, thoroughly permeated with the evil power of the moon bitches.

You and your brothers require extra discipline in case you start thinking you're better than everyone else."

"And how on Aerthlan were we all born Embraced?" Bran ground out. "You have punished us for it all our lives when it was you and your brother who intentionally impregnated women in hopes of having Embraced children! You even gave them a tonic to induce their labor—"

"Enough!" Master Lorne's eyes flashed with anger as he seized Bran's shirt in a bony grip. "We created you so we could use you to fight evil, but clearly, you have too much evil inside you. Do I need to start flogging you again?"

Bran swallowed the bile that had risen up his throat. What was the use in railing against the reality of his life? There was no escape from it. There was nothing he could do but comply. "Nay, Lord Master."

With a shove, Master Lorne released him. "Be grateful that the love I hold for my dearly departed brother is keeping you alive."

Bran nearly choked on the hypocrisy. When his father, Lord Morris, had committed suicide twenty years ago, Lorne had been quick to take control of his older brother's network. Lorne had even helped himself to his brother's mistresses. So while Lord Morris had fathered Bran and Arlo, Lorne had fathered Zane with the same mistress who had given birth to Arlo.

Technically, Zane was Bran's cousin, but since Arlo was a half brother to both Bran and Zane, they had always simplified their twisted lineage by calling themselves brothers.

The three of them had never known their mothers. The mistresses had been sent away once they'd fulfilled their purpose. Of course, a few of the mistresses had failed to produce an Embraced child or a male child. There had been two daughters. One worked as a spy at Lourdon Palace, in the capital of Tourin, and the other at Ebton Palace in Eberon.

Master Lorne eyed Bran as if determining his worth. "You said you learned something important today?"

He was tempted to say nothing. But he didn't want Father Saul to be considered a failure when the mission had been impossible to begin with. "The mission never could have succeeded. We would have realized that if we'd known the nature of the princess's Embraced power. She can easily stop any attack."

The master's eyes widened. "How? Do you know what her power is?"

Bran nodded. "If she claps her hands, everyone in her vicinity falls asleep, and they remain unconscious for hours. That is how she escaped."

Excitement glinted in the master's eyes. "She could put an army to sleep? Her parents?"

"Aye. Only animals and birds, such as myself, are immune." Bran wasn't sure why, but he didn't want to mention the eagle.

"This is fantastic!" Master Lorne paced toward the fireplace. "We shouldn't kill her, then, not when we can use her." He spun around to face Bran. "Where is she?"

"I'm not sure. I flew straight here from Bramblewood." Bran didn't want to mention that he'd stayed late there so his friend wouldn't have to die alone. Then during the flight to the monastery, he'd been so overwhelmed with grief at one point that he'd had to stop and rest for a while. Greer had left right after Saul had taken the poison, so he'd managed to beat Bran back to the monastery.

The master rubbed his bony hands together. "We have to know where the princess is. Fly to Ebton now to see what your sister Vera knows."

"Yes, Lord Master." He would also ask her what she knew about the eagle shifter. When Master Lorne waved a hand in dismissal, Bran bowed his head and strode toward the door.

Behind him, the master chuckled. "This is rich. We can use the princess against her own family!"

Bran winced inwardly, imagining how he'd feel if his brothers died because of him. He wrenched open the door and stepped outside. As he trudged back to his room, his heart grew heavy, for no matter how he secretly railed against his orders, no matter how much he questioned himself, he knew he would still do as he'd been trained. He would be obedient.

The monks who had raised him were correct.

He was evil.

Chapter 10

Two days later, Eviana peered through the narrow window of the covered wagon as it passed by the army camps around Benwick Castle. The wagon was little more than a rectangular, wooden box on wheels, designed more for protection than comfort. The window on each side was a narrow slit to make it difficult for anyone to shoot an arrow inside. A barrel of water sat in each corner in case someone shot a flaming arrow at the wagon.

A wide bench ran along each side of the interior, topped with a thick velvet cushion. The back door was barred shut from the inside and had a small grated window with a shutter that could be closed and locked in place. A similar window was at the front of the wagon, so the people inside could communicate with the wagon's driver. Even though the windows were open now, to allow some air to flow through, Eviana found the interior too dark and stuffy.

She'd never liked small, enclosed places. At first, they had reminded her of the dragon imprisoning her in its giant talons and pinning her against its scaled body. But as time went by, she was reminded more and more of her daily life enclosed in the private apartments of Ebton Palace or her grandfather's small privy chamber. Every aspect of her life had been predetermined from the moment of her birth. *Trapped.*

She took a deep breath to steady her nerves and focused on the blue sky overhead. Pendras and Lennie would be up there flying. And about five miles down the road, Quentin, Elam, and Olana would be waiting for her arrival.

Her pulse picked up at the thought of traveling with Quentin and seeing him every day. She'd hardly seen him at all the day before. He'd gone somewhere to get a cart and workhorse, and after he'd returned, he'd been busy, filling the large cart with straw, several crates of wine, a small supply of food, and two small trunks filled with clothing suitable for servants and a poor merchant. Then this morning, before dawn, he and his group had departed quietly while most everyone had been asleep.

According to the plan, they would travel five miles down this main road until it intersected with another smaller road. There was a small pasture nearby, surrounded by forest, and there, they would hide the cart and horses. That was also where Eviana would secretly join them.

Eric and Dominic had left the day before to begin their official investigation. Her father, King Leo, had brought this covered wagon to Benwick himself, so he could see his wife and daughter before they set off on their adventures. In case there was a spy at Benwick, they had staged a big farewell in the courtyard. After hugging her husband, Luciana had climbed onto the driver's bench of the wagon, where she would sit next to the driver. And after a tearful embrace with her father, Eviana had stepped into the wagon, along with Faith, disguised as a lady's maid in a plain woolen gown and travel cape, the hood drawn over her head to hide her face.

Eviana had dressed in the manner befitting a princess: a blue silk gown and matching cape, the hood lined with white fur. But as warm and stuffy as it was inside the wagon, she'd quickly had to remove the cape.

She glanced over at the other bench, where Faith was sitting and gazing out a window. The poor girl would have to travel all the way to Vindalyn in this wooden box.

As Faith removed her woolen cape, she let out a big yawn, and Eviana found herself yawning, too.

"Sorry." Faith gave her a sheepish smile. "The warmth in here is making me sleepy."

"Me, too." Eviana smiled back. "I was too excited to sleep very well last night."

Faith nodded. "I could hardly sleep, either."

Eviana glanced out the narrow window. The campsites were gone, and a seemingly endless line of trees ran alongside the road. "I appreciate your doing this, but I'm afraid being stuck in this wagon will be very boring for you."

"That's what my parents are hoping for. A boring trip where nothing dangerous happens."

"That would certainly be for the best." Soon they would reach the rendezvous point, so Eviana closed the windows in the back door and front wall. "We should change clothes now."

Faith, being six years younger than Eviana, was a little bit shorter and thinner, but Eviana was able to pull the laces tighter around her torso to insure a good fit. Soon, Faith was dressed in the silk petticoats, stockings, and blue silk gown and slippers, while Eviana was wearing a plain gown of wine-colored wool, along with the matching cape and a sturdy pair of black ankle boots. After braiding her hair, she tied off the end with a dark red ribbon. The final touch was a cream-colored kerchief that covered her hair and knotted at the base of her neck.

"There." She smoothed down her skirt, grateful to be rid of all the petticoats. "Now you look like the princess, and I look like a . . . a merchant, I hope."

"Or a peasant," Faith teased her, then laughed. "You're

the prettiest merchant I've ever seen. The men will be flocking around you to buy wine."

"I hope so." Then Olana could touch them, and they would reveal their secrets. But there was something wrong with her plan, Eviana realized as she reopened the windows. It was the priest of each village whom they should be targeting. "I need to come up with a story that will explain why we're seeking out all the priests."

She gazed out the window, considering that, as the wagon lumbered along. Just as a marvelous idea struck her, she heard her mother tapping at the front window.

"Quentin is circling overhead," Luciana told them softly. "We're close to the rendezvous point."

"All right." Eviana's heart raced. This was it. The beginning of her mission and her adventure. With Quentin.

As the wagon slowed to a stop, Luciana announced in a loud voice, "My daughter and I need to go into the woods for a moment. Please give us privacy while we attend to our needs."

"Yes, Your Majesty," the colonel in charge replied, then called for his troops to halt.

Eviana slid the bolt on the door and opened it. In the space between the wagon and the nearest troop, Lennie landed and spread her dragon wings to shield the women from view. Eviana waved at her best friend; then she and Faith descended the wooden steps to the ground. When Luciana joined them, they hurried into the woods on the eastern side of the main road.

Elam emerged from behind a large oak tree and bowed. "Your Majesty."

Luciana shook his hand. "Take good care of my daughter." She turned to give Eviana a hug. "Be careful."

"You, too." Eviana embraced her mother as she blinked back tears.

"We'll be fine," Luciana assured her. "I'll be traveling inside the wagon from now on with Faith. We'll probably do something exciting like take a nap."

With a smile, Eviana nodded. "Thank you for believing in me."

"May the goddesses keep you safe." Luciana touched her daughter's cheek. "And may you follow your heart." With tears glistening in her eyes, she dashed back toward the wagon.

"Good luck!" Faith gave her a quick hug, then ran after Luciana.

"This way." Elam motioned for her to follow him.

Eviana glanced back to see her mother and Faith disappear from view. *Goddesses, please keep them safe. And us, too.* She took a deep breath, then strode after the colonel.

"I'll be traveling on horseback," Elam told her as he led the way. "Olana is driving the cart. You can sit next to her, or ride in the back of the cart."

"And Quentin?"

"He'll be flying overhead, watching for any sign of an ambush."

Ambush? "Who would attack us?" Eviana asked. "No one will know who we are."

"There are thieves who make their living by preying on travelers and merchants," Elam explained. "Much like the ruffians who attacked your barge. I doubt you've ever had to deal with them on your trips to Vindalyn. They would never attack a royal convoy guarded by soldiers, but our small group will be considered fair game."

"I see." Pretending to be a merchant was not going to be as simple as she had thought.

"If Quentin sees anyone suspicious, he'll land on the back of the horse pulling the cart," Elam continued. "That will be your cue to use your gift."

"I understand." It was better to play it safe, of course, but she was going to find it very frustrating if Quentin was flying high in the sky for most of the trip. How could she even have a conversation with him?

Elam paused at the edge of a clearing. "Your Highness, from now on I will be your servant, Elam. And I will call you Mistress Evie."

"Yes, Elam." As she followed him into the clearing, she spotted the cart and horses.

Olana and Quentin were standing by the cart, their backs to her as they helped themselves to some fruit and cheese. *Good goddesses.* Even from the back and from a distance, she could instantly recognize him. The sun shone off his burnished golden hair, and the breadth of his shoulders reminded her of how easily he had swept her into his arms. Her gaze dropped to his breeches as the memory of his bare rump slipped into her mind. *Don't think about that!* Too late, she thought with a wince. Her face was already growing warm.

As if he could feel her gaze, Quentin glanced over his shoulder. "She's here," he said softly as he turned toward her.

Even his voice was lovely. And those eyes . . . Eviana's heart swelled. He was barefoot, his shirt unbuttoned and hanging loose around his breeches, and his hair looked mussed as if he'd just climbed out of bed. Compared to the noblemen at court who spent hours grooming themselves, he looked so . . . real. No pretense. No lame attempt to impress her. It was as if he was telling her, *This is who I am. Take it or leave it.*

Good goddesses, she could no longer deny it. She *was* attracted to him. She wanted to know him. She wanted to touch him. This was definitely more than gratitude for his daring rescue.

"Good morning, Mistress Evie," Olana said, stepping into her role.

Eviana stopped a few feet away. "Good morning, Olana. Quentin."

He bowed his head, then turned his back to her to rummage through the basket of food. Was he not going to speak to her?

"Would you like a bite to eat before we go?" Olana asked.

"Ah . . . yes." Eviana cleared her throat. "Do you have an apple?"

"Of course." Olana spun around to grab an apple from the basket, just as Quentin tried to hand one to her. When their hands came close to touching, he dropped the apple and jumped back, letting the apple plummet to the grassy meadow.

He winced. "Sorry."

Olana glanced at Eviana, then gave Quentin a wry look.

Was he hiding something? Eviana wondered what it could be as she leaned over to retrieve the apple.

Unfortunately, Olana leaned forward at the same time, and they bumped heads.

Olana straightened with a gasp. "Oh, I'm so sorry."

"I feel trapped by my own life," Eviana confessed, then groaned inwardly. *Oh, dear goddesses, this is so embarrassing.* With her face blushing, she bent over and snatched up the apple. "I shouldn't have said that. Please don't tell anyone."

Olana gave her a sympathetic look. "Your secret is safe with us."

Eviana slanted a glance at Quentin. He was watching her intently but said nothing. What on Aerthlan was *his* secret?

Olana heaved a sigh. "I'm afraid it's going to be difficult for all of you to travel with me."

"Then perhaps we should get all the embarrassment out of the way," Eviana suggested as she rubbed the apple against her skirt. "Why don't we confess our secrets now? Then we won't have to worry about it later."

"No, thank you!" Elam dashed over to his horse.

Quentin looked equally horrified. "I'm going to shift now." He ran to the far side of the clearing and disappeared amongst the trees.

"Look at that," Eviana muttered. "I certainly know how to scare people off."

"It's not your fault." Olana's shoulders slumped as she turned to secure the food basket in the back of the cart. "It's me they're running from."

Eviana winced. She'd never realized before how lonesome Olana must be. "Well, since my secret is out, there's no need for me to avoid you. I'll be right by your side." She wrapped an arm around Olana's shoulders to give her a hug. "I feel trapped." She made a face. "And blah, blah, blah, woe is me."

Olana laughed. "I believe that's the best confession I've ever heard."

"Thank you." Eviana bit into her apple. An eagle soared over them, and she glanced up at Quentin. What could his secret be? Everybody already knew about the unfortunate circumstances of his birth. Was he hiding something worse than that?

"I'll fetch his clothes, and then we can leave." Elam strode toward the woods where Quentin had shifted.

"I should relieve myself before we go." Munching on her apple, Eviana headed toward the trees in the opposite direction. She glanced up at Quentin and saw him flying off toward the narrow road they would be taking. They would be traveling mostly east and only slightly south, while her mother and Faith would be on the main road, going straight south to Vindalyn.

Once she was done, she headed back to the cart. Olana was climbing onto the driver's bench when her skirt caught beneath her foot.

"Oh!" Her arms flailed as she fought to maintain her balance.

"Olana!" Elam ran toward her and just as she fell backward, he caught her in his arms. He stiffened, an alarmed look spreading across his face. "I've been in love with you for twelve years."

Olana gasped. "What?"

"Ack!" He jumped back, dropping her on the ground. "Oh! Olana, I'm sorry." He leaned toward her. "Are you all right?"

"What did you say?" She scrambled to her feet, and he sprang back.

"I-I believe you heard me." He retreated another step, his face turning red. "I know you don't return my feelings, so there is no point in discussing it. Please forget I ever said anything." He rushed to his horse and mounted up. "We should be going now."

"But—" Olana stared at him as he steered his horse toward the narrow road.

Eviana came out of her shock and ran toward Olana. "Are you all right? I-I saw you fall."

Olana gave her a blank look.

"He's leaving. We need to follow." Eviana took her by the arm to help her onto the cart. "I still feel trapped, blah, blah, blah."

"Woe is me," Olana whispered, her gaze shifting back to Elam.

"Are you sure you're all right?" Eviana asked.

"I'm . . . stunned." Olana clambered onto the cart and settled on the driver's bench.

Eviana sat beside her. "It was rather shocking."

"You heard him?" Olana turned toward her. "I didn't imagine it?"

"I heard him." Eviana passed her the reins. "Let's go. He's getting too far ahead of us."

With a shout, Olana gave the reins a flick, and the work-horse started plodding along slowly.

"Perhaps we shouldn't be so surprised," Eviana murmured. "After all, you said yourself that what people are hiding most often is love."

"But I never imagined I would be the object of that love." Olana shook her head. "Twelve years? He should have told me." As she maneuvered the cart onto the narrow road, she winced in pain. "My shoulder is hurting. Would you mind taking the reins?"

Eviana hesitated, then took them. "You must have hurt yourself when you fell."

"You mean when he dropped me." Olana snorted. "The coward."

"I'm sure he had his reasons."

"For twelve years?" Olana glared at Elam's back as he rode a good twenty yards in front of them.

"I have another confession," Eviana admitted. "I've never driven a cart before."

"Oh." Olana gave her a wry smile. "Don't worry. You're doing fine. Daisy—that's the horse—she'll stay on the road, and she really has only one speed."

"Slow?"

"Exactly." Olana sighed, then muttered under her breath, "He should have told me."

"I think you need to have a talk with him."

"How?" With a snort, she motioned toward him. "As far as I can tell, he's going to spend the entire journey trying to avoid me."

Eviana glanced up at the sky where Quentin was zigzag-ging back and forth. "I know the feeling."

Olana heaved another sigh, then remained quiet as she glared at Elam's back.

"A lovely day for travel," Eviana said, enjoying the blue

sky and the trees turning red, orange, and gold. She took a deep breath of the crisp autumn air. This was so much nicer than being stuck inside that boxlike wagon. "I hope we can complete our mission before winter comes."

Olana remained quiet.

Eviana tried again. "I was so excited about our mission, I could hardly sleep last night." She glanced at Olana, who was still glowering at Elam in silence. *Great.* A long trip with people who were refusing to talk to one another? This was going to be awkward.

Chapter 11

Bran was ready to throttle his sister, Vera. Yesterday afternoon, he'd arrived at Ebton Palace and there, he'd landed on the windowsill of her bedchamber. Not seeing her inside, he'd waited and waited until, finally, she'd returned to her room. He'd tapped on the glass with his beak, but instead of letting him in as she usually did, she'd fled the room.

After that, he'd flown to the church of Enlightenment in the village of Ebton. Father Roland was one of the Brotherhood, so he'd given Bran some clothes to wear. Dressed in the plain leather sandals and black robes of a priest, Bran had returned to the palace, where he had gained entry to the outer courtyard and requested a meeting with the lady-in-waiting, Vera. Not only had she refused to see him, but she'd asked the guards to throw him out!

Bran had returned to the church, and Father Roland had given him supper and a cot to sleep on for the night. Even though Bran was pissed, he'd managed to hold his tongue and not mention to Father Roland what had happened. If the priest reported Vera's disobedience to Master Lorne, she would be in huge trouble. The master had people killed for less.

But Bran still needed to know the location of the princess.

Father Roland didn't know. The last he'd heard, Princess Eviana had left for Norveshka, traveling by barge, but Bran knew that trip had been canceled. He'd spotted the royal barge docked at the pier behind Ebton Palace. And before arriving at Ebton, he'd flown by Benwick Castle. He'd seen no sign of the princess there. If she was at Benwick, she was being well hidden and no one was talking.

As one of the princess's ladies-in-waiting, Vera had always been his best source of information on the royal family. He didn't know why she was avoiding him now, but he would not give up.

So, this morning, he'd come up with a new plan. He stuffed a black robe into a canvas bag, then flew over the palace with the bag straps clutched in his talons. After dropping the bag into the square-shaped garden, he flew down, shifted, and put on the black robe.

Blending into the dark shadows of the hallway and stairwell, he made his way to Vera's small room on the top floor. He let himself in and waited.

Finally, Vera strode into the room, a lit candlestick in her hand. With a sigh, she placed the candle on the small table next to her narrow bed.

Bran stepped out of the shadows, and she gasped, jumping back. "Don't scream," he muttered.

"Oh!" She pressed a hand to her chest. "You scared me half to death. What are you doing here? How did you get in?"

"Shouldn't I be the one asking questions?" he growled. "Why are you avoiding me?"

Her eyes flashed with anger. "I don't want to see any of you again. I told Father Roland about the barge trip, and then the princess was attacked!"

Bran sighed as his own anger faded away. So Roland must have told Greer, and Greer had rushed over to Bramblewood to give Father Saul the mission.

Vera's eyes glistened with tears. "Do you have any idea how guilty I have felt?"

He stepped closer to his sister. "It's not your fault, Vera. You have no say over what the priests do with the information you give them. Besides, the royal family is our enemy. You mustn't forget that."

"I know, but . . ."

"Where is the princess now?"

Vera shook her head. "I don't want to tell you."

"You have to—"

"I don't want you to hurt her!" A tear rolled down Vera's cheek. "She's always been so good to me. And the queen, too. They give me nice clothes and this lovely room all to myself."

"You're letting material things sway you."

Vera took in a shaky breath as more tears flowed. "If any of the courtiers try to say or do something bad to me or any of the ladies or maids, Queen Luciana yells at them and bans them from court. I feel safe here, Bran. Safer than I've ever felt before."

Bran narrowed his eyes. "You didn't feel safe at the monastery? You never had to endure the whippings that my brothers and I did."

Her face crumpled. "There were times I would have preferred to be whipped. But . . ." She turned away, squeezing her eyes shut. Her voice came out as a whisper. "The master had other ways to torment the girls."

A chill ran down Bran's spine. *By the Light, no.* "What did he do to you?"

"He . . . he let the other priests . . ."

Bran clenched his fists. That spidery bastard.

"He said it was part of our training," Vera whispered. "In case we were given a mission to seduce someone. He let them touch us, but not . . ." She wiped the tears off her face. "He insisted we remain virgins so we could give up our virginity for the cause."

That bloody bastard. Bran paced across the room, tempted to destroy something. All this time, he'd thought it was only the boys at the monastery who were abused. Since Vera was the daughter of Lord Morris and one of his many mistresses, Bran had always believed that his half sister had been treated with respect. Master Lorne was her uncle, damn him! He should have been protecting her, not . . . "Give me the names of the bastards who hurt you. I will make them pay."

Vera gave him a sad look. "You can't do that, Bran. The master would hurt you, if not kill you."

"I'll find a way!" He banged a fist on the wall. "They have to pay." The rage inside him made his gut feel as if it was twisted into knots.

"I'm all right now," Vera said softly. "I . . . I escaped. You're the one who has to keep going back."

He took a deep breath. "You can't be all right. Your scars must run deeper than my own." He turned toward her. "I am sorry. I am so sorry, Vera."

She wiped the tears from her face and perched on the edge of her bed. "I know I was sent here to spy on the royal family. But in the five years that I've been here, the queen has promoted me from being a mere maid to a lady-in-waiting. People call me Lady Vera. I . . . I am so happy here. I didn't even know what happiness was until I came here."

He nodded. It was little wonder that she'd been swayed. How could she not have been?

"At first, I thought the spying was exciting." She snorted. "But the things I reported were so harmless—what the royal family ate for dinner, who was invited to their parties, what they wore. But now, it seems terribly different."

"True," Bran agreed. "Master Lorne is finally making his move."

"Does he really mean to destroy the royals?" Vera grimaced. "I was horrified when I found out the barge was attacked. Thank the Light the princess wasn't harmed."

"You didn't know about her Embraced gift?"

"No." Vera shook her head. "It's always been a secret. What is it?"

"She can make people fall into a deep sleep."

"Oh." Vera shrugged. "That seems rather harmless."

"Actually, it can be extremely dangerous." Bran recalled his surprise at seeing everyone fall unconscious during the barge attack. Everyone except the eagle. "Why didn't you tell me about the eagle shifter?"

"Quentin?"

"That's his name? What else do you know?"

She waved a dismissive hand. "He's nobody special. A messenger boy. The illegitimate son of a stable hand and a scullery maid who was lucky enough to be born on the night the moons embrace."

Bran had always suspected Vera was resentful toward those who had been born Embraced. Lord Morris had used dangerous potions to assure that the women he'd impregnated would give birth at the correct time. Unfortunately, Vera's birthing had been so slow that she'd arrived after sunrise the following day. A normal baby. Her mother had died soon after as a result of being overdosed with the powerful potion.

"This Quentin seems to know the royal family very well," Bran said.

Vera nodded. "He's one of the children from the Isle of Secrets. I suppose we have our father to thank for that. The king and queen of Norveshka took pity on him and raised him. Now he's a courier amongst the royal families."

"You should have told me about him."

Vera gave him a wry look. "Why? Are you curious about him because he's a bird like you?"

Bran shrugged. Maybe he was, but he couldn't let his curiosity interfere with the Brotherhood's mission. "You'll have to tell me something. Master Lorne sent me here for information, and if you don't deliver . . ."

Vera frowned. "He'll consider it a failure."

She didn't have a poison-filled ring, thankfully, but Bran knew the master would find some way to punish her. Or even kill her, if he knew how compromised she had become. All Lorne had to do was send his favorite assassin, Greer.

Vera heaved a big sigh. "Very well. I can tell you that the royal family was outraged by the attack. Eric and Dominic are leading an official investigation. They left yesterday."

"And the princess? Where is she?"

Vera hesitated, then lifted her chin with a defiant look. "Fine. I'll tell you what I know. But it won't matter, because the queen and princess have four troops and two dragons to protect them on their journey."

"Where are they going?"

"Vindalyn." Vera rose to her feet. "They're too well guarded to be attacked. The master won't be able to get any of his nasty priests close to her. And even if he does, she can use her gift to put them to sleep."

"We'll see about that." Bran opened the window.

"You—" Vera stepped closer. "You won't tell the master that I . . ."

He glanced at her. "That you're now siding with the enemy?"

She winced. "I've lived with them for five years, Bran. They're not evil. They truly care about this country and its people."

He gritted his teeth. "I won't tell on you."

"Thank you." She touched his shoulder. "They would never abuse young children."

"I don't want to hear it." He shot her a warning look, then softened his eyes. "Stay safe, Vera. Turn around now so I can leave."

"Very well." She stepped back and turned. "Stay safe, Bran."

He dropped his robe and shifted. As he took off into the air, her words kept repeating in his mind. *They would never abuse young children.*

Chapter 12

This was the problem with long flights, Quentin decided as he flew overhead: There was too much time for thinking, and unfortunately, his thoughts kept returning to Eviana and her unwilling confession. *I feel trapped by my own life.*

For the last two hours, he'd seen nothing remotely dangerous. A few deer in the forest, a few rabbits. His keen eyes could even detect a field mouse. About two miles ahead of them, a farmer was taking a wagonload of cabbages and turnips to the next village. Behind them, nothing.

What exactly was making her feel trapped? he wondered for the hundredth time. Did she not want to be the duchess of Vindalyn? Or was she upset that she was expected to marry soon? Just thinking about that made his talons curl.

And what had happened when she was thirteen? There was so much he wanted to know about her, but he didn't dare ask. That was something a friend would do, and he could certainly never be that. Better to avoid any conversation with her. And stay as far away from her as possible.

They looked a bit weary down below. Elam was still sitting stiffly on his horse, keeping about twenty yards ahead of the cart. Eviana held the reins, and she and Olana had been silent for a long time. They probably needed a break, and with the sun high in the sky, it was about time for a midday meal.

He searched for a good spot. There. Not far ahead was a

green meadow, surrounded by trees with a small creek running close by. Circling back to the others, he descended to about seven feet off the ground and let out a squawk to get their attention.

"What is it?" Elam asked.

With a second squawk, he headed back to the meadow and landed beside the road to wait for them.

"You need to rest?" Elam asked as he drew near. "This looks like a good spot." He steered his horse into the meadow.

The cart slowly followed, with Olana giving Eviana directions on how to turn and come to a stop. The horse, Daisy, bent her head and started munching on grass.

Eviana scrambled off the cart. "What a wonderful place for a picnic!"

Quentin flew to the cart and landed on the top of a trunk of clothing.

She smiled at him. "You want your clothes, don't you?" She turned to help Olana off the cart. As she touched her friend, she said, "I feel trapped." Then the two of them smiled at each other and said together, "Blah, blah, blah, woe is me."

With a laugh, Eviana looped an arm around Olana's shoulders. "Shall we set up the picnic?"

Quentin's heart warmed at the sight. Instead of wallowing in the shame of her untimely confession, Eviana was using the situation to befriend Olana. What a kind heart she had. *You fool, you're falling for her even more.*

"Come along, Quen." Elam grabbed his bundle of clothes from the cart and dashed for the woods before Olana could reach the back of the cart.

With a huff, she glared at him as he ran away.

Was she angry with Elam? Quentin wondered as he flew to the woods. He shifted and pulled on his breeches. Elam remained close by, staring mindlessly at a tree, as if he were reluctant to go back to the cart. "Something wrong?"

"No," Elam grumbled. "I-I'll go stand guard by the road."

That wasn't really necessary, since there was no one behind them on the road, but Quentin said nothing as Elam trudged away. Something must have happened that he wasn't aware of. But what? He would have heard his fellow travelers if they'd had an argument. But they had been mostly silent on the road.

He relieved himself, then wandered over to the small creek to wash his hands. After pulling on his shirt, he buttoned it as he walked barefoot back to the cart.

The women had laid out a blanket and topped it with a basket of fruit, a wooden tray of cheese and bread, and a set of four wooden plates and cups.

"That looks great." He motioned to the woods. "There's a small creek there if you'd like to wash up."

"Oh, yes! Thank you." Eviana strode toward the woods with Olana.

Quentin found the jug of cider in the back of the cart and brought it to the blanket. He sat in one corner, poured himself a drink, and filled a wooden plate with food. After a while, Olana came back and settled on the blanket a few feet away from him.

He glanced back at the woods. "Where is Eviana?"

"You mean Mistress Evie," Olana reminded him. "She's fine. She wanted to wash her face and re-braid her hair." She put some cheese and fruit on her plate, then tore off a piece of bread. "Is that the cider you have there?"

"Aye." Quentin poured a cup and passed it to her.

"Thank you." Very carefully, she took it by the rim to avoid touching him.

After a long sip, she set down her cup. "Shush." She waved her hand at a fly that hovered over her plate. When the fly moved over to Quentin's plate, she waved her hand at it just as he did.

He jerked his hand back to keep from touching her.

She winced. "Sorry."

"Leave some food for me!" Eviana called out with a grin as she approached.

Damn. Quentin swallowed hard. That had been too close. How was he going to make it through this entire journey without his secret coming out?

He slanted a wary look at the princess. As she strode toward the blanket, she shook out a damp piece of cloth. He recognized it as the kerchief she'd worn over her head. Apparently, she'd used it to wash up at the stream. Her cheeks were pink from a good scrubbing. Her eyes were sparkling, and her neatly braided hair swayed from side to side as she walked.

Her gown was made of plain, unadorned wool, but she still looked regal to him. And more beautiful than ever.

She smiled at him, and his heart nearly stopped. He quickly looked away. *Keep your distance. Don't even talk to her if you can help it.*

"I'm so glad we're all able to eat together." She settled on the edge of the blanket and spread the kerchief on the grass to dry. "I was afraid Quentin would remain a bird for the entire trip."

He scoffed, keeping his head turned away from her. Was there something wrong with being a bird?

She grabbed a wooden plate and filled it with bread, cheese, and fruit. "What a relief you're eating real food and not flying about, hunting for a tasty field mouse."

He gave her an annoyed look. "I don't eat mice."

She laughed. "I was teasing you. Actually, you make quite a magnificent-looking eagle. Don't you think so, Olana?"

She nodded quietly as she ate.

Quentin's heart squeezed. Eviana thought he looked magnificent?

She glanced over her shoulder at Elam, who was standing by the road. "Isn't he going to join us?"

Olana shot him an annoyed look. "Apparently not."

"He's on guard duty," Quentin said and bit into an apple.

"Guarding us from what?" Olana muttered.

Once again Quentin wondered if Olana was upset with the colonel. "Is something wrong?"

"No," Olana said at the same time Eviana said, "Yes."

Eviana heaved a sigh of exasperation. "You need to talk to him. Here." She offered her plate of food to Olana. "He'll be hungry. Take this to him so he can eat."

Olana hesitated. "Should I?"

"Yes!" Eviana pushed her plate of food into Olana's hands. "Go."

"Very well, then." Olana stood and walked slowly toward Elam.

"What's going on?" Quentin asked softly as Eviana began loading food onto the last wooden plate.

She glanced over her shoulder to check on Olana's progress, then sidled closer to Quentin.

Good goddesses, did she need to be this close? He glanced to his right, but he was already on the edge of the blanket.

She extended a wooden cup toward him. "Could you give me some cider?"

"Oh." He had the jug, and she was thirsty. That was all there was to her closeness. "Of course." He poured some cider into her cup.

"Can you feel it?" she whispered. "There's romance in the air."

Crap! His hand wobbled, and cider spilled onto the blanket. Dear goddesses, did she know how he felt about her? "Wha-what?"

"Oh, my, you filled it to the brim." Carefully, she took the cup from him, then placed her lips on the edge of the cup to slurp down some cider.

He swallowed hard. Damn but her mouth was beautiful.

"Mmm." She licked her lips.

Was she purposely trying to torture him? His breeches were already feeling a bit tight. "What did you say about . . . ?"

"Romance?" She set her cup down on her plate. "Well, this should be the start of a glorious romance, but I'm afraid it's just terribly . . . awkward. Doesn't it seem awkward to you?"

"Maybe." He glanced down to make sure his untucked shirt was providing cover.

She picked up the last of the loaf of bread and tore it in two. "We might as well finish this. Otherwise it will just go stale."

"All right." He took the heel end and bit into it. Dammit, how much did she know?

She glanced at Elam and Olana, then heaved a sigh. "I wish people would just say what they're thinking and feeling instead of hiding it. I find that extremely frustrating. Don't you?"

He swallowed his bread with a gulp, then drank some cider.

She leaned toward him and whispered, "Someone's been hiding his feelings of love."

He choked.

"All you all right?" She patted him on the back as his eyes watered.

"What?" He cleared his throat. "How did you know?"

"How could I not know?" She gave him a confused look. "But I don't understand it at all. Shouldn't something as wonderful as love be celebrated? Why hide it? What kind of man loves a woman for years without telling her?"

"I . . ." Dammit, what could he say? He concentrated on

refilling his cup without his hands shaking. "There could be many reasons."

"You mean excuses." She waved a dismissive hand. "Faith was right. It's cowardly."

Cowardly? He set the jug down with a thud and turned toward her. "I don't think you should judge someone when—"

"Fine!" Her green eyes flashed. "But it still makes me angry. Think about all that wasted time when they could have been happy."

"But the woman may not return the man's affections—"

"How would he ever know if he doesn't speak up?" She huffed. "It's so frustrating! Twelve years wasted—"

"No, only six."

"What?" She frowned. "I'm quite sure Elam said twelve."

"Elam?"

"Yes, Elam." She tilted her head. "Who did you think I was talking about?"

His heart fell back into his chest and thudded loudly in his ears. She wasn't talking about him. She must not know his secret, after all. "Are you saying Elam is in love? With whom?"

"Olana, of course." She gave him an exasperated look. "Do try to keep up."

He snorted. But dear goddesses, this was a relief. He should have realized she didn't know his secret. Unfortunately, he was so afraid of her finding out that he was becoming paranoid.

Her mouth twitched. "Some spy you are. You didn't even know what was happening right below you."

He gave her a wry look. "I'm an excellent spy when it comes to things that are important."

"What could be more important than love?"

He paused, momentarily lost in her wide-eyed, innocent gaze. Damn, how could she be so beautiful?

Her cheeks turned pink as she looked away. "Oh, Olana's coming back." She leaned toward him and whispered, "Act normal."

He snorted. Normal as the heart attack she'd nearly given him.

Without a word, Olana settled on the blanket, picked up her plate, and resumed her lunch.

Eviana cleared her throat. "Were you able to talk?"

Olana scoffed. "Yes, we talked. About the weather. And the mission. He said it should take three or four days to reach Arondale."

"I've always wanted to see that place." Eviana nibbled on some cheese. "I've heard it's lovely, and the hot springs are supposed to be very good for one's health."

Olana nodded. "People from all over Aerthlan make pilgrimages there to pray in the chapel and bathe in the waters."

"A pilgrimage," Eviana repeated softly. "That's it."

"That's what?" Quentin asked.

"The reason why we're traveling to Arondale," she replied. "I've been coming up with a scenario to explain what we're doing in case anyone asks."

He shrugged. "I thought we'd already figured that out. You're a traveling wine merchant."

"Yes, but why would a wine merchant seek out the priest in each village?" She slanted a mischievous look at him. "I've come up with a marvelous idea."

He narrowed his eyes. What was she going to propose now?

"Is there any cider left?" Elam asked as he approached, carrying his now empty plate.

"Sure." Quentin filled the last cup and handed it to Elam as the colonel sat next to him. He couldn't help but notice that Elam was trying very hard not to look at Olana.

Elam took a sip, then put more food on his plate. "Didn't you say Arondale is where Victor was murdered?"

Quentin nodded as he finished his apple. "Aye. And the guard who caused Uma's death was also killed there."

"Then that priest is a likely suspect," Elam concluded.

"I believe so." Quentin thought back to the scene he'd witnessed. "I saw the priest, though, and he wasn't behaving in a suspicious manner."

"Perhaps he is simply a good actor," Olana said. Her gaze met Elam's, then they both looked away.

Quentin noted the blush on their faces. Eviana was right, there was definitely romance in the air. He'd been so immersed in the struggle to hide his own feelings that he hadn't noticed what was happening right in front of him.

An awkward silence fell over the group; then Eviana broke it with a question. "I suppose you knew Victor and Uma from the Isle of Secrets?"

"Aye," Elam answered. "But not very well. They were only four years old, so they were living in the castle nursery."

Olana finished her cider, then stared at the empty cup in her hands. "I was twelve years old when the final battle took place. Naomi and I were put in charge of the little ones, and we took them to the far side of the island for a picnic. Much like this one." Her eyes glistened with tears. "Uma and Victor had so much fun playing in the sand and the water."

"We'll find the murderers and make them pay," Elam said softly, giving Olana a fervent look. "I promise you."

She gazed back at him, blinking away her tears.

Eviana ate the last of the cheese on her plate. "I have to admit, I've always been fascinated by the story of your lives on the Isle of Secrets."

Elam snorted. "The final battle was exciting, but life before that was . . ."

"Awful," Quentin finished for him.

"I was going to say boring," Olana added. "But awful is true enough. Every day was exactly the same. I was either taking my turn at the spinning wheel or working in the fields."

Eviana winced, then turned to the men. "Did you work in the fields, too?"

"I did for a few years," Quentin admitted. "And I also helped Bettina gather seaweed." He smiled. "She didn't really need my help, but she knew how much I loved going to the beach."

"But then you turned eight, and the Sea Witch assigned you to the blacksmith's shop where Elam was working." Olana gave the two men a sympathetic look. "It was the hardest job on the island."

Elam nodded. "It was rough." He gave Quentin a wry look. "At least it was for me. Quen had a habit of disappearing."

Quentin felt warmth rising to his face. *Dammit.* Now Eviana would think he'd been a lazy good-for-nothing just as the soldiers had always claimed. "It's not because I was lazy. It was bloody hot in the shop. And stifling. Sometimes I felt like I couldn't breathe. So I would run to the nearest beach to sit in the cool water. And I would look out at the sea and wish I could escape."

Olana nodded sadly. "We all wanted to escape."

"I thought maybe the Sea Witch had lied to us, and we weren't on an island, after all, and I could escape by land," Quentin continued. He knew he should shut the hell up, but the feelings had been held back for so long that they were now bursting out in a flood. "Whenever I could, I would sneak out of the village to explore the countryside and every inch of coastline. But there was no way off the island. Then I started watching the soldiers and memorizing their movements. I thought perhaps I could sneak past them and hide onboard the Sea Witch's ship. I had no idea where it would go, or how I would survive. All I knew was . . . I was desperate. But then, Nevis and Elinor arrived, and for the first time I had real hope."

"How old were you?" Eviana asked, her eyes wide as she listened to his story.

Damn. Why had he spilled his guts like this? "I . . . I was nine when we had the final battle. I'm afraid I was a bit of a troublemaker."

"No," Eviana whispered, and her eyes filled with tears as she looked at him. "You felt trapped."

His breath caught as her words and gaze seemed to cut right through him to envelop his heart. And then he recalled her earlier confession: *I feel trapped by my own life.* Once again, he seemed to have something in common with her. Once again, he felt his soul reaching out to hers. And once again, he knew it was impossible.

She touched his arm. "What they did to an innocent group of children is horrendous."

"Your High . . . Evie, don't let it upset you." Damn, but he hated to see tears in her eyes. "It's all over now."

With a sigh, she looked away. "Is it? We lost Uma and Victor. And a priest poisoned himself for failing to kidnap me."

"Well, then." Olana blinked away the tears in her eyes as she reached for the platter of cheese. "We'd better pack up, so we can continue our mission."

"Aye." Elam jammed the cork back into the jug of cider. "We should be on our way."

Quentin took a deep breath, closing his eyes briefly, as his pulse slowly returned to normal. Why the hell had he felt compelled to share so much of his painful past? Was it because Olana and Elam had lived that past with him, so he felt comfortable with them? Or had he secretly longed to open his heart to Eviana? If that was the case, he'd made a foolish mistake. But there was nothing he could do now to change it.

When he opened his eyes, he noted that Olana and Eviana

had already stuffed all the food, plates, and cups back in the basket. Elam was putting the cider jug into the cart.

"I'll take this." Olana picked up the basket, then started for the cart. "You two can fold up the blanket."

Quentin scrambled to his feet.

Eviana picked up one end of the blanket and shook it out. "Can you grab the other end?"

He nabbed a corner in each hand, then brought his hands up to meet hers. As they pressed the corners together, their fingers touched. His pulse quickened, and he glanced at her to find her looking at him.

She glanced away, her cheeks growing pink. "Don't let go."

Oh, he wished he would never have to let her go. He held onto the corners, his arms stretched wide, while she bent over to grab the edge below. Folding a blanket together was such a domestic task, one that a husband and wife might do. *Don't even think about that. It can never happen.*

He cleared his throat. "You said something earlier about a marvelous idea?"

"Oh, that." She brought the edge up and once again their fingers touched. "I thought it was marvelous, but now . . . I'm not so sure."

"Tell me what it is." He brought his arms together along with the edges of the blanket.

"Well." She stepped back as he finished folding the blanket into a neat square. "I thought we could pretend we were on a pilgrimage to Arondale, and we were selling wine along the way to finance our trip."

He nodded. "That makes sense."

"Yes, but none of us look ill enough to need the special healing of the sacred springs. So I made up a story. I've been married five years, but I'm heartbroken over the fact that I have yet to bear children. I'm hoping the sacred waters will help me. And along the way, I'll seek out every priest to ask for his blessing. It makes perfect sense, don't you think?"

Alarm pricked at his gut. "But in a situation like that, a young wife would probably be traveling with her husband."

"Exactly." She gave him a triumphant look. "I'm so glad we see eye to eye on it."

"What?"

"And so I have another proposition for you."

Good goddesses, no. He stepped back. "You can't be . . ."

"You can play the role of my beloved husband."

The blanket slipped from his hands to fall on the grass. *Oh hell, no.*

She winced. "You needn't look so horrified."

"I can't."

"Well, I can't ask Elam, not when he's in love with Olana."

"I can't do it."

"It's for the sake of the mission."

"No! We can come up with a different story." He picked up the blanket as he racked his brain for a new idea. "We . . . we could say your husband recently passed away, and you're making the pilgrimage to pray for his soul because he was so . . . bad."

She snorted. "You want to make me a widow? And give me an evil husband?"

"At least he's dead."

She shook her head. "My idea is much better."

"It's not happening."

She gave him a frustrated look. "Is it that hard to pretend to love me for a few days?"

He winced. It wouldn't be hard at all. It would be so easy, he could completely lose control. He handed her the blanket. "They're waiting for us. I need to shift." He ran to the woods as if his life depended on it.

That blasted man. Eviana glowered at the eagle flying overhead. They'd been on the road now for two hours, and she was still angry. Or to be honest with herself, she was hurt. And embarrassed. She had suitors all over Aerthlan who were eager to marry her, and Quentin couldn't even pretend to be her husband.

She had assumed he would agree out of a sense of duty, but no. Even his loyalty to the king wasn't great enough to make him suffer through the pretense of being her husband. Did he dislike her that much? Just the thought made her heart ache.

But it had to be true. Because if he actually liked her, he wouldn't have hurt her feelings like this. He wouldn't have given her such a horrified look when she'd made her proposal.

Oh, that blasted man!

What was really embarrassing was that she'd let herself imagine that the intense looks he gave her actually meant something. That he actually liked her. Maybe even felt desire for her.

She groaned inwardly. How foolish of her! Dear goddesses, could this day get any worse?

Next to her, Olana heaved a sigh as she glared at Elam. "Men," she muttered.

"Exactly," Eviana agreed. She took a deep breath and relaxed her hands. In her frustration, she'd been clenching the reins for too long.

Suddenly, Quentin made an abrupt turn and headed straight for her. She sat up, her heart quickening.

"Dear goddesses," Olana whispered. "Is there something wrong?"

Eviana pulled on the reins to stop the cart just as Elam halted his horse. With a swoosh, Quentin landed on Daisy's back, his golden eyes focused on a batch of evergreen trees lining the road.

A half dozen men dropped down from the branches and

aimed their bows and arrows at Eviana and her friends. They were all dressed in green and wore green kerchiefs to cover the bottom half of their faces.

A huge man drew his sword as he strode to the center of the road. "Give us the goods from your cart, or you'll die."

Yes, Eviana thought, the day could get worse. She clapped her hands three times.

Chapter 13

Quentin turned his head to watch the show. One after another, the highwaymen dropped their weapons and collapsed on the road. Good. Elam plummeted off his horse and landed with a thud. *Ouch.* Not so good. Olana slumped over and tilted slowly to the side, her head falling into Eviana's lap.

"I'm hurt and embarrassed," Eviana confessed, then winced and looked away, her face blushing.

Her confession had changed, Quentin thought with a gulp. And it was his fault.

"What do we do now?" she asked, her head still turned away from him.

He flew to the back of the cart and shifted. "Don't look back." He grabbed his breeches from the cart and pulled them on. "I think we should go to the nearest place of safety."

She remained still, not looking back. "You mean the next village?"

"No." He winced as he quickly buttoned the breeches. Dammit, he hated this option, but it was the best course of action. "Northam Dales is the closest place."

"Baron Northam's estate?"

"Aye." Quentin gritted his teeth. The milkmaid-impersonating baron who was one of Eviana's suitors. But the man was loyal to the crown and definitely knew how to keep a secret.

Quentin quickly shoved the wine crates and trunks to each side of the cart to leave a bed of straw in the middle. He'd have to stash Elam and Olana . . . oh shit, he was going to have to touch Olana, and Eviana was right there.

He cleared his throat. "We won't be stopping until we reach Northam Dales, so if you need to relieve yourself . . ."

"Oh, I do need to do that." Carefully, she lowered Olana's head onto the bench, then scrambled off the cart.

Quentin strode toward Elam. "I'll have everything ready to go by the time you get back."

"All right." Eviana dashed toward the woods, hesitating a moment to look at the fallen highwaymen before disappearing into the trees.

He would have to work fast, Quentin thought. He hefted Elam over a shoulder and nabbed the reins of his horse, then led the animal to the back of the cart. After tying off the reins, he settled Elam onto the bed of straw. Then he hurried back to Olana. As he pulled her into his arms, the unwanted confession surged upward, demanding to be released.

"My heart is forever lost to—" A feminine gasp made his heart lurch up his throat. "*Eviana!* You're back."

She was standing by the trees with a shocked look on her face.

Crap! She must have heard him. Had he managed to disguise his confession in time? His heart pounded and his hands shook as he quickly set Olana in the back of the cart. It was a narrow space, so she was lying right next to Elam.

He glanced quickly at Eviana. She still looked stunned. Had she heard him? Did she know how he felt?

She motioned behind her. "I think you should see this."

She headed back into the woods.

What the hell? He followed her, and just beyond the line of trees, they entered the thieves' campsite. A few weapons and green blankets were strewn around a firepit that had gone cold hours ago. "Aye, I knew about this. I spotted it from the sky before I saw them hiding in the trees."

"I don't think you saw this." She stopped by a small crate filled to the brim with a stack of papers. A rock on top kept them from being blown away. With a trembling hand, she moved the rock to the side, removed the top page, and handed it to him.

He stiffened at the sight of the words in bold, black ink.

RISE UP AGAINST TYRANNY!
THE KINGS AND QUEENS OF AERTHLAN
ARE USING THEIR EVIL EMBRACED GIFTS
TO RULE OVER US, STEAL OUR LAND
AND RESOURCES, AND KEEP US POOR
AND POWERLESS. HOW MUCH LONGER
MUST WE TOIL UNDER THEIR EVIL
OPPRESSION? IT IS TIME TO RISE UP AND
RID THE WORLD OF THE EVIL
EMBRACED WHO PERSECUTE US.
JOIN THE REBELLION NOW!

"They want to kill my parents," Eviana whispered in a shaky voice. "They want to be rid of all of us who are Embraced."

He touched her shoulder. "It will be all right. We won't let this happen."

"Why do they hate us? We can't help what time we were born." Her eyes filled with tears. "My parents aren't oppressors! They love this country and its people. Papa is constantly trying to come up with ways to help people have better lives. They worry so much . . ." A tear rolled down her cheek.

"I know, I know." Damn, he hated to see her cry. "Eviana, it's not personal. Your parents happen to be in power, and there will always be others who resent that. Mainly because they want power for themselves."

She wiped her cheek. "You're right. I shouldn't let that . . ." She took a deep breath. "I need to be stronger than this."

"You *are* strong." He squeezed her shoulder, and when she looked at him, he had to fight the urge to take her into his arms. He released her and leaned over to examine the rest of the papers. "They all appear to be written by the same hand."

She shuffled through the stack. "You're right. And they all say exactly the same thing. Do you think one of the highwaymen wrote these?"

He glanced around their campsite. "It wasn't done here. I suspect someone else did the writing, and the highwaymen are simply being paid to spread the papers about."

"Like the ruffians who were paid to kidnap me?" Eviana grabbed one of the handbills and looked it over. "Oh, no." She pointed at a bottom corner on the backside. There was a small sun with eight rays.

Quentin swallowed hard. The same group that had tried to kidnap Eviana was behind the handbills.

"Maybe a priest wrote them." Eviana returned the paper to the crate. "My father has opened schools all over the country, but still, there are many who don't know how to read or write."

Quentin nodded. "We should take the ringleader with us and let Olana question him when he wakes up. I'll take these, too." He lifted the crate and headed back to the cart.

"I'll be there soon." Eviana slipped deeper into the woods.

By the time she returned to the cart, Quentin had finished tying up all the unconscious highwaymen. He'd used their kerchiefs to fasten their hands behind their backs, and their belts to secure their ankles. He'd broken their arrows and had thrown their knives far into the woods.

While tying them up, he'd checked their forearms for the sun tattoo, but none of them had one. It confirmed his theory that these men were being used as delivery boys. If they were illiterate, they might not even know what the handbills said. The crate of papers was stashed in the cart, along with Elam and Olana, and the ringleader was slung over Elam's horse and tied down.

"Ready to go?" he asked as she quietly approached. Her eyes seemed a bit red and swollen. Dammit, had she been crying? He'd been so busy, he hadn't realized that she'd taken a while to return. "Are you all right?"

"I'm fine." She barely glanced at him before climbing onto the driver's bench. "Am I driving?"

"I can do it. I know the way to Northam Dales."

She glanced at him again. "Before we arrive, you might want to finish getting dressed."

He winced, just now realizing that he was half naked. "You're right. Just a minute." He threw on a shirt, then leaned against the cart to pull on his boots.

"So you tied up the rest of the thieves," she said, looking at them spread out alongside the road.

"Aye. I'll ask Baron Northam to pick them up."

She slanted another quick glance at him as he climbed onto the bench and sat beside her. "We'll have to convince the baron to keep our identities and mission a secret. But I'm sure he'll be eager to please my father."

And eager to impress the princess, Quentin thought as he flicked the reins to get Daisy moving. "He'll do whatever we ask. Or I'll be telling everyone his secret."

"He has a secret?" She turned toward him. "What is it?"

"If I tell you, it won't be a secret."

With a huff, she looked away. "As far as I can tell, everyone has a secret."

He swallowed hard. Had she heard his confession or not? It wasn't something he could simply ask. *Damn.* He glanced at her, but her head was turned away from him, her lips pressed shut.

Was she upset? You dunce, of course she's upset. They'd discovered an underground rebellion. The group of priests who had tried to kidnap her also wanted to kill her parents. Her brothers. All the kings and queens. Hell, he was Embraced, so they'd want him dead, too.

"It will be all right. Whoever these evil people are, we'll stop them." He reached over to touch her hand.

She moved her hand away and slid to the edge of the bench.

What the hell? His heart squeezed in his chest. She must have heard his confession after all.

And she was rejecting him.

How could a day keep getting worse? Eviana dug her fingers into her woolen gown. *Don't cry anymore. You have to be strong.*

Her tears had escaped in the woods, and once they had started, she'd had a hard time stopping them. She had so looked forward to today and her daring adventure, but nothing was happening the way she had imagined it would.

Her rump and back were aching from hours of sitting on hard wooden benches. Her feelings had been hurt when Quentin had refused to play the role of her husband. Then, the sudden attack of the highwaymen had forced her to use her gift. If that wasn't terrifying enough, now she was reeling from the news that her entire family was marked for death.

And whom could she talk to? Olana and Elam were upset with each other and staying silent. Good grief, they were unconscious now.

She certainly couldn't talk to Quentin. She had been so excited about traveling with him and getting to know him better. Her plan had seemed to be working, too. At the picnic, he'd talked about his childhood, and her heart had ached to hear how much he had suffered. He even knew the pain of feeling trapped, just as she did. She'd truly thought they were getting closer. She'd thought he would accept playing the role of her husband. But no. He'd rejected her.

And now she knew why.

He was in love with someone else.

My heart is forever lost to . . . Oh, dear goddesses, his words kept repeating in her mind, torturing her.

When she'd discovered the stack of treasonous papers at the campsite, she'd stumbled back to the road in shock, and there, she had heard his confession. Two shocks in a row that had left her reeling.

It had been too much to deal with, and her brain had shoved the second shock to the far reaches of her mind to allow her to come to grips with the first one. But once Quentin had taken the papers back to the cart, leaving her alone in the woods, his confession had hurtled back, mentally slapping her.

My heart is forever lost to . . .

She'd stumbled deeper into the forest as the words skittered through her. And then, the pain had begun. The tears had started. He was in love with someone else. She hadn't realized how strongly she was attracted to him until he'd been whisked away and she'd lost her chance at ever being with him.

And now, she was being tortured, forced to ride next to him when there was no way she could ever have him. *But I wanted him!* Oh, how pathetic she sounded. She should have realized earlier that he was attracted to someone else. It explained why he'd refused her initial offer of friendship. He was being loyal to his true love, whoever she was.

Who was she? Was she from Draven Castle?

Eviana sighed. She had no idea. Quentin had managed to cut his confession short when she'd emerged from the woods, so she hadn't heard the woman's name.

Actually, now that she thought about it, she realized this relationship of his shouldn't have come as a surprise. The man was gorgeous. Strong, intelligent, trustworthy, honorable. Not to mention his habit of forgetting to wear a shirt. *Argh.* The man had muscles on top of muscles and bronze skin that looked so warm and inviting. He probably had women pursuing him all over Aerthlan.

She was too late. She could never have him, and it hurt. It hurt so much she suspected she must have been falling in love with him.

She'd lost him, and she was in danger of losing her entire family. Even her adopted aunts and uncles, who were ruling the other countries of Aerthlan. They, too, were in danger from these unknown villains.

She glanced at Quentin, then at Olana and Elam in the back of the cart. Could the four of them discover the villains and defeat them?

She was beside herself with worry, Quentin could tell, but he didn't know what he could say or do to give her comfort or reassurance. Not when she would just reject him.

Why did it hurt so much? He'd always known he wasn't good enough for her. He'd always known there was no hope for him. He'd always known she would marry a nobleman. Her rejection came as no surprise, but it still hurt like hell.

Stop feeling sorry for yourself. There was too much at stake. The villains wanted all the Embraced dead, and all four of them on this cart were Embraced. He needed to stay alert and prepared for whatever might happen next.

A four-foot-high rock wall started on the left-hand side of the road, marking the beginning of Baron Northam's land. Some vines had intertwined along the rocks, the green leaves starting to turn red and gold. After a few miles, there was a break in the wall, the gate left open to make visitors feel welcome. Northam Dales was the largest dairy farm in Eberon, and people came from miles around to buy the cheese produced there.

Quentin turned the cart onto the road. It was a grand entrance, lined on each side with huge oak trees that formed a tunnel. The sun shone through, dappling the road with sunlight. Beside him, Eviana let out a sigh, and he hoped the beauty of nature was giving her some comfort, although the thought of her enjoying the baron's estate was aggravating to say the least.

The last thing she needed was more land. The Duchy of Vindalyn was huge, comprising nearly a fourth of Eberon. When she became its duchess, she would own more land than anyone in the country, including her twin brother, who would someday be king. It was the reason why old King Frederic had forced Luciana to marry his nephew Leo, whose lightning power killed anyone he touched. Frederic had figured Luciana would die, and then all he had to do was kill Leo and he could have the duchy for himself.

Even today, Vindalyn was the most sought-after prize in Eberon. Eviana was right to assume all her suitors were more interested in the duchy than in her. It was no wonder that her father had been upset over the number of less-than-worthy nobles. He had to make sure her future husband was trustworthy and loyal to the crown.

The road curved as it ascended a big hill, and they left the huge oak trees behind. When they reached the summit, a spectacular view spread out before them: acres of rolling hills, green fields dotted with black-and-white dairy cows, sparkling ponds, and an elegant manor house made of butter-colored limestone, partially hidden with green ivy.

"Oh, my," Eviana whispered.

Quentin suppressed a groan. Of course she was impressed. Northam Dales was famous for being one of the most picturesque estates in the country. "We should be safe here for the night. Northam has good security."

Eviana nodded. "When I danced with him at my father's birthday party, he told me his warehouse of aging cheese is worth a fortune."

Quentin rolled his eyes. No doubt the baron had kept quiet about dressing up as a milkmaid. "Let me talk to him first so he won't reveal your identity. If the servants find out who you are, the news could spread, and our entire mission would be jeopardized."

"I understand." As they neared the manor house, she pulled the hood of her cape over her head to partially conceal her face.

The cart rolled to a stop about twenty feet from the doorstep. Quentin jumped down and hurried over to knock on the door.

After they waited a few minutes, the door opened to reveal an elderly butler.

"How do you . . ." Quentin blinked. The man's livery boasted black-and-white spots like a cow.

The butler gave him a dismissive look. "If you're here to buy cheese, the shop is behind the house."

"No, I . . . wait!" Quentin raised his voice as the butler started to close the door. "I need to see Baron Northam."

The butler glanced at him and their cart, then sniffed. "I doubt he wants to see you."

"Tell him Quentin is here with a milkmaid. He'll come."

The butler snorted. "We have plenty of milkmaids here already." He shut the door in Quentin's face.

"That wasn't very friendly," Eviana muttered from the cart. "Are you sure the baron will see us?"

"Aye, he will." Quentin descended the steps and stopped in the middle of the gravel driveway. As far as he could tell, Northam seemed to thrive on drama. So he would give the baron a big dose of it. "Any second now . . ."

The door was flung open and Baron Northam charged down the stairs. He skidded to a stop in the gravel and lifted his chin in defiance. "What are you doing here, Messenger Boy?"

Quentin glanced at the open door, where the elderly butler and several young footmen had gathered to see what had caused their master to move so quickly. All of the servants were dressed in black-and-white-spotted livery. "I need a word with you, Northam." He gestured for the baron to follow him farther away from the door.

"What is it?" Northam whispered as he rushed to keep up. "Have you come to threaten me?"

"No." Quentin halted suddenly and turned his head to give the young nobleman a fervent look. "I've come to beg your assistance on a royal matter of great importance. Can you be trusted, my lord?"

Northam's eyes widened. "What is happening?"

Quentin lowered his voice dramatically. "Something deadly serious. Once again, I ask if you can be trusted?"

"Of course! My family has been loyal to the crown for generations." A horrified look came over the baron's pudgy face. "Is the king doubting me?"

"Not at this time. And I know very well how good you are at keeping a secret."

The baron hissed in a breath. "You needn't threaten me. I will gladly do anything I can for the king."

"Very well." Quentin gestured toward the cart. "My companions and I are on a secret mission."

Northam glanced at the cart. "Who is that? Is that Her—"

"Don't say it!" Quentin interrupted. "No one must know she is here."

Northam stiffened with alarm. "Is she in danger?"

"She could be if her identity is revealed. For now, she is playing the role of Mistress Evie, a wine merchant from Vindalyn." Quentin gave the baron a wry look. "I'm sure you understand the thrill of donning a costume?"

The baron winced, then slapped a pudgy hand to his chest.

"I swear to you on all that is holy that I will take this secret to the grave. I would do anything for the princ—"

"Shh."

"I mean her," Northam corrected himself. "What can I do to help?"

"Not far from here, we were attacked by a group of high-waymen."

"Oh, those bastards!" Northam cried. "They are the scourge of our county. I've had to double the number of my guards to make sure they don't steal one of my precious cows."

"They won't bother you anymore. That is the ringleader there." Quentin pointed at Elam's horse. "And the rest of the gang is tied up and unconscious beside the road."

"How . . . how did you do that? We've been trying to capture them for months."

Quentin shrugged. "It's a long story. Could you lock up the ringleader somewhere secure and collect the rest of the gang?"

"Of course! Just a moment." The baron ran back to the front door as fast as his pudgy legs could take him. He talked to his servants, wildly gesturing toward Elam's horse. One of his footmen dashed across the front lawn to a large stone building next to a stable. Soon a dozen guards emerged.

Northam hurried back to Quentin. "The guardhouse has several holding cells. They'll keep the highwaymen there. What else do you need?"

"There are two unconscious people in the back of the cart: Colonel Elam and Lady Olana."

Northam gasped. "The Confessor?"

"Aye. As soon as she wakes up, she'll need to question the prisoners." Quentin glanced at the cart. One of the guards had taken the reins of Elam's horse and was leading it back to the guardhouse. Meanwhile, a troop of guards on horse-back led some extra horses as they charged down the road to collect the rest of the highwaymen. After they passed by,

Quentin continued. "It may take a few hours for Elam and Olana to wake up. They'll need a place to rest. In fact, it would be for the best if we all spent the night here."

"Of course!" Northam's eyes lit up. "I would be delighted for Her High—for you all to stay here. I'll have my best guest-rooms made ready." He turned to run back to the butler, but Quentin grabbed him by the arm.

"No, you won't. We're traveling merchants. You'll put us by the servants."

"Oh, right." Northam dashed over to the butler to give him some orders, then returned.

"Come with me." Quentin led him toward the cart.

As they drew closer to Eviana, the baron stopped and started to bow. Quentin grabbed the back of his shirt to pull him straight. "My lord, may I introduce Mistress Evie, a wine merchant."

"Oh, right." Northam nodded, then gave Eviana an awkward wave. "Hey, there."

Eviana bowed her head. "Good day, my lord. Your estate is quite lovely."

"Why, yes, it is!" Northam beamed. "I must say I'm delighted that you're here. It would be my greatest pleasure to take you on a tour of the farm and cheese factory. I don't mean to boast, but my dairy cows are the happiest cows in the world! And you haven't lived until you've tasted my special aged Northam Cheddar!"

"Enough, Northam," Quentin growled under his breath. "Would a baron act that way with a merchant?"

"I don't care," Northam hissed. "This is my chance to impress her!"

Quentin leaned close. "If you can't manage to keep our secret, then what will happen to yours?"

Northam winced. "You bastard. All right." He turned back to Eviana and raised his voice, speaking in a nonchalant manner. "Mistress Evie, if you have the time, would you mind going for a little tour?"

From behind the baron, Quentin shook his head at Eviana, silently signaling her to refuse.

She gave him a wry look, then smiled at the baron. "I would love to, my lord."

"Yes!" Northam grinned; then when Quentin cleared his throat, the baron added, "It's damned inconvenient, but I suppose I can spare an hour or so from my busy schedule."

Quentin groaned inwardly. He wished they could just leave, but he had to wait for Olana to wake up so she could question the ringleader. And by then, it would be past sunset.

He strode to the back of the cart. The crate of treasonous papers was there, covered with the blanket they had used earlier for the picnic. "Northam, I need this cart carefully guarded. The wine here is quite expensive."

"Yes, of course." Northam waved for his footmen to approach. He reached the back of the cart and recoiled at the sight of Elam and Olana. "Wha-what is wrong with them? Are they dead?"

The two footmen exchanged a worried look and slowed their steps.

"They're not dead," Quentin assured them. "They're just sleeping."

"Are they sick?" Northam grimaced. "It won't affect my precious cows, will it?"

Quentin snorted. "Are you more worried about your cows than your servants?"

Northam huffed. "My cows are the best in the world. Servants can be replaced."

"Even milkmaids?"

Northam shot him an annoyed look.

"Please don't be alarmed by my companions," Eviana told the baron and his footmen. "They were knocked unconscious by those horrid highwaymen. I'm sure they'll wake up soon."

Northam nodded, then turned to his footmen. "Have the bedchambers been made ready?"

"Aye, my lord," the taller one answered.

"Good." Quentin pulled Elam out of the cart, carefully avoiding Olana.

Northam scoffed. "What are you doing? I have servants for that."

"I'm stronger than they are," Quentin replied as he hefted Elam over his shoulder.

Northam glanced at Eviana, then declared, "I'm strong, too!" He reached for Olana, then jumped back with a gasp. "Oh, you!" He pointed at the taller footman. "You carry her."

"Aye, my lord." The footman pulled Olana into his arms, then stiffened. "The master treats his cows better than he does us." He gasped, nearly dropping Olana. "Oh, my lord! I didn't mean that. I don't know—"

"Hush!" Northam gave Eviana a wary look, then laughed nervously. "Just a jest we have around here. You, uh, Morton—"

"Matthew," the shorter footman murmured.

"Yes, Matthew, stand here and guard the cart," Northam ordered. "I'll take the rest of you to your rooms."

Eviana climbed off the cart. "Thank you, my lord, for allowing us to stay overnight. I simply couldn't travel anymore after that horrible attack by the highwaymen. We were lucky to have escaped with our lives."

"Not to worry, Mistress," Northam told her as he escorted her to the front door. "You'll be safe here."

Quentin followed them, and not far behind him was the footman carrying Olana.

"My family has been here for ten generations," Northam announced as he led them into the Great Hall. "Lovely, isn't it? Construction on this part of the manor house was begun over three hundred years ago. You'll note the fine wood paneling on the walls." He stomped a booted foot. "And we still have the original floor!"

"How marvelous," Eviana murmured.

Quentin groaned inwardly. Just what he needed: a reminder that he had nothing to offer Eviana. As they climbed several flights of stairs, the baron continued to boast about his home, his ancestry, his land, and his business. Finally, they reached the top floor, and the baron showed them two small rooms.

He winced. "I hope these humble accommodations will do."

"They're good." Quentin strode into the second room and noted there were two narrow beds and a small desk with one chair. He dropped Elam on one of the beds. As he left, he heard the baron talking to Eviana in the hallway.

"I'll let you rest for a little while," Northam told her. "Then I'll come take you for the tour."

"Yes. Thank you, my lord." Eviana turned to go into her room, barely glancing at Quentin as he passed by.

Dammit. She was going to let that chubby weasel court her. Quentin dashed down the stairs and out the door to the cart. The footman was there, standing guard.

"Matthew, could you take this trunk to the women?" He pointed out the trunk containing female clothing.

"Aye, sir." Matthew picked it up and started toward the house.

"I'll go with you." Quentin grabbed the crate of handbills and followed the footman up the stairs.

In his small room, he set the crate on the desk. Somehow, he needed to let the king know about these treasonous handbills. But it was a long flight back to Ebton Palace. Benwick was a little closer. Queen Luciana and her caravan even closer.

Yes, he would take one of these papers to Luciana, and she would make sure her husband saw it. Then Quentin wouldn't have to leave Eviana alone for too long.

He certainly couldn't let her be courted by someone like Baron Northam. The man might have a great deal to offer, but he was all wrong for her.

Chapter 14

That afternoon, the Raven located the queen's caravan.
After leaving Ebton Palace that morning, he'd flown
southeast until the main road to Vindalyn had come into
view. From there, it had been a straight shot south until he'd
spotted the two dragons circling about.

It was his first time to see dragons, since they normally
stayed in their home country of Norveshka. He circled wide
so he could admire them. The afternoon sun gleamed off
their scales in shimmering hues of green and purple. Their
wings were wide and powerful, their necks long and graceful.
Clearly, with all the circling they were doing, they were accustomed to traveling at a much quicker speed. As Bran studied them, he noted that one was slightly smaller than the
other and its purple color was tinted with more pink.

Down below, the long caravan of mounted soldiers and
supply wagons moved slowly down the road. In the middle
of the train, he spotted a covered wagon. No doubt, that was
where the queen and princess were hiding.

As the caravan passed through a small village, the people
stopped their labor to wave. But the soldiers were soon forgotten when the villagers spotted the dragons overhead. They
grew still, their mouths gaping in awe, their gazes fixed on
the magnificent creatures. No doubt, like him, it was their
first time seeing dragons.

He flew into the village, keeping low under the canopy of

trees to remain undetected. Then he landed on a windowsill of dark timber where he could blend in and remain unnoticed. Not only did he need rest after hours of flight, but this spot gave him a great view of the caravan as it passed by.

Four troops of soldiers, well armed, but bored and weary. Only two supply wagons. No doubt they planned on buying more foodstuffs as they traveled. As the covered wagon lumbered past him, he focused on the windows. Luckily, the shutters were open to allow air to flow through, so he caught a glimpse of two women inside with black hair. One had her hair piled on top of her head, and the other . . . Her long black hair fell loose down her back. The queen and the princess.

He waited until the caravan had moved down the road, then launched himself into the air and flew quickly southwest toward the monastery.

At the slow pace the caravan was moving, he figured it would take two more days for it to reach the ferry at the Ron River. At that point, the queen's party would be only about ten miles east of the monastery. If the Brotherhood of the Sun waited until half of the troops had crossed the river, it would be easier for them to attack a caravan that was divided.

But with the dragons airborne, ready to breathe fire on any attackers, such a venture would be suicidal. And the princess could always put all the humans to sleep. Vera was right: kidnapping the princess was impossible. And any poor priest who was given the mission would end up dining on poison.

With a heavy heart, Eviana gazed out the window of her small room. It was still afternoon, but she was ready for this day to be over. Too much had happened, and she was still struggling to cope with it.

There was nothing she could do about her aching heart, so

instead she needed to focus her attention on their mission. And that meant she would have to work with Quentin, no matter how difficult that might be.

She glanced over at Olana, sound asleep on one of the narrow beds. It could be sunset before she woke up.

A knock at the door caught Eviana by surprise. Had Northam returned already for the tour?

As she walked to the door, she grabbed her cape off her bed and steeled her nerves to put up with the unwanted suitor. She opened the door and gasped. The cape tumbled from her hands to the floor.

Quentin was there, and the blasted man was shirtless once again. Was he purposely trying to torment her?

He glanced around the hallway, then whispered, "I know you don't want to see me, but . . ." He lifted two of the handbills. "We have to deal with this."

"Aye, we do." She picked up her cape and motioned for him to enter. After a quick glance outside to make sure no one had seen a half-naked man sneaking into her bedchamber, she closed the door. "I do wish you would dress properly—"

"I'm going to shift and take these papers to your mother. She's the closest of your family to us, and it should be fairly easy to find her caravan with the dragons overhead."

"That makes sense." Eviana nodded as she dropped her cape on the bed. It was a good plan. "And then my mother can have a soldier deliver the papers to my father in Ebton."

"Exactly. I have two here: one for your father and one for Nevis." Quentin used the desk to fold the papers lengthwise once, then twice, making a long narrow strip. "Once I shift, I need you to roll these tightly around one of my legs and tie it off. Do you have a ribbon you can use?"

"Yes." She dug into the trunk of clothing and located a green ribbon.

"Excellent." He handed her the folded papers, then opened the window wide. "Leave this open, so I'll be able to return."

"All right." Her eyes met his briefly; then she looked away. *He loves someone else.*

"I would have asked Elam to do it, but he's—"

"Asleep. I understand." She studied the papers and ribbon in her hands. "How . . . how long do you think you'll be away?"

"I'm not sure. An hour or two, at the most." He shifted his weight, then dragged a hand through his hair.

Such a simple move, but it made the muscles in his arms bulge. *Goddesses, help me.* She turned to pace across the floor, but the room was so small, she couldn't get more than a few feet away from him.

"I . . . I wish you wouldn't go on the tour," he murmured.

"How could I refuse? Northam is being very generous and cooperative."

"True, but . . ."

She glanced over her shoulder. Quentin seemed genuinely worried. "Is this related to the baron's secret? Does he . . . wet his bed or talk to chipmunks?"

"Not that I know of."

"Does he become violent?"

"No." Quentin shook his head. "I believe he's harmless."

"Then there's nothing to worry about." She sighed. Before Quentin's confession, she would have imagined his concern meant he actually cared for her, but now she knew better. He was simply doing his duty of protecting the princess.

"I will return as quickly as I can." His hands went to the waistband of his breeches. "I should shift now, so I can be on my way."

"Ah . . . yes." She quickly turned away, clutching the papers more tightly in her fists. Good goddesses, he was stripping right behind her! Her heart lurched into a quick rhythm. If only he would approach her slowly, then wrap his arms around her and whisper in her ear that he loved her. *Stop imagining things that can never happen!*

He let out a soft squawk, and she spun around. He was perched on the desk next to the window, his enormous wings folded under. He planted a foot forward to give her easier access.

With her heart still racing, she sat in front of the desk. She'd never been so close to him before in eagle form. He tilted his head, his golden eyes watching her.

Her hands trembled slightly as she smoothed the folded papers on the desk's surface, smushing them as flat as possible. Slowly, she placed one edge against his leg, then wrapped the papers around and around as tightly as she could. His skin was softer than she had expected. And warmer. Holding the paper in place, she looped the ribbon around several times, then pulled the ends tight and tied them off.

He made a soft noise that she assumed was a thank-you or good-bye, then leaped out the window. His wings extended, and soon he was soaring up and away.

She watched until he was a tiny speck in the sky. With a sigh, she turned and noticed his discarded breeches on the floor. She smiled. What did she expect? He couldn't fold them and put them away while in bird form.

Good goddesses, just picking up his breeches made her heart pound. She shook them out, then draped them over the back of the chair by the desk.

She glanced at Olana, still fast asleep. What would happen now if she touched the Confessor? Would she say she had a broken heart? Or would she say she'd fallen in love?

Did she dare find out? She took a step toward Olana, but just then a knock sounded at the door.

"Mistress Evie?" Northam called. "Are you ready for the tour?"

Not really. "Yes, just a moment." She settled her cape around her shoulders and headed for the door.

*　*　*

An hour later, her mouth was sore from smiling and her brain was tired of coming up with new compliments. When the baron had walked her through the rooms on the ground floor, she'd called the drawing room exquisite, the sitting room charming, and the dining room magnificent.

Unfortunately, she'd made the tragic mistake of calling the portrait gallery fascinating. That ill-chosen compliment had inspired Northam to launch into a detailed description of every ancestor for the last three hundred years. As far as she could tell, all of his family had been a bit on the stout side.

The paintings actually were interesting, though, she had to admit. A few of the male ancestors had posed next to black-and-white cows, and quite a few of them held a large wedge of cheese in their pudgy hands. Oddly enough, some of the female ancestors had dressed up as milkmaids.

It had been a great relief when they'd gone outside to tour the estate. The fields were a gorgeous green, the sky a clear blue, and the trees were brilliant with fall color. But alas, Northam had been more interested in showing her the milking barn and cheese factory than the bucolic countryside.

The man loved his cows, there was no doubt about that. He knew them all by name, although he rarely called a servant by the right name. And when it came to cheese, the baron could easily talk for hours.

Will this ever end? She smiled and nodded, hardly listening anymore as her thoughts kept returning to Quentin. Had he managed to locate her mother? Was he on his way back yet? How could time drag by so slowly?

When they emerged from the cheese factory, she noted the sun was lowering toward the horizon. *Thank the goddesses.*

"Ah, they have the picnic ready!" Northam announced with a grin. "I thought we would dine outside, so we can admire the spectacular view."

She spotted a table and two chairs on top of a nearby hill.

Servants were bustling about, setting glassware and china on the white tablecloth. Other servants brought covered dishes from the manor house. It was lovely, but so different from the simple picnic she'd enjoyed earlier with Quentin, Olana, and Elam.

Glancing up at the sky, she wondered once again if Quentin had made it back safely.

"What do you think?" Northam asked as they ascended the hill.

"It's lovely. Your entire estate is lovely. I'm sure you must be very happy here."

"I am." Northam waved his hand at the servants to shoo them away. "But I do get lonesome here. My parents passed away five years ago, and I have no siblings." He pulled out a chair for her to sit. "Of course, I will need an heir."

She gritted her teeth as she sat down. Somehow, she'd fallen into the Courtship from Hell.

Northam sat across from her and showed her a wine bottle. "I'm sure you recognize this."

She forced a smile. "Yes, a Vindalyn wine. That's my grandfather's favorite."

"Mine, too!" He pulled the cork and filled her glass. "I must say, your fabulous wine pairs beautifully with my special aged Northam Cheddar. Doesn't that make us the perfect couple?"

That had to be the most unromantic thing she had ever heard. She took a long drink, hoping the wine would deaden her pain.

Northam appeared oblivious as he continued to brag about this and that. She nodded every now and then as she ate. There was cheese, of course, but also some roast beef, crusty bread, and fruit.

"I believe family traditions are very important, don't you?" the baron asked and when she nodded, he added, "I'm sure you noticed how some of the portraits in the gallery showed the women in my family dressed as milkmaids. My mother and my grandmother were both fond of dressing up like that." He sighed. "I do miss them so much."

Oh, the poor man was lonesome, Eviana thought.

"I so look forward to having a lovely wife and several daughters who can continue that tradition."

Eviana blinked. He would want his wife to dress up as a milkmaid?

A shadow swept over the table, and she glanced up. Quentin! Her heart fluttered as she watched him circle overhead. Thank the goddesses, he was back.

"That damned bird," Northam muttered. "Here, my dear, have some more wine while I tell you about some of my new experimental cheeses."

The process had something to do with old wine vats, but Eviana barely listened as she kept an eye on Quentin. After circling overhead a dozen times, he landed on a nearby boulder.

"Shoo!" Northam scolded, but Quentin merely gazed at him with his golden eyes. "Why doesn't he leave?"

"Don't let it concern you," Eviana said as she popped a grape into her mouth. "It's part of his job to make sure I'm protected."

"But you're safe here." Northam aimed an angry look at the eagle. "We're fine! Go!"

Quentin folded his legs and sat.

"Damned bird," Northam muttered.

"He takes his duty very seriously." Eviana took a sip of wine.

"If you ask me, he's jealous."

She choked. "Excuse me?"

Northam nodded. "Look at the way he's glaring at me. He's acting like a jealous lover."

Her hand trembled as she set her wineglass down. "I—I don't think so."

The baron frowned at her. "Is there something going on between the two of you?"

"No!" She glanced at Quentin. *Jealous?* That couldn't be right. If he was jealous, then that meant he wanted her for himself. And that would be terribly wrong when he was in love with someone else. "I believe you are mistaken, my lord."

"Well, I'm relieved you have no feelings for him." Northam slanted a suspicious look at Quentin. "But he is certainly obsessed with you."

She scoffed. "I don't think so."

"You're perfectly safe here, and he must know that, but he refuses to leave us alone." Northam shook his head. "The man is smitten, to be sure. Luckily, he cannot compete with someone like me." He spread his arms to indicate his large estate. "I have so much, and he has nothing."

Eviana swallowed hard. Quentin had everything she wanted: strength, intelligence, courage, loyalty, honor.

Or she had thought he did. Now she had to wonder. For if he was actually attracted to two women at once, then he wasn't honorable after all.

When the dinner was over and Northam was escorting Eviana back to the manor house, Quentin took off and flew back through the window of her bedchamber. He checked to make sure Olana was still unconscious, then shifted and pulled his breeches back on.

Back in his own room, he finished dressing, then waited in the hallway. And waited. What was taking Eviana so long to return? Was that chubby weasel trying to lure her into his bedchamber to try on costumes and play milk the cow?

Dammit. He started for the stairs but halted when he heard footsteps coming up. She reached the landing just below, and he exhaled with relief. "I was getting worried."

She said nothing but shot him an irritated look as she trudged up the stairs.

Was she angry with him? He'd kept his distance during her dinner with the weasel. He'd stayed so far away, he hadn't been able to hear them. "I told your mother about the highwaymen, and that we would have Olana question them after she wakes up."

"Are Mother and Faith all right?" Eviana asked as she reached the top of the stairs.

"Aye. Your mother is writing a report of everything I told her, and she'll send it to Ebton Palace along with the handbills. By tomorrow, your father and Nevis will know what happened."

"That's good." Eviana opened the door to her bedchamber, then paused. "I asked Northam to have more food prepared. I'm sure Olana and Elam will be hungry when they wake up."

"I'm starving, too." He followed her into her room. "It was damned hard to watch you eat when I was so—"

"Then why?" She spun around to face him. "Why did you watch?"

"I-I was guarding you."

"I wasn't in any danger." She planted her hands on her hips and frowned at him. "You were trying to intimidate the baron, weren't you?"

Quentin scoffed. "If I hadn't, he might have tried something strange."

Her eyes narrowed. "You got rid of my suitors the other night, and now—"

"I did you a favor. They're not good enough for you."

"So you're deciding who's good enough?" She snorted. "Is anyone good enough?"

He came close to saying *no* but stopped himself in time.

"Oh, dear goddesses." A pained look crossed her face. "Northam is right. You're jealous."

"What? No, I . . ." Dammit, he was.

"And that must mean you . . . you have feelings for me." Tears glistened in her eyes. "How could you? How could you care about me when you're in love with someone else?"

He flinched. "What?"

"I'm so appalled. You . . . you're cheating on that poor woman!"

"*What?* What other woman?"

She paced over to the desk, then turned toward him. "I heard your confession earlier. I know . . ." She blinked back tears. "I know you're in love with someone else."

She'd heard him? But she hadn't realized he'd meant her. His heart tightened in his chest. *Crap!* He'd covered up the truth too damned well.

She sniffed. "I thought you were an honorable man, but now I can see I was terribly mistaken."

"What?"

"There is only one conclusion I can make: you're an unfaithful scoundrel!"

"What?"

"Is that all you can say? *What?*"

He gulped. What could he say? He couldn't tell her the truth. Dammit, but the answer was right in front of him. All he had to do was confirm that he was, indeed, in love with someone else. That he was a two-timing bastard. That he could never be worthy of her. Then she would go on with her life and forget he'd ever existed.

But when he looked at her, he couldn't make the words come out. He was unworthy, dammit. He had no family, no home, no land. All he had was his sense of honor. If he confessed to being dishonorable, then he had nothing.

The only other choice was to tell her the truth. *Damn.* He'd never expected to do that. His heart thundered so loud, it echoed in his ears. "There is only one woman I love. And I have loved her for six years."

A tear rolled down Eviana's cheek. "Then why aren't you married? Does she not feel the same way?"

"I've never told her."

Eviana wiped her cheek. "Why not?"

"Her family will never accept me. And they are correct. I am not worthy."

"Hogwash!" Her green eyes flashed with anger. "You're intelligent, brave, strong, and handsome."

"I am not a nobleman."

"You have a noble character!" She huffed. "Who are these people? I have a mind to set them straight."

His heart squeezed. She would fight for him? Damn, but he loved her so much. His beautiful Eviana with her pure and lovely heart. *She deserves the truth,* an inner voice told him. The need to tell her suddenly felt so compelling, he couldn't resist.

He walked over to where Olana lay, still asleep on her bed. "If I touch her, I will have no choice but to tell the truth." He glanced at Eviana. "Do you want to hear it?"

She stared at him, her eyes wide. "Yes."

He reached for Olana until his fingertips touched her shoulder. Closing his eyes, he felt the confession well up inside him, demanding release.

As his eyes opened, he whispered, "My heart is forever lost to . . ." He turned to face her. "Eviana."

Chapter 15

Her mouth fell open. "What?"

He watched her, his golden eyes filled with wariness. "Is that all you can say? *What?*"

She didn't know how to respond. Her mind raced as she pressed a trembling hand against her chest. Goodness, she could hardly breathe. His heart was forever lost to *her*? And what had he said earlier? *There is only one woman I love. And I have loved her for six years.* Then she was that woman?

He bowed his head. "I apologize for burdening you with an unwanted confession."

Unwanted? She gave him an incredulous look.

He winced. "You look shocked. I must have done a good job of hiding my feelings."

Not really. Now that she thought about it, there had been moments in the past when she'd caught him watching her. And in the last few days, there had been times when his intense looks had made her wonder and made her wish. She'd wanted him to care about her. Her shock right now was due to the surprise of her wish coming true.

She hadn't lost him after all. A burst of joy shot through her chest, and her heart lurched into a fast rhythm. He loved her!

He shifted his weight. "I hope this won't make the mission awkward for you. I should have kept my feelings to myself, but I . . ." He paused, frowning. "I couldn't bear to be labeled unfaithful. Not when my heart has been yours for six years."

"Oh, Quentin." Tears came to her eyes. He was such a sweet and honorable man.

"Please don't cry. You needn't worry that I might be a bother in the future. I know very well that I have no right to be attracted to you. And I know you don't return those feelings. Your family would never approve of me. And I have nothing to offer you—"

"Wait a minute." She lifted a hand to stop him from continuing. His dreadful words had dried up her tears in an instant. "You just admitted that you love me, but now you're rejecting me?"

"I could never reject you, Eviana, but it is obvious, given our circumstances, that *you* must reject *me*."

"Why?"

"Because I'm unworthy."

She grimaced. "Shouldn't I be the one to decide if you're worthy?"

He paused, considering that. "You make a valid point, but in the end, you know your family will have the last word. Your father, especially. As it is, I had to promise your brother before we left that I would not . . . harm you in any way."

"What? Did Eric tell you to stay away from me?" When Quentin hesitated to answer, she huffed with anger. "It's none of his business!"

"He's your brother. He has every right to be concerned—"

"But not to interfere!"

"He was worried that you might mistake a sense of gratitude for something more serious."

She snorted. "As if I'm too young to know my own feelings. I'm the same age as he is." She paced across the room, wondering what exactly her feelings were. She was so stunned now, it was hard to think. Definitely, she was attracted to Quentin. And she was grateful to him. She respected him.

Admired him. Enjoyed being with him and talking to him. When she'd thought he was in love with someone else, it had hurt something awful. She'd assumed that had meant she was falling in love.

But was she ready to declare her undying love for him? Once she said it, she couldn't take it back. And she definitely didn't want to hurt him. Or hurt herself. Maybe she needed a little time to think this over. After all, she'd never been in love before. Small steps, that was what she would take.

She turned toward him. "I won't ask you to be my friend anymore."

A pained look crossed his face. "I understand."

Oh, no! Did he think he was being rejected? "What I meant is I won't ask because I believe we already are friends."

He gave her a doubtful look. "We are?"

"Yes. Definitely. We talk to each other. Rely on each other." She hesitated, feeling warmth rush to her cheeks. "Care about each other." Something hot flared in his eyes, stealing her breath.

He looked away. "The situation is worse than I thought. I'll spend most of my time as an eagle, so we can stay apart—"

"I disagree. Friends should never have to avoid each other."

He glanced back at her, his eyes heated and intense. "I do need to keep my distance. My feelings go far beyond friendship."

Her heart fluttered. Good goddesses, just knowing that he desired her sent a thrill ricocheting through her. "Then, given the circumstances, I have a new proposition."

He winced. "What now?"

"I believe we should give ourselves a chance to become better acquainted. So . . . I propose a courtship."

He flinched, stumbling back a step.

She moved closer to him. "What do you say, Quentin? Would you like to court me?"

He stared at her, a stunned look on his face.

"Oh, good grief, say yes," Olana muttered.

Quentin spun around. "Olana! You're awake."

Eviana winced. "For how long?"

"Long enough." Olana sat up. "I pretended to be asleep for a while so you could talk, but I really can't wait anymore. I desperately need to use the chamber pot!"

"Oh, of course." Eviana headed for the door. "We'll step outside."

Quentin followed her, and she shut the door.

He glanced at her, then looked away. "As soon as Olana is ready, I'll take her to the guardroom so she can interrogate the highwaymen."

"I understand." Eviana folded her arms across her chest. "Meanwhile, I'm waiting for your answer."

He sighed. "I cannot court you. You should know that."

Her nerves tensed. Why was this man so stubborn? "Why not?"

"You are . . ." He glanced around to make sure they were alone. "You know what you are, and I'm a servant."

She scoffed. "You think I'm not a servant? I've been trained my whole life to serve my country and the Duchy of Vindalyn."

"There is a huge difference in rank."

"So?" She frowned at him. "I outrank all my suitors. I outrank the baron. Why should I care if I outrank you?"

He gritted his teeth. "You *should* care. People would consider it a disgrace—"

"People will always talk." She waved a dismissive hand. "I've learned that the hard way. I'd rather be with someone who is genuine and honest. Someone who will allow me to be me." *So I won't feel trapped.* "Since you love me, shouldn't we at least try? Court me, Quentin."

Pain and sorrow glinted in his golden eyes. "I cannot."

Blast him for being so stubborn. She lifted her chin. "Very well, then. I shall court you."

He blinked. "You . . . you can't."

"I can. And you can't stop me."

He raised a hand, pointing at her. "You . . . you can't force yourself on a man."

She stepped closer and lowered her voice. "I don't expect to use force." She placed her hand on his chest. "See how gentle—"

He grabbed her by the wrist to stop her. "Don't tempt me, Evie. I won't be gentle."

Her heart pounded as she gazed into his eyes, hot as molten gold. Goddesses help her, she did want to tempt him. When his gaze lowered to her mouth, she moved closer. *Yes, please.*

The door to his bedchamber burst open, and Quentin jumped back, releasing her.

Elam ran into the hallway with an alarmed look on his face. "Where are we?" He raised one of the treasonous handbills that was clenched in his fist. "And what the hell is this?"

"I can explain," Quentin started, but stopped when Olana stepped into the hallway.

"I want to know, too," Olana said, casting a quick glance at Elam.

"We're at Northam Dales," Quentin explained. "It was the closest place of safety to the ambush."

"And the baron has been very cooperative," Eviana added. "He has the highwaymen locked up in the guardhouse."

"And this?" Elam motioned with his head to the handbill.

Before Quentin could answer, heavy footsteps sounded on the nearby stairwell. A small army of servants was carrying up a metal bathtub, a dozen buckets of hot water, and a basket filled with towels and soap.

Elam quickly stuffed the handbill in a pocket.

One of the footmen carrying the tub nodded at Eviana. "The master told us to bring this for you."

"Oh, how kind of him." Eviana smiled as she opened the

door to her bedchamber. And how wrong of him to make such a big fuss over a wine merchant. "I must say, the baron is trying his best to persuade me to lower the price on my wine."

The servants said nothing as they tromped into her room and set the tub and buckets on the floor.

The maid carrying the basket placed it on the desk. As they filed out, she asked, "Do you need any assistance, my lady?"

"No, no, I'm fine," Eviana replied. "Could you have a meal prepared for my servants?"

The maid nodded. "We'll leave some food for them in the kitchen." She followed the other servants down the stairs.

Eviana glanced at the bathtub. A bath would feel heavenly after sitting all day in the wagon. But she also wanted to go to the guardhouse with the others. Unfortunately, by the time she returned, the water would be cold.

"Go ahead," Quentin told her. "Enjoy your bath."

"But I want to hear the interrogation," Eviana whispered as the last of the servants disappeared down the stairs.

"We'll report back to you," Quentin reassured her. "As it is, I need to catch Olana and Elam up on everything, and that would just be boring for you."

"Very well." Eviana gave Olana an encouraging smile. "Good luck."

As her three companions headed down the stairs, Eviana could hear Quentin explaining how they had come to Baron Northam's estate. He loved her, she thought as she slipped back into her room. He loved her.

No doubt he was determined to avoid her for the rest of the mission, but she wouldn't let the stubborn man get away with it. Not when she was planning on courting him.

She poured six buckets of hot water into the tub, then undressed and climbed in. He loved her. With a sigh, she sank into the hot water. The thought of falling in love seemed so thrilling. A bit frightening, but definitely more thrilling.

As she smoothed the rose-scented soap over her body, she wondered what Quentin would think of her. Did he consider her beautiful? He hadn't said. What was it about her that had attracted him? And he'd fallen for her six years ago? She would have been seventeen then, barely even aware of his existence. And over the years, they'd hardly spoken to each other.

But he had always watched her. He loved her.

She smiled as she lathered up her hair. With his glorious confession, the whole day had been transformed. Earlier, she had been in tears, but now she couldn't stop smiling. Earlier, the scene with the highwaymen had seemed horrific, what with the discovery of the treasonous handbills. But now, she could see several reasons why she should be happy that the encounter had happened. One: none of them had been harmed in any way. Two: they had found the handbills before they could be distributed. And three: they could now question the highwaymen and find out more about the villains.

In all, the day that had seemed horrible now seemed like a wonderful success. In one day, they had learned the villains' main objective. Insurrection. It was a frightening prospect, but luckily, they had discovered it early.

So far, her mission had been successful. And her wish to become closer to Quentin was coming true, too.

After rinsing off, she climbed out of the tub and reached for a towel. Now she had two missions: defeat the villains and court Quentin. As for the latter, she wasn't exactly sure how to go about it, but somehow, she would break through his defenses.

Unworthy? What hogwash.

*   *   *

What the hell was she thinking? Courtship? As Quentin strode toward the guardhouse, his mind was a jumbled mess. It had been damned stressful when he'd made his confession. He'd tensed up, not knowing which he should fear the most—that she would reject him or accept him.

Apparently, she accepted him. She believed they were friends. She'd even admitted to caring about him. Good goddesses, he had thought his heart would explode. But the situation was even worse than that. Now she'd decided to court him!

Didn't she know how unworthy he was? How could she even suggest something so foolhardy? Good goddesses, did this mean she was in love with him?

His heart lurched. *Don't get your hopes up, you fool.* She hadn't said anything about love.

He shook his head. She couldn't have feelings like that for him. She barely knew him. It had to be what her brother had feared, that she was mistaking gratitude for love. Or, perhaps, it had to do with her feeling trapped by her life. She might be rebelling against that feeling by pursuing someone who was totally unsuitable.

Damn. It was more imperative than ever for him to stay away from her.

"Quen?"

He jerked to his senses and noted that Elam was standing by the guardhouse, holding the door open. "Yes?"

Elam gave him a wry look. "I called your name three times. Where were you?"

"Oh, sorry." Quentin winced. He needed to focus on the matter at hand.

"Olana has already gone inside." Elam motioned with his hand.

"Let's go." Quentin strode into the guardhouse with Elam close behind.

One of the guards led them down the stairs to the base-
ment that served as the estate's jail. There were three prison
cells. The ringleader was in the first one, and his gang of six
was divided evenly between the next two. Each thief was
shackled at the ankle to a cell bar to make sure they couldn't
escape.

The guard chained the ringleader to the front wall of bars,
so it would be easy for Olana to touch him. Then the guard
left, and the heavy metal door clanged shut.

The prisoners scrambled to their feet, looking over the
newcomers.

"Who are you?" the ringleader asked.

"Can you get us out of here?" another thief asked.

"Aye." The leader nodded. "We'll pay you well. We have a
stash of gold, and I'll give you half of it if you—"

"I guess you don't know who we are," Quentin interrupted. "We're the last people you tried to rob."

The leader winced. "Well, no hard feelings, right?"

"It was all a big misunderstanding!" a second thief
claimed. "We were . . . we were just going to ask directions."

"That's right!" the leader agreed. "There's no proof that
we're thieves. We never robbed you."

"We didn't do anything!" a third thief cried. "We don't
even know how we got here."

"Right," a fourth one said. "We were on the road, asking
directions, then all of a sudden, we woke up in jail."

A fifth thief pointed at Olana. "She put a spell on us. She's
a witch!"

"We're innocent!" A sixth thief rattled the bars of his cell.
"You've got to save us before they hang us."

"That's right! We're innocent!" The leader flinched when
Olana touched his arm. "We've been robbing people on the
road for eight months." With a gasp, he slapped a hand over
his mouth.

"Cap'n!" the second thief cried. "What are you saying?"

"We're not robbers!" the third one declared. "We're heroes. We steal from the rich to give to the poor."

The leader stiffened when Olana touched him again. "But we always keep the money."

"Cap'n!" the thieves cried in unison.

The leader gave Olana a suspicious look as he tried to back away. But with his short leg chain, he could only move a few inches. "I think she's making me talk."

"She's a witch!" the fifth thief yelled again, and all the men repeated, "A witch! A witch!"

"Enough!" Elam growled at them. "She's a lady, and you will treat her with respect!"

Olana glanced up at Elam with a startled look.

"She's doing something strange to me," the leader muttered.

"I am." Olana nodded. "I'm called the Confessor."

The thieves gasped and exchanged frantic looks.

"I've heard about her," one whispered.

"We're all going to die," another one whimpered.

"You should be afraid," Elam warned them. "I've seen greater men than you piss on themselves when she enters the room."

The thieves gasped again, and Olana's eyes softened as she glanced at Elam.

The colonel might win her over, Quentin thought as the thieves all started to whine and complain at once. But even if a romance between Elam and Olana flourished over the next few days, there was no way he could pursue a similar relationship with Eviana.

Stop thinking about her. He refocused his attention on the interrogation.

Elam pulled the handbill from his pocket and showed it to the leader. "What is this?"

With a collective gasp, the prisoners all went silent.

The leader affected an innocent look. "I know nothing. Nothing." He stiffened when Olana touched his arm. "A priest paid us five gold coins to spread the handbills around the nearby villages. Damn!" He glared at Olana. "Bitch!"

Elam slammed a fist into his face.

"Do you know what the handbill says?" Quentin asked.

"Ow." The leader rubbed his jaw. "How would I know? I can't even read."

"They're prayers!" a second thief declared. "Prayers for a good harvest."

"That's right." The leader nodded, then winced when Olana touched him. "They're inciting a rebellion against our evil oppressors."

"Cap'n!" the rest of the thieves cried.

"Dammit," the second thief growled. "Now we'll be executed as traitors."

"We're already going to hang as thieves," the third one muttered.

"Why do you think the king and queen are oppressing you?" Olana asked.

The leader thought a while and scratched his head. "Well, they don't like us robbing people. And . . . and the priest said they were. Shouldn't we believe him?"

Quentin snorted. "Tell me more about the priest. Where does he live? What does he look like?"

The leader shrugged. "I don't remember." Olana touched him, and he winced. "Dammit. He was average height, brown hair, brown eyes, about twenty-five years old."

Quentin stepped closer to the cell. "What is his name?"

"No idea." The leader gritted his teeth when Olana tapped his arm. "Father Greer."

Could he be the Raven? Quentin wondered. "Can he shift into a bird?"

The leader blinked with surprise. "No, I don't think so."

He grimaced. "But he said if we messed up, he would come back and kill us. And then he grabbed an apple in his bare hand, and it froze solid! It was covered with ice!"

Quentin grabbed one of the cell bars. "Are you saying he's Embraced? His gift is freezing things?"

The leader nodded. "Aye. We . . . we were forced!" He looked at his gang. "We were all in fear for our lives."

"Exactly!" the second thief agreed. "We had to take the handbills, or he would have killed us. We're innocent!"

"But you accepted the gold from him," Elam muttered.

"We'll give it to you if get us out of here," the leader offered.

"Is there anything else you can tell us about this priest?" Quentin asked.

"Nothing. I know nothing." The leader sighed when Olana tapped his arm. "He's a member of the Brotherhood of the Sun."

Quentin exchanged a look with Elam and Olana. Now they knew the name of the villains. "Where can we find the Brotherhood of the Sun?"

The leader scoffed. "They're everywhere. And nowhere. No one knows where they're hiding. We only know that if you mess up, you're dead." With a sigh, his shoulders drooped. "Like we are."

Chapter 16

That evening, the Raven arrived at the tower room where he lived with his brothers, only to find the place empty. He dressed and hurried down the spiral staircase to the ground floor. Two priests were headed to the dining hall and spotted him as he crossed the Great Hall.

"You should go to the master's library," the eldest whispered, motioning to the room.

"Aye, your brothers and Greer are there," the other priest added.

Bran nodded, keeping his face blank even though a sliver of alarm was creeping down his spine. Why would Lorne want to see his brothers?

He strode to the library door and knocked. His youngest brother, Zane, opened the door. With excitement dancing in his dark eyes, he motioned for Bran to come inside.

"It's about time," Master Lorne drawled from behind his massive desk.

Arlo was standing by the hearth, his brow wrinkled with worry, while Greer was lounging in a chair, watching the blazing fire with a sneer on his face.

"The princess has been located," Zane whispered to Bran as they approached the desk.

"Aye." Bran bowed his head to the master. "Greetings, Lord Master. May the Light be with you. I just came from the queen's caravan. It's on the main road south, headed—"

"I know, I know." Lorne waved a dismissive hand. "Several of the village priests sent reports. What took you so long?"

Bran didn't want to get Vera in trouble for causing a delay. "I learned about the caravan this morning, but I wanted to confirm the information before coming here. There are four mounted troops, two supply wagons—"

"Yes, yes, we know." Lorne gave him an annoyed look. "The question I want answered is how do we capture the girl?"

Bran winced. "Even if we hired every criminal in the country, I'm not sure they could defeat four troops of trained soldiers. Also, the two dragons would most probably roast any attacking force. And if we somehow managed to get past the troops and the dragons, the princess could stop everyone with a mere clap of her hands."

Lorne narrowed his eyes. "So you don't even want to try."

"But we have to do it." Zane tugged on Bran's sleeve. "We'll figure out a way."

Bran shook his head. "I don't believe it's possible."

"If I say I want it done, then it will be done." Lorne stood slowly, anger flaring in his dark eyes. "Once again, you're making me question your loyalty."

Greer rose to his feet, a smirk on his face. "Then make Father Bran prove his loyalty. Put him in charge of the mission."

"No!" Arlo stiffened with alarm.

The bloody bastard. Bran strode toward Greer. "Is this the cowardly way you rid yourself of your enemies? You foisted an impossible mission on Father Saul so he would die."

Greer shrugged, his mouth curling with amusement. "Did I?"

Bran grabbed his robe to jerk him forward. "You bastard. If you want to kill me, be brave enough to try it in person."

"Any time." Greer gripped Bran's wrist in a tight hold.

Soon Bran felt the invisible jab of icy needles piercing his skin, freezing everything in their path. He ripped his hand free. Even though his fingers ached with cold, he curled them tightly, ready to slam his fist into Greer's face.

"Enough!" Master Lorne hissed. "You damned Embraced with your evil powers. I look forward to the day I can rid the world of you all."

"Why, thank you, Uncle," Bran muttered. He glanced over at Zane. The poor boy was hearing this from his own father.

Lorne paced across the room. "I had thought it would take several years to destroy the royal family and take over the country. After all, we have only a handful of monks who are trained to fight. Not nearly enough to defeat the army, even if we pay every criminal we can find to help us. That was why we started distributing the handbills. If we can get enough people on our side, we can defeat the army. But it will take time. Too much time."

He turned and faced the others. "The discovery of the princess and her unique power is a gift from the Light. If we don't use that gift, it will be an insult to our god. Once she puts the army and her family to sleep, we can easily kill them all. The country can be mine in one day!"

It would be a bloodbath, Bran thought. How could a god want that? And would Master Lorne rule the kingdom the same way he had ruled the monastery? Would children all over the country be whipped to learn obedience? Vera's words about the royal family came back to him. *They would never abuse young children.*

Master Lorne pointed a bony finger at Bran. "You will take on this mission."

Bran stiffened as his brothers gasped and Greer smirked.

"I made my position clear," Bran said with gritted teeth. "The mission is not possible."

Lorne strode toward him. "If you give up now, it will be a failure, and you know—"

"I'll do it!" Arlo exclaimed as he stepped forward.

"No!" Bran reached out to stop him, but Arlo shoved his hand away.

"I want to do it," Arlo insisted. "I want to prove myself. I'm sure I can succeed."

When Bran found himself believing his brother, he realized what was happening. Arlo had activated his Embraced gift, and even though he was aiming it at Master Lorne, the gift was powerful enough that Bran could still feel the effect.

Arlo had the unusual ability to make people believe anything. He could make someone agree that the sky was green and cows could fly, but normally, he did not use his power to play tricks on people. With his kind heart, he only used his power to help people believe in themselves if they were suffering from self-doubt. It was the main reason Bran had always known that his brother would make an excellent priest.

But now, Arlo was using his power to make the master believe a lie. And he was doing it to save Bran's life. At the cost of his own.

"Arlo, stop it." Bran grabbed onto his brother's arm. "Don't do this."

Arlo kept his focus on Master Lorne. "I can accomplish the mission. Give it to me."

"Arlo!" Zane's eyes filled with tears as he ran toward his brother and grabbed his other arm. "Don't do this!"

Master Lorne nodded slowly. "Very well. The mission is yours."

Bran stepped back, his head reeling. This couldn't be happening.

"Arlo." Zane wiped a tear from his cheek.

"It will be all right." Arlo patted his younger brother on the back.

Master Lorne blinked, as if he were coming out of a trance, then gave the three brothers a wary look. "Why do I feel as if you three are more loyal to each other than to the Brotherhood?"

Greer smirked. "If Arlo fails, their little threesome will be over."

Bran was too devastated even to consider pummeling Greer's face. All he could think about was the likelihood of his brother having to die. He couldn't let it happen. He wouldn't. By all that was holy, he would keep his brother alive. "You won't fail, Arlo. I won't let you." *I won't let you die.*

The next morning, Eviana glared at the stubborn eagle flying overhead. He was doing an excellent job of avoiding her. They had been on the road for over an hour now, and Quentin hadn't so much as squawked at her.

The night before, she'd been so exhausted from the long day of travel that she'd fallen asleep right after her bath. So she had missed seeing him again last night. And she'd missed him this morning as well. Northam had insisted she eat breakfast with him in the dining room. By the time she'd managed to escape, the others had already eaten in the kitchen and had the cart packed and ready to go. Quentin had already shifted and was perched on a trunk in the cart.

They'd said their farewells and had started down the road to the village of Butterfield. According to Northam, the best butter in Eberon was hand-churned there. He'd encouraged her to stop at the local bakery for freshly baked bread slathered with the village's famous butter. The idea had so appealed to him that he'd wanted to go with them, so Eviana had been forced to remind him in a whispered voice that she and her companions were on a secret mission. The baron had relented then, but he'd made sure they had a basket full of cheese and fruit and a new jug of cider in the back of the cart. She, in turn, had given him half a crate of wine, claiming in a loud voice for all to hear that she'd given him the best price she could.

During the next hour, while Olana drove the cart, she explained everything that had transpired inside the guardhouse. Elam rode alongside the cart so he could add his comments. Occasionally, he would give Olana a look of sweet longing that made her blush.

Apparently, she was no longer angry with the colonel, Eviana thought. The two were talking to each other and exchanging glances. Their relationship was progressing, unlike her relationship with the stubborn birdbrain overhead.

"So they're called the Brotherhood of the Sun," Eviana concluded when they finished their report. "They're priests, inciting a rebellion." She glanced over her shoulder but couldn't see the crate. "What happened to all the handbills?"

"Late last night, Quen and I took most of them to the kitchen and burned them," Elam replied. "We saved a few, in case we need them for evidence, and hid them in our trunk of clothes."

"That's good." Eviana thought over all the new information she'd just learned. "So we know the name of one member of the Brotherhood. Father Greer, who can freeze things to death."

"Right." Elam nodded. "But we don't know where to find him. We're not even sure if all the Brothers live in one place."

Eviana considered that issue for a while as the cart lumbered slowly down the road. "If the priests are living together, then they might be in a monastery, right? How many monasteries are there in Eberon?"

Elam shrugged. "Not sure. But that is definitely something we should ask in each village. The villagers would know if there is a monastery close by."

"I've been thinking about what we should do when we reach Butterfield," Olana said. "If we see the priest, Elam could trip him. Then I could rush over to help him up, and he would confess."

"Sounds like an excellent plan." Eviana smiled at her two companions. "You make a good team."

Olana blushed, slanting a shy look at Elam.

"I suppose you've known Elam most of your life?" Eviana asked.

Olana nodded. "We both lived in the village on the Isle of Secrets, but I was always closest to the children near my age, who grew up in the nursery with me: Naomi, Peter, and Quentin." Her hands tightened on the reins. "They felt like my brothers and sisters."

"What happened to everyone after the big battle?" Eviana asked. "I imagine you were eager to leave the island behind."

"We were," Olana admitted. "I was with the younger group. We went to the Isle of Moon with Brody, Maeve, and Princess Elinor. They gave us rooms in the castle and tutors so we could catch up on our education. Maeve hired the two oldest girls, Bettina and Catriona, to be her ladies-in-waiting."

"When Nevis was offered an earldom and promoted to general, he decided to go back to Eberon," Elam explained. "Elinor wanted to go, too, since it was there that she and Luciana could track down the parents of the Embraced children. I decided to join the army and stay with Nevis." He shrugged. "It turned out that both my parents had died from the plague."

Olana gave him a surprised look. "My parents died from the plague, too."

"Really?" Elam's eyes softened. "I am sorry."

Olana sighed. "It is hard to miss them when I never knew them. And it seems to me that being taken to the Isle of Secrets saved our lives. If we had remained with our parents, we might have died, too."

Elam nodded. "True. The plague never made it to the island."

Eviana glanced up at Quentin. "I suppose Quentin didn't go to the Isle of Moon with you?"

"No." Olana shook her head. "He wanted to go to Norveshka." She smiled, glancing up at him. "He thought he could become a dragon."

Elam snorted.

Olana's smile widened. "I was so happy when I finally saw him again. He was sixteen, I believe, when he made his first flight to Ebton."

How old was he now? Eviana wondered. If he'd left the island at the age of nine, then he had to be twenty-nine now. Six years older than she.

"I was fifteen when I came to Ebton," Olana continued. "Since my parents were gone, and they were never able to find Naomi's parents, we decided to work as ladies-in-waiting. We were so excited when your mother hired us." A pained look crossed Olana's face. "Naomi and I wanted to stay together. We shared the same birthday, so we'd lived with each other since we were babes."

But Naomi was no longer at Ebton, Eviana thought. "I can barely remember Naomi. What happened to her?"

Olana winced but didn't reply. Elam gave her a worried look.

Hadn't Elam said he'd fallen for Olana twelve years ago? Eviana thought back. She'd been eleven at the time and apparently oblivious to romance. "Was this around the time when Elam fell for you?" Eviana asked, but Olana remained silent.

Elam frowned. "We rarely saw each other. I was busy with the army at Benwick."

"Then how . . . ?" Eviana glanced at one and then the other, but they had both clammed up. As the silence stretched on, Eviana sighed. Now it was awkward again. They weren't talking. And Quentin was still avoiding her.

How much farther to Butterfield? she wondered.

"Twelve years?" Olana muttered, then gave Elam an injured look. "Why didn't you tell me?"

He winced. "When would I have told you? We hardly ever saw each other."

"If you never saw me, how could you fall in love?" She glowered at him. "You should have told me. You should have made some effort—"

"You were still in love with Logan!"

Olana gasped. Her hands gripped the reins hard as she struggled to breathe.

Eviana looked away, not wishing to stare. But good goddesses, these two were hurting and needed help. As silence fell over them once again, she felt an overwhelming urge to do something, say something. "Who is Logan, may I ask?"

Olana remained silent, but tears had gathered in her eyes.

Elam sighed. "He's a few years older than Olana. On the Isle of Secrets, he was put in the Embraced army because he can run at a tremendous speed. When he runs past you, all you see is a blur. Later on, he joined the Eberoni army and was stationed at Benwick. Because of his speed, he ran messages back and forth between Benwick and Ebton."

"I see." Eviana glanced at Olana. "And I suppose you must have seen him whenever he came to Ebton?"

Olana nodded. A tear rolled down her cheek, and she angrily swiped it away. "I thought I was in love. The summer when I was eighteen, I finally mustered up the courage to tell him."

Eviana leaned close. "What happened?"

Olana scoffed. "He ran away."

"At a tremendous speed," Elam added wryly, and Olana shot him an annoyed look.

"He didn't run that fast," Olana muttered. "He couldn't, because he wasn't alone. Naomi went with him."

Eviana sucked in a breath. "Your best friend? Didn't she know how you felt about Logan?"

Olana nodded. "She did. His rejection hurt, of course, but I think her betrayal hurt even worse. That, and knowing that it was my gift that made him run away. What man would want to wed the Confessor?" She slanted another injured look at Elam. "I suppose it was my gift that kept you away, too."

Elam stiffened. "No. Not at all. I have nothing to hide."

"But you did hide! For twelve years!"

He winced. "It's not as if I fell for you overnight. The feelings grew very slowly. It was five years before I even realized I had fallen in love. At first, I could only see how hurt you were, and I . . . I felt terribly sorry for you."

Olana flinched. "You pitied me?"

"No!" Elam looked affronted. "That's when I saw how strong you were. You kept going. You kept smiling, even though you were in pain. I didn't pity you. I admired you."

Olana's eyes widened.

"I saw so many people avoiding you because of your gift," Elam continued. "But you never gave in to self-pity. You were always eager to help whenever a king called on you. I . . . I thought you were amazing."

Tears gathered in Olana's eyes once again. "Why didn't you tell me?"

"I thought you were still hurting because of Logan. And Naomi."

"That was twelve years ago!" Olana huffed. "How long did you expect me to suffer because of them?"

Elam frowned at her. "I know you don't return my feelings."

"You never gave me a chance!"

"You've known me most of your life, Olana. If you were never attracted to me before, why would I—"

"I always admired you. And respected you. I thought of you as the older brother I could always trust."

He scoffed, looking away. "Right. An older brother."

"A very handsome older brother," Olana added, and he glanced at her once again. "Back when I was a child, you did seem much older. But I turned thirty-three just a few days ago, and you must have turned thirty-nine. A difference of six years seems like nothing now."

Six years? Eviana thought. It was the same age difference between her and Quentin.

"Then you . . ." Elam watched Olana closely.

More tears streamed down her cheeks. "I'm so tired of being shunned. And feared. And so damned lonesome!"

Elam inhaled sharply. "Olana. I . . ."

"You should have told me." She wiped her face. "If you can love me, despite my gift, then I want to try. We should at least try, don't you think?"

Elam's eyes glistened with tears, and he guided his horse closer to the cart. "Lady Olana." He reached for her hand, and when she placed it in his, he whispered, "I have loved you for twelve years."

Olana made a muffled noise, halfway between a tearful sob and a joyful laugh.

Eviana pressed a hand to her mouth, trying her best not to ruin the beautiful scene by bawling.

"May I court you?" Elam asked.

"Yes," Olana replied, smiling through her tears.

As they continued to smile at each other, Eviana wiped away her tears and took a deep breath. Elam and Olana had forged ahead with their relationship, and all it had really taken was a good honest talk.

She glanced up at Quentin flying ahead of them, zigzagging back and forth. How could she make any progress with him if he stayed away and refused to talk? She was still determined to court him but was beginning to see how difficult it would be.

It obviously took two to make a courtship work.

Chapter 17

An hour later, Eviana noticed the sky above them was empty. "Where is Quentin? Has something gone wrong?"

Elam scanned the sky. "Most probably he's flown ahead to check out the village of Butterfield. We're getting close to it now."

After a few tense minutes, Eviana exhaled with relief when she sighted the eagle once again. Quentin landed in the road about twenty yards ahead of them.

"He probably wants to get dressed," Elam said. "Let's stop for a moment."

"All right." Olana pulled the cart to the side of the road.

Elam dismounted. "Need some clothes?" He retrieved Quentin's clothes from the back of the cart, then headed into the woods.

Eviana's pulse quickened as she watched Quentin fly into the woods to shift. Now, at last, she would have a chance to talk to him. While he was getting dressed, she dashed into the woods on the opposite side of the road to relieve herself. When she returned, Olana took her turn.

As Eviana climbed back onto the cart, Quentin emerged, fully dressed, from the woods. She smiled. "Good morning."

With a frown, he turned toward Elam.

She scoffed. Was the stubborn man going to ignore her?

"I flew over the village," he said, still frowning. "But I couldn't see anyone. No one drawing water from the well, no children playing on the village green, no one hanging laundry."

Elam blinked. "You mean the town is empty?"

Quentin shrugged. "They could all be inside buildings, I suppose."

"That seems odd when the weather is so nice," Eviana added, determined not to be cut out of the conversation.

"It certainly has me curious," Olana said as she returned to the cart. "We should be on our way." She planted a foot on the cart step to heft herself back onto the driver's bench, then paused. After glancing at Eviana and then Quentin, she set her foot back on the ground. "Actually, I'm so tired of sitting that I would prefer to walk a bit. Would you mind driving the cart, Quen?"

"Me?" Quentin slanted a wary look at Eviana, and she gave him a wry one back.

"Thank you, Quen." Olana patted his arm as she passed by.

Eviana inhaled sharply. Now he would have to confess!

Quentin winced, then ground out the words through gritted teeth. "My heart is forever lost to Eviana."

"What?" Elam stared at him, dumbfounded. "You . . . ?"

"Forget what I said," Quentin snapped, then shot Olana an annoyed look. "You did that on purpose."

"Did I?" Olana affected an innocent look.

"You're in love with Her High—Mistress Evie?" Elam asked, his eyes still wide with shock.

With a muttered curse, Quentin crossed his arms across his broad chest and looked off into the woods.

"He claims to love me," Eviana muttered. "But as you can see, he's doing his best to ignore me."

"Don't talk about it," Quentin grumbled. "It's none of their business."

Eviana made a face at him. *The blasted man.*

Elam looked them over, then turned to Olana and whispered, "What should we do?"

She smiled at him. "Let's leave the happy couple alone. Would you like to walk with me?"

"I would love to," Elam replied. Taking the reins of his horse in one hand, he extended his other hand to Olana. When she clasped it, he said softly, "I've been in love with you for twelve years."

She looked away, blushing, as they strolled down the road toward the village.

"You won't grow tired of hearing me say that?" Elam asked.

Olana shook her head. "No. Because it will change. Next year, you'll say you have loved me for thirteen years."

He grinned. "True."

As they walked farther away, their low voices could no longer be heard.

Eviana glanced over at Quentin, who was still standing next to the cart, glowering at Olana. "Shouldn't we be leaving?" She patted the bench beside her. "Let's go."

With an angry grunt, he climbed onto the cart and settled at the far end of the bench. "She did that on purpose. She thinks she's a bloody matchmaker."

"You can hardly reach the reins over there," Eviana muttered.

He scooted a few inches closer and took the reins. "Aren't you tired of this hard bench? You could sit in the back on the straw."

"No, thank you." She gave him a little smile.

He looked away as he flicked the reins and gave Daisy a shout. The cart moved slowly forward.

Eviana motioned to the couple far ahead, who were still holding hands. "Did you see how well Elam and Olana are progressing with their courtship? All it took was a good, honest conversation."

Quentin didn't answer.

"So . . ." Eviana sighed. "We could spend this time getting to know each other better, don't you think?"

He remained quiet.

Was she going to have to clonk the man over the head to get some words out of him? "Ever since last night, I've been wondering a few things. For instance: if you fell for me six years ago, then I was seventeen at the time. Was there something I did that drew your attention? What was it that attracted—"

"Actually, there *is* something we need to discuss," he interrupted.

He speaks! She shifted on the seat to face him. "Yes?" Had he decided to accept their courtship?

"If we're going to travel together, we need to set some rules," he began.

She blinked. "Rules?"

"Yes. For example, we will speak to each other only when necessary and only about the business of our mission."

Her mouth dropped open.

"I will take your silence as agreement. Also, we should be extremely careful to avoid any touching."

With a huff, she swatted his shoulder.

He stiffened. "You're breaking the rules."

"I didn't agree to your stupid rules."

"We need the rules. Without them, we could end up . . . well, it would be a disaster."

She scoffed. *A disaster?* "What exactly would this dreaded disaster entail?"

"We . . ." His jaw shifted. "You know what I meant."

"Do I?" She blinked innocently at him. "How would I know? I don't believe I've ever done anything disastrous with a man before."

Something hot glimmered in his golden eyes; then he looked away to focus on the road.

"Perhaps you could elaborate on what specific activities I

need to avoid?" she asked. "Could it be . . . touching? Or kissing?"

His jaw clenched, but he remained silent.

The blasted man. He wasn't taking the bait. With a nonchalant shrug, she faced front. "Actually, now that I think about it, I *have* kissed a few men."

"What?" He turned back toward her.

Now he's talking. She counted off all the princes on her fingers. "Reynfrid of Tourin, Pendras of Norveshka, Rudgar of the Isles, and Brendelf of Woodwyn."

"All of them?" He gave her an incredulous look. "You can't come across a prince without kissing him?"

She bit her lip to keep from laughing. "I kissed them on the cheek to say farewell."

"Oh." Quentin's mouth started to curl up into a smile, but he quickly stopped it. "That's a greeting, not a kiss."

"Then I suppose I will never experience a real kiss," she said, giving him a pointed look. "Since it would be such a terrible disaster."

His gaze dropped to her mouth; then he looked away. His jaw shifted as if he were grinding his teeth.

But what a lovely jaw he had, Eviana thought, admiring the strong line of it. This close, she could even see some golden whiskers. She leaned toward him and kissed his cheek.

He jerked and scooted away, giving her a shocked look. "What the hell was that?"

"It was a greeting, not a kiss."

He scoffed. As he moved closer again, he mumbled, "A greeting like that could give a man a heart attack."

She smiled to herself.

He slanted a curious look at her. "So you're . . . well acquainted with every prince in the world."

She nodded. "They're like younger brothers to me."

"They're of equal rank to you."

"Yes." She glanced at him. "If you're thinking one of them would be the best match for me, then you're totally mistaken."

"You're not attracted to any of them?"

"No, I'm not, but that's actually beside the point." She shifted once again to face Quentin. "My father would never allow me to marry any of them. For example, if I married Brendelf, then the Duchy of Vindalyn would merge with Woodwyn, and Eberon would lose about a fourth of its land."

Quentin sat back with a stunned look.

She snorted. "You never thought about that, did you? You were too busy with your *Woe is me.*" She waved her hands in the air. "*I'm so unworthy!*"

He glowered at her. "That's not amusing."

"No, it's not." She glared back. "None of this is amusing. Do you think I enjoy being a difficult match? To keep Vindalyn a part of Eberon, my parents want me to marry an outstanding Eberoni nobleman. But there aren't any! You saw what happened at the party. You damned well caused it!"

He winced. "I am sorry about that."

"I'm not. I didn't like any of them anyway." She heaved a sigh. "I like you, Quentin. So I'm going to court you whether you like it or not."

With a frown, he studied the road before them. When an awkward silence stretched out, she was tempted to break it. But she could tell he was in deep thought. Maybe she should leave him alone for a while. Let him think about everything she'd said.

And then maybe, just maybe, he would follow his heart instead of his stubborn brain.

As they approached the village of Butterfield, Quentin struggled to stay focused on the mission. She liked him! She'd admitted it.

Stop thinking about it! But why hadn't he realized the dilemma she was in? Her parents were not going to let the Duchy of Vindalyn fall into foreign hands. Now that he thought about it, he could see that most of Eviana's life had been determined by the fact that she was the heiress. Was that why she'd said she felt trapped?

Did she believe that somehow he presented a solution to her problem? But that was a terrible error on her part because her parents would never accept him. It was too late for him—he was already in love. But Eviana only liked him at this point. It would be terrible if she fell in love, only to have her heart crushed by her parents' rejection of his suit. To safeguard her heart, he needed to make sure her feelings weren't allowed to develop any further.

There was only one solution: He had to keep his distance, no matter what. Unfortunately, it was going to be a great deal harder than he'd ever realized. Every time she admitted to liking him or caring for him, every time she touched him, every time she gazed at him fondly with her beautiful green eyes, he longed to pull her into his arms. He wanted to hold her, kiss her, touch her. He wanted to hear her sigh with pleasure and cry out with passion.

He wanted the disaster.

Don't think about it! Doing so would only make him want it more. As the cart reached the outskirts of Butterfield, he shook himself mentally so he could focus on the task ahead of them.

"You're right," Eviana said softly beside him. "I can't see any villagers working in their gardens or hanging laundry. No children playing."

Where have all the people gone? Quentin wondered as he steered the cart into the town square. Ahead of them, Elam and Olana had stopped by the well. It was a circular pool built of stone. In the center, a stone column encased an iron tube with a spigot. A handle could be pumped to make water pour from the spigot into the pool. Using a large wooden ladle, Elam transferred some water into a nearby trough, so his horse could have a drink.

"Even the tavern appears empty," Eviana observed as they passed by.

All the businesses seemed closed, Quentin thought as he scanned the village. There was a tavern and bakery on this side of the square. Across the village green, there was a church of Enlightenment and a school. The playground and benches were empty.

The only sign of life was in center of the village green, where tables and chairs had been set up. A long table looked as if it might be loaded with food, but tablecloths were covering it all.

Quentin stopped the cart close enough to the horse trough that Daisy could have a drink.

"What do you think is going on?" Elam asked as Quentin jumped down from the cart.

"Not sure." He remained by the cart to make sure Eviana climbed down safely.

"The tables in the village green have the look of a party," Olana said as she washed her hands with fresh water that poured from the spigot.

"But where are the—" Quentin stopped when the doors to the church suddenly burst open, and a crowd of people headed down the steps, smiling and talking to one another. Children scampered ahead toward the tables on the green, where they pulled out hidden baskets from underneath a tablecloth.

"Oh, my." Eviana watched, her eyes wide. "The entire village was in the church."

"It seems like an odd time for mass." Olana dried her hands on her skirt.

"Oh, look!" Eviana pointed, a smile spreading on her face.

Quentin spotted a young couple at the top of the church

steps, both dressed in white. The villagers gave them a cheer as they descended the stairs, and the children threw flower petals at them from their baskets.

"It was a wedding!" Eviana exchanged a grin with Olana.

"How lovely!" Olana clasped her hands together. "Look how happy everyone is."

"We should congratulate them." Eviana rushed over to the well and washed her hands.

"Don't forget we're on a mission," Quentin warned her.

"There's the priest." Elam motioned toward the church door, where a thin, elderly man in black robes had emerged from the building. He remained there, smiling as he looked over his flock.

Olana narrowed her eyes as she looked him over. "I don't think we should trip him. He looks too frail."

"We'll see if he'll talk to us," Quentin said, glancing at Olana. "If not, you could still touch him."

"While you question the priest, I'll see what I can find out from the villagers," Eviana said as she pulled out a bottle of wine from the back of the cart. "I'll give the happy couple this as a gift." She sauntered toward the tables.

"Elam." Quentin motioned with his head toward Eviana. The villagers were probably harmless, but they still had to be careful with the princess.

Elam nodded, then hurried to catch up with Eviana.

"Let's go." Quentin led Olana toward the church. The priest was alone there, now, watching and smiling as the villagers filled their cups with wine so they could toast the happy couple. Tears glistened in the priest's eyes, and as he turned away to wipe his eyes, he spotted Quentin and Olana.

He gave them a welcoming smile, then headed slowly down the steps. "You picked the right day to be passing through our village. We're celebrating a wedding, and there is always room for more at our tables."

"That is very kind of you, Father," Olana responded with a bow of her head.

The priest reached the bottom of the stairs and swayed on his feet for a moment. He leaned over, rubbing his brow with his right hand.

"Father, are you all right?" Olana rushed toward him.

"I'm fine," the priest mumbled as he slowly straightened. "Perfectly fine."

"That's a relief." Olana touched his arm.

"I have a terrible wasting disease," the priest confessed, then sucked in a breath. "I shouldn't have said that. Please don't tell any of my flock. This is a happy day for them, and I don't want to ruin it with the news that I will not be here much longer."

"We won't say a word," Olana assured him, her eyes filled with worry. "I'm so very sorry to hear about your illness."

The priest shrugged, then gave them a smile. "I cannot complain. I've had a long and good life, thanks be to the Light. I've been blessed to serve this village and its people for over forty years, and I love them all dearly. Please join us. I expect your travels have made you hungry."

"Thank you," Quentin replied. "We appreciate your kindness but cannot tarry for long. We hope to make it to the village of Rushing Falls by tonight."

"Ah." The priest nodded. "You are merchants, I gather?"

"Aye, wine merchants," Quentin replied. "And you are . . . ?"

"Father Titus." The priest shook Quentin's hand. "The Light be with you. With you both." He smiled at Olana.

"Would you happen to know a Father Greer?" Quentin asked, and the priest's smile immediately vanished.

Father Titus stepped back, a look of suspicion and fear crossing his face. "Are you spies? Did Master Lorne send you?"

Master Lorne? Quentin wondered if he was the leader of the Brotherhood of the Sun.

The priest lifted his chin in defiance. "You can tell Lorne that I refuse to join him. I refused his brother twenty-five years ago, and my answer remains the same. They can go to hell."

"We don't know any Master Lorne," Olana said quietly.

"But you *could* call us spies," Quentin admitted. "Not for the Brotherhood, but for the king." He motioned to Elam. "Our companion there is a corporal in the Eberoni army. I'm the official courier for the royal family, and Olana here is known as the Confessor."

"Oh, my." Father Titus looked them over, then focused on Olana. "I have heard of you. So it was your touch that made me confess to my illness?"

"I'm afraid so." Olana bowed her head. "I am sorry, Father."

"No, no, that's quite all right." Titus waved a dismissive hand. "No doubt you weren't sure whether I could be trusted."

"Unfortunately, that is true," Quentin agreed. "Any information you could give us would be greatly appreciated. And I'll be sure to let the king and queen know how helpful you were."

Titus snorted. "I don't need a reward to do what's right." He motioned to the church behind him. "Sixteen years ago, a terrible storm blew through this village. It ripped the church's roof to shreds and shattered the windows. We were distraught, for we couldn't afford the costly repairs. I wrote a letter to the king and queen, asking for their help, but several weeks passed by, and I feared they had no interest in our poor village. But then, a troop of soldiers arrived with wagons filled with building supplies, baskets of food, and bolts of fine wool and linen. Not only did they rebuild the church, but they built a school for us, too."

The priest's eyes filled with tears. "And that was when we realized how much our king and queen care about us. We will always be loyal." He placed his hand over his heart. "You have my word."

"Thank you." Quentin glanced over at Eviana, who seemed to be enjoying herself with the villagers. "I can confirm that the royal family is worthy of your devotion."

"What can you tell us about the Brotherhood of the Sun?" Olana asked.

Titus motioned for them to follow as he led them toward the nearby schoolyard. "I don't want the villagers to hear about this. They are innocent, hardworking people."

"Father!" one of the village women called out. "Bring the guests over so they can eat!"

The priest smiled at her. "Maddie, if you would be so kind, please bring some food and wine to us here."

Several women busied themselves, filling up three trays. Then they brought the trays to the schoolyard, where the priest had settled on a bench.

Olana sat on the opposite end of the bench, and Quentin settled on the grass in front of them. They ate and drank while they waited for the women to return to the party.

Quentin bit into a slice of freshly baked bread, slathered with butter. Damn, Northam was right. This was the best butter he'd ever tasted. He took a drink of wine and noticed the priest was not eating. "Please enjoy your food, Father."

Titus shrugged. "I don't have much of an appetite these days."

"You mentioned a Master Lorne?" Olana asked.

Titus nodded. "He is the head of the Brotherhood. That much I know for sure. His elder brother, Lord Morris, started the—" He narrowed his eyes. "I can see that you know who Lord Morris is."

"Aye, we do." Quentin bit into a slice of cold roast beef. "But we didn't know he had a brother."

Titus took a long drink of wine. "It helps with the pain.

Anyway, twenty-five years ago, Lord Morris tried to recruit me as one of his spies. I refused, of course. I didn't want my flock to get involved with his nefarious plan."

"He and the other members of the Circle of Five wanted to take over the world," Quentin muttered. "I assume that has remained the goal?"

"Unfortunately, yes." Titus reached in a pocket and pulled out a folded sheet of paper. "A week ago, when I rose before dawn to prepare for the sunrise mass, I found this tacked to the doors of the church. I was horrified. I ran around the square and found the same note pinned to the door of every business. I ripped them all down and burned them before anyone could see them."

"May I see it?" Quentin took the paper and unfolded it. It was similar to the handbills the highwaymen had possessed. A call to rebellion with a small sun pictured on the backside.

"I didn't know what to do," Titus continued. "I kept this one copy as proof of the Brotherhood's evil plans. I was afraid to send one of the villagers to Ebton with it, since having something so treasonous on his person could get him killed. I thought of taking it myself, but my health is not up to the journey. And I needed to be here for the wedding."

"Don't worry." Quentin folded the paper and stuffed it into a pocket. "We'll make sure King Leo and General Nevis know about this."

"Yes." Olana gave the priest a sad smile. "Please relax and enjoy your time here."

Titus's eyes filled with tears. "I will. And I can see now that my prayers have been answered. The Light, in his mercy, sent you here today. Not only so I could give you that paper, but so I could finally be free of the secrets that have been burdening me for so many years."

He took a deep breath. "So, where was I? Ah yes, after the Circle of Five was defeated, everything was peaceful and quiet. I hoped that meant the Brotherhood had dispersed and disappeared, but now I realize they were merely biding their time."

"Why?" Olana asked. "Why would they wait twenty years?"

Titus shrugged. "I'm not sure. But I suspect they were waiting for people like Father Greer to grow up."

"Who is he?" Quentin asked. "I hear he can freeze things to death."

"That is true. He is Master Lorne's favorite assassin." Titus grimaced. "A priest using his gift to intimidate people and commit murder. It is an abomination."

"Where is the Brotherhood located?" Quentin asked.

"I'm afraid I don't know that." Titus frowned. "It is a well-kept secret. Most of what I've heard is merely rumor. None of the members want to be caught actually divulging any information. Any mistake on their part means they must commit suicide."

Quentin nodded. They'd seen that with the death of Father Saul. "Do you know anything about a raven shifter?"

"Ah." Titus nodded. "I have heard about him. The priest in Rushing Falls told me. Father John. He's on our side."

Quentin leaned closer. "And the raven?"

"Rumor has it that he's one of Lord Morris's sons," Titus whispered. "They say there are three sons, and they are all Embraced."

Quentin sat back. "That old priest had sons?"

Titus nodded. "I'm not sure if you know the story, but for years, Lord Morris traveled around Eberon, gathering up Embraced babies to send them to a secret place where they could be trained to use their powers to help the Circle of Five take over the world."

Quentin exchanged a look with Olana. "We've heard about that."

Titus set his plate of uneaten food on the bench beside him. "Apparently, Lord Morris was worried that the other members of the Circle would turn on him someday and try to kill him."

"That probably would have happened," Quentin muttered.

"Exactly," Titus agreed. "That is the problem with being in cahoots with a group of villains. None of them trust one another. So Morris stopped sending Embraced babies to the secret place and instead sent them to the Brotherhood. But that still wasn't good enough. He took on several mistresses, hoping to produce Embraced sons of his own who would be loyal only to him."

"So they could protect him?" Olana murmured.

"Yes." Titus nodded. "Of course, that never happened, since Morris died twenty years ago. But Master Lorne was all too happy to step into his brother's place."

"And then Master Lorne waited for the Embraced children to grow up." Quentin exchanged another look with Olana. Now there was another Embraced army that would have to be defeated?

What had happened twenty years ago was about to be repeated.

Chapter 18

The sun was lowering toward the horizon by the time Eviana and her companions drew near to the village of Rushing Falls. The first hour of the journey had passed quickly, for she had been fascinated by everything Olana had told her. She hadn't discovered anything interesting from the villagers of Butterfield, but luckily, Father Titus had turned out to be a fount of information.

Unfortunately, once Eviana had heard all the news, there was nothing left to do but sit and watch the trees go by. For hours. Quentin was flying overhead in a zigzag pattern. The minute they'd left Butterfield, he'd gone into the woods to shift back into his eagle form. So she had no idea if she'd made any progress with him or not.

She sighed. Her back was tired. Her rump sore. The only thing of interest in the last few hours had been the slow and gradual change of terrain. The farther southeast they traveled, the hillier the land became. The pastures dotted with oak and beech gave way to thicker forests of scented pine.

Before entering the village, they stopped by a heavily wooded area so Quentin could shift and get dressed. After the rest of them relieved themselves, they gathered around the cart to drink some cider and make their plans.

"I spotted an inn in the village with a tavern," Quentin said as he retrieved a few gold pieces from the men's trunk of clothing. "We can stop there for the night. I'll rent a room for the ladies; Elam and I can bunk in the stable next to the cart. We can't leave the wine or our small stash of gold unattended."

Eviana groaned inwardly. What he was saying made perfect sense, but it also meant that he planned to stay far away from her for the rest of the day.

"Actually, I would be happy to keep Elam company for a while," Olana said, giving him a shy smile. "It would give us a chance to talk."

Elam smiled back at her. "I would love that."

"Then it's settled." Eviana gave Quentin a wry look. *Try to weasel out of this.* "Quentin and I will have dinner in the tavern and ask the innkeeper to send some food to you in the stable."

"That would be lovely, thank you." Olana gave Quentin an amused look.

He frowned back at her and Eviana. "I'm not sure I should even stay. We learned so much today from Father Titus. I should probably fly west and find the queen's caravan so I can make a report. But they'll be farther away now, and the idea of flying all night . . ."

"You need to rest so you can fly tomorrow," Eviana insisted. "The news can wait a day or two. Besides, we might learn more tomorrow from Father John."

"That's true," Olana agreed. "You made the journey yesterday, and we had a long day today. We all need to sleep tonight." She turned toward Elam. "Let's go. I feel like walking."

Eviana smiled to herself as Olana and Elam sauntered up a hill toward the village, leaving her alone with Quentin. She climbed onto the cart. "I hope the food will be good. I'm famished."

Without a word, he climbed onto the cart and took the reins. Within a few minutes, they began to pass houses and small farms. Then, down in a green-pastured valley, a rushing stream was lined with more houses. Daisy's hooves clip-clopped over the stone bridge, and Eviana had a good view of the small falls the village was named after. Up on the next hill, they found themselves in the town square. On the south side of the square, a large wooden building housed the inn and tavern.

Quentin drove the cart around back to the stable.

"We'll take care of everything," Elam said as he began to unhitch Daisy from the cart. "You two enjoy your dinner."

"Don't forget the trunk." Olana pointed at the trunk containing women's clothes.

Still silent, Quentin hefted the small trunk onto a shoulder and strode toward the entrance.

Eviana hurried past him and opened the door. The booming clamor of loud male voices rolled out. Goodness, it sounded like every man in the village was here tonight. She followed Quentin into the foyer. To the left, there was a long hotel counter in front of a wall where a row of keys dangled from hooks. Straight ahead, a narrow hallway was next to a flight of stairs. And to the right, a wide entrance gave into the tavern.

She peeked inside. Almost every table was crowded with loud, boisterous men.

Quentin rang the bell. No one came.

Eviana joined him at the counter. "Maybe they didn't hear you."

He set the trunk on the counter and rang the bell again.

"Oh, my, I'm sorry." A maid rushed from the tavern with a tray filled with dirty dishes. "I couldn't hear over all the noise."

Eviana smiled at her. "It looks very busy tonight."

"It's a madhouse." The maid set her tray on the counter and skirted around it. "The local farmers have finished the fall harvest, so they're celebrating. What can I do for you?"

Quentin set two gold pieces on the counter. "We would like a room for the night. Your best room, if you don't mind."

The maid's eyes lit up. "Oh, of course." She snatched up the gold and grabbed a key off the wall. "This is room number three, right at the top of the stairs. Your wife will love it!"

Quentin blinked.

"Oh, I'm sure I will." Eviana couldn't resist teasing him. "Thank you, sweetheart." She wrapped her hands around his arm and leaned against him. Ha! So much for his rule of no touching.

With barely a glance at her, he hefted the trunk onto his shoulder and grabbed the key. "I'll take this up to the room."

"I'll find a table for us in the tavern," Eviana offered, then touched his arm again. "See you soon, dearest."

He slanted her an annoyed look, then trudged up the stairs.

Smiling to herself, she hurried into the tavern. Goodness, there was only one table that had two empty chairs together.

"Over here, pretty lady!" a drunk young farmer yelled as he motioned to the empty chair beside him.

"No! You can sit by me!" another young farmer shouted as he perched on a nearby windowsill to leave his chair vacant.

Oh dear, Eviana thought. It would probably be safer for her to continue the pretense of being married. And it would serve Quentin right for constantly rejecting her. In a loud voice, she announced, "My husband will be joining me soon."

As the single men in the room moaned, she rushed over to the occupants of the table with two empty chairs. "Would you mind if my husband and I joined you?"

"No, of course not," a friendly-looking older man said. His plump cheeks were bright pink from too much beer.

"Please have a seat," the other man said. Not only was his face pink, but his balding head was, too. He motioned toward the groaning bachelors. "Don't let them worry you. They've had too much to drink, but they're a harmless lot."

"Aye, completely harmless." The first man hiccoughed. "We've known them all of their lives. By the way, my name is Wilbur."

"And I'm Dewey." The second man slapped a hand against his stout chest. "I own the largest farm in the county."

Wilbur snorted. "But I had the biggest crop."

Dewey shrugged and gave Eviana a wry look. "What can I say? His land is better than mine."

Wilbur patted his friend on the back. "I'm glad you were finally able to admit that."

Dewey scoffed. "It only took ten beers."

"And twenty years!" Wilbur claimed, then attempted to focus his bleary eyes on Eviana. "So, are you passing through Rushing Falls or looking to stay?"

"We're traveling wine merchants," Eviana explained. "My name is Evie, and my husband is Quen."

As the maid approached their table, Dewey motioned to the empty bowls in front of him and his friend. "You should get the beef stew like we did."

"Is it good?" Eviana asked, and the men laughed.

"It's all there is," Wilbur said, and the men laughed some more.

As they finished their beer, Eviana turned toward the maid. "I'd like a jug of cider, some bread and butter, and two bowls of beef stew."

Dewey wiped his mouth with the back of his hand. "More beer for us!"

"Oh, and I need two bowls of stew sent to the stable for my servants," Eviana added.

"And more beer!" Wilbur thumped his empty tankard on the table.

"I understand." The maid rushed away.

Wilbur lifted his tankard to drink, then remembered it was empty. "Oh, damn." He set it down and gave Eviana an apologetic look. "Excuse my cursing, dear lady. So, are you planning to sell some wine here?"

"Actually, we were hoping to meet Father John." Eviana glanced around the crowded room but couldn't spot a priest.

"Why do you need a priest?" Dewey's bloodshot eyes narrowed. "Is there something wrong?"

Eviana wasn't sure how to answer, so she fell back on the scenario she had invented the day before. "We're hoping he can bless us. You see, we're on a pilgrimage to Arondale so we can bathe in the healing waters there."

Wilbur looked her over. "You seem healthy to me. It must be your husband who is ill?"

"No, he's—" Eviana spotted Quentin entering the room and waved a hand. "Sweetheart, over here!"

Quentin gave her a warning look as he walked toward her.

"Lucky bastard," one of the single men muttered.

"He doesn't look ill to me," Dewey mumbled.

"Oh, no, he's perfectly healthy." Eviana wrapped a hand around Quentin's arm as he sat beside her. Goodness, but his arm practically bulged with muscle. "I ordered some beef stew."

He glanced down at her hand, then at her. "Is it good?"

"It's all they have." She looked at the men across from her and they all laughed. "Quen, this is Wilbur and Dewey."

Quentin nodded at them and smiled. "Nice to meet you."

Wilbur sat back, eyeing Quentin. "So I hear you're on a pilgrimage."

When Quentin hesitated, Eviana jumped in. "Yes. We're going to Arondale for the healing waters. Right, sweetheart?" She gave him a look that said *play along!*

He shook his head slightly as if to say *no.*

The blasted man. She tightened her grip on his arm.

He nudged her leg with his knee.

She was debating whether to kick him when the maid returned with a tray. She set two large pewter tankards of beer in front of the farmers, then a jug of cider and two cups in front of Quentin, along with a basket of bread and a crock of butter.

As the maid hurried away, Eviana gave Quentin a wry look. "Please have some bread, sweetheart."

He arched a brow, then poured the cups full of cider.

As he drank, Eviana pulled off a hunk of bread. "You see, my husband and I have been married for five years but have yet to be blessed with any children."

Quentin sputtered his drink, then wiped his mouth. "There is no need to discuss our private matters." He gritted his teeth. "Sweetheart."

"But how can I stay quiet when I'm so devastated!" Eviana pressed a hand to her chest and took on a forlorn look. "I can only pray that the sacred spring will render me more fertile."

"Now, now, young lady." Wilbur gave her a worried look. "I'm sure it will all work out."

Dewey gulped down some beer, then thumped his tankard on the table. "I hate to see you blaming yourself for this. Maybe the problem lies with . . ." He gave her pretend husband a pointed look.

Eviana gasped. Oh dear, she hadn't expected this sort of reaction. "Oh, no! It couldn't be my dear husband's fault."

Quentin ripped off a piece of bread with more force than necessary. "This is not something we should be discussing with strangers." He glowered at the bread as he buttered it. "Besides, our lovemaking is perfect."

Wilbur sat back with a huff. "That's what all the men say, but let me tell you, the wives can tell a different story."

"That's true." Dewey nodded, giving Eviana a sad look. "So, you have to be honest with yourself, dear lady. Is your man getting the job done?"

"Of course!" Eviana wrapped her arms around Quentin's arm. "No one could be more . . . capable in the bedroom than my husband."

"Capable is one thing." Wilbur pointed a finger. "But a woman needs more than that. My wife always told me that only a fully satisfied woman can get with child." He puffed out his chest. "And I have seven children."

"I have eight!" Dewey boasted. "Thank the Light you two found us tonight. We have the expertise to help you with this problem."

"That's really not necessary—" Quentin began, but was interrupted by Wilbur.

"Now, first you need to tell us if you want a boy or a girl."

"A boy," Eviana said at the same time Quentin said, "A girl."

"Ah." Dewey nodded, giving his friend a knowing look. "They're not of one mind yet. That could be the problem."

"I want a boy who resembles his handsome father," Eviana said, slanting a nervous look at Quentin.

His golden eyes flared hot. "And I want a little girl as beautiful as her mother."

Her heart thundered in her chest. Did he mean that? Would his eyes burn with so much intensity if he was only pretending?

"Holy Light," Wilbur whispered, then leaned close to his

friend. "Do you see how much they love each other? We need to help them."

Eviana gulped. Could even strangers tell that she and Quentin were . . . what were they? Were they good actors? Or were they truly in love?

Dewey rested his elbows on the table. "So what will it be? A boy or a girl?"

Eviana's cheeks burned with heat as she glanced at Quentin again. "A boy, and then a girl?"

He nodded, his eyes simmering like molten gold. "As you wish."

She took in a shaky breath, then gulped down some cider to cool off.

"A boy, then." Wilbur hiccoughed. "It's your lucky day! I have five boys, so I know exactly what you need to do."

There was a pause as the maid returned and set two bowls of stew on the table.

As she walked away, Quentin asked, "So are you saying there is a different . . . strategy to use depending on whether you want a boy or a girl?"

"Exactly!" Dewey pointed at him. "Girls are beautiful and loving, so to create a girl, you have to make love slowly and gently, but with great passion, of course."

Wilbur nodded. "You have to take your time and make your wife feel like she's the most precious treasure in the entire world."

Quentin looked at Eviana and said softly, "I can do that."

Her heart lurched up her throat. Holy Light and goddesses. She gulped down the rest of her cider.

Quentin took her hand in his own and gave her a wry look. "And how would we make a son?"

The blasted man. When she'd started this pretense, she'd thought it would be amusing to annoy him, but now, he was turning the tables to see how flustered he could make her.

"For a robust baby boy, you have to engage in some robust lovemaking," Wilbur claimed.

Dewey nodded. "Aye, that makes perfect sense."

Wilbur took a long drink, then leaned toward Quentin. "I'll be blunt with you, boy. To create a man, you have to use some manly positions."

"Here, here." Dewey thumped a fist on the table. "Take her from behind. Throw her over a chair."

"Or up against a door," Wilbur added.

Eviana sat back. "Is that even possible?"

Dewey gasped. "You didn't know?" He frowned at Quentin. "You've been too lax on the job, boy."

Quentin's cheeks turned pink.

"Oh!" Wilbur pointed at him. "He's blushing! That's the problem. He's too shy!"

"You need to be more courageous," Dewey insisted. "Women love a man who is bold. And powerful."

"Exactly!" Wilbur agreed. "Powerful lovemaking will lead to a powerful son."

Quentin's hands gripped the edge of the table. "I do just fine, thank you."

Dewey snorted. "I doubt—"

"My husband is very courageous." Eviana rushed to his defense and placed her hand on his. "And so powerful. He's quite . . . insatiable, really. And so creative. Why, we've tried all sorts of positions. And in so many places. I can hardly remember them all."

Dewey blinked. "What kinds of places?"

"Well . . . there was the time . . ." Eviana glanced at Quentin for help, but he just gave her a wry look. "We were on horseback."

Wilbur hiccoughed. "The horse didn't mind?"

Eviana shrugged. "It did try to bolt when we screamed

with passion, but Quen is so masterful, he kept the beast under control."

Dewey snorted. "Which beast?"

Quentin's mouth twitched. "I appreciate your wanting to help, but we'll figure this out on our own. Meanwhile, I'd like for my wife to be able to eat while the stew is still hot."

"Of course, of course." Wilbur nodded. "You need to keep your strength up."

"Aye, you have a long night ahead." Dewey finished his tankard.

"We'll tell Father John that you need his blessing," Wilbur said. "And don't worry. We'll help you all we can."

"Thank you." Eviana ate a few bites of stew and soon the two men rushed off to find the priest.

Quentin gave her a wry look, then dug into his stew. "I told you that story was not a good one."

She scoffed. "On the contrary, they believed every word of it."

He glowered at his stew. "They believed I was . . ."

"Impotent?" She winced when he shot her an angry look. "I'm sure you're not! Although I really wouldn't know."

He snorted, then went back to eating.

"I came to your defense. Remember?"

He kept eating.

After a sigh, she spooned some stew into her mouth. "I tried to make you sound very skillful and talented. But my knowledge of the subject is severely limited."

His mouth twitched. "On a horse?"

She frowned at him. "You weren't helping."

He smiled, then went back to eating.

She ate a few more bites, then muttered, "I suppose a bathtub would have been more believable."

He shook his head. "Too crowded."

"Ah." She wondered if he was speaking from experience, blast him. Leaning closer, she whispered, "Is it really possible to make love against a door?"

He choked, then swallowed his food. "We shouldn't discuss—"

"So you've never tried it?"

He gave her an incredulous look. "Why would you think I had?"

"Well . . ." Her cheeks grew warm. "I've always suspected, as handsome as you are, that you have a group of women chasing you. Hordes of women. From every corner of the globe."

He set his spoon down. "Even if something that ridiculous were true, it would not signify to me. How could it when my heart has been yours for six years?"

Her heart lurched into a quick rhythm. "Then you . . . you will agree to our courtship?"

He watched her with his intense golden eyes, then replied, "No."

Her heart sank like a rock.

With a wince, he looked away. "If you're done eating, I'll take you to the room."

She set her spoon down. "You mean *our* room."

"I can't stay there. I'll bring Olana to you." He rose to his feet, then led her back to the foyer. "It's room number three, at the top of the stairs." He removed a key with a bright red tassel from his pocket and lowered his voice to a whisper. "You can lock the room from the inside and wedge a chair beneath the door latch."

She gave him an annoyed look as they climbed the stairs. "If you're that worried about my safety, why don't you stay and guard me?"

He scoffed. "And who will guard you from me?"

Her pulse raced. "Are you referring to the dreaded disaster?" They reached the top of the stairs, and she watched him unlock the door. "I'm not at all convinced it would be a disaster. Not if we both want it."

His knuckles turned white as he gripped the door latch hard in his fist. "Don't . . . don't tempt me. I promised your brother I would not harm you in any way."

"You harm me every time you reject me. It makes my heart ache."

His golden eyes burned with frustration. "Your heart will ache even more if we—"

"We're back!" Loud voices sounded below.

Eviana and Quentin spun around. Down in the foyer, Wilbur and Dewey were entering the front door, and they had a group of men with them. One had a fiddle, and the others had jugs of beer.

Wilbur waved at them and grinned. "Thank the Light we caught you just in time! We've brought Father John!"

A portly priest in black smiled up at them and pressed his thumbs and fingers together to form a circle, signifying the sun. "May the Light shine his blessings on you tonight."

"Huzzah!" the men shouted and drank more beer.

"And may the seed you plant tonight take root!" the priest exclaimed.

"You can do it!" Dewey yelled, and all the men cheered, shaking their fists in the air.

The rest of the men from the tavern crowded into the foyer to see what was happening, then joined in with the cheering.

Eviana turned around, her cheeks burning with embarrassment.

Even Quentin's face was pink. He waved at the men. "Thank you. You're too kind. You can go now." He yanked open the door, and Eviana scurried inside.

He followed her, then slammed the door shut and locked it. "I . . . I'll stay here until they leave."

She nodded. "They did what they came to do. They had the priest bless us. So they should be going soon."

Fiddle music started, and the men started singing a bawdy song about a cowherd and a milkmaid.

"Oh, no," Eviana whispered. "I think they're on the stairs."

Quentin winced. "We're being serenaded by a pack of drunkards."

"Maybe when the song ends, they'll leave." But her hopes dwindled by the time they launched into the sixth verse. How many verses did this song have? And what on Aerthlan was the cowherd doing with that cowbell? "Do they actually think this song is romantic?"

"I don't think they're aiming for romance," Quentin muttered.

"What do you mean?"

He inhaled through gritted teeth. "It's a lusty song."

"Oh." She swallowed hard.

He glared at the door for a few seconds, then made a fist and banged on it.

Outside, the men cheered.

She stepped closer and whispered, "What are you doing?"

He banged on the door again. "We're making love against the door."

"We are?"

He gave her a wry look. "We're pretending. We'll give them what they want, and then they'll go away. And then I can leave."

"Oh." She nodded, while a small voice inside her asked, *Does it have to be pretend?*

He hit the door again. "Make a loud noise. A cry."

"Me?"

"Is there someone else in the room? Do it now."

She made a face at him. "I'm not accustomed to this sort of thing, so you'll have to be patient."

"There is no patience when you're in the throes of passion. Now scream."

Goodness, he was making her face feel hot. "Argh!"

"Not like you're in pain," he hissed. "They'll think I'm hurting you."

"Oh, sorry."

"Cry like you're finding it pleasurable."

Pleasurable? More heat rose to her face, and she took a deep breath. "Aaaaah!" Then she laughed and covered her mouth. "Sorry."

His mouth twitched. "Laughter is good."

"Is it?"

He nodded. "It would mean you're really enjoying yourself."

"Oh?"

His gaze grew wary. "Don't look at me like that."

She licked her lips.

"Don't do that." He looked away and started banging on the door faster and faster. Then he shouted with a final hard slam against the door.

A loud cheer sounded outside.

"What was that?" she whispered. "I thought you weren't supposed to sound like you're in pain."

"I wasn't." He gave her an annoyed look. "I just experienced the most intense lovemaking of my life. And it was a damned *pretense.*"

She winced. "I'm sorry." She pressed an ear against the door. "I think they're leaving now. I can hear their footsteps going down the stairs."

"Good." He inhaled deeply and blew it out. "I'll wait a few minutes, then leave."

"All right." She turned to look around the room. There was a large four-poster bed in one corner next to a table with a lit candle. Her trunk of clothes had been placed at the foot of the bed. In another corner, a screen of blue damask was stretched across it, most likely hiding the chamber pot. Curtains of matching blue damask covered the windows. And on the far side of the room, a fire was burning in the hearth.

"It's a lovely room." She motioned toward the fireplace. "And they started a fire for us."

"I did that before going down to eat."

"Oh, thank you." She turned toward him. He was still lingering by the door, as if he couldn't wait to escape.

She fingered the red silk tassel on the key. "Are you sure they weren't making that stuff up just to play with us?"

"You mean the stuff about conceiving a boy or a girl?" He shrugged. "I think they were drunk."

"No, I mean the . . ." She waved a hand at the door. "Doing it there. It just doesn't seem possible to me. What do you think?"

"I think we shouldn't talk about it."

"I'm only asking out of intellectual curiosity." She leaned her back against the wall. "Of course my knowledge of such matters is severely limited, but I would assume it would require both parties to be standing. And then, the . . . alignment would be completely off, don't you think?"

He frowned at her. "Evie—"

"Unless, of course, the couple is of the exact same height. But I would think that would be a rare occurrence. I mean, you're a good six to eight inches taller than me." She glanced down at his breeches, then looked away. "I can only conclude that they were jesting."

"I would have to lift you."

She glanced back at him. "You mean hold me up? That seems terribly burdensome. And awkward. I can't imagine how that would be—" She gasped when he suddenly seized her by the waist and lifted her up till her face was even with his.

"What . . . ?" She grabbed onto his shoulders. "What are you doing? I'm too heavy. You'll strain—"

"Wrap your legs around me." He pressed her back against the door, then moved his hands to her rump.

"Oh." She hooked her feet together around his waist. "I . . . I suppose it could work after all."

His fingers pressed into her rump as his eyes simmered with heat.

She gulped. "Are . . . are you still pretending?"

"No." He moved closer, and she felt the rub of his hips dragging her skirt up her inner thighs. "Are you?"

"No." She gasped when he nestled against her most private parts. Good goddesses, she could feel a hard bulge pressing through the layers of fabric.

He leaned closer, his gaze shifting to her mouth. "I want to kiss you."

Her hands gripped his shoulders. Holy Light and goddesses, this was actually happening! "Quen."

His eyes met hers, searching them as if he were seeking a reason to stop. "If you don't want this, tell me now."

She shook her head. "I won't stop you."

His eyes glistened with tears as he refocused on her mouth. "Just one. I've wanted one for so long." Slowly he leaned forward until his lips pressed gently against hers.

She gasped at the sweetness and the feel of his breath mingling with hers. He kissed her again, this time molding his lips against hers. Oh, so soft and sweet, she thought her heart would melt.

Suddenly, he pulled back and set her on her feet. "Forgive me. I never should have . . ." He stepped back, dragging a hand through his hair. "I have dreamed of doing that. But I shouldn't have . . ."

Was he going to reject her again? She lunged forward, wrapping her arms around his neck. "If you won't kiss me, then I'll kiss you. And you can't stop me." She pressed her mouth against his.

He stiffened, and for a tense few seconds, she was afraid he would try to stop her. But then, a low growl rumbled in his throat, and his arms enveloped her, pulling her tight against him. He kissed her back, wildly. Feverishly, as if he meant to devour her.

She dug her fingers into his hair and pressed against him. This time, her heart wasn't melting. It was on fire!

A knock sounded on the door, but they ignored it. Another knock, this time louder.

He broke the kiss and leaned his brow against hers as they caught their breath.

Another knock. "We've brought a bath for the mistress," a male servant shouted.

Quentin strode to the door, unlocked it, and cracked it open. "We didn't order a bath."

"It was a gift from Wilbur and Dewey," the servant explained as he pushed open the door. A dozen servants barged into the room, carrying a tin tub and buckets of hot water. They set it all down in the middle of the room, then filed out the door.

"Well, that was very kind of Wilbur and Dewey," Eviana murmured.

Quentin sighed. "I don't know if they're angels or demons."

"Angels," she told him, then eyed the tub. "I don't think it would be too crowded."

"We're not—"

"We proved it would be possible against the door." She lifted her chin. "I think we could—"

"Nay." Quentin frowned at her. "I'm going now to check on Elam and Olana. I'll send her up here—"

"Quen—"

"We can't let this happen again." He gave her a sad look. "I'm sorry."

Oh, dear goddesses. He was still determined to reject her. "It will happen again, Quen. We're in love—"

"Don't say it." He backed toward the entry. "Lock the door behind me. Wedge a chair beneath the latch." He slipped outside and closed the door.

She trudged slowly toward the door and turned the key. As she dragged a chair over, her eyes filled with tears. Their little moment of passion had been glorious. Wild and desperate and so filled with love.

How could he reject that?

Chapter 19

What a fool he was, Quentin thought as he rushed down the stairs. Had he really thought that giving in to the urge for one kiss would satisfy the longing that had built up for six years? That one kiss had only made him hungry for more. Hell, it had left him desperate. Thank the goddesses, the tavern was empty now, and no one could see him roaming about with a bulge in his breeches.

He stepped outside and paused for a moment to let the cool night air chill the heat that had overwhelmed him. He should have resisted. He never should have kissed her.

It will happen again, Quen. We're in love.

No, it couldn't happen again. But hadn't she admitted that she loved him?

It makes no difference, he quickly reminded himself before his heart could sing with joy. Her parents would never accept him. Her brothers would want to kill him. Hell, the entire country would want him exiled for daring to touch their princess.

This harsh dose of reality made the swelling in his groin go down as he headed for the stable. It was dark inside, with only a little light from the stars and twin moons shining through the open windows. Luckily, his vision was still good, and he was able to maneuver around the buckets of water and piles of straw. He spotted Daisy in a stall, sleeping, and

Elam's horse in the next stall. At the far end of the stable, the cart had been parked.

Quentin approached quietly and peeked into the wagon bed. Elam had shoved the crates of wine and the trunk of male clothing to one side and set the baskets of food on top, leaving more space in the bed. He'd added more straw as a cushion, and he and Olana were snuggled up together beneath the picnic blanket.

With his military training, Elam was a light sleeper, and he woke, his eyes narrowing on Quentin in the dark as he reached for a knife wedged between the two crates.

"It's just me," Quentin whispered. "Olana can go sleep with Eviana now."

"She's already asleep." Elam let go of the knife handle and adjusted the blanket around Olana's shoulders. "Go. You can't leave the mistress unguarded."

Quentin winced. "I can't spend the night alone with her."

"Why not? Are you going to be dishonorable?"

"Of course not."

"Then go." Elam waved his hand at him in a shooing gesture. "Leave us."

With a sigh, Quentin trudged out of the stable. What to do? Elam was right that they couldn't leave Eviana unguarded. But she was taking a bath right now. An image of her removing her clothes popped into his mind, and he quickly squelched it before his lust could be reawakened.

He strode toward the inn, looking around and spotting no one. The villagers had all gone home and were probably fast asleep. All he could hear was the occasional hoot of an owl and the sound of rushing water from the nearby falls.

That was what he needed, he decided as he jogged toward the stone bridge. A quick dip in cold water would keep him in check. Next to the bridge, he found a footpath that went upstream. He followed the rushing water until he reached a spot where large boulders had created a deep pool. He stripped and lowered himself into the water.

Icy cold. He hissed in a breath, then quickly washed himself and dipped beneath the surface to rinse off his hair.

Back on shore, he pulled on his clothes, but they quickly became damp, keeping him chilled to the bone. His frozen feet ached as he pulled on his boots. With his teeth clenched, he hobbled back to the inn. By the time he made it up the stairs, his teeth were chattering.

He knocked softly on the door. "Evie?" He heard some splashing noises. Was she still in the tub?

"Quentin?" she whispered on the other side of the door.

"Aye." A shudder racked his body. "It . . . it's me."

"Just a minute."

He waited, hugging himself and pacing back and forth to try to warm himself up.

The door cracked open, and she peered out at him. "What is it? I thought Olana was—are you all right? You look a little blue."

"I-I'll be guarding you tonight."

"You're shivering." She opened the door wider. "Come in."

He headed straight for the hearth and added another log. The fire grew hotter, and with a shaky breath, he turned, letting the heat seep into the back of his legs.

Eviana had closed the door and turned the key. She had on a nightgown, covered with her woolen travel cape. Her feet were bare, and her hair damp and loose down her back. She must have dressed in a hurry when he'd knocked on the door.

"What happened?" She approached him, looking him over. "Your clothes are damp and clinging . . ." Her eyes lingered on his wet shirt for a moment; then she quickly retrieved a towel from the back of a chair. "I already used this, but perhaps it will help."

"Thank you." He rubbed the towel over his wet hair.

Her eyes narrowed. "Did you fall into the creek?"

"Yes. On purpose."

She scoffed. "If you wanted a bath, you could have had it here." She motioned toward the tub.

That would have been dangerous. He turned to face the fire and rubbed the towel over the damp shirt that had molded itself to his chest. "Olana is fast asleep in the cart with Elam. And we couldn't leave you unguarded for the night. So . . ."

Eviana joined him by the fire. "You're spending the night here?"

"I'll be your guard." He handed her the towel. "I'll stay here by the fire. You can go to bed and forget I'm here."

She gave him an incredulous look. "You expect me to forget? After what you and I—"

"Don't talk about it. Or even think about it."

"By *it,* are you referring to that glorious moment of wild and passionate kissing?"

He shot her a look of warning. "That is not helpful."

"I haven't been able to think about anything else but our glorious moment of wild and passionate kissing."

He gritted his teeth. "Evie—"

"Especially while I was in the tub naked."

"Go to bed."

She hesitated, watching him closely. "Is that what you want?"

"I want you to sleep. We have to travel tomorrow." He sat cross-legged on the floor in front of the hearth. "Good night."

With a sigh, she walked toward the bed. He glanced sidelong at her when she paused for a moment to drape the towel over the back of a chair. The room darkened as she blew out the candle. He refocused on the fire in the hearth, and soon, he could hear the rustle of bedsheets.

He pulled off his boots and stretched his chilled feet toward the fire. More rustling noises behind him. She seemed to be tossing and turning quite a bit. He unbuttoned his still-damp shirt. Once she fell asleep, he would take it off so it could dry.

"This won't do," she announced behind him, and he glanced back to find her pulling the down-filled comforter off the bed. Her cape was off, and he couldn't help but notice how thin her nightgown was. He could actually see the outline of her legs, the contour of her hips.

This was dangerous. "What are you doing?" he asked as she dragged the comforter toward him.

"You have to fly all day tomorrow, so you need to sleep, too." She laid the comforter out on the floor beside him, then dropped a pillow on top. "There."

"Won't you be cold without it?" he asked as she returned to the bed.

"I'll be fine. I have a blanket. And this cape." She spread her cape on top of the blanket, then climbed back into bed. "Good night."

"Good night." He watched her for a while. She was curled up with her back to him.

When he thought she was asleep, he removed his damp shirt, then stretched out on the comforter close to the fire. He watched the flames for a while, then fell fast asleep.

Sometime in the night, after the fire had dwindled down, he awoke to find Eviana trying to quietly add a log.

He sat up. "Let me do that."

"I didn't want to wake you," she whispered. "Sorry, but I was cold."

"It's my fault." He took the log from her. "I should have kept the fire going." He built up the fire until it was roaring, then looked up, surprised to see that she had brought the other pillow and blanket back to the hearth. "What are you doing?"

"The bed is cold. And it's nice and warm here." She settled on the comforter next to the fire and shook out the blanket so it would be on top of her.

"This is not a good idea, Eviana."

She snuggled under the blanket, her head on her pillow. "I'm not afraid of you, Quen."

"You should be."

"Oh, I'm scared," she muttered, then closed her eyes.

She didn't think he was dangerous? Somehow that pricked at his pride, and he was tempted to rip her blanket off and warm her up with kisses. But he wouldn't, dammit. She was right. He loved her too much to take advantage of this situation.

With the fire blazing, he stretched out on his back on the far side of the comforter, trying to leave as much space between them as possible. He lay still, listening to the sound of her breathing and wondering if she was asleep.

"One of the problems with long hours of travel is I have too much time to think," she said softly.

So she wasn't asleep but thinking. "I have that problem, too."

She rolled onto her back, and he looked at her. She was watching the flickering firelight that danced across the ceiling. "I was truly touched by your story of growing up on the Isle of Secrets."

Because she also felt trapped? He was tempted to ask her about that, but kept his mouth shut. The last thing they needed was to feel closer.

"I'm so glad you were able to escape," she said softly.

He recalled the tremendous surge of freedom he'd felt when he'd first gone to Norveshka with Silas and Gwennore. "When I went to Norveshka and saw the huge mountains and forests spreading out as far as I could see, I was awed by the vastness of it all. It felt like nothing could ever trap me again."

"That's how I felt." She smiled as she rolled over to face him. "But the adjustment must have been difficult for you."

He shrugged. "I had to learn Norveshki. Gwennore hired a tutor to help me catch up with my schooling. It was challenging, but I never found it too difficult. I had been so starved for knowledge on the island that I devoured my lessons as fast as I could."

"And you learned to read and write all four languages?"

He glanced at her. "You had to do that, too. Didn't you?"

She nodded. "When did you shift for the first time?"

"I was fourteen." Once again, he wondered what had happened to Eviana when she was thirteen. Was that when her gift had manifested itself?

She cushioned her head on the crook of her arm. "While we were traveling, something occurred to me. I kept thinking about your story and how much you wanted to escape the island, and I realized that even if Nevis and Elinor had never arrived there, you would have escaped eventually on your own when you shifted. You would have been able to fly away."

He'd never thought of that. "That's true."

"So it was never in your destiny to remain trapped by the circumstances of your life. Your gift gave you exactly what you wanted. What you needed. The ability to escape and be free."

He turned onto his side to face her. "And you? You said you felt trapped, too."

She glanced away, looking embarrassed.

"Is it because you're a princess? And an heiress?"

She sighed. "That's part of it. All my life, it has felt like my entire future was already decided for me."

He could definitely understand that. The circumstances of his birth affected everything in his life, too. He could never be more than a servant.

"And part of it is because of my gift," she continued. "Papa has always worried that I could be used as a weapon, so I was kept somewhat . . . isolated."

She'd been made into an outcast, Quentin thought with a prick of annoyance. He, too, knew how that felt.

She rolled onto her back to stare at the ceiling. "I think the feelings of entrapment actually began when I was kidnapped at the age of three. When the dragon snatched me up, it wrapped its claws around me so tight. I couldn't escape. I could hardly breathe. The terror I felt was overwhelming. I remember thinking over and over, *Make it stop. Make it stop.* And then I blacked out."

Quentin sat up and could see the tears glistening in her eyes. "Evie . . . it grieves me that you had to experience such terror."

She blinked away her tears and looked at him. "But what occurred to me is now, I *can* make it stop. If something dangerous threatens me, I have the power to stop it. My gift gave me what I most needed. Just as yours did."

He widened his eyes. "I never thought of it that way. Are you saying we somehow chose the gifts we received?"

"I think it might be possible. Or perhaps the goddesses simply gave us what we needed the most."

He sat back, thinking that over. "I doubt your father would have ever asked for the power of lightning."

"No. He never would have wanted it. But didn't he need it? King Frederic tried several times to kill him, and it was his lightning power that protected him. And I doubt Uncle Rupert would have survived without his power. Or my uncles Brennan and Brody."

Quen nodded. "It's an interesting idea, though I'm not sure if it works in every case."

She shrugged. "Maybe not. But in our cases, I definitely

think we both unconsciously asked for our gifts and were fortunate enough to receive them. And we both needed our gifts so we wouldn't feel trapped."

How could he have so much in common with a princess? As he gazed down at her, so lovely in the firelight with her long black hair strewn across the white pillowcase and her eyes looking at him so softly, he could feel the pull. The longing. The promise of a lifetime of love and passion.

He couldn't let it happen.

"Good night, Evie." He jumped to his feet and retrieved her cape from the bed. Using it as a blanket, he curled up on the edge of the comforter, his back to her. Her scent was in the cape, and he breathed it in deeply, willing himself to sleep.

Exhaustion, together with the heat of the nearby fire, lulled Eviana into a deep sleep. But sometime before dawn, when the fire had dwindled and her body had sought heat, she'd rolled closer to Quentin. Slowly she became aware that one of her legs was hooked over his and her arm was draped across his bare chest.

She blinked awake. The cape must have fallen off him when he'd rolled onto his back. He seemed sound asleep. The steady rise and fall of his warm chest beneath her hand was comforting and felt so right. Wasn't this how she wanted to wake every morning?

The memory of their passionate kissing hovered in her mind, refusing to be ignored. She'd felt so loved, so desired, so overwhelmed with a need to love Quen back. She'd wanted to fall headlong into the dreaded disaster he had warned her about. Didn't she want that same feeling every night?

And the closeness she had felt when they'd talked—didn't

she want that every day? There was no point in denying it anymore. This wasn't a passing phase, a temporary infatuation. It felt as natural as breathing, but as essential as air. She wanted him in her life every day. She loved him.

But he kept rejecting her.

She eased away from him, moving her leg back and slowly retracting her hand. Suddenly, he grasped her hand to stop her. With a small gasp, she glanced up at him and found him looking at her.

"Sorry," she whispered. "I thought you were asleep."

He said nothing, just looked at her, his golden eyes growing more heated with desire.

She licked her lips, and when his gaze lowered to her mouth, her heart started pounding. Were they about to have another bout of wild and passionate kissing? "Are . . . are you thinking about the dreaded disaster?"

"Aye."

"Does it have to be disastrous? Surely, a few kisses would be—"

"I would want more."

Her heart lurched. "What if I want more, too?"

His grip on her hand tightened. "Do you?"

Tears burned her eyes as the confession welled up inside her. "I'm in love with you, Quen."

Heat flared in his eyes. "Are you sure it's not just gratitude? Or a rebellion against feeling trapped? Or—"

"Stop." She jerked her hand from his grasp as she sat up. This blasted man. "It took a great deal of courage for me to confess my feelings, and you don't even believe—"

"I believe you." He sat up. "The problem is me. I'm not—"

"Don't!" She glared at him. "Don't you dare say you're unworthy. So help me, I'll . . . I'll . . ." She scoured her brain for a suitable punishment, but only one thing came to mind. "I'll seduce you."

His eyes grew wide. Then his mouth twitched. "In that case, I'm extremely unworthy." He spread his arms to the sides. "Do your worst."

Her cheeks flamed with embarrassment. But she'd tossed the gauntlet; she could hardly stop now. And it served him right for constantly rejecting her.

She reached out to cup his cheek, and he tilted his head to rest in her hand. The slight tickle of his whiskers against her palm made her pulse race even faster. What now? she wondered. With her other hand, she dragged her fingers down his neck, across his shoulder, then down his chest. His muscles were taut, his skin smooth and warm. Leaning forward, she planted a kiss on his chest and felt it instantly expand.

"Eviana." He gently moved her back. "You should stop now."

"But I've barely started."

"Sweetheart, I'm already seduced. I've been that way for six years."

Her heart swelled. "What was it that attracted you? Was it love at first sight?"

"Nay. When I first saw you, you were only three. We were in the Great Hall at Aerie Castle, and Maeve used her magic to make it safe for your father to embrace you and your brother for the first time."

She smiled. "I remember that. You were there?"

He nodded. "And then later, when I was in Norveshka, I asked Gwennore about you, and she told me how you had been kidnapped. I thought you must be incredibly brave. And then, years later, I saw you on the Spring Embrace when you turned seventeen. You were so beautiful, so happy, so full of life—how could I not fall for you?"

The warmth of a blush stole across her face. "Over the last few years, I kept catching you looking at me. And I wondered if it was simply part of your spying, or if you actually liked me."

His eyes widened in shock. "I didn't think you even knew I existed."

She snorted. "I was fascinated with the handsome and mysterious spy who could shift into a magnificent eagle." She smiled as she repeated his words. "How could I not fall for you?"

He looked away with a grimace. "I don't know if this is a miracle or a disaster. I don't want you to become too attached to me. Your family will never accept me, and I cringe to think how much you could suffer because of me. I don't want that for you. I love you too much."

He loved her. "Quen." She wrapped her arms around his neck and ran kisses along his jawline.

"Evie." He grasped her by the upper arms. "I'm barely—" He moaned when she brushed her lips against his mouth.

"I want you," she whispered.

His grip on her arms tightened for a few tense seconds, and she prayed for his resistance to finally break. Suddenly he pushed her down onto the comforter and planted his mouth on hers.

Yes! She returned his kiss, reveling in the way he molded his mouth against hers. Goodness, but she'd had no idea that a kiss could be this interesting. Or last this long. There was nibbling and sucking and then, the shock of his tongue entering her mouth. And somehow, the sensations in her mouth made her feel sensitive over her entire body.

She wanted him to touch her. "Quen." She broke the kiss to breathe heavily against his mouth. "I want more. I want it all."

"Evie." He trailed kisses along one side of her neck while dragging his hand down the other side, finally coming to rest at the low neckline of her nightgown.

"Tell me when to stop." He moved his hand slowly over the thin fabric, and she gasped as his fingertips grazed her nipple.

"Don't stop."

He quickly undid a few buttons, then pushed aside the fabric to expose one of her breasts.

"Quen." She didn't know which was more exciting—the look of adoration on his face or the soft groan that escaped from his mouth.

He gently cupped her breast, then leaned down to flick his tongue against her tightening nipple.

"Oh." She delved her hands into his hair. "Yes," she gasped when he sucked her nipple into his mouth.

A knock sounded at the door, and they both froze for a second. With a gulp, she realized that the sun was shining brightly through the window. How long had they been kissing?

Another knock. He sat up with a wary glance at the door.

"Quen?" Olana called softly from the hallway. "Mistress Evie, are you awake?"

Eviana sat up, quickly rebuttoning her nightgown. "We're . . . Just a minute."

Quentin jumped to his feet, looked down at his breeches, and muttered a curse.

Eviana's eyes widened at the sight of the bulge. Goodness, if they hadn't been interrupted, they might have . . . she quickly scrambled to her feet.

"The trunk of women's clothing is in there," Olana said softly. "I'd like to change into a new gown."

"Of course." Eviana bundled up the blanket and comforter and quickly dumped them back on the bed. Then she tossed the pillows on top.

Meanwhile Quen had thrown on his shirt, leaving it untucked to cover the bulge. He sat in the chair to pull on his boots.

Eviana found her cape on the floor and settled it over her shoulders. Holding the edges together with one hand, she unlocked the door with the other. "Olana, please come in."

Olana slipped inside. "Good morning." As she scanned

the room to locate the trunk, her gaze lingered on the bed for a moment.

Eviana winced. The bed looked like the site of a wrestling match. She strode toward the foot. "The trunk is here."

"I see." With her cheeks turning pink, Olana glanced over at Quentin, then back to Eviana.

Quentin strode toward the door. "I'll leave you two alone then."

"Wait." Olana raised a hand to stop him. "Elam wanted me to tell you that he woke early and saw Father John before the sunrise mass. Father John confirmed everything Titus told us. He said we should head straight to Arondale. The priest there, Father Renard, has the sun tattoo on his forearm, and he wears the ring of poison. If I question him, we might learn where the Brotherhood is located."

Quentin nodded. "Then we should leave as soon as possible. I'll buy some fresh bread—"

"That's not necessary," Olana interrupted. "Elam has already bought some supplies and he sold one of the crates of wine to the tavern owner here. I hope you don't mind." She glanced at Eviana. "Elam thought it best for us to act like real wine merchants."

"He did the right thing," Eviana agreed. "And it was very kind of him to take care of so much business this morning."

"Yes, well . . ." Olana glanced at the bed once again. "He thought we should leave you alone for a while."

Eviana's face heated up, and even Quentin's cheeks were a bit rosy.

"I'll see you outside." He hurried out the door, closing it firmly behind him.

Ignoring the blush on her cheeks, Eviana opened the trunk and pulled out two plain woolen gowns. "Which one would you like?"

"This one will do." Olana pointed at the dull brown one, then turned her back to Eviana. "Could you untie my laces?"

"Of course." Eviana's hands trembled a bit as she realized the full import of the night she'd spent with Quentin. The confessions had been made; the resistance had shattered. They both wanted each other, and they both knew it.

"Are you all right?" Olana asked softly.

Eviana drew in a deep breath. "I've fallen in love."

Olana nodded. "I believe I have, too."

Chapter 20

This plan could actually work, Bran thought as he helped his brothers unload crates of wine and cider at the only tavern in the small village of Southbrook, located on the main road to Vindalyn.

Two days ago, Bran had teetered on the edge of despair when the mission had been given to his brother, but Arlo had remained calm. The trick to defeating an Embraced person was to render their gift useless, Arlo had claimed. Since Princess Eviana's power could put people to sleep, they had to put her to sleep first. And if the soldiers and dragons guarding her were also sound asleep, then it would be a simple task to abscond with her.

Bran and his brothers had spent all day yesterday at the monastery concocting a potent sleeping drug that could be mixed with wine and apple cider. After bottling the tainted concoctions, they had filled ten crates. Early this morning, they had loaded the crates into a wagon, and, dressed as merchants, Arlo and Zane had started driving to Southbrook. Bran had flown off in raven form, so he could locate the queen's caravan.

When he found it, the soldiers had broken camp and were filing onto the main road to begin their journey for the day. He estimated they would arrive in the village of Southbrook by midafternoon. Since Southbrook was the last village before reaching the Ron River, it was the obvious place for the caravan to replenish its supplies.

By this evening, the caravan would arrive at the ferry that crossed the Ron River. The ferry was closed at sunset, so the caravan would have to make camp for the night. Then they would drink the wine and cider laced with the powerful sleeping potion.

After checking on the queen's progress, Bran had flown south till he spotted his brothers. He'd swooped down to land in the wagon bed, then he'd dressed in the merchant's clothes that Arlo had left for him. Soon after that, they had arrived at the tavern in Southbrook where they were now unloading the crates and stacking them on the front porch.

The door opened and the tavern owner peered out at them. "What are you doing?" He stepped out onto the porch, giving them a wary look. "I've never seen you before."

"This is the wine and cider you ordered." Arlo activated his gift as he approached the tavern owner. "We make deliveries to you every month."

The owner looked confused. "You do?"

"Yes. You ordered all of this a week ago," Arlo replied, looking into the man's eyes. "And a good thing you did, since the queen's caravan will be coming through today. You'll be able to sell this to the travelers and make a handsome profit."

The owner nodded slowly. "Yes, we will."

"What is all this?" The owner's wife peered through the doorway. "I don't remember paying for it."

"You did a week ago." Arlo broadened the focus of his power. "And you should be able to sell it all to the queen and her soldiers this afternoon."

The wife blinked. "Oh. That's good."

"We'll leave you, then." Arlo climbed back onto the

driver's bench alongside Bran, and Zane settled in the wagon bed.

"So far, so good," Bran whispered as they drove away.

They headed down the main road toward the ferry and the campsite where the caravan would have to stop for the night. Bran and his brothers would hide in the woods, waiting for the queen and her daughter and their troops to drink the potion and fall asleep.

It was possible that some of the soldiers on duty might not drink, so Arlo had planned for the likelihood of a small skirmish. They had an assortment of weapons in the wagon, and they had asked ten young monks who had been trained in warfare to assist them. The monks were supposed to arrive before nightfall.

If all went well, they would kidnap the princess tonight and transport her to the monastery, which was only ten miles west of the ferry.

This could work, Bran thought once again. It had to work, for a failure would cost Arlo his life.

Late that afternoon, Quentin spotted the village of Arondale up ahead. It seemed uncanny to him that it had been only five days since he had last been there. Five days since he'd rescued Eviana from the Ebe River. On that day, he'd managed to fly from Ebton to Arondale and back to Benwick, but now, he had to maintain the snail-like speed of the cart below.

It had taken them three days to make their way back to Arondale, and in those three days, so much had happened. So much that shouldn't have happened, he reminded himself for the hundredth time. Six years of longing had overwhelmed him last night. He shouldn't have capitulated, but his resistance had crashed when Eviana had kissed him and told him she wanted him.

How could he resist her when he loved her? But at the same time, how could he set her up for heartbreak when he loved her?

They had stopped briefly for a picnic lunch that had proven somewhat awkward, with each couple stealing silent glances as they avoided speaking about last night's sleeping arrangements. Quentin had outlined his strategy for dealing with Father Renard in Arondale. As soon as they discovered where the Brotherhood of the Sun was hiding, he would fly to the queen's caravan to let her know. Then the two dragons could report to Leo and Nevis, and within a few days, the Brotherhood would find themselves surrounded by the Eberoni army.

After lunch, he began to see more traffic on the road. Arondale was not only a pilgrimage site for the ill and infirm, but a place of relaxation and rejuvenation for those who enjoyed the hot springs. And so, as they drew closer to the village, he saw more people on horseback, a few wealthy merchants and nobles riding in expensive coaches, and farmers driving wagons with an ill or crippled family member lying on a bed of straw.

About a mile from Arondale, he swooped down to land beside the road, where he could go into the woods, shift, and dress. Olana was tired of driving, so she climbed into the wagon bed, while Quentin sat beside Eviana and took the reins. The land had become much more hilly and the pine forests were now thick on either side of the road. The air was chilly and crisp with the scent of pine.

As they reached the outskirts of the village, Eviana murmured, "What a lovely place. But it's much more crowded than I had expected it to be."

"Is this where the Ron River begins?" Olana asked.

"Not exactly," Quentin replied. "The river actually starts about twelve miles upstream, but it's just a tiny creek until the five springs here feed into it."

Elam steered his horse close to the wagon. "Can you tell us more about how Victor was murdered?"

"Aye," Quentin answered. "He drowned in the river, which I thought was odd, since it's only about four feet deep. And then I found out his gift was the ability to hold his breath for a long time, so his death seemed even more odd. When they pulled him out, they discovered his head had been bashed in."

Eviana shuddered.

Olana sighed. "I'll make the priest tell us what he knows."

The traffic became more congested and they had to wait their turn to cross the narrow stone bridge over the rushing river. On the other side, they followed the main road and discovered a dozen taverns and inns.

Soon, they had two rooms reserved in a modest-looking inn, and they sold the last of the wine to the owner. They locked their trunks in the rooms and left the horses and cart in the stable. Quentin and Elam each stuffed a small pouch of gold coins into their pockets; then they all set out for the springs and nearby chapel.

The road was filled with tourists buying food and knick-knacks, and ill people hobbling with canes toward the springs. A few crippled people were being pushed in small carts.

A drunk tourist bumped into Olana, nearly falling on top of her. When she pushed him off, he announced, "I took a piss while I was in the first pool."

The crowd of people yelled at him, and he dashed away with a few angry people chasing him.

With a wince, Olana pulled her travel cape tighter around herself. From then on, Elam made sure to place himself between her and the crowd.

They soon discovered that the entrance to the chapel was locked and the springs were fenced off. No one could bathe in the springs or see Father Renard without first paying an

admission fee. Those who were deemed healthy were required to stand in line, while the crippled and infirm were allowed to go to the front of the line. Apparently, the springs
had become so popular, the villagers had decided to limit
how many people could partake of the healing waters at one
time.

The sun was lowering toward the horizon by the time
Quentin and his companions made it to the front. There was
a table set up and six village men, armed with knives, were
guarding the iron caskets filled with coins.

The woman seated at the table looked them over. "All four
of you want to experience our sacred healing waters?"

"Actually," Quentin replied, "we would like a word with
your priest."

"We're on a pilgrimage," Eviana added. "And we hope to
gain his blessing."

The woman nodded with a bored look as if she'd heard it
a million times before. "No one can see Father Renard unless
they partake of the healing waters first. Your body and soul
must be purified before you can fully receive his blessing. Entrance to the springs will be two gold coins apiece."

Eviana gasped. "And what happens to those who are ill
but poor?"

The woman shrugged.

Quentin exchanged a wry look with Elam, then they counted
out eight gold coins and set them on the table.

The woman snatched them up and dumped them into the
nearest iron casket. "In order to maintain the purity of our
healing waters, you will be required to wash off first in our
bathhouse and then put on one of our clean white robes. The
bathhouse is right over there." She pointed at a nearby building. "Women go to the middle door, and men to the one on
the left. The rental fee for the robes is one gold coin apiece."

Eviana gasped again. "This is outrageous—"

Quentin placed a finger on her mouth to stop her. "It's all

right, sweetheart. If the healing waters can help us have a child, then it is certainly worth it."

She nodded, then turned to the woman. "And after we experience the healing waters, we can see the priest?"

The woman shrugged. "His schedule is full, but he should be able to fit you in tomorrow morning."

"Tomorrow?" Quentin frowned. He was tempted to forget this nonsense and simply break into the chapel. But apparently, he would have to go through six armed men first.

The woman smirked. "Father Renard might be able to fit you in earlier if you're on the list of priority pilgrims."

With a sigh, Quentin pulled out his bag of coins once again. "How much?"

The woman smiled. "Another two gold coins apiece."

"They're worse than the highwaymen," Olana muttered, and the six men glared at her.

By the time Quentin paid, he was completely broke. But he wasn't too concerned, since he knew Elam had some coins on him, and there were a few more in the trunks locked in their room. Besides, they might learn everything they needed to know soon, and then their mission would be over.

The woman dumped their coins into the casket. "This one is full." She slammed the lid shut, then turned to the six men. "You can take it to the office."

The casket was so heavy, it took two of the armed guards to carry it off. As Quentin and his companions strode toward the bathhouse, he noted that the guards were headed the same way. They went into the door on the right, so that had to be the office.

Quentin and Elam went through the door on the left, and after they had washed and dressed, they met the women outside by the entrance to the first spring. He and his companions were all barefoot and dressed in plain white robes that buttoned down the front to the waist.

"After you." Quentin motioned for the women to enter

the pool first. Holding on to the wooden handrails, they descended the short staircase into the first pool.

As Quentin followed them, he was surprised by how large the pool was. It was still rather crowded, though. Since most of the infirm and disabled were unable to climb the steep staircase to the next pool, they remained in the first one.

He held onto Eviana's arm to keep her steady as they crossed the uneven stone floor. The brilliant blue water was pleasantly warm and reached to their thighs. The mist that hovered over the water's surface swirled around their waists and lent the pool a magical appearance. He could see why people thought the area was sacred. Along one side of the pool, a small waterfall poured into it from the next pool higher up the hill.

As he led Eviana toward the stairs, he heard Elam's whispered confession behind them. He must have grabbed onto Olana.

After climbing the steps, they reached the second spring and pool. It was a bit less crowded. Quentin kept ascending the steps until he and Eviana arrived at the fifth and last spring, surrounded on three sides by a thick pine forest. This pool was smaller, the water hotter, and the mist thicker. Unfortunately, it didn't have the privacy he was hoping for, since there were three other couples already there.

"Oh, how lovely." Eviana smiled as she settled on a stone bench that circled the perimeter of the pool.

"I do hope it will cure my leprosy," Quentin announced as he sat beside her, and the three other couples gasped and scurried down the steps.

Stifling a laugh, Eviana swatted his arm. "That was naughty."

He leaned close and whispered, "You haven't seen naughty yet."

She gave him a challenging look. "Is that a threat or a promise?"

"It depends on whether you want it or not."

"Oh. I definitely—shh." She hushed him as Elam and Olana arrived.

"Sorry it took so long," Elam muttered. "We couldn't get to the steps. There was a herd of people rushing down them."

"Yes," Olana agreed. "Everyone seems to be leaving for some reason."

"How interesting," Eviana murmured, casting an amused look at Quentin.

Beneath the water's surface, he felt her hand brush against his thigh. He grabbed her hand and laced his fingers with hers.

"Oh, my, what a beautiful place." Olana looked around, her eyes wide.

"And experiencing it only cost us a small fortune," Elam added.

Olana settled onto the stone bench. "The water does feel very soothing, but I'm not sure how long I can endure the heat."

Elam sat beside her. "We can leave whenever you want. The sun is close to setting, so you might want to have dinner."

She nodded. "I hope the priest can see us tonight."

Elam snorted. "He must be the wealthiest priest in all of Eberon."

"I suspect some of the wealth is going to the . . ." Quentin glanced around but didn't see anything moving in the forest. "His fellow monks."

"The priest might be used to hearing confessions, but he'll be the one baring his soul tonight." Elam smiled at Olana with admiration in his eyes. "I can't wait till he meets the Confessor."

"I've been thinking about it all day," Olana admitted. "And coming up with all the questions I need to ask."

"I did some thinking, too, on the way here." Quentin leaned forward, and his companions moved closer in. "Once we learn the location of the Brotherhood and I leave to report it, the rest of you may have to leave, too. Our identities may be exposed at that point."

"True." Elam nodded. "There is an army fort northeast of here on the way to Mount Baedan."

Eviana held up a hand. "We should head south toward Vindalyn. We'll be safe there."

"It could take more than a day to get there," Elam countered.

"I know where you can go," Quentin said. "Peter's farm is southwest of here, and it's on the way to Vindalyn. No one would expect you to be there."

"Oh, I would love to see Peter again." Olana smiled. "And meet his family. He's told me so much about them in his letters."

"Then that's what we'll do," Elam agreed. "When Quentin returns, he'll be able to find us at Peter's house."

"If I'm delayed for some reason," Quentin added, "continue your journey toward Vindalyn. I'll be able to spot you from above."

"All right." Olana yawned. "I'm going to get sleepy if I stay here. Maybe I should wander around a bit and find out what the villagers know about Victor's murder." She stood up and smiled at Elam as he immediately stood beside her. "I think I'd like to try one of those meat pies they're selling along the main road."

"Sounds good." With a smile, Elam headed toward the steps. Suddenly, he halted, his eyes focused on the forest in front of him.

"Did you see something?" Olana stopped beside him.

"I'm not sure," Elam replied. "It's too dark."

Quentin spotted something furry scampering off into the woods. "Not to worry. It's just an animal."

Elam and Olana said their good-byes and headed down the steps to the next pool.

As the sun set, it painted the sky with brilliant reds and pinks and yellows. Quentin relaxed on the stone bench next to Eviana. He knew he should stay focused on the mission, but being here in this beautiful place with his beautiful Eviana, all he could think about was her.

When the last of the sun disappeared over the horizon, a loud voice shouted below, "The springs are now closed! Everyone should leave!"

Eviana huffed. "For as much as we spent, we should be able to stay as long as we like."

Quentin smiled. "Shall we be naughty and ignore them?"

"Yes, please." She returned his smile. "My back and rump are sore from sitting in the cart for three days, and this hot water feels wonderful."

He nodded. "I'm enjoying it, too." It was a hell of a lot better than last night's dip in the icy stream.

"Good." She lounged against the bench, dropping her head back to gaze at the stars. "Tell me more about yourself. How does it feel to fly? Was it scary when you first learned how?"

He shrugged. "I never found the flying that hard. It's the landing that can hurt."

She snorted.

"Tell me about yourself," he said softly.

"What's there to tell? Most of my life has been boring. Though I do seem to have something dramatic happen every ten years."

He figured she was referring to the kidnapping at age three. And now, at the age of twenty-three, she'd survived another attack. "What happened when you were thirteen?"

She glanced at him with a surprised look. "How did you know about that?"

"Your brother Eric mentioned it."

She scoffed. "Eric talks too much."

"He didn't say much, other than the fact that it was traumatic. Was that when your gift was first manifested?"

"Aye." With a sigh, she rested her head back, once again gazing at the stars overhead. "We were in the family drawing room, celebrating Dominic's birthday. I don't even remember what made us laugh so much, but I clapped my hands, and then suddenly, everyone collapsed."

She winced. "At first, I thought it was a jest of some kind and they were playing a game with me. But then . . ." She closed her eyes briefly. "No matter how hard I tried, I couldn't wake them up."

"That must have been terrifying," Quentin murmured.

She sat up and faced him. "For a few horrible seconds, I thought they had all died. But soon I realized they were simply asleep. I rushed off to find the castle physician, but everyone I passed in the castle was asleep—the guards, the servants, everyone. I couldn't understand why I was the only one awake. And that was when it hit me: I was awake because I had caused it."

Quentin drew in a deep breath. He couldn't imagine the fear she must have felt, being left entirely alone and feeling that she was to blame. "What happened? Did you wait until they woke up?"

Tears glistened in her eyes. "When I realized all the guards were asleep, I went into a panic. I was afraid someone from outside the castle could come in and kill my family. But then, as my panic grew, I wondered if there was anyone awake in the entire country, or the entire world. What if no one ever woke up, and I was doomed to be alone forever?"

Quentin squeezed her shoulder.

She blinked away her tears. "I finally decided I would have to protect my family. So I locked everyone inside the drawing room and took the key with me. I knew if my father woke up, he could use his lightning power to open the door. Then I saddled a horse and rode all the way to Benwick Castle. Everyone there was awake, thank the goddesses. Nevis took me and half the army back to Ebton. By then, my family was awake and frantically looking for me. And I had to tell them what had happened."

She looked away as a tear rolled down her cheek. "I think that was the worst part: seeing my father's face when he realized how dangerous I could be."

"Ah, Evie." Quentin pulled her into his lap and hugged her.

She leaned her head on his shoulder. "From then on, my gift was a closely guarded secret. My parents told everyone in the castle that we'd all been struck down by a mysterious illness. Since no one was hurt and it never happened again, it was soon forgotten." She sighed. "Of course my father never forgot. He's always been worried that I could somehow bring destruction to the family and the entire country."

Quentin rubbed her back. "That doesn't mean he ever loved you any less. Your whole family adores you and worries about you."

"They'll adore you, too."

He snorted. "They'll want to kill me for touching you."

With a smile, she laid her palm against his cheek. "Then you should do all you can to deserve that terrible fate."

"You want me to die?"

"No!" With a laugh, she gave his shoulder a playful shake. "I'm trying to convince you to kiss me again."

"Ah." He leaned forward and gave her a peck on the lips. "There you go."

She wrinkled her nose. "I thought you promised to be naughty."

He kissed her nose.

"If you can't be naughty, then I'll do it." She started unbuttoning his robe.

"Eviana, this is not—"

"Of course, I've seen your chest before." She reached the

fourth button. "Several times. Even so, it never ceases to amaze me."

Damn, but his resistance was crumbling. He never should have pulled her into his lap. He'd done it out of sympathy, but now the feel of her rump resting on his thighs was causing his groin to swell. "You should stop."

She kept going. "All those muscles are so enticing. Whenever I see them, I want to touch—"

"Evie." He put his hands on her shoulders to push her back, but after a few tense seconds, he pulled her close.

With a sigh, she wrapped an arm around his neck. "Doesn't it feel right to you, Quen? As if our whole lives have been waiting for this moment?"

He leaned back to look at her. The light of the twin moons reflected off her pale skin, making her look like a goddess. And the mist hovered around her as if she had magically appeared from the heavens. "I've never seen you so beautiful as tonight. No man on Aerthlan could be good enough for you."

Her eyes filled with tears. "I have no interest in other men. I can only see my golden eagle with his noble soul."

He leaned forward to kiss her gently. Then again. And again. Soon, his hands were tangled in her hair as he molded his lips against hers and invaded her mouth. His groin stiffened as she responded, moaning and stroking his tongue with her own.

Her hand slid inside his unbuttoned robe, and she smoothed her fingers over his chest and nipple. He reacted, dragging his hand down her wet robe till he could fill his palm with her breast. As he trailed devouring kisses down her throat, he rubbed his thumb over her nipple. Her robe was in the way, so he quickly unbuttoned it to the waist.

"Face me." He lifted her up so she could straddle his lap.

As she settled onto his thighs, she rested her feet on the stone bench, and her robe bunched up around her hips.

When he leaned forward to kiss her breasts, she groaned and held his head, her fingers delving into his hair.

His groin grew harder, and his heart pounded faster and faster. He needed more groans from her, more shudders, more panting breaths. He wanted to make her scream. As he suckled her breasts, his right hand smoothed up her leg and slid beneath her robe.

Her leg quivered as he caressed the soft skin of her inner thigh.

"Quen, what—" She gasped when he cupped her between the legs. "Oh."

After one last flick of his tongue on her hardened nipple, he sat back and looked at her. Her hair was wild, her cheeks pink, her mouth swollen, and her eyes wide with wonder.

He stroked her.

She gasped again, but now her eyes were filling with passion. "Quen."

"Do you want to be pleasured?"

She shuddered. "Yes. What do I do?"

"Close your eyes. Enjoy." He nuzzled her neck as he began to stroke her more firmly.

Soon she was panting and clutching at him, moving her hips in rhythm with him. He quickened his pace, and she stiffened, letting out a keening cry.

The feel of her shattering in his arms was more than he could bear, and he lost his seed against the robe he still wore. They held each other tight, and slowly, their breathing became more normal, and her sweet little shudders faded away.

"I had no idea it would be so . . . glorious," she whispered.

"We didn't actually . . . I mean, we did, but not . . ."

She sat back and looked down. "You . . ."

He winced. "So much for the purity of their sacred waters."

She snorted. "Quen."

"Yes."

She gave him a shy smile. "I have another proposition."

Oh, great. What was she going to propose now?

"Will you marry me?"

He flinched. *What the hell?* How could she even think of something that . . . wonderful. No, impossible.

Her smile faded. "Why do you look so shocked? After what we just did, I would think—"

"You don't propose marriage to a man just because he gave you a feeling of sexual fulfillment."

She frowned at him. "That seems like a good reason to me. Besides, there is much more to us than that, and you know it. So will you marry me?"

His heart clenched in his chest. "No."

Chapter 21

The plan was working, the Raven thought as he watched the nearby campsite from his perch in a tree. Just as he had figured, the queen's caravan had stopped before sunset to make camp on the north side of the Ron River, close to the ferry. Once the campfires were blazing, everyone had settled around them for food and drink. And now, shortly after sunset, almost all of them were sound asleep.

The door to the covered wagon was open, but no one had come out, so he assumed the queen and princess were inside asleep. A few guards were on duty, and they wandered around the perimeter of the camp, carrying torches, apparently not concerned that everyone had fallen asleep so early. By the weary looks on their faces, they were probably wishing they could sleep, too.

The Raven took flight to circle the campsite. He couldn't spot the dragons anywhere. Hopefully, they were asleep. According to the Brotherhood's spies in Norveshka, the dragons were shifters. Male shifters. That meant two of the men below were actually the amazing dragons he'd seen earlier in the day.

A thick braid of long white hair caught his eye, and he swooped around to get a better look. It was a woman. She was dressed in a tunic and breeches, like the other men around her campfire, but there was nothing masculine about her. On the contrary, the tight breeches only served to accent her curves. And even though her hair was white, she was young. Her ears were slightly pointed. An elf?

He circled again, fascinated, for he'd never seen an elf before. They were rumored to be beautiful, and that was certainly true. She was the most beautiful woman he'd ever seen.

What was she doing here, camped out with the Eberoni army? And what the hell was he doing? He needed to focus on the mission. Arlo's life was at stake.

He flew up higher for a bird's-eye view and counted six guards marching around the perimeter of the camp. The ten warrior monks from the monastery would be able to take them by surprise.

The Raven headed west and spotted his brothers on the narrow path that led to the monastery. They were still dressed as merchants and were waiting by the wagon they had used to haul the crates of wine and cider earlier in the day. If all went according to the plan, they would be putting a sleeping princess in the wagon soon and taking her back to the monastery.

As the Raven swooped down, he spotted the warrior monks waiting in the woods that lined the narrow path. They were not easy to detect, since they were dressed in black shirts and breeches. Their faces were visible now, but before attacking, they would cover the lower portion with black kerchiefs. Each one was armed with a sword and a few knives.

After landing beside the wagon, Bran shifted and pulled on the clothes he'd worn earlier in the day.

"Well?" Arlo approached him. "Are they asleep?"

"Aye. We can move in now." Bran motioned for the warriors to gather around. "There are six guards you will need to—" He paused, his nerves tensing when he spotted two more men in black emerging from the woods. Father Greer and his faithful hound dog, Father Horace. "What the hell are you doing here?"

"They came with the warriors," Arlo muttered.

"Master Lorne gave us permission," Greer said with an amused sneer. "He was concerned, as we all are, about the success of this mission."

Bran gritted his teeth. No doubt the bastard was hoping they would fail so he could make Arlo swallow his poison. "Stay out of our way."

With a worried look on his face, Zane tugged on Arlo's shirt. "Let's get started. We can't be sure how long the sleeping tonic will work."

"Aye, let's go." Arlo motioned for everyone to follow him.

As they hurried through the forest, Bran described the campsite and location of the six guards to the warriors.

"Knock them out if you can," Arlo told the warriors. "Killing should be the last option."

Greer snorted. "They're our enemy. We should kill the guards and as many of the soldiers as we can."

"While they're asleep?" Bran shot him a look of disgust.

"Shh." Arlo hushed them as they reached the edge of the forest. The campsite lay before them, well lit with numerous campfires.

Bran pointed out the guards with their torches, and the warrior monks spread out, moving quietly toward their marks. As one torch was extinguished after another, Bran and his brothers dashed toward the covered wagon.

They climbed inside, and, thanks to an oil lamp hanging from the ceiling, discovered the two sleeping women on the padded benches. On the floor, Bran spotted a half-empty bottle of tainted wine, alongside two wooden cups that were lying on their side as if they'd fallen when the women had collapsed.

"This one is the queen," Bran whispered as he pointed at

the older woman. She was dressed in a blue woolen gown with a matching cape trimmed with white fur.

So this was the woman who had earned his sister's loyalty by making her feel safe. Vera's words echoed in his head. *They would never abuse young children.*

A sharp jab of guilt struck him, and he suddenly felt too wretched even to gaze at the queen's kindly face. How could he do this? He was about to steal her daughter so the princess could be forced to assist in the murder of her own family. He'd avoided thinking about it all day, keeping his thoughts strictly focused on his brother Arlo's survival, but now, now that he saw the queen and her daughter lying here defenseless, he felt a terrible onslaught of shame. And deep down inside him, a sense of rage that had been slowly simmering for years.

"Then this is the princess." Zane leaned over the other sleeping woman. The way she had fallen onto the bench had caused the hood of her dark green cape to cover most of her face.

"I'll carry her," Arlo said.

A noise behind them made Bran spin around. Greer had climbed into the wagon.

"Get out," Bran growled.

Greer snorted. "Once again, you prove you're not worthy of inheriting the Brotherhood."

"That's not your decision to make," Arlo snapped. "Now go, so we can leave with the princess."

"Fools." Greer pulled a knife from his belt. "You would let an opportunity like this go to waste?" He stepped toward the queen. "The royal family is our enemy. If we kill the queen now, that's one less to worry about later." He adjusted his grip on his knife so he could plunge it into the queen's heart.

"No!" Bran grabbed him by the wrist to stop the downward strike.

Greer struggled to rip his arm free, but Bran held on. Then with a sneer, Greer activated his power, and shards of freezing ice stabbed Bran's hand.

"Bastard." Bran released him, then smashed his cold fist into Greer's jaw.

Greer stumbled back, and Zane grabbed him by the neck and shoved him against the wall.

"If you hurt my brothers, you will answer to me," Zane hissed.

Greer gulped. His freezing power didn't work well on the youngest of the brothers, since Zane's hands could heat liquid to a boil.

"Enough," Arlo told his brother.

As Zane released his hold, Greer glared at the three brothers. "Fine, then. I'll tell the master that you refused to kill the queen when you had the chance."

While Arlo and Zane exchanged a look as if they were wondering whether they should actually commit murder, Bran racked his brain for a reason why they shouldn't. Not just to protect the queen, but to keep his brothers as innocent as possible.

"We'll kidnap both of them," Bran suggested. "We can use the queen as leverage. The princess will do whatever we ask of her if we threaten to harm her mother."

Arlo's eyes widened. "You're right. If we take the princess alone, she might refuse to cooperate, even if it means her own death."

Zane nodded. "But she won't be able to watch her mother being harmed."

"Let's do it, then." Arlo scooped the princess up in his arms. The hood of her cape fell back, exposing her face.

Bran stiffened. *What the hell?* "Wait." He stopped his brother and took a closer look at the woman in his arms.

"What is it?" Arlo asked.

A chill skittered down Bran's spine. This was not the princess. For a few seconds, he considered keeping his mouth shut. If the master believed this was the princess, then Arlo would be safe. But this girl, whoever she was, would not have the princess's gift. The truth would eventually come out, and then Arlo would be expected to poison himself.

Bran's gaze shifted to the silver ring his brother was wearing. The real princess had to be found. Tonight, if possible.

"Get the queen," Arlo told his brother Zane.

"Wait a minute." Bran took a deep breath. "The royal family must have figured something like this could happen. This . . . this girl is not the princess."

Arlo stiffened. "What?"

Zane grabbed Bran's arm. "She has to be. You're mistaken."

Bran shook his head. "I saw Her Highness at the attack on the barge. This is not Princess Eviana."

Arlo's face grew pale.

Greer chuckled. "Then the mission is a failure, and you know what that—"

"The mission is not over yet," Bran growled. "It will succeed. Arlo and I will find the princess and bring her to the monastery. Zane, take the queen there for now. And keep her safe."

Zane nodded. "I will."

Greer smirked. "I'll return to the monastery, too, so I can tell the master how you failed."

Bran grabbed Greer by the shirt and jerked him forward. "We will succeed. If you tell the master otherwise, I will kill you myself." He pushed Greer away, and the bastard clambered out of the wagon.

Arlo looked deathly pale as he laid the girl back onto the bench. "How . . . how will we find the princess?"

Dammit to hell. Bran didn't know. The princess could be

hiding anywhere. A seed of panic took root in his heart, but he quickly smothered it. He had to keep his wits about him. Arlo's life depended on it.

"Don't worry," Zane said as he scooped up the queen in his arms. "I'll tell the master that you're bringing the princess. And he'll be very pleased to have the queen for a prisoner. All will be well." His eyes glistened with tears. "It will be all right, Arlo. We won't let anything happen to you."

"That is true," Bran agreed. "Come on. The princess might be here in the camp somewhere." He recalled the beautiful woman he'd seen before dressed in men's clothing. "She could be disguised as one of the soldiers."

As Zane carried the queen back to the wagon, Bran and Arlo dashed around the camp, checking each person. There was no woman with long black hair. The six guards were alive, but unconscious, and two had been seriously wounded. After doing their job, the warrior monks had returned to the wagon.

"Good luck," Greer called to Bran and Arlo; then he and Father Horace chuckled as they slipped into the woods.

"They're right," Arlo whispered, his face downfallen. "I failed."

"Don't say that." Bran gave his brother a shake. The rage deep inside him flared hot. "We have to fight this, Arlo. You can't give up!"

Arlo's eyes filled with tears. "But we have no idea where to even look."

"We will not accept failure." Bran wrenched his brother's silver ring off and threw it into the woods. "We'll take two of the horses here and be on our way." No matter what it took, he had to find the princess. And save his brother.

Eviana was ready to scream. Why did the blasted man keep rejecting her? It was obvious that he loved her. Tears blurred her eyes as she dashed into the women's room of the bathhouse.

Quentin had followed her as she hurried down the series of pools, and several times, he'd reminded her to be careful. Finally, in her frustration, she'd splashed water in his face. Why did he care if she fell and broke something? He'd already broken her heart. Wounded her pride. Stomped on her feelings.

Calm down, she told herself as she entered the dark changing room. Since the springs were closed, all the lamps in the bathhouse had been extinguished. There was only the light of glowing embers in the hearth to guide her across the room to the shelves where women stashed their clothes.

Luckily, her clothes were still there. But then, her woolen gown was such a drab color brown, who would want it? She removed her sodden white robe and grabbed a clean towel from the stack by the hearth. As she dried off, the sight of her bare skin brought back the memory of Quentin touching her. Kissing her. Pleasuring her. How could he make love so wonderfully and then reject her? *Don't think about him!*

But how could she not think about him? Their lovemaking had been so heavenly. She'd thought her proposal would be the perfect ending for such a beautiful night.

Was he next door in the men's room getting dressed? Maybe if she talked to him, she could convince him—She shook her head. She was not going to beg the blasted man.

She pulled on her plain white shift, and then the ugly brown gown on top. Reaching behind her back, she struggled to tighten the laces. Argh, could this night get any more annoying?

Loud voices interrupted her thoughts, and she realized the noise was coming from next door, where the office was located. She moved soundlessly across the floor and pressed her ear against the wall. It had to be thin, for she could hear every word the two men were saying.

"Father, you can't leave like this! How can we charge the pilgrims for your blessing if you're not here?"

"I'll send another priest. Now give me my gold!"

"You're taking too much!"

"This was all my idea! I made you fools rich. Now hand me that bag!"

There was a gasp. "Father Renard, put away the knife."

"You think I won't kill you? I killed two last week!"

Eviana pressed a hand to her mouth to keep from making any noise.

"Fine! Take the gold."

"About time."

Eviana heard heavy footsteps and then the slam of a door. Silently, she inched back to her clothes and slipped on her shoes and travel cloak. She tiptoed to the door and pressed her ear against it. It seemed quiet outside. Still, it might be wise to wait a minute before leaving.

Father Renard was definitely dangerous. He'd admitted to murdering two people, and one of them was probably Victor. He had also started the ruse here to get rich by taking advantage of the ill and disabled. But why did he want so much gold all of a sudden?

He was running away! Somehow, he must have known that he was about to be caught.

She cracked open the door and peered out. No one in sight. She made a mad dash for the main street and nearly collided with Quentin, who was waiting for her with Elam and Olana.

He grabbed her by the forearms. "Is something wrong?"

"I overheard Father Renard talking to another man in the office," she whispered. "He admitted to killing two people, and he took a lot of the gold. I think he's running away tonight!"

Quentin looked in one direction on the main street, while Elam and Olana scanned the other direction.

"Is that him?" Elam pointed at a thin man in the black robe of a priest. Behind his saddle, he had two bulky bags strapped across the horse's back. "He's the only priest I see."

"Get your horse and follow him," Quentin said. "I'll shift so I can track him from above."

As Elam ran for the stables, Quentin turned to Eviana and Olana. "Wait for us at the inn. We'll bring him back."

Eviana nodded. "Good luck."

He stepped into a dark alleyway. "Take my clothes back to the room."

"I will." Eviana turned her back so he could strip and shift. Soon, a large eagle swept overhead. She watched as he flew away, headed in the direction Father Renard was fleeing.

Please keep him safe, she prayed to the moon goddesses. For even though her pride was still stinging from his rejection, there was no way she would give up on him.

It took only a minute for Quentin to catch up with the man they assumed was Father Renard. He had to be the priest, Quentin thought. Not only was he wearing a black robe, but it looked as if he'd crammed too much gold inside his bulky saddlebags. His poor horse was struggling to keep a quick pace under the burden of so much weight.

The priest crossed the bridge to the north bank of the Ron River, and then turned onto a dirt road that followed the river in a westerly direction. Was he headed toward the place where the Brotherhood lived?

Quentin circled back to check on Elam's progress and guide him in the right direction. Elam followed him across the bridge and onto the road the priest was taking.

From there, Quentin sped up till he was flying over Father Renard. Elam urged his horse into a fast gallop. Soon, he passed by the priest, then turned and halted his horse to block the road.

"What are you doing?" the priest yelled. "Are you a bloody thief?"

Elam drew his sword. "Are you Father Renard?"

The priest gulped. "Pick on someone else." He planted a hand on his chest. "I'm just a poor servant of the people. I have nothing."

Elam glanced up at Quentin, who was circling overhead. "He's wearing the ring." He moved his horse closer and pointed his weapon at the priest. "If you don't want a taste of my sword, you will return to the village with me."

"Who are you?"

"I'm a colonel in the king's army, and you are a traitor to the crown."

The priest gasped. "No, I—" He looked around frantically. "You can't catch me!" He jumped off his horse, and his black robe landed in a puddle as a furry red fox emerged and dashed into the woods.

A shifter! Quentin flew after the fox as it darted through the forest. The priest must have been the animal that had hidden by the fifth pool to listen in on his conversation with Elam, Olana, and Eviana. Once the priest had realized he was in danger, he'd planned to escape in the dark of night.

The fox's eyes glinted in the moonlight as it spotted the eagle closing in. It zigzagged frantically through the trees, but Quentin could see the animal in the dark no matter how fast it moved. He zoomed down, weaving around the trees, getting closer and closer. Behind them, Elam was running through the forest, crashing through bushes to keep up with them.

After a sudden burst of speed, Quentin was able to drop down and dig his talons into fur. With a yelp, the fox pulled loose and dove under some bushes, but Quentin caught the animal's hindlegs in his grip.

The fox shifted into human form and kicked to get his legs free. "Get away from me!"

As Quentin shifted, he lunged forward to grab Father Renard's arms and pin him down.

The priest squirmed. "Let me go!"

"Don't even think about shifting," Quentin warned him. "My eagle loves the taste of fox."

The priest grew still, his eyes wide with fear.

Elam reached them and hauled the naked priest to his feet. "You're coming with us."

"You bastards," Father Renard hissed. "Who do you think you are, abusing a priest like this?"

"We'll be asking the questions." Elam dragged Father Renard back to the horses.

"You won't get anything from me," the priest boasted.

"We could get your gold," Quentin said wryly, and, with a growl, the priest lunged at him.

Elam jerked Father Renard back, twisting his arm behind his back, and the priest yelped in pain. "Cooperate, or we'll give all your gold away."

With a sullen look, the priest put his robe back on and climbed onto his horse. Quentin noted the sun tattoo on the man's forearm. His ring of poison must have fallen off when he'd shifted.

Elam took the reins of the priest's horse and tied them to his saddle. As the two started back to Arondale, Quentin shifted so he could fly overhead, keeping close to the priest so he would be afraid to shift.

Back in the village, Elam took Father Renard straight to the constable's office, while Quentin landed on the windowsill of his room at the inn and tapped the glass with his beak.

Eviana opened the window, and he jumped onto the floor.

"Here." She set his clothes beside him. "Olana's next door. I'll fetch her." She grabbed the key on the way out the door.

Quentin shifted and quickly dressed. As he stepped into the hallway, he found Eviana and Olana waiting for him.

"Did you bring the priest back?" Olana whispered.

"Aye, Elam took him to the constable," Quentin replied. "We should go there now."

After Eviana locked the door, she followed them down the stairs and into the main street. "Can we trust the constable? He might be one of the greedy villagers in cahoots with Father Renard."

She made a good point, Quentin thought. "Once Elam reveals that he's in the army and that the villagers' scam will be reported this evening, the constable will have to do what's right, or he'll find himself in prison." He gave the women a worried look. "It may not be safe for you to remain here tonight. You should go to Peter's house."

"We will," Olana assured him. Her eyes sparkled with excitement. "I have a feeling our mission will be over tonight."

Eviana nodded. "Thank the goddesses Quen and I stayed late at the springs, or I never would have heard the priest planning his escape." She gave Quentin a pointed look. "At least something good happened tonight."

He winced inwardly. She was still upset with him. He'd tried to explain himself at the springs, but she'd refused to listen. Instead, she'd hurried down the series of pools, her face flushed with embarrassment. And now, there was no time to talk.

He opened the door to the constable's office. A young deputy was on the night shift, and he had locked the priest into the one jail cell.

"This is Darren," Elam introduced the deputy. "He was Victor's best friend."

Darren bowed his head. "Thank you for investigating Victor's murder. The constable just brushed it off, saying a tourist probably did it, but I knew that couldn't be right."

"I'm afraid the constable may be in league with the priest," Elam muttered.

Quentin nodded. "You will have to be careful, Deputy."

Darren lifted his chin. "I'm not afraid of those bastards. And most of the villagers are sick of them ordering us about and keeping all the money for themselves. This used to be a holy place where poor pilgrims could seek help and be blessed. That was when Father Simon was in charge. But he died, and this . . ." He pointed at the priest in the jail cell. "This Father Renard replaced him and brought in his ruffians to get rich."

"Lies! All lies!" Father Renard shouted as he shook the bars of his jail cell. "Let me out. I'll pay you in gold!"

"Quiet," Elam ordered. "If you don't behave, I'm throwing your gold into the street for the villagers to collect."

The priest hushed but glowered at them all.

"We have some questions for you." Quentin reached through the bars to grab the priest's arm so he couldn't move out of reach. "Who killed Victor?"

"I already told that colonel I don't know," Father Renard hissed, then stiffened when Olana touched him. "I did it. The little sneak was going to report us to the king."

"You bastard," Darren growled. Whipping out his knife, he lunged toward the prison cell.

Elam grabbed his arm to stop him. "He'll pay for his crime, I promise you. But right now, we need to know more. And we need you to be our witness."

Darren took a deep breath. "Very well. But when we're done here, I'm telling everyone what this bastard did."

Father Renard's face grew pale. "The villagers will want to lynch me."

Quentin shrugged. "Then we'd better be quick with our questions. Did you kill the guard from Ronford Castle who murdered Uma?"

"I have no idea what—" Father Renard winced when Olana touched him. "Yes. I paid him well to do the job, but then the asshole came here and threatened to turn me in if I didn't pay him more."

Darren sat at his desk to take notes. "So he's confessed to two murders, and he financed a third murder."

"Where is the Brotherhood of the Sun hiding?" Olana touched the priest's arm.

He gritted his teeth as if he was fighting the compulsion to respond. "They . . . they're in the Monastery of Light, ten miles west of the Ron River ferry. Dammit!"

"And the leader?" Olana asked.

"Master Lorne. He's Lord Morris's younger brother." Father Renard sneered at them. "Do you think this will make any difference? The Brotherhood is everywhere. You'll never be rid of all of us. You can kill ten of us, and ten more will find you in your sleep and slit your throats!"

Olana grabbed his arm again. "What is your goal?"

"To take over the world and get rid of Embraced bitches like you!" Father Renard yelled, and Elam slammed a fist into his jaw.

He reeled back, and Quentin yanked him forward till he smashed into the iron bars.

With blood trickling from his mouth, Father Renard glared at them. "You will pay for this."

"Big talk for someone about to be lynched," Quentin muttered. He released the priest and turned to Darren. "I'll report this to the army tonight. Until the soldiers arrive, stand firm. Don't let anyone in here who might try to help the priest escape."

"I understand." Darren jumped to his feet and saluted.

"Oh, and he can turn into a fox," Quentin added.

Darren blinked. "What?"

"That's nothing!" Father Renard yelled, pointing at Quentin. "That bastard can turn into an eagle! And he threatened to eat me!"

Darren blinked again. "What?"

Eviana made a face. "You were going to eat him?"

Quentin gave her a wry look, then turned back to Darren. "He may try to escape as a fox, so be careful. Have your knife ready to skin him alive."

"What?" Father Renard yelped. "You can't do that!"

"I believe I can." Darren picked up his knife and gave the priest a speculative look. "For Victor."

"Let's go." Quentin opened the door, and he and his companions filed out onto the main street while the priest screamed for help.

A few villagers were passing by, and they stopped when they noticed their priest in jail.

"What's going on?" one of them asked.

"Some soldiers will be here soon," Elam told them, showing them the badge that identified him as a colonel. "The priest has confessed to the murder of Victor."

The villagers gasped, and soon they were running about spreading the news. Quentin figured the priest would be lucky if he was still alive by the time the soldiers arrived.

Back at the inn, they gathered in one of the rented rooms to make their plans. Elam would take Olana and Eviana straight to Peter's house for the night. Then, after they were well rested, they would resume their journey toward Vindalyn. It would not take long, since they were already on the south side of the Ron River.

"I'll fly west to find the queen," Quentin said. "Once I tell the dragons where the Brotherhood is located, they can report the location to the king and General Nevis. The four troops with the queen can march straight to the monastery. This could all be over by tomorrow."

Olana took a deep breath. "I hope you're right."

"Tell my mother that we're fine and not to worry," Eviana said.

Quentin nodded. "I will." He didn't know if Eviana was still angry, but he took a chance and reached for her hand. She didn't pull away. "I hate leaving you like this. I'll be worried about you the entire time I'm away."

"We'll be fine." Her eyes filled with tears as she gazed up at him. "The information we learned won't do any good unless you report it." She squeezed his hand. "Please be careful."

"You, too." He kissed her hand, then stepped behind a dressing screen to strip and shift.

They waved good-bye as he flew out the open window. As he raced in a westerly direction, his nerves tensed. If all went well, the threat of the Brotherhood would soon be over. But he had a terrible feeling that things would not go well at all.

Chapter 22

"**I** have an idea," Arlo said.

Bran drew in a sharp breath. Thank the Light, his brother was coming back to his senses. The shock of their initial failure to kidnap the princess had hit Arlo hard, and Bran had been terrified that his brother had given up.

The two horses they had stolen from the sleeping troops were saddled and ready to go, but Bran wasn't sure which direction to ride. His first inclination was to hide his brother someplace where he would be safe.

When Arlo took off running, Bran chased after him. "What are you doing?"

"There were six guards on duty." Arlo located the first guard, but one of the warrior monks had knocked him out cold.

The second guard was also unconscious, but the third one was awake. Barely. He had fought back and been wounded. The slash across his thigh was deep, and he was bleeding profusely, his face pale and clammy.

"He's a colonel," Bran said softly. "He could be in charge here."

Arlo took off his shirt and ripped it into strips.

"Who . . . who are you?" The colonel fumbled for his knife as he struggled to sit up.

Arlo knelt beside him and activated his power. "I'm your

general. What happened here?" He looped one strip a few inches above the wound and pulled it tight before tying it off.

"Nevis," the colonel whispered. "I think everyone was drugged. Two men attacked me." He grabbed Arlo's arm. "You have to hurry. They took Her Majesty."

"We'll find her. Don't worry." Arlo folded up another strip and pressed it against the wound. "Is the princess all right?"

The colonel nodded. "She'll be safe. Elam and Quentin will protect her."

The eagle shifter? Bran's pulse sped up. "Where are they?"

The colonel gave Bran a confused look. "Who . . . ?"

"He's with me." Arlo glanced up at Bran. "Hold this."

Bran knelt to hold the pad in place while Arlo tied another strip around the wound.

"Where did they take the princess?" Arlo asked.

The colonel closed his eyes. "Arondale."

Bran jumped to his feet. *Thank the Light.* "Let's go."

Arlo followed him, glancing back at the colonel. "With some luck, he might live, but I'm afraid he could lose the leg."

Bran scoffed. Even when his brother was in danger of losing his life, he could still worry about a complete stranger. It was just more proof that everything he and his brothers had been taught was a lie. All their lives, they'd been told that being Embraced meant they were evil, but Bran could no longer stomach the sick and perverted ways of the Brotherhood. They'd whipped his brothers, molested his sister, and now they would insist his brother commit suicide to show his damned obedience.

For all his life, Bran had accepted the hell they had raised him in. He'd complied while a kernel of rage had eaten at his guts. *No more!*

They mounted their horses and charged east along the dirt road beside the Ron River. With each mile that took them farther away from the monastery, Bran felt a sense of relief calming the fury inside him.

After about an hour, they reached the Earl of Ronford's estate, and Bran spotted Ronford Castle on a hill overlooking the river. A mile down the road, he turned north, taking a narrow track into the forest.

"Are you sure this is the way to Arondale?" Arlo asked as he followed.

"We're making a stop on the way." After a few minutes, Bran halted in front of a small hunting lodge and swung off his horse.

"Why are we here?" Arlo dismounted. "Aren't we in a hurry?"

"We are." Bran tied their horses to a hitching post. "And I can get there much faster if I fly."

"Then I'll follow—"

"No," Bran interrupted him. "When the princess figures out she's in danger, she'll clap her hands to put everyone to sleep, and that would include you. As the Raven, I'll be immune. Then I can shift and knock her out. But if you're there, I'll have to deal with two unconscious bodies."

Arlo frowned. "Then I'll use my power on her and convince her that we're friends."

"She'll clap her hands before you can get close enough," Bran argued.

Arlo huffed with frustration. "I don't want you to have to do this on your own."

Bran placed a hand on his brother's shoulder. "It will be easier for me if I know that you're safe. No one will ever know you're here."

Arlo glanced at the cabin. "What is this place?"

"The Earl of Ronford's hunting lodge. He's in mourning now for the death of his daughter, so he won't be using the cabin for a while." Bran rolled a large stone over and retrieved the key that had been hidden underneath.

"How do you know all this?" Arlo asked.

Bran shrugged as he unlocked the door. "I'm a spy." He

stepped inside. "After a day of flying, it becomes too difficult to shift back into human form in a village. There's the problem of having to steal clothes, and then I have no money for food or lodging. Knowing about places like this is how I get by."

Arlo gave him a sad look. "I didn't realize how lonely your life must be."

Bran snorted. "I never felt lonely, not when I knew I could always go home to you and Zane." Tears stung his eyes, and he blinked them away. "Wait for me here. I'll be back with the princess, and then we'll take her to the monastery."

Arlo nodded and gave him a quick smile. "Thank you, Bran."

As Bran headed out the door, the tears threatened to come back. He didn't know what he would do without his brothers. Without them, he would have succumbed to the rage inside him and either gone insane or committed mass murder at the monastery.

Calm yourself. He still had a long night ahead of him. After stripping, he left his clothes beside the front door. Then he shifted and flew toward Arondale.

When Quentin located the queen's campsite close to the ferry, his talons clenched. Something was wrong. There were no guards marching the perimeter. All the campfires had dwindled down to glowing embers, and everyone appeared to be asleep.

As he swooped around, he noticed that the man in charge, Colonel Miller, was injured. He landed beside the colonel and shifted. Someone had slashed the man's leg, but strangely enough, someone else had bound it up.

"Colonel Miller?" He tapped the man's shoulder.

"General Nevis," the colonel murmured. "Did you catch them?"

Nevis? "The general is here?" Quentin asked, but Miller had passed out again.

Quentin rose to his feet, looking around. A few of the guards were regaining consciousness, sitting up and rubbing their heads. He spotted Lenushka and Pendras on the ground by a nearby campfire and ran toward them. Pendras had a bag of clothing next to him, so Quentin pulled out a pair of breeches and put them on.

"Pendras." Quentin gave the dragon shifter a shake, and Pendras opened his eyes briefly before closing them again. "Pendras, wake up! What happened here?"

Pendras blinked as he struggled to stay awake. "I . . . I don't know."

Had they all been drugged? Quentin located a canteen and sniffed the contents. The water smelled fine. He pulled Pendras into a sitting position and handed him the canteen. "Drink."

Meanwhile, one of the guards stumbled toward them. "We were attacked. Caught by surprise."

"Who?" Quentin asked. "Was it the Brotherhood?"

"Don't know. There was a man dressed all in black. He came out of the woods so fast, I barely saw him before he clobbered me." The guard rubbed his head and winced.

Lenushka groaned as she sat up. "What happened?"

"You tell me." Quentin passed her the canteen of water. "I think you were all drugged. What did you drink?"

"Some wine we bought in the last village," Pendras replied.

Lenushka stiffened suddenly and looked toward the covered wagon. "They must have been searching for the princess."

Quentin's blood ran cold as he noted the open door. He dashed for the wagon with the dragon shifters stumbling after him.

Faith was starting to stir on one of the benches. The other bench was empty. Quentin's heart stuttered as he stared at it in shock.

"Holy Light," Lenushka whispered. "They took Luciana."

"What?" Faith asked in a groggy voice.

"The bastards took the queen," Pendras growled.

"*What?*" Faith sat up with a jerk, looking at the empty bench in horror.

Quentin clenched his fists tight, then forcibly relaxed them. "Pendras, I want to you to fly to Ebton to tell the king. And Lenushka, go to Benwick to tell Nevis. They'll bring the army here as quickly as they can."

Lenushka nodded. "All right."

"But we don't know where they've taken the queen," Pendras muttered.

"Most probably they took her to their monastery," Quentin replied. "I've learned its location, so we can catch them by surprise. It's only ten miles west of here."

Pendras's eyes lit up. "Then the four troops here can have the place surrounded by dawn."

Faith jumped to her feet. "I'll go fetch Colonel Miller."

Quentin winced. "He's badly wounded. Who's next in line?"

"That would be Captain Drew." Faith gave them a wry look. "I grew up at Benwick. I know everybody. Shall I go find him?"

"Yes, please," Quentin told her.

She paused at the open door. "I'm also a trained army medic. I'll have the colonel brought here so I can treat his wound." She hurried down the steps.

"What are you going to do?" Pendras asked Quentin.

Good question, Quentin thought as he left the wagon. Part of him wanted to join the force that would go to rescue the queen. But the other part, a more urgent part, was telling him to hurry back to Eviana. The Brotherhood had failed to capture her here. They would be desperately searching for her now.

Remain calm, he told himself. *Take this logically, one step at a time.* "First I need to do reconnaissance on the monastery, so I can report back to Captain Drew."

Lenushka nodded. "Good plan. I wonder if these four troops will be enough? It could take the army a few days to arrive."

"Vindalyn is closer." Quentin nodded at Captain Drew as he dashed over to join them. After telling the captain their plans, he added, "I'll fly to Vindalyn. The duke knows that his daughter's caravan is on the way, so he'll already have some troops headed in this direction. I'll find them and tell them to join yours at the monastery."

Captain Drew nodded. "Excellent. Thank you."

Faith returned with several soldiers carrying the wounded colonel, and they climbed into the wagon.

"Oh, one more thing." Quentin quickly told the captain about the fox-shifting priest in Arondale's jailhouse, who had admitted to committing murder twice before confessing the location of the Monastery of Light.

"I'll send some soldiers there," Captain Drew said; then he strode away, shouting at everyone to break camp.

Lenushka and Pendras ran into the nearby forest to strip and shift, and soon, the two dragons were zooming north.

Quentin ducked into the woods to shift. As he flew west, looking for the monastery, he prayed that the queen was all right. His nerves tensed, knowing that Eviana could be in danger, too, and he was not there to protect her.

Dammit, what else could he do? Any trouble Eviana faced was only a possibility at this point, while the queen's peril was definite. Even Eviana would be furious if he ignored her mother's deadly situation. By the time he scanned the monastery and reported it, then located the Vindalyn troops, it would be almost dawn.

She'll be all right, he assured himself for the hundredth time. *She has her gift. If the Brotherhood attacks, she can put them all to sleep and flee to Vindalyn.*

His talons clenched with fear. Her gift wouldn't work if the Raven went after her.

After an hour of flight, the Raven arrived at Arondale. At this time of night, he'd expected the villagers to be asleep, so he was surprised to see a small crowd gathered in front of the constable's office, shouting and waving their kitchen knives.

"Bring the bloody priest out here!" one of the villagers shouted.

"Aye!" another yelled. "We have a surprise for him!"

Were they talking about Father Renard? The Raven landed on the rooftop of the building across the street. He had planned on going to the chapel to ask the priest for information, but apparently Father Renard's dastardly ways had caught up with him.

The man on duty inside the constable's office cracked open a shutter on the window and peered out at them. "I told you to go home! Soldiers are coming here to handle the—"

"I want justice now!" a villager yelled. "That bastard murdered my son!"

"I know! Victor was my best friend," the young man on duty replied, pushing the shutters open wider. "Father Renard will get what he deserves. Now go home and stop your yelling. You're disturbing the other villagers."

The irate father scoffed. "They should be disturbed. When the village priest is a murderer—" He stopped with a jerk as the Raven flew a few inches over him, zooming at a great speed toward the open window.

The man on duty reeled back to keep from getting stabbed in the face with a sharp beak. "What the hell?"

The Raven landed on the constable's desk and spotted Father Renard in the prison cell.

The priest's eyes lit up. "Have you come to rescue me? Let's go!" He shifted into a fox and slipped through the prison bars. As he made a mad dash for the open window, the man on duty quickly turned to close the shutters and latch them.

The Raven shifted, picked up the knife on the desk, and clonked the man on the back of the head with the metal handle. As the man slumped onto the floor, the fox shifted back into human form.

"Great job! Let's get out of here." The priest ran back to the jail cell to grab his black robe. "There's a back door we can use."

"Where's the princess?" Bran asked.

"Who?" Father Renard pulled on his robe and motioned to some bags on the floor next to the desk. "We need to take the gold—"

"Where's the princess?" Bran repeated more loudly.

"What princess?" The priest buttoned his robe. "I'll give you some of the gold—"

Bran grabbed the priest by the neck and shoved him against the wall. "Where is she?"

"I-I don't know a prin—"

"She was with the eagle shifter."

"Oh." The priest swatted at Bran's hand. "I'll tell you. Just let me go."

Bran didn't let go but relaxed his grip. "Talk."

Father Renard swallowed hard. "It was that damned eagle and a colonel who caught me and brought me here. You have to get me out of here before they lynch—"

"Was there a woman with them?"

"Yes, that damned Confessor!" The priest's gaze darted from one side to the other. "But I didn't tell her anything."

"You must have confessed to murder if they want to lynch you."

The priest winced. "Well, yes. But I didn't say anything about the Brotherhood."

Bran scoffed. "And the princess? Was there another woman with them?"

Father Renard tilted his head, thinking. "Yes, but she didn't say anything."

"What did she look like?"

"Young, pretty, long black hair, ugly brown gown."

"And where would I find her? Is she still here in town?"

The priest frowned as he tried to remember. "I think they were going to leave. But I was too upset about being lynched to pay much—"

"*Where?*" Bran tightened his grip. "You have about three seconds to prove you are still useful."

"All right! I'll tell you." The priest winced. "I eavesdropped on them while they were in one of the hot springs. The eagle wanted the others to leave town tonight. He was flying off to report what I told the Confessor. They were going to a farm on the way to Vindalyn. Peter's farm."

Bran inhaled deeply. Thank the Light. He'd be able to kidnap the princess before dawn. "You will take me there."

"Me?" Father Renard asked. "But I need to—"

"Do I need to report to the master what you told the Confessor?"

The priest gulped. "I'll take you. Let me get my bags—"

"No. They will slow us down." Bran released the priest so he could pull the breeches off the man he'd clonked on the head. As he put them on, he noticed the priest sneaking a few gold coins out of the bag.

He grabbed the priest's arm and dragged him toward the back door. "We'll use that gold to buy two horses at the stable."

"What?"

Much to the priest's dismay, Bran actually bought the horses instead of stealing them. Soon, they were headed southwest, and as they rode silently in the dark, Bran formulated a plan for kidnapping the princess.

Once they arrived at the farmhouse, they would need to convince Princess Eviana that she was surrounded by a large group of ruffians, intent on destroying the house and everyone inside. If they made her desperate to save everyone she was with, she would clap her hands to put the attackers to sleep.

But her gift wouldn't work on a fox and a raven. She would be defenseless when they came in to grab her.

Chapter 23

It had to be well past midnight, Eviana thought as the adults in Peter's house finally started to fall asleep. Peter's wife, Suzy, had taken the youngest four children off to bed hours earlier, but the oldest boy, Liam, had stayed up, begging to hear how his father and friends had helped defeat the Circle of Five twenty years ago.

The boy had eventually fallen asleep by the fireplace while Elam, Olana, and Peter had continued to reminisce about their childhood on the Isle of Secrets. Eviana had found it all fascinating for this was Quentin's childhood, too.

But now, Peter was starting to doze off in his comfy chair by the fire, and Olana had fallen asleep, her head cushioned in Elam's lap. He was still awake on the settee he shared with Olana, since he was determined to remain on guard duty all night.

"You should sleep," he told Eviana softly. "We have a long ride to Vindalyn tomorrow."

Eviana nodded as she curled up in a big comfy chair. She was terribly tired after three long days of travel. Actually, she thought, this was already the fourth day. So much had happened in those few days. Elam had apparently won Olana's heart, although Eviana suspected Olana had desperately wanted to be loved.

As for Quentin, Eviana's relationship with him was proving to be more difficult. But she was not going to give up.

Where was he now? she wondered. Was he on his way back? He was going to be so tired.

A loud crashing noise startled her. A nearby window shattered, glass flying everywhere as a large rock shot through and plummeted to the floor.

Dear goddesses. Eviana froze for a second, not believing her eyes. They were under attack?

As Olana jerked awake, Elam jumped to his feet and grabbed his sword.

"What—" Olana began, but a loud voice interrupted her.

"We have your house surrounded! Send the princess out, or we will attack!"

With a gasp, Eviana rose to her feet.

Peter ran to the door to make sure it was bolted.

"What's happening?" a sleepy Liam asked as he sat up.

A second window shattered when another rock flew into the room. A thud shook the door as someone slammed against it.

Elam ran to the edge of a shattered window and peered out. "I can't tell how many people there are. It's too dark."

Eviana drew in a shaky breath. "I should clap my hands."

"No!" Elam told her. "We can't defend you if we're asleep."

"Send out the princess before we attack!"

Eviana winced. How could she let this innocent family be harmed?

"I'll try to get rid of them." Peter closed his eyes and concentrated. Soon, loud knocking noises sounded overhead as the roof was struck over and over.

"Papa." Liam scrambled to his feet, looking up at the ceiling. "You're making it hail."

"What's going on?" Peter's wife, Suzy, dashed into the room.

"Send out the princess or we will burn your house to the ground with everyone in it!"

With a gasp, Suzy collapsed onto the floor. "No."

Liam's face turned pale. "Papa?"

Tears stung Eviana's eyes. She couldn't let this innocent family suffer because of her. She clapped her hands three times.

Everyone fell to the floor, unconscious.

She inhaled deeply to steady her nerves. It would be all right. The attackers outside would be unconscious, too. She would tie them all up, then take one of their horses and ride—

Her thoughts were interrupted when a black raven swooped through one of the shattered windows.

The Raven! She ran toward Elam to grab his sword. When she turned, she found the Raven had shifted and was holding an unconscious Liam in front of him with a knife at the boy's neck.

"Drop the sword or I slit his throat," the Raven said.

She dropped it. As it clattered onto the floor, she moved her hands to clap.

"The boy will be dead before you clap again!"

Dammit. She needed to put the Raven to sleep while he was still in human form.

"Raise your hands where I can see them," the Raven hissed. "Move slowly to the door and slide the bolt with one hand."

As she inched slowly toward the door, keeping the Raven in sight, she quashed the growing panic inside her. *Think!* She had to escape. Any human attackers outside would be asleep, so it was only the Raven she needed to get away from.

She slid the bolt with her right hand. The Raven had moved closer, dragging Liam with him.

"Open the door," he ordered.

She turned the knob and as the door swung open, a furry creature leaped at her, its sharp teeth bared and its claws extended.

"Oh!" She stumbled back in surprise. A fox? Pain erupted

on the back of her head, and she barely had time to realize she'd been struck hard before everything went black.

When Eviana slowly awakened, she was first aware of a throbbing pain at the back of her head, but that was quickly overpowered by terror as she realized the full import of her situation. She was a prisoner. Her father's worst fear was going to happen. The Brotherhood would try to use her power to destroy her family and country.

Without moving, in case she was being watched, she cracked her eyes slightly open. She was on a horse, her right hand tied to the saddle horn, her left hand covered with some sort of woolen material and tied behind her back. Her captors were making sure she couldn't clap her hands.

A man was sitting behind her . . . the Raven? The warmth of his broad chest seeped into her back, keeping her from getting too cold in the night air. He had one arm wrapped around her waist to prevent her from falling off the horse.

Where was he taking her? The monastery that Father Renard had told them about? Had the priest been the fox that had jumped at her? She slanted her gaze right and left and couldn't see anyone else. Was she alone with the man behind her?

"You're awake," the man said softly.

She lifted her head, her eyes wide open. "Are you the Raven?"

"Yes." He loosened his hold on her.

How could she escape? She tugged at the hand tied to the saddle horn. The rope was tight, but she'd gladly rub her skin raw if it helped her get loose.

"There's no point in hurting yourself," he said as if he were reading her mind.

She took a deep breath to quell the panic that threatened to consume her. Quentin would find her. And he would have already reported the location of the monastery, so her father and Nevis would bring the army to rescue her.

The sky had lightened, so the sun would be rising soon. Quentin would be returning to Peter's house any minute now. And then he would fly like a bat out of hell to rescue her. *Be careful, Quen.*

Her hands clenched as an alarming thought struck her. "You didn't hurt anyone at the farmhouse, did you?"

There was a pause before he answered, "No."

She glanced around and saw no one. "Was it just you and the fox?"

"Yes."

Damn. What a fool she'd been. She shouldn't have clapped her hands. Elam and Peter could have fought off the priest and the Raven. The damned Raven had tricked her. But he had threatened to burn the house down, and it was full of children. What else could she have done? "What is your name?"

No answer.

She tried again. "What happened to the fox?"

"I let Father Renard go."

She scoffed. "He's a murderer."

"He wanted to go back to Arondale to get his gold. I figure he'll be recaptured there and get what he deserves."

"You don't mind if he's executed for his crimes?"

"No."

This seemed odd to Eviana. The Raven didn't seem to feel very brotherly toward the others in the Brotherhood. "You won't be able to get away with this. Father Renard told us the location of your monastery, and by now my father and General Nevis will know. They'll bring the army—"

"That's the plan," he interrupted. "And then you will put them to sleep."

Her heart clenched in her chest. She couldn't let Papa's

worst fear happen. "I will not be used to destroy my own family and country." She would escape somehow. And if she couldn't, she would escape through death.

Tears stung her eyes. It wasn't a bluff. If there was no way out, she would have to kill herself. The Brotherhood probably meant to kill her anyway after using her. The least she could do was keep them from killing her parents and brothers.

"We have your mother."

She gasped, and a chill skittered through her bones. *Mother.* She and her mother would both have to die. And it was all because of her damned gift. *Oh, Mother, I'm so sorry. I should never have been born.*

Tears streamed down her face. If she and her mother died, they could keep Papa and her brothers safe. But how would they be able to live, knowing that they'd failed to protect the women of the family? How would Quentin survive? *Oh, Quen, I wanted to have a life with you.*

"You're crying."

She sniffed. "My mother and I will gladly die for our family and country. And once we're gone, my father will destroy you with his lightning power. The dragons will breathe fire on anyone who tries to escape. By doing this, you are bringing about your own doom and destruction."

The arm around her tightened. "If you destroy the monastery, I will dance on its ashes."

She stiffened. What was this? He hated the monastery? "Why are you taking me there, then?"

"If I don't deliver you, they will kill my brother."

"You have a brother?"

"Aye. Two brothers. It was Arlo's mission to kidnap you. If he fails, he'll have to kill himself. I can't let that happen."

She took a deep breath. "I have two brothers, too. So you will understand that I'll do anything to save them."

There was a long pause; then he simply said, "Aye."

Eviana thought back over everything she had learned. Father Saul had committed suicide for failing in his mission. And his back had been scarred. "Did they whip you?"

He flinched.

That had to be a yes, Eviana thought. The priests of the Brotherhood must have abused him and his brothers. And now they were threatening to kill one of them.

"Raven." She turned her head. "I could take you to the army, and we could rescue your brothers. And my mother. It would be easy for me to put the Brotherhood to sleep. Let me help you."

"I have no choice—"

"There is always a choice," she insisted. "If your heart is good, you will know the right choice. Please, let us help you."

There was a long silence.

As time stretched out, she wondered if he was considering her offer.

As she debated what she could say next, she realized that the sun had finally breached the horizon. It was behind her, so they were definitely headed west. The dirt road they were on was bordered by a thick forest on the right. The sun glinted off the broad strip of water to her left. That had to be the Ron River.

Wouldn't the troops from her mother's caravan be up ahead? If she could escape and reach them . . . but that kernel of hope dwindled when the Raven suddenly turned onto a narrow footpath that led into the forest. Soon a small cabin came into view with four horses tied up at the hitching post.

Behind her, the Raven stiffened, and his arm around her tightened.

"Is something wrong?" she whispered.

A man in a black robe sauntered out of the cabin and gave them an amused look. "Ah, so you found the princess."

"Get lost, Greer," the Raven growled at the other priest,

leaning forward so he could silently slip off the rope that had tied Eviana's hand to the saddle horn.

What was he doing? Eviana wondered. Was he making it easier for her to escape?

"Why should I leave?" Greer smirked. "Especially after Horace worked so hard to track you and your brother."

The Raven dismounted. "I thought you would be at the monastery trying to take credit for capturing the queen."

Greer scoffed. "Zane will get the credit. Master Lorne is always partial to his own son. But when I bring the princess, the master will finally realize who deserves to be his heir."

"Arlo and I will deliver the princess. You can get lost." The Raven tied the reins loosely to a flimsy tree branch.

Could she reach the reins? Eviana wondered.

Greer shrugged. "Arlo has already agreed to give us the princess."

"You lie," the Raven hissed as he strode toward Greer.

Greer opened the cabin door. "Go see for yourself."

"You bastard, what have you done?" The Raven ran into the cabin.

Eviana's blood chilled at the evil, satisfied smirk on Greer's face. This man was a murderer, she had no doubt. She leaned forward to grab at the reins, but with her left hand still tied behind her back, she could only reach one. She gave it a tug, but the horse shook his head, pulling it from her grasp. Dammit, she had to escape. This might be her only chance.

"No!" A heartrending scream came from the cabin, and Eviana panicked. Grabbing onto the saddle horn, she slipped off the horse. With her one useful hand, she pulled her skirt up to her shins and ran.

The scream was suddenly cut off. Good goddesses, had they killed the Raven? She kept running down the footpath toward the river road.

"Horace, get out here!" Greer shouted. "She's getting away!"

When Eviana reached the river road, she could hear the pounding of horse hooves behind her. She couldn't outrun her pursuers. *Dear goddesses, help me!*

This is it, a quiet voice inside her said. This was the moment she had to make her choice.

If your heart is good, you will know the right choice.

With tears in her eyes, she plunged through the bushes on her right. She would not be used to harm her family or destroy her country. Her father's greatest fear would not happen.

She reached the river and plunged into the chilly water. Soon, her body was trembling, her teeth were chattering, but she kept going until the current swept her away.

"Get her!" Greer yelled as he and Horace charged into the river on horseback.

Dammit, couldn't they let her die in peace? Eviana struggled to keep her head above water. Ahead of her was Ronford Castle, perched on a hill. Would a guard spot her from the battlements and send help? Could she survive this ordeal?

She waved her right hand frantically in the air and screamed, hoping to draw the attention of a guard.

A horse pulled up beside her, and one of the priests hauled her out of the water.

"Bitch!" Greer tossed her over his lap and headed back for the riverbank.

Eviana coughed as she tried to catch her breath. The chilly air made her gown feel like ice, and her head throbbed with pain.

It's just as well, she thought as her vision grew blurry. *If all goes well, I will freeze to death before they can—*

Everything went black.

The sun was just coming up as Quentin spotted Peter's house up ahead. He was exhausted from being up all night, but with the queen in danger, there was no time to waste.

To his surprise, Luciana's father had been leading the duchy's troops to the border of Vindalyn. The elderly man was not in good health, so Quentin had hated breaking the news to him about his daughter. Dismayed, the duke had immediately issued orders to break camp and proceed north.

As Quentin drew nearer to Peter's house, his nerves tensed. Eviana had to be all right. Hopefully, she had slept well and was ready to travel south into Vindalyn.

But as he swooped down toward the farmhouse, his breath caught at the sight of broken windows. Good goddesses, no! He landed outside a shattered window and shifted. Inside, Olana and Suzy were sweeping up glass, while the children huddled together on the settee.

His blood ran cold. Eviana wasn't there.

Olana spotted him. "Quen!" She ran toward the window, heedless of the glass crunching beneath her shoes. "Hurry! They've taken Eviana. Elam left not long ago. You should be—"

Quentin immediately shifted and took off.

Olana shouted after him. "—able to see Elam on the way!"

Quentin's talons clenched with panic, but he tamped down on the fear and attempted to turn it into more energy. He had to fly faster than he'd ever managed before.

Whoever had captured her would probably be taking her to the monastery. And they would in all likelihood be following the road that ran along the north bank of the Ron River. Since the river had a serpentine course, the road did also. That would be to his advantage, because he could take a straight shot west.

He'd catch up with them. He had to. He had to rescue her before they reached the monastery. Captain Drew was moving the troops in that direction, but Eviana's captors might manage to sneak around them. Once they had Eviana and her mother both captive at the monastery, it would be a disaster.

Eviana, I'm coming! He never should have left her alone. He shouldn't have sent her to Peter's house. Dammit, he shouldn't have rejected her proposal.

He wanted a life with her. Why was he letting his stupid feelings of unworthiness get in the way? Instead, he should be even more determined to prove that he was worthy.

Dammit, if she was harmed in any way, he would never forgive himself. And if she ever made another proposal, he would accept it. Hell, he would make the proposal himself.

Eviana, hold on! I'm coming!

Chapter 24

Bran's head hurt like hell as he gained consciousness. That damned Horace must have hit him from behind when he'd—

With a gasp, he scrambled to his knees.

No, he hadn't imagined it. Arlo was lying beside him, collapsed on the floor. Not breathing.

"Arlo!" He tapped his cheek.

It was freezing cold.

"Arlo?" Bran thumped at his brother's chest. "Don't die. Arlo . . ." His hand curled into a fist.

His brother was already dead. Frozen by that bastard Greer.

Denial paralyzed him for a short moment. No, Arlo couldn't be dead. This couldn't be happening. He couldn't lose his brother like this. *No, no.* He shook his head, but the truth slammed into him with a viciousness that gripped his heart.

His brother was dead.

"*No!*" The rage inside him shattered the walls he'd erected around it. "*No!*" He jumped to his feet, grabbed a wooden chair, and hurled it against a wall.

"I will kill you, Greer," he hissed. "You and Horace." He turned to look at his brother. "I will avenge you. I'll kill them all, every bloody priest who ever hurt you!"

As he paced across the room, he thought his head would

burst from either pain or rage—he wasn't sure which was worse. First, he would destroy that damned monastery. No, first, he would kill Greer and Horace. *Think!* He tamped down on the rage. If he didn't think this through, he'd end up dead before he could avenge his brother. He'd end up dead like Arlo.

Tears burned his eyes. *Arlo.* How would he manage without him? His two younger brothers had kept him sane all these years. *Zane.* Zane had to be saved from the hell they had grown up in.

"I will avenge you, Arlo. And I will keep our youngest brother safe."

What should he do first? A dim memory popped into his mind. After Horace had clobbered him, he'd fallen to his knees. There had been a flash of metal as Horace had lifted his sword to make a killing blow. But then, Greer had shouted that the princess was getting away, and Horace had dashed out the door.

Her sudden escape had saved his life.

Did they whip you? Her words came back to him, and he glanced at Arlo, who had suffered the whippings alongside him. The princess had been the first person ever to show concern. And her mother had made Vera feel safe for the first time in her life. *Please, let us help you.*

A tear rolled down his face as Bran fell to his knees beside his brother. "I am sorry for all the pain you endured. I should have rescued you and Zane. I'm so sorry."

He shouldn't have left his brother here alone. He shouldn't have underestimated Greer's evil cruelty and ruthless ambition. By now, Greer had probably recaptured the princess. He would take her to the monastery. And there, they would torture her mother to force the princess to use her power.

Could he stop it? If he attacked Greer and Horace as the Raven, he would have no weapons, while they were both armed. But his chance of success would double if he wasn't alone. And there was someone who would be even more desperate than he to rescue the princess.

There is always a choice, she had told him. And if he had a good heart, he would make the right one.

"Arlo." He rested his hand on his brother's head. "I think you would agree with the choice I have made."

He stripped off his clothes as he headed for the door. Outside, he shifted, then flew back toward the farmhouse, looking for the eagle.

It didn't take long for Quentin to catch up with Elam, although he was surprised to find the colonel in the company of two soldiers. They were racing along the river road as fast as they could.

He swooped down in front of them to let Elam know he was there.

"Quen!" Elam shouted at him. "We have to rescue the princess!"

Quen gave a squawk as he circled around them.

"I came across four soldiers just west of Arondale," Elam yelled. "Captain Drew had sent them. I brought two of them with me."

Ah, these were the soldiers he had asked the captain to send. Quen gave another squawk, then zoomed ahead of the riders, putting distance between them since he could fly straight while they had to follow the curves of the river. He scanned the dirt road and neighboring woods carefully as he went, searching for any sign of Eviana.

A cawing sound drew his attention up to the sky, and he spotted a black spec headed straight for him. The Raven? What was the bastard doing here?

With a screech, Quentin shot toward him.

The Raven swerved to avoid a collision. He dropped down to land on the dirt road, and as he shifted, Quentin landed beside him.

He shifted and grabbed the Raven by the neck. "Where is she?"

The Raven raised his hands in a motion of surrender. "I'll help you."

"The hell you will, you bastard!" Quen tightened his grip. "Didn't you kidnap her?"

The Raven winced. "She escaped from me. But now, Greer and Horace have her. At least, I think they do."

Quentin shoved the Raven away. "You're trying to slow me down, aren't you? This is all a ruse."

"No!" The Raven's eyes glinted with tears. "They killed my brother. I want them dead before they can kill my other brother. And we can save the princess! We'll have a chance if we attack together."

Quentin clenched his fists as he tried to figure out whether the Raven was telling the truth. "You're not leading me into a trap?"

"No!" The Raven groaned with frustration. "We'll be in the air. If you don't like what you see, you can just fly away. Now come with me!" He shifted and took off, flying west.

Dammit. Quentin hesitated only a second, then shifted and flew after the Raven. If the bastard was lying, he'd find out soon enough.

They flew, one on each side of the road, searching the forest and river. Soon Quentin spotted Ronford Castle atop a hill on the south side of the river. A wooden drawbridge on the south bank had been pulled up, but when it was down, people from the river road could cross the bridge to the gatehouse, located on the castle's outer curtain wall.

He turned his attention back to the road, and there, almost three miles in front of them, two horses were moving at a quick trot. Two men were riding, wearing all black, and one of them had a woman thrown over his lap.

With a low screech, he zeroed in on them. Beside him, the

Raven sped up. As they narrowed the gap, one of the men glanced up and spotted them.

"Greer, look!" The figure motioned toward them, and the other priest looked up.

"Into the woods!" Greer shouted.

They headed into the forest, weaving through the trees, but Quentin and the Raven kept advancing on them.

"Dammit, Horace," Greer growled below. "I told you to kill Bran."

"I was just about to," Horace whined. "But then the princess escaped."

Bran? Quentin glanced at the Raven. Was that his name? As they drew closer, he could see that Eviana's gown was soaked through. Had she fallen into the river while trying to escape? His heart clenched. She might have been desperate enough to throw herself in.

Anger seethed inside him, and as soon as the riders below reached a small clearing, Quentin swooped down and knocked Greer off his horse.

The Raven landed on Horace's shoulders and dug in his talons. The priest screamed, thrashing his arms at the attacking bird. His horse reared up in fright, dumping Horace onto the ground.

Quentin quickly shifted and caught the reins of the horse carrying Eviana. "Evie!" He patted her face, and she moaned. Thank the goddesses, she would be all right.

He turned to go after Greer. The priest had hit the ground hard enough to knock the air out of his lungs, so now he was floundering on the ground as he tried to stand up. With a running kick, Quentin knocked him back down.

"Damn you." Rolling onto his back, Greer pulled a knife from his belt and slashed at Quentin.

Jumping back, Quentin narrowly missed the blade. Then, as Greer scrambled to his feet, Quentin kicked the knife out of his hand. He dashed over to grab the weapon.

"Come at me again, and I'll run you through!" Greer shouted as he drew his sword.

Quentin glanced over at Horace and the Raven. Horace had a knife and was swinging wildly at the Raven, who was ducking and dodging. Meanwhile, Eviana was trying to slide off the horse. She was shivering from the cold and had one hand tied behind her back. When her feet hit the ground, her knees gave out and she collapsed. Still, she didn't give up, and stumbled back onto her feet.

He stepped toward her, but Greer charged at him, lifting his sword. As it swung down, Quentin ducked and rolled. The blade hit the ground hard enough to get stuck in the soil, and while Greer struggled to pull it out, the Raven leaped at him from the side, knocking him down. Before he could do more, Horace charged at him with his knife.

The Raven caught Horace's wrist to keep the knife from plunging into his chest. As the two struggled for control of the blade, Greer sneaked up behind the Raven, ready to stab him in the back.

"Behind you!" Quentin yelled.

The Raven grabbed Horace and swung around, keeping Horace in front of him as Greer charged. Horace stiffened with a gasp as the sword ran him through.

"No!" Greer stumbled back in shock as his companion collapsed on the ground, taking his sword with him.

Eviana gasped.

Quentin ran over to her and used his knife to cut the rope binding her. She was icy cold and shivering. He wished he had a blanket—for the first time, he realized he was butt naked.

The Raven picked up the knife Horace had dropped and moved toward Greer. "Now it's your turn."

Greer jumped back, pulling another knife from his belt.

"Go!" the Raven yelled at Quentin. "Take her and leave!"

"You're helping them? You traitor!" Greer growled.

"Can you get back on the horse?" Quentin helped her mount Greer's horse, then swung into the saddle behind her.

As they left the clearing, Greer leaped onto the other horse and charged deeper into the forest. The Raven shifted and flew after him.

"Evie, are you all right?" He wrapped his arms around her as violent shudders racked her body.

"I—I'm not dreaming? You're really here?"

"I'm here." He held her close as he steered the horse back to the river road. "You're safe. And I'm never leaving you again."

"Oh, Quen." She gripped his arms tight with her icy hands. "I was so terrified. And I felt so stupid for letting the Raven capture me."

"I felt stupid for leaving you."

"You couldn't help that. You had to make your report to my mother—Oh! The Raven said the Brotherhood has captured my mother. Is that true?"

"I'm afraid so, but don't worry. We'll save her."

Another shudder skittered through her as a sob escaped. "I thought I would have to kill myself. I thought Mother would have to, too."

"Evie." He lifted a hand to caress her face while he kissed her cheek. "I won't let anything happen to you. You're safe. And your mother will be safe, too." When he reached the river road, he turned east.

She stiffened. "What are you doing? The monastery is the other way."

"We're going to Ronford Castle. You need a hot bath and some dry clothes."

"No, I'll be fine. I'm too worried about Mother to stop now." She shivered again.

"You'll be no help if you freeze to death, so we're going to the castle first."

She huffed. "You're going there naked?"

He winced. "You noticed."

"How could I not notice? You and the Raven were both naked."

He gritted his teeth. "You shouldn't have looked at him."

She scoffed. "I may be frozen, but I'm not frigid."

His mouth twitched. She was getting her spunkiness back. Nothing could keep his Eviana down for long. "Have I told you that I love you?"

"Hmm." She leaned her head back against his shoulder. "I believe you have. Many times. Though not often with words."

"Ah."

"But I am delighted to hear the words. And I'm amazed how warm you can be when you're naked."

"You seem to be fixated on that."

She sighed. "I would rather think about that than the fact that I was nearly driven to the point of committing—" Her voice broke.

Suicide? He finished her sentence in his thoughts. Was this why her gown was soaked through? Had she purposely thrown herself into the river? "Evie." Tears blurred his vision. "Thank you for staying alive. I could never forgive myself if I lost you."

"I love you, too, Quen."

Should he ask her to marry him now? Or should he wait until she had recovered from the day's trauma?

"Quen!" Elam shouted as he charged ahead of the two soldiers following him. "Your Highness!"

"We're going to Ronford Castle." Quentin pointed at the nearby drawbridge. "Evie is nearly frozen from falling into the river while trying to escape."

Elam pulled his horse to a stop in front of them. "You escaped?"

"Only briefly," Eviana explained. "Quentin and the Raven rescued me."

"The Raven?" Elam's eyes widened.

"I believe his name is Bran," Quentin said.

The other two soldiers reached them, and they gasped at the sight of a naked man on horseback with his arms around the princess.

Elam dismounted. "I figured this would happen, so I came prepared." He opened a saddlebag and retrieved a pair of breeches and a shirt. "I suggest you get dressed while we proceed to the drawbridge."

As Quentin dressed behind some trees, Elam called to the guards at Ronford Castle, introducing himself and Princess Eviana. The drawbridge was quickly lowered and the gate opened so they could cross the river and enter the castle. By the time Quentin ran barefoot into the courtyard, Lord and Lady Ronford had arrived to welcome them. The earl and his wife were dressed all in black, and the servants, as well.

"Oh, my poor dear, you're shivering." Lady Ronford removed her woolen cloak and placed it over Eviana's shoulders. "I'll have a hot bath prepared for you and a feast for everyone!"

"Aye." The Earl of Ronford nodded. "It's not often that we're visited by a member of the royal family."

"Please," Eviana objected. "Don't go to any trouble. We cannot stay long. My mother is in grave danger."

"The queen?" The earl looked appalled. "What has happened?"

"I can explain," Elam said. "But please take care of Her Highness first."

"Of course!" Lady Ronford motioned for a maid to approach. "Take Her Highness to Uma's room and have a bath prepared for her." She looked Eviana over quickly. "I believe my poor Uma's clothes will fit you."

"I was very sorry to hear of her passing," Eviana said, then followed the maid into the castle keep.

Lady Ronford's eyes filled with tears. "I should go to the kitchens now." She dashed across the courtyard.

"May I offer my condolences?" Elam asked the earl. "I knew Uma on the Isle of Secrets. She was a lovely child."

Lord Ronford nodded sadly. "Then you grew up on the island, too? You must be Embraced?"

"Aye, I am." Elam motioned to Quentin. "And so is Quentin. He's an eagle shifter and the official courier of the royal families of Aerthlan."

"Ah." The earl's eyes widened. "I have heard of you. Welcome to Ronford Castle. Please come inside."

As he led them across the Great Hall to his library, Elam quickly explained everything that had happened. Then he asked the two soldiers to stand guard by the door.

"Thank the Light you were able to rescue the princess." The earl closed the doors after Elam and Quentin had filed into the library.

Quentin sat in a comfy chair in front of the fireplace and suddenly realized how exhausted he was. He closed his eyes, listening to the conversation.

"And you say the monastery of this Brotherhood is not far from here?" Ronford asked.

"Aye, my lord," Elam answered. "It's only ten miles west of the ferry. We believe that is where they are holding the queen prisoner."

"Those bastards," the earl muttered.

Elam sighed. "I hate to say this, but you should know, my lord, that the Brotherhood was behind the death of your daughter."

"*What?*" the earl bellowed, and Quentin jerked fully awake. "Why would they target my sweet Uma? She never hurt anyone."

"She was Embraced," Quentin said. "They hate the Embraced, especially those in the royal families."

"Why?" Ronford asked.

Quentin shrugged. "They claim the Embraced use their gifts to wield power over others, so they must be destroyed."

The earl scoffed. "You mean this Brotherhood wants the power for themselves."

"Exactly." Quentin nodded.

Ronford clenched his fists. "We won't let the bastards get away with it. I have a dozen men here trained in battle, including myself. We will join you to help save the queen and destroy the Brotherhood."

Lady Ronford entered the library with Eviana, now dressed in a dark green gown of warm wool with matching leather slippers.

Quentin and the other men in the room jumped to their feet and bowed their heads.

"I couldn't help but hear your kind offer," Eviana said to the earl, then looked everyone over, her gaze lingering on Quentin. "After we have a bite to eat, we'll head straight to the monastery."

"Yes, Your Highness," the men replied.

Quentin gave her an assuring smile, but as Lord Ronford rushed forward to escort the princess and Lady Ronford to the dining room, his smile faded.

With a sigh, he fell in line far behind them as suited his position. She was no longer Evie, his friend and lover. She was back to being Princess Eviana.

And no one, other than Eviana, was going to believe he was worthy of her.

Chapter 25

Bran shifted and followed Greer through the forest as the bastard weaved amongst the trees, trying to escape on horseback. Each time the Raven swooped down to harass him, Greer swiped at him with a knife.

"I'm going to kill your brother Zane, too!" Greer bellowed.

Zane. The Raven realized he needed to get to the monastery before Greer so he could protect his brother. So he shot off, headed home as fast as he could. As he drew nearer, he noticed the troops from the queen's caravan had moved closer to the monastery. Hidden in the nearby forest, they were quietly surrounding the Brotherhood's secret residence.

The monks in the courtyard were going about their business as usual, so apparently the Brotherhood had no idea that they were about to be attacked. He flew through the tower window into his bedchamber and landed on the wooden floor.

Zane looked up from the book he was studying. "Bran!" He scrambled off his cot. "What happened? Did you find the princess? Where's Arlo?"

Bran shifted and retrieved a pair of black breeches and shirt from the trunk at the foot of his cot. "Zane, I came back to get you. We need to leave." He pulled on the breeches. "The Eberoni army has surrounded the monastery."

"What?" Zane's eyes widened. "Why hasn't someone struck

341 WHEN A PRINCESS PROPOSES

the gong to alert everyone? Do they not know?" He strode for the door. "We need to tell—"

"Zane, we're leaving." Bran put on his shirt. "Pack some clothes—"

"What are you saying?" Zane gave him a confused look. "Are you taking me to Arlo? Where is he? Hasn't he come back with the princess?"

Bran paused in the middle of buttoning his shirt. "We don't have the princess."

Zane stiffened. "You . . . you failed? Arlo . . . ?"

Yes, he'd failed his brother. Tears stung Bran's eyes. "I tried to hide Arlo somewhere safe. Then I went and kidnapped the princess. But when I brought her to Arlo, Greer was there. He'd used his bloodhound Horace to track Arlo. And they . . . Greer had already killed our brother."

Zane stumbled back a step, his face turning pale. "He . . . he's . . . gone?"

Bran nodded. "Greer froze him, then stole the princess. I flew after them to kill them. Horace is dead. The princess escaped. Greer is on his way here now, and he has vowed to kill you, too."

Zane clenched his fists as he breathed heavily. Soon, his face flushed a bright red as his gift burned inside him. "The bastard can't kill me. I'm killing him first!"

"He's not even here yet, so calm down." Bran could already feel the heat radiating from his brother. He'd always worried that Zane's gift was too volatile. Too powerful. If Zane lost control, he could burn himself to death along with the person he was targeting. "We will avenge our brother, I promise you. But right now, we need to get out of here. The army will destroy this place along with everyone in it. We have to live if we're going to kill Greer."

Zane's power slowly ebbed. He took a deep breath. "They can't attack us. We have the queen."

"And how long can that last?" Bran grabbed some clothes

from Zane's trunk and rolled them up. "The monks can threaten to torture her, but they can only kill her once. And once the queen is dead, nothing will stop the furious king from slaughtering us all." He tied off the bundle of clothes. "This is a lost cause, Zane."

His brother gasped. "How can you say that? Master Lorne was given this holy task by the Light—"

"Bullshit! He's a master of lies who wants to rule the world."

Zane stepped back with a stunned look on his face. "You—you've been compromised, swayed by our enemies."

"How could I not be?" Bran cried. "I only had to think for myself."

"They're evil!"

"No, the Brotherhood is evil," Bran hissed. "The monks whipped us, molested our sisters, and twisted our brains until we couldn't tell what was good or evil anymore! We—" He thumped his chest with tears in his eyes. "We are the bad guys, Zane."

"No." Zane stepped back, shaking his head. "No."

"We have to escape."

"No!" Zane wrenched open the door and ran.

"Zane!" Bran called after him. *Dammit.* He sat on his cot and quickly slipped on his leather sandals. A tear rolled down his cheek when he glanced at Arlo's empty cot. "I'll save him, Arlo. I promise."

He grabbed the bundle of Zane's clothes and dashed down the spiral staircase. How could he make his brother leave with him? Would he have to knock him unconscious? Zane might hate him for a while, but once he adjusted to life outside the monastery, he would eventually realize how wrong their lives had been.

As Bran ran across the Great Hall, he noticed the monks were going about business as usual, so Zane must not have told them about the troops outside. Bran opened the door to the master's office and strode inside. He stopped, nearly bumping into Zane, who was standing still in shock.

Greer was behind the desk, and Master Lorne was in his chair as usual, but he was covered with frost, his eyes wide open, his expression frozen with a look of terror.

"You killed him," Zane said softly.

Greer lifted his chin. "I'm following the rules. The army has come to destroy this place. The master failed in his mission, so he had to die."

"You killed my brother, and now you've killed my father!" Zane stalked toward Greer. "You'll die now, you bastard!"

Greer pointed his knife at Zane. "Try it. Once I kill you, the Brotherhood will be mine."

"You can have the damned Brotherhood!" Bran jumped forward to stop his brother, but Zane pulled away and charged toward Greer.

"No!" Bran ran after him.

Zane dodged the knife Greer swung at him, then grabbed his arm and activated his power. Heat burned through Greer's sleeve, singeing the fabric, and with a cry of pain, he dropped the knife.

"I'll kill you." Greer used his other hand to grab hold of Zane's neck. "And I will be the next master." Frost appeared on Zane's skin as Greer tried to freeze him, but it quickly melted as Zane's skin turned red with heat.

"Stop it!" Bran plowed a fist into Greer's face, and Greer fell back, releasing his hold on Zane. *Damn.* Bran shook his hand. That had felt like hitting a block of ice.

"He has to die!" Zane lurched toward Greer.

Bran pulled him back, wincing at how hot his brother was. Dammit, if Zane didn't cool down, he might boil himself to death.

The door burst open and two monks ran inside.

"Master!" one of them yelled. "There are dra—" He stopped at the sight of Master Lorne frozen to death.

The two monks exchanged stunned looks, then one of them said quietly, "There are dragons flying overhead. And soldiers surrounding us. What do we do?"

"Take the queen to the battlements," Greer ordered as he dashed for the door. "Then threaten to kill her if they advance."

As the monks ran after Greer, Bran threw off his clothes.

"What are you doing?" Zane asked. "You're not running away, are you?"

"I want to see for myself what's happening. Don't worry. I won't leave here without you." He shifted and flew through the open door.

"Papa!" Eviana slid off her horse and ran to embrace her father. "How did you get here?"

Leo held her tight. "I hitched a ride on a dragon." He motioned to the general beside him. "Nevis did, too. I didn't expect to see you here."

"I had to come," Eviana insisted. "For Mother."

"Aye." Leo released her, and his expression grew hard as he glared at the monastery in the distance. "Eric is bringing the army here, but he doesn't expect to arrive till tomorrow. I couldn't wait. I have to rescue her today."

Eviana glanced through the trees at the monastery. It was a small castle, surrounded by fields of grain, a vegetable garden, and a vineyard. Apparently, the monks grew their own food and made their own wine.

Above the castle, Pendras and Lenushka were circling the tower in dragon form, scaring the monks on the battlements. The priests cowered and hid whenever a dragon passed overhead. But where in that castle was her mother? Father was right. They needed to rescue her today.

"Father." Eviana motioned to her companions to come forward. "The Earl of Ronford has brought his men to help us."

The earl bowed. "We will do everything we can to save Her Majesty."

Leo's jaw clenched. "They will rue the day they took her."

"And you know Colonel Elam and Quentin." Eviana motioned to them, and they bowed.

"Thank you for keeping my daughter safe," Leo told them.

Eviana winced and exchanged a look with her friends. Papa didn't know yet that she'd been captured.

"Have you seen my daughter?" Nevis asked. "Is she all right?"

"Aye, general," Elam answered. "She's still at the campsite just north of the ferry. We passed by there on our way here."

Leo nodded. "Captain Drew told us he left the wagons there with some guards, so he could move the troops here without being detected."

Eviana assumed Nevis's daughter was all right, but she hadn't actually seen her. She and her companions had only stopped at the campsite for a minute, and one of the guards there had told them that Faith was in the covered wagon tending to Colonel Miller's wounded leg.

"I located the Duke of Vindalyn and his troops last night," Quentin reported. "They expect to reach the ferry by this evening."

Leo's eyes widened. "The duke is leading them himself?"

"Aye, Your Majesty." Quentin winced. "I told him that the queen had been captured."

Eviana drew in a sharp breath. Poor Grandpa. The news must have devastated him. "Is he all right?"

Quentin looked at her, and she felt her heart tighten in her chest. During the ride here, he had kept his distance, letting her ride alongside the earl. And now, she realized that her thoughts had been so focused on her mother, she'd never heard what he'd done the night before. He'd been up all night, working, and then he'd rushed to rescue her. He had to be utterly exhausted.

"He was shocked, of course," Quentin replied. "But he rallied quickly, driven by his love and concern for her."

Leo turned toward Eviana. "As happy as I am to see you, I don't want you here while we go into battle. I'll have you escorted back to the campsite." He glanced toward the monastery, and his gloved hands clenched. "Once I have Luciana back, I will destroy the Brotherhood."

"Papa." Eviana took a deep breath. "May I have a word with you and the general in private?"

"Yes, but we must be quick about it." Leo turned to go into the woods with Nevis.

Eviana motioned for Quentin to come with her. He gave her a questioning look but followed her into the woods.

"What is it?" Leo asked impatiently. "Every second that my wife is in their hands . . ." Lightning energy crackled around him, and Nevis jumped back.

"Get control of yourself," the general warned Leo. "We can't just attack them. They might—"

"I'm sure they haven't harmed her," Eviana said quickly. "Their goal was to kidnap me. Once they had me at the monastery and the army arrived, they were going to torture Mother to make me use my power to put you all to sleep."

Leo grew pale.

"Thank the Light they didn't manage to kidnap you," Nevis growled.

Eviana exchanged a look with Quentin. "They did, but Quentin rescued me."

Nevis hissed in a breath. "Damn."

Leo remained silent, his face pale.

Eviana's eyes stung with tears. "I know that is your worst fear, Papa. You've always been afraid that my gift could be used to destroy our family and country. But I can do the opposite! I can actually save Mother. And our country."

He shook his head. "I don't want you involved."

"Papa!" She grabbed his sleeve. "All I have to do is clap my hands and everyone in the monastery will fall asleep. Then Quentin can fly in, find Mother, and bring her out. The answer is so simple! Just let us do it!"

Leo looked stunned.

"It's a good plan," Nevis said. "A hell of a good plan."

"The dragons will be immune, too," Quentin added. "They can assist us."

Leo hesitated while he considered. "Your gift will put the troops here to sleep, too."

"We can retreat about five miles," Nevis suggested. "Then we'll be out of range of Eviana's power."

Leo nodded. "And once we have Luciana back, we will invade the monastery and take all the monks prisoner."

Eviana's heart lurched. "Then you'll let me do it?"

"Aye, I will." Leo grabbed her by the arms. "You've been wrong all these years, Evie. We kept your gift a secret to protect *you*, not ourselves. My greatest fear was not that you'd be used against us, but that if you were captured, you would kill yourself to keep us safe."

Tears streamed down her face. She would never tell him, but she had been prepared to do exactly what he'd feared. She sniffed and wiped her face. "We'll rescue her, Papa. Trust me."

"I do." He gave her a quick hug, then turned to Quentin and clasped him on the shoulder. "Thank you for saving my daughter. And my wife."

"Your Majesty!" Elam called. "We can see the queen."

They ran back to the edge of the woods. On the battlements of the Brotherhood's castle, a monk was dragging Queen Luciana along the wall walk. She elbowed him in the ribs and pulled away from him, but then another monk grabbed her. As she struggled, his hood fell back, revealing a shock of carrot-red hair. When he pressed a long blade against her neck, she grew still.

"If you attack us, she dies!" the redheaded priest shouted from the battlements. "Take your troops and your dragons away!"

Leo stepped into the clearing and dropped his sword. "Do not harm her! We are retreating!"

He stepped back into the woods. "Retreat!" As the men mounted up, the dragons landed by the edge of the woods and made their way between the trees.

Eviana stopped them before they could shift and told them her plan. With a nod, they huddled down beneath a thick canopy of trees to remain hidden.

As her father, Nevis, and the troops rode away, Eviana turned to Quentin. "Can you let me know when they're far enough away?"

"Aye." He stepped behind some trees to shift. As he flew away, Eviana paced nervously beside the dragons.

Lennie made a small huffing noise, and when Eviana turned toward her, the female dragon reached out a wing to tap her on the shoulder as if to say, *All will be well.*

Eviana nodded at her best friend. All *would* be well.

When Quentin saw that the king and his followers had stopped about halfway to the ferry, he circled back and flew to Eviana as fast as possible.

As he drew closer, he swooped down to the cover of the trees so no one on the battlements of the monastery could see him. He landed beside Eviana, and she gave him a nod.

"Let's do it." She eased close to the edge of the woods. Her mother was still there, standing very still, her face pale. Eviana clapped her hands three times.

Everyone on the battlements, all the monks and her mother as well, collapsed into a deep sleep. Quentin took off with Lenushka close behind. He landed on the battlements next to the fallen queen and shifted. After picking her up in his arms, he looked toward the woods and spotted Eviana waving at him. Pendras was beside her, ready to transport her to her father and the troops.

Quentin hurried down the stone steps, carrying the queen, while Lenushka landed in the courtyard. When Quentin reached the foot of the stairs, the sound of a creaking door made him stop and turn. Coming out of the Great Hall was Bran, fully dressed and carrying a young man in his arms. He must have been in raven form when Eviana had clapped her hands. The raven shifter halted abruptly at the sight of the dragon.

Lenushka snorted, a small puff of smoke coming from her nostrils as she glared at Bran. His gaze shifted from the dragon to Quentin, who still had the queen in his arms.

"Let him go," Quentin said.

Lenushka glanced at Quentin, then huffed again, and took a step toward Bran.

"Let him go," Quentin repeated. "He helped me rescue Eviana."

Lenushka stopped and tilted her head as she gave Bran a curious look.

Bran gave Quentin a nod, then, after one last glance at the dragon, he hurried down the steps and ran for the stable.

Quentin carried the queen over to Lenushka, and she reared up onto her hind legs so she could grasp Luciana in her forelegs. Carefully, she cradled the sleeping queen against the glimmering pink scales on her chest. With a flap of her wings, she took off, carrying the queen to her waiting husband.

Quentin shifted and as he circled the courtyard, he noticed Bran leaving the stable on horseback, leading a second horse with the unconscious young man tied over the saddle. That had to be the other brother he had worried about. Meanwhile, Pendras had also taken flight, holding Eviana in his forelegs. Quentin followed them, and within a few minutes, they were all landing in front of King Leo and Nevis.

"Luciana!" Leo ran forward to pull the sleeping queen into his arms. With tears in his eyes, he held her tight.

Pendras set Eviana down, and she dashed toward her mother. "Mama!"

Leo pulled her into the embrace, and the two of them hugged with the queen between them.

"Thank you," Leo told his daughter, then turned to Quentin and the dragons. "Thank you."

"Mount up!" Nevis ordered the troops. "We're going back to capture the bastards!"

The troops cheered and swung back into their saddles.

"Elam," King Leo called. "Take a few soldiers and escort my wife and daughter to the Duke of Vindalyn and his troops. Then I want you all to go to Vindemar. I'll join you there as soon as I can."

"Aye, Your Majesty." Elam took the queen in his arms. "I'll keep them safe."

As Quentin flew over to where Eviana was readying her horse, the king called to him. "Quentin, can you identify the man who kidnapped my wife? And my daughter?"

Still in eagle form, Quentin nodded his head. With any luck, Greer would be one of the sleeping monks at the monastery.

Leo waved at him as he mounted his horse. "Then you're with me."

Quentin nodded again, then glanced at Eviana.

She winced. "You must be exhausted."

"Let's go!" Leo shouted, and the mounted troops charged toward the monastery.

Eviana leaned over to touch Quentin's feathered head. "I'll see you at Vindemar."

He nodded. As he took off flying, he heard her sneeze. *Damn.* He hoped she hadn't caught a cold.

With each flap of his wings, his muscles ached. But that was the least of his worries. He was back to being a servant now, at the beck and call of the kings of Aerthlan. How could he see Eviana whenever he wanted? He couldn't, and that hurt a great deal more than any tired muscles.

When he arrived at the monastery, he and Pendras shifted so they could open the gate and let the king and his troops ride into the courtyard. Quen was given a pair of breeches, and while the soldiers tied up sleeping monks, he checked each one, hunting for Greer.

Leo raced up the stairs to the battlements to find the young redheaded monk who had held a knife to his wife's throat. There was a flash of lightning that hurtled the monk over the battlements; then he crashed onto the courtyard below.

They found the man they assumed was Master Lorne, the younger brother of Lord Morris. He was seated at his desk in the library, frozen to death.

As the hours went by and Quentin scoured every room of the castle, he couldn't find Greer anywhere. The bastard must have realized that Eviana would clap her hands, so he had escaped as soon as he heard of the troops' approach.

Utterly exhausted, Quentin trudged toward the Great Hall to make his report to the king. With Greer on the loose and other priestly spies scattered about the four mainland kingdoms, the battle against the Brotherhood was not over.

Chapter 26

That evening, the priests of the Brotherhood awakened to find themselves in the Great Hall of the monastery with their feet tied together and their hands bound behind their backs. The army had stashed the thirty monks together so they would be easier to watch, but when a few tried to access the poison from a neighboring monk's ring, Captain Drew had them separated and their rings removed.

The monks who threatened to kill them all were locked up in the dungeons, while those who were willing to cooperate were left in the Great Hall.

After making his report that Greer was not there, Quentin found the nearest room with a cot and fell fast asleep.

The next day, as the king and Nevis questioned the prisoners, they soon realized that the monks didn't actually know very much about the organization. Apparently, they'd spent their days working in the fields, cooking, and making wine.

When Nevis discovered that the young acolytes had fresh scars on their backs, the priests admitted that they whipped the novitiates during the Loyalty Ceremony that occurred on the nights the moons embraced. Infuriated, Nevis wanted to flog the monks, but he soon discovered that they all had scars. Only the dead Master Lorne was unmarked.

Since the monks didn't know much, Leo went to Master Lorne's library to search for answers. Quentin spent most of the day with the king as they scoured the room for a list of the master's spies in the four mainland countries. Leo even used his lightning power to blow apart the master's desk in case something had been secreted away in a hidden compartment. But they found nothing. Apparently, Master Lorne had burned all his reports, and his secrets had died with him.

While Quentin assisted the king, his thoughts kept returning to Eviana. She would be traveling the whole day, but if all went well, she and her companions would arrive at Vindemar Castle tonight. Vindemar was the main residence of the Duke of Vindalyn, and it was situated on the coast, overlooking the Southern Sea.

Quentin had been there before while delivering messages, and he'd always thought it was one of most beautiful places in Eberon. The coast was rocky and jagged. The hills close by were green with vineyards and olive groves. And the weather was always sunny and pleasant. If Eviana had caught a cold, she would recover quickly there.

But would he be able to see her? The dragons had already been sent off to tell the other kings what had happened and to warn them to be on the lookout for Greer and any spies. Quentin had told the king about the Raven and that he suspected the bird shifter might actually be on their side. But now he feared the king would order him to search the entire mainland for the Raven, when all he really wanted to do was go to Vindemar to see how Eviana was faring.

Late that night, Eric arrived with half of the army. Dominic had taken the other half to guard Ebton Palace, the royal seat of Eberon. At Eric's arrival, Leo announced that he would set out for Vindemar the next day as he was eager to make sure his wife was all right.

With his nerves tense, Quentin requested to go with him, and to his great relief, the king agreed.

And so, the next day at dawn, the king left with two troops

while Quentin flew overhead. With no wagons to slow them down, they made it to Vindemar that evening shortly before sunset.

Luciana met her husband in the courtyard, and he leaped off his horse to pull her into his arms. Not wanting to appear naked before the queen, Quentin had remained in eagle form. He scanned the courtyard, but Eviana was nowhere in sight.

"Quen!" Elam waved at him, then strode over to the Duke of Vindalyn. As the two talked, Elam motioned to the eagle, and the duke smiled and nodded at him.

Elam must have bragged about him, Quentin thought, for soon there were servants bringing a trunk of clothes and fresh bedding to one of the tower rooms. Elam climbed the stairs to the battlements and waved at Quentin to join him.

"This will be your room." Elam pointed at the tower room as the last of the servants left. "After you're dressed, we can go to the dining hall."

Quentin flew inside and shifted. It was a cozy room with a window overlooking the Southern Sea. "Is Eviana all right?"

"She's in bed with a cold," Elam answered as he waited outside the open door. "After I delivered her and the queen to the duke and his troops, I took a few soldiers back to Peter's house to help him with repairs. Then I brought Olana here. She's taking care of the princess now. So what happened at the monastery?"

Quentin brought him up to date as he dressed. "Oh, the soldiers who were sent to Arondale returned last night. They said they caught Father Renard trying to sneak back into the constable's office to get his gold. The villagers nabbed him and lynched him."

Elam scoffed. "Well, I would say he deserved it. What will happen to all the priests at the monastery?"

"That's the problem Leo and Nevis have been discussing."

Quentin pulled on a pair of boots, and luckily, they fit fairly well. "Out of the thirty prisoners, about a third of them are still threatening to kill us all. They're being kept in the dungeons and will probably be executed for treason. We found the room where they had been writing the handbills."

"And the others?"

Quentin stepped onto the battlements, fully dressed. "The young acolytes are begging for mercy and being very cooperative. They claim they were brought there as orphans and abused. Nevis wants to give them a chance to prove themselves in the army or navy. Leo agreed, but insists that they be separated from one another and carefully monitored."

Elam nodded. "They're in a similar situation to the one we were in when we left the Isle of Secrets. Hopefully, they can lead happy and productive lives."

Quentin gazed out at the sea. "That leaves about ten monks they're not sure what to do with. The one in charge of the vineyards and winemaking was begging to be allowed to work here in Vindalyn. Leo will ask the duke if he's willing to take him in."

"And the Raven? What happened to him?"

Quentin shrugged. "Not sure." He suspected Bran had taken his youngest brother back to the hunting lodge to bury their other brother, but he'd kept his mouth shut about it. With any luck, the kings would not have to worry about Greer for very long. He believed Bran would be hunting for the man who had murdered his brother. "What's been happening here?"

"Not much. It's a peaceful place." Elam led him toward the stairs. "I do have good news, though." He blushed. "I asked Olana to marry me."

Quentin blinked. "That fast?"

"I'm thirty-nine. She's thirty-three. Why would we wait?"

"Then . . . she agreed?"

Elam grinned and nodded. "Aye."

Quentin slapped him on the back. "You rascal. That has to be the quickest courtship on record."

Elam snorted. "I think you were making quick progress, too."

Quentin's smile faded. "I don't know about that." Right now, he wasn't sure when he would ever see Eviana again. Dammit, he should have proposed to her when he'd had the chance.

Elam started down the stone steps to the courtyard. "Olana wants to go to Butterfield and have Father Titus marry us. I think she was really touched by the old priest."

"Aye, he's a good man." Quentin recalled the elderly priest who had been so helpful.

"She told the queen about Father Titus, and Luciana said when they return to Ebton, she'll make sure that she and Leo pass through Butterfield to thank the priest in person."

"Ah." Quentin's heart squeezed as he reached the base of the stairs. Meeting the king and queen would mean so much to the old priest who was deathly ill. "I'm afraid they'll need to hurry."

"I know," Elam agreed sadly.

Quentin stiffened as he spotted Colonel Miller across the courtyard, walking easily into the dining room. The man wasn't even limping. "How . . . how did Miller recover so quickly?"

Elam shrugged as they started to cross the courtyard. "I guess his wound wasn't that bad."

The hell it wasn't. Quentin had seen the wound, and he was surprised the man still had his leg. "Is Faith here?"

Elam nodded as he walked. "Aye. But I haven't seen her. Luciana said she's in bed, feeling under the weather."

"She has a cold like Eviana?"

Elam shrugged. "I don't know. I suppose so."

Quentin tilted his head in thought as they neared the dining hall. This was strange. Faith had treated the colonel's wound, and now it was miraculously healed? Could Faith be Embraced? If she was, her parents had managed to keep it a secret.

As they entered the dining hall, the Duke of Vindalyn spotted them and called them over. The elderly duke still sat a horse well, but when on foot, he used a cane and moved slowly.

Quentin and Elam bowed and made their greetings.

"I've been wanting to thank you." The duke reached out to grab Quentin's hand and shake it. "You rescued my daughter and my granddaughter. I can't thank you enough, young man."

Quentin felt his face grow warm. "I was doing my duty—"

"Hogwash." The duke chuckled. "You went far beyond duty, and you know it. You are welcome here anytime. And if there is anything I can ever do for you, don't hesitate to ask."

Could he marry the duke's granddaughter? Quentin was tempted to ask.

"Quentin!" Queen Luciana moved gracefully toward them, smiling. "Eviana told me about all your brave deeds. Thank you." She smiled at Elam. "Thank you both."

His face grew hotter as Quentin bowed. "It is an honor to be of service, Your Majesty. I am relieved to see you well."

A pained look crossed the queen's face, but she quickly hid it and resumed her smile. She was still suffering from the trauma she'd endured, Quentin thought.

Servants came in carrying trays of food, and Luciana helped her father onto the dais. King Leo arrived, dressed in a clean set of clothes, and joined them at the head table. Quentin and Elam moved toward the back of the room to take a seat at one of the lower tables.

The servants brought food to the head table first, and then began serving the lower tables. As Quentin waited, he glanced at the dais where they had already started eating.

That's where Eviana would sit, too, if she wasn't in bed with a cold. In the same room as he, but miles apart. Once again, he wondered how he would ever see her again.

Eviana blew her nose and set the hanky beside her on the bed. On her lap was a tray of food, but she was more interested in asking questions than eating. "So Quentin came here with Papa?"

Olana nodded. "That's what I heard from one of the maids. They arrived about two hours ago while you were napping."

"And how was he?"

"Your father?" Olana asked dryly.

Eviana huffed. How she hated being sick with this darned cold. "I meant Quentin. The poor man was flying all over the country for days without any rest. He must be terribly sore and exhausted."

Olana sighed. "Yes, I've heard about this several times over the last few days."

Eviana groaned and forced herself to eat another spoonful of chicken soup. No doubt Olana was tired of being stuck in this room taking care of a princess with a snotty nose. "I'm sorry. I know you'd rather be spending this time with Elam."

Olana blushed. "I told your mother I wanted Father Titus to officiate the wedding in Butterfield, and she said that she and your father would be happy to attend."

"Oh, that's wonderful!" Eviana smiled. "I want to go, too." Her smile faded. "And I want Quentin to go with me. I miss him so much."

Olana tsked. "I'll tell you what. Finish your soup, and when I take the tray back to the kitchen, I'll find out all I can about your Quentin."

"Oh, thank you!" Eviana wolfed down the last of her soup, and as she handed the tray to Olana, their fingers accidentally touched. "I'm in love with Quen—" She bit her lip as her parents suddenly barged into the room.

Olana winced and stepped back, holding the tray.

"We just finished dinner and thought we would check on you," Luciana said as they approached the bed. "How are you feeling now?"

"I'm better, thank you." Eviana gave them a wary glance. Had they heard her confession? "How are you, Mother?"

"Much better now that Leo is here." Luciana smiled at her husband, then turned to Olana. "And how are you, my lady? You must be very excited."

Olana blushed as she smiled. "I am, Your Majesty. If you'll excuse me now, I'll take this tray back to the kitchen."

Luciana perched on the edge of the bed while Leo leaned against a bedpost and crossed his arms over his chest.

When the door closed, Luciana leaned forward to whisper, "So I hear your journey became quite a romantic adventure."

Eviana gulped. They must have heard her confession. "No. I mean, yes. But we didn't really . . ." She winced.

"You didn't . . . know that Olana and Elam were falling in love?" Luciana asked.

Eviana blinked. "Oh. Were you talking about them? I . . . Yes, Quentin and I knew they were falling in love. We tried to help them by leaving them alone as much as possible."

Luciana sat back. "So that means you spent time alone with Quentin?"

"Well, yes." Eviana felt her face growing warm. "But we didn't really . . . I mean we came close . . . so I thought the most appropriate response was to propose marriage."

"*What?*" Leo straightened up from the bedpost and stepped closer.

Luciana's eyes widened with shock. "You . . . what?"

Eviana took a deep breath. "I proposed to him."

"And what motivated you to do that?" Leo demanded.

"Well, given the circumstances at the time . . ." Eviana's face grew hotter.

Luciana grabbed her hand. "Are you all right? You weren't harmed in any way?"

"No, it was quite nice." Eviana winced. "I mean—"

"Damn," Leo growled.

"Papa, I'm in love with him. And he's loved me for six years. He has the most noble character of any man I've ever met." Eviana hesitated as she noticed the fierce glint in her father's eyes. "I mean, other than you, of course."

"And you proposed marriage?" Leo asked.

Eviana nodded. "Aye."

Luciana squeezed her hand. "What did he say?"

Eviana winced. "He refused."

"Bloody hell," Leo growled, then stormed out of the room.

"Oh dear," Luciana murmured.

"Mother." Eviana grabbed her mother's hand with both her own. "Quen's not in trouble, is he?"

Chapter 27

Am I in trouble? Quentin wondered the next day when he suddenly received a summons to attend the king in the library immediately. Surely not, he thought, as he quickly selected the best clothes from the trunk the servants had placed in his room. As far as he could tell, he was currently in favor. He'd been given this nice room in the tower and a trunk full of excellent clothes, and last night, after dinner, a servant had taken him to the bathhouse so he could wash up.

But as he strode along the battlements, he noticed the sun was barely rising over the horizon. What had happened to make the king demand to see him so early?

He arrived at the library and knocked on the door.

"Come in!" the king yelled.

He sounds a bit angry, Quentin thought as he stepped inside and quickly bowed. When he straightened, he saw Eviana, and his heart filled with joy. She was looking well. Even her red nose looked adorable.

She lifted a hanky to her face, supposedly to wipe her nose, but hidden behind it, she grimaced at him. What was she trying to tell him? He glanced over at the king and queen, who were frowning at him. Oh, crap. The king was even wearing his sword belt.

"Come forward," Leo ordered, glowering at Quentin.

"Aye, Your Majesty." Quentin stepped closer. Apparently, his time of being favored had come to an abrupt end.

Leo clenched his gloved fists, and Luciana touched his arm as if to keep him from committing murder.

Quentin swallowed hard.

Leo took a deep breath. "So I hear my daughter proposed marriage to you, and you refused. Why?"

Oh, shit. Quentin glanced over at Eviana, who looked pale and worried. "It grieves me that I may have hurt Her Highness's feelings. I am deeply aware that I am not worthy of her."

Eviana huffed. "There you go again. Papa, he keeps claiming he's unworthy, and no matter how much I try to convince him otherwise, the stubborn birdbrain insists—"

"Birdbrain?" Quentin gave her an incredulous look.

She winced. "Sorry. I'm just so frustrated that you keep rejecting me."

Quentin sighed. "What else can I do? I'm a servant—"

"I told you that might be the problem," Luciana warned her husband.

With a grunt, Leo pulled out his sword.

"Papa, don't kill him!" Eviana leaped in front of Quentin, but he quickly moved her aside.

"Please don't punish her," Quentin asked. "It was all my fault."

"No, it wasn't." She jumped in front again. "I was courting you."

Luciana covered her mouth as if she were hiding a smile.

"Stand aside, Evie," the king ordered. "Both of you, kneel."

Quentin flinched. "It wasn't her fault."

"*Kneel now!*" Leo bellowed.

Quentin fell to his knees and as Eviana kneeled beside him, he took her hand and squeezed it tight.

Leo tapped his sword on Quentin's shoulders. "I dub thee Sir Quentin, a royal knight of the realm."

Quentin gasped.

"And you." Leo tapped his sword on Eviana's shoulders. "In gratitude for your successful completion of a dangerous mission, I dub thee Lady Eviana, the first female knight of the realm."

Quentin exchanged a stunned look with Eviana.

"There." Leo stepped back and sheathed his sword. "Now you have the exact same rank. What do you say, Sir Quentin?"

Still stunned, Quentin glanced at the king. "Thank you?"

Leo gave him a pointed look as he angled his head toward his daughter.

"Oh." Quentin came to his senses and swiveled on his knees to face Eviana. "When you were kidnapped and I was so frantic to find you, I realized I should have never rejected you. I can't live without you. Will you marry me, Evie?"

"Yes!" She flung her arms around his neck. "Yes, of course."

"Up on your feet," Leo grumbled. "You're getting married today."

Quentin stiffened. Today?

"Today?" Eviana asked.

Luciana's mouth twitched. "Yes, given the circumstances, we feel it should happen as quickly as possible."

Quentin gave Eviana a questioning look. What on Aerthlan had she told her parents?

She was a married woman, Eviana told herself for the hundredth time as she and Quentin ate breakfast together on the dais in the dining hall. After Quentin's lovely proposal, her parents had whisked them straight to the chapel, and there the Duke of Vindalyn had given them his blessing. Elam and Olana were there, grinning, and Olana had handed Eviana a bouquet of flowers she'd picked from the castle garden. And then, they'd found themselves saying their vows before a priest.

"Am I dreaming?" she whispered to Quentin.

"I think we're awake." He shifted in his chair, glancing down the table at the king, queen, and duke. "This feels so strange."

She frowned. "Being married?"

"No, eating at this table."

"Oh." She smiled. "You'll get used to it."

He glanced at her. "I will try my best to be worthy of you."

"Oh, not that again." She reached for her goblet. Wine at breakfast? She took a sip. "Can you believe it? We're actually married."

Quentin nodded and drank some wine.

She leaned close. "I told you my family would accept you."

He gave her a wry look. "Then why did you leap in front of me, begging your father not to kill me?"

She winced. "Well . . ."

"A toast!" Halfway across the room, Elam stood at the table where he was eating with Olana. "May the newly-wedded couple enjoy many years of peace and contentment!"

"Huzzah!" Everyone cheered and drank some wine.

"And may these halls be filled with young children!" another man yelled, and everyone cheered again.

Eviana's mouth fell open. She'd been a married woman for less than an hour, and everyone was already expecting her to be a mother? She drank more wine.

But now that she thought about it, she and Quen would now be able to make love whenever they wanted. She glanced at him and found him looking at her.

Under the table, he took her hand in his. She nudged her knee against his. He tapped the edge of his boot against her slipper. Goodness, was it always this hot in the dining hall?

He leaned close to whisper in her ear. "How long are we expected to eat?"

"I really can't eat," she whispered back. "I'm much too . . ." She glanced at his beautiful eyes, and they were heated like molten gold. "Shall we go?"

"Where? To my tower room?"

"My bedchamber is closer."

"Let's leave." He stood, and she jumped up beside him.

He bowed to the king and queen. "If you will excuse us—"

"We're exhausted," Eviana finished.

He grabbed her hand, and as they stepped off the dais, the queen turned to her husband.

"They lasted longer than I thought they would," Luciana whispered.

Leo grunted.

As Eviana and her husband rushed out the door, the crowd in the dining hall cheered. Wincing, she glanced at Quen. "Do you think they know what we're—"

"Yes."

"That's a bit embarrassing." She glanced at him again, then they both laughed.

"This way." She pointed to a staircase, and they both ran to the next floor. Then she led him to her room, and they hurried inside and locked the door.

He pulled her into his arms and as he leaned down to kiss her, she realized she was still recovering from a cold. She jumped back. "You'll catch my cold."

"I don't care."

"I do." She glanced at her bed, afraid that it was still covered with dirty handkerchiefs. But thankfully, while she was getting married, some maids had come in and cleaned everything. Fresh linens were on her bed, and the coverlet had been folded back.

Quen pulled her into his arms again and before she could object, he was kissing her.

Oh, how glorious, she thought as she melted in his arms. Soon his kisses became more demanding as if he couldn't get enough of her, and she loved it.

Running her hands into his hair, she returned his kiss, stroked his tongue when he stroked hers, and answered his moan with a moan of her own. They were both hungry. Both desperate. Both so in love, she couldn't help but think that they were absolutely perfect for each other. And making love would be just as perfect.

He broke the kiss, breathing heavily against her neck. "Evie."

"Yes."

"Why were your parents in such a hurry to see us wed? Do they think that we already . . ."

She kissed his cheek. "I may have hinted that we did."

He leaned back to give her an incredulous look. "But we didn't. Evie, they'll think I took advantage of you."

She shrugged. "It all worked out."

"They'll think I'm a scoundrel!"

"No, they think you're a hero. You saved me and my mother."

He paused, frowning at her. "Will you tell them later that I didn't—"

"Yes, yes, I will." She frowned back at him. "Are you unhappy that we were married so quickly?"

"No." His eyes softened. "I'm delighted to be your husband."

"Ah." She dragged her hands up his shirt to the top button. "In that case, take off your clothes."

He glanced around the room. "Should we close the curtains? It's a little bright in here."

She shrugged as she unbuttoned his shirt. "I've seen you naked before, Quen. This is not going to be a big surprise."

His jaw shifted. "You don't sound like you were very impressed."

She shoved his shirt off his shoulders. "Oh, your chest is quite remarkable. All these muscles." She finished pulling off his shirt and tossed it aside.

He frowned at her. "Only the chest is remarkable?"

"Well, you were fighting at the time. So all I could see were these odd dangly bits flopping about."

He snorted. "I think you'll be surprised after all." He dropped his breeches and she gasped.

"Oh! Goodness, that's not at all floppy."

"No." He stepped toward her, and she backed away.

How on Aerthlan had he gotten so big? "How did that . . . what happened?"

"We were kissing, remember?"

"That's all it takes?"

"Evie, sometimes I get hard just thinking about you." He turned her around to unlace her gown. "Now it's my turn to see you naked."

She glanced over her shoulder to get another look at his erection. It was not only long and stiff, but surprisingly thick. "Are you sure I'm going to like this?"

"As your husband, it is my duty and privilege to make sure you do."

"Ah. I'm afraid you'll have your work cut out for you."

With a snort, he shoved her gown down to the floor. On the way back up, he grabbed the hem of her shift and pulled it over her head.

Her breath caught. Maybe she should have closed the curtains after all.

"Oh, Evie." He wrapped his arms around her, pulling her back against him. "You're so beautiful."

She was about to complain that he was stabbing her in the rear, when his hands cupped her breasts and his thumbs flicked against her nipples. "Oh." He was taking his husbandly duties quite seriously.

"I love you." He nuzzled her neck with heated kisses, and her knees grew weak.

Before she could melt onto the floor, he picked her up and laid her on the bed. As he proceeded to kiss her and touch her all over, she clutched at him. Her heart pounded faster and faster, and soon she was feeling desperate.

She struggled to breathe. "Touch me like you did before."

"Here?" He slipped his hands between her legs.

"Yes." She opened her knees wide for him. "Please, I want you to pleasure me again."

"I intend to." He stroked her gently. "I intend to do it whenever you like." He kissed her neck and whispered in her ear. "And I know you like it. You're hot and wet."

She moaned.

He moved between her legs and before she could question what on Aerthlan he was up to, he stroked her with his tongue.

"Oh!" The familiar sensation grew inside her, swirling her around faster and faster, higher and higher. When he suckled on her, she shattered, letting out a keening cry.

Good goddesses, she couldn't even see straight. As her body continued to shudder, he pressed himself against her.

"I'm taking you now," he whispered.

"Huh?"

"It might hurt a little."

"Huh?"

He eased inside her.

She blinked, and he suddenly came into focus. "Quen?"

He plunged.

"Ow!"

"Sorry." He gritted his teeth.

"I knew you were too big."

"Evie—"

"Maybe we should try again when you're smaller."

"Evie." He cradled her face. "Relax."

"I feel stuffed."

His mouth twitched. "We'll make it through this."

"We will?"

He nodded and kissed her gently, molding his mouth against her. Soon the pain had faded away, and she had to admit to herself that feeling stuffed was actually quite pleasurable.

When he slowly moved inside her, she decided it was extremely pleasurable, and soon she was panting and convinced she was in heaven. Suddenly, his pace quickened and the whirlwind carried her up once again. He cried out, emptying his seed inside her.

As he collapsed beside her, he pulled her into his arms. "Are you all right?"

"Yes. And you? You cried out."

He shrugged one of his big, beautiful shoulders. "That happens."

"Oh." She smoothed a hand down his back. "And it can happen again?"

He smiled. "Whenever we like."

She reached lower so she could caress his rump. "You know, I saw your rear end the day the barge was attacked."

"You did?"

She nodded. "I was hiding under the willow tree and saw you putting on a pair of breeches."

His eyes widened. "Naughty princess."

She gave his rump a playful squeeze. "I thought you looked like a bronze statue, all glorious muscles and golden skin."

"And I saw your wet gown molded to your beautiful breasts with the nipples hard and begging to be kissed."

She gasped. "Naughty eagle."

His mouth twitched. "Now that we've established how naughty we are, we should enjoy it."

"Hmm." She kept exploring with her hand. "Definitely."

He sucked in a breath when her hand circled his manhood. "Naughty wife."

She laughed. "I'm going to enjoy being married."

"Me, too."

Epilogue

One week later . . .

It was a glorious sunny afternoon as Quentin stood on the battlements of Vindemar Castle and looked out over the Southern Sea. Already, Vindemar was starting to feel like home.

Three days ago, the king and queen had left to return to Ebton Palace. Elam and Lady Olana had decided to remain in Vindemar for a bit longer, but Faith, now completely recovered, had gone with the king and queen so she could return to her home at Benwick. Luciana had promised Lady Olana that they would stop at Butterfield on the way so they could personally thank Father Titus. Leo was even considering knighting the old priest.

The struggle with the Brotherhood of the Sun seemed far away now, but Quentin knew they remained a problem. Greer was still out there, and the Raven and his brother. There could also be spies who were still loyal to the cause. But both the king and the duke had informed Quentin that now his most important duty was to learn all he could about the management of Vindalyn so he could assist his wife in the future. The threat of the Brotherhood would be dealt with by other members of the royal families of Aerthlan.

As part of his training, Quentin took a ride with the Duke of Vindalyn every day to learn about the vineyards and villages. Two days ago, Eviana had recovered enough from her cold that she was able to join them on their daily outings. And everywhere they went, the duke happily introduced Quentin as the future Duke of Vindalyn.

A duke? Never in his wildest dreams had he imagined that would happen. He'd always wanted a home and a family to call his own. And for the last six years, he'd wanted Eviana. But for her to want him—that still seemed like a miracle.

"There you are." Eviana wandered up to him, smiling. "You seem to like this spot. I've seen you up here every afternoon."

He nodded. "I've always liked the ocean."

She turned to gaze out at the sea. "It doesn't give you bad memories of the Isle of Secrets?"

"No. I may have hated the island, but I was always drawn to the sea. It signified freedom."

She nodded. "The vastness of it makes it seem as if anything is possible."

"True." He turned toward her. "And how do you feel? Do you still feel trapped?"

She inhaled the sea air deeply. "No. I think what really bothered me was my fear that I would have to marry someone who wanted Vindalyn more than me. And then I would be trapped in a loveless marriage, and being a duchess would feel miserable and lonesome." She turned toward him and smiled. "But I love my life now that I can share it with you."

He took her hand. "All my dreams have come true because of you."

"Then I have one last proposition for you."

He snorted. "Another one? Don't tell me, you want to do it against a door?"

She grinned. "Perhaps later."

"In a bathtub?"

She gave him a wry look. "You seem to be fixated on love-making."

"I am, actually."

She glanced down at his breeches. "So I see."

"What are you looking at?"

Her mouth twitched. "Well, you kept claiming that you were unworthy. I have to make sure you don't have any shortcomings."

"There are no problems there, and I'll be happy to prove it." He motioned toward the nearby tower. "I happen to have a room right there. I propose we retire immediately."

"I accept."

"Good." He led her toward the tower.

"But wait a minute." She halted. "Have you forgotten that I have a proposal, too?"

"What is it?"

She smiled. "I propose that we live happily forever after."

"I accept."

"Good." She took his hand and led him toward the tower room.

With a laugh, he grabbed her around the waist. "Eviana," he whispered in her ear. "Forever after begins now."

Don't miss any of the Embraced by Magic novels!

HOW TO LOVE YOUR ELF

Raised in isolation on the magic-shrouded Isle of Moon, five girls became five sisters. Now women, they are ready to claim their places in the world—and perhaps change it forever . . .

Flame and Fortune

Sorcha knew the mission was dangerous. Leaving the safe grounds of her brother's kingdom and parlaying with the elves across their border . . . well, treachery seemed at least as likely as true peace. But to support her sister, Sorcha would brave far more than the underhanded ways of the elves. Or so she thought, before she was taken hostage.

Of course, her captors didn't count on her particular abilities—or on the help of the Woodsman, the mysterious thief who made his home in the forest. He saw the battle from the trees, saw the soldier attacking against incredible odds to save a comrade—and then saw the valiant fighter revealed as Princess Sorcha of Norveshka. He can't tell if he wants to kidnap her or kiss her. But despite Sorcha's stubbornness, his inconvenient honor, and a rebellion on the cusp of full war, something burns between them that neither can let go . . .

THE SIREN AND THE DEEP BLUE SEA

Four sisters have become queens, rulers of all that
Aerthlan's two moons embrace. The last sister will forge her
own path . . .

Signs and Seals

Raised on the magic-seeped Isle of Moon, Maeve is used to
unusual powers—and the way they fuel the politics of her
world. But when she discovers an ability to shape-shift at
will, she knows who she wants to share it with first. Brody,
the enigmatic, infuriating shifter-spy has always made time
for Maeve. But it's been almost two months since she's seen
him. And though no one else believes Brody is in danger,
Maeve is more than ready to rescue him herself.

The rumors Brody's investigating are terrifying: a secret
army of magic-users, in the service of the cruel Circle of
Five. But when he uncovers the identity of one of the Five,
the mission becomes personal. Cursed as a boy by the Sea
Witch, Brody can spend only two hours a day in his human
form, a restriction that limits his future and muzzles his
heart. Plus Maeve teases him for being such a pretty doggy
instead of appreciating his manly charms. To win his freedom, he must take on a terrible disguise. And when Maeve
finds out, she'll unleash a tempest like no other . . .